The DARK ENQUIRY

DEANNA RAYBOURN

The
DARK ENQUIRY

A LADY JULIA GREY NOVEL

MIRA®

Recycling programs
for this product may
not exist in your area.

ISBN-13: 978-0-7783-1237-6

THE DARK ENQUIRY

Copyright © 2011 by Deanna Raybourn

For questions and comments about the quality of this book please contact us
at Customer_eCare@Harlequin.ca.

www.MIRABooks.com

Printed in U.S.A.

First Printing: July 2011
10 9 8 7 6 5 4 3 2 1

To Pam, agent, friend, and fairy godmother. Thank you.

The FIRST CHAPTER

I will sit as quiet as a lamb.

—*King John*

London, September 1889

"Julia, what in the name of God is that terrible stench? It smells as if you have taken to keeping farm animals in here," my brother, Plum, complained. He drew a silk handkerchief from his pocket and held it to his nose. His eyes watered above the primrose silk as he gave a dramatic cough.

I swallowed hard, fighting back my own cough and ignoring my streaming eyes. "It is manure," I conceded, turning back to my beakers and burners. I had just reached a crucial point in my experiment when Plum had interrupted me. The table before me was spread with various flasks and bottles, and an old copy of the *Quarterly Journal of Science* lay open at my elbow. My hair was pinned tightly up, and I was swathed from shoulders to ankles in a heavy canvas apron.

"What possible reason could you have for bringing manure into Brisbane's consulting rooms?" he demanded, his voice slightly muffled by the handkerchief. I flicked him a glance. With the primrose silk swathing the lower half of his face he resembled a rather dashing if unconvincing highwayman.

"I am continuing the experiment I began last month," I explained. "I have decided the fault lay with the saltpeter. It was impure, so I have decided to refine my own."

His green eyes widened and he choked off another cough. "Not the black powder again! Julia, you promised Brisbane."

The mention of my husband's name did nothing to dissuade me. After months of debating the subject, we had agreed that I could participate in his private enquiry investigations so long as I mastered certain essential skills necessary to the profession. A proficiency with firearms was numbered among them.

"I promised him only that I would not touch his howdah pistol until he instructed me in the proper use of it," I reminded Plum. I saw Plum glance anxiously at the tiger-skin rug stretched on the floor. Brisbane had felled the creature with one shot of the enormous howdah pistol, saving my life and killing the man-eater in as quick and humane a fashion as possible. My own experiences with the weapon had been far less successful. The south window was still boarded up from where I had shattered it when an improperly cured batch of powder had accidentally detonated. The neighbour directly across Chapel Street had threatened legal action until Brisbane had smoothed his ruffled feathers with a case of rather excellent Bordeaux.

Plum gave a sigh, puffing out the handkerchief. "What precisely are you attempting this time?"

I hesitated. Plum and I had both taken a role in Brisbane's professional affairs, but there were matters we did not discuss by tacit arrangement, and the villain we had encountered in the Himalayas was seldom spoken of. I had watched the fellow disappear in a puff of smoke and the experience had been singularly astonishing. I had been impressed enough to want some of the stuff for myself, but despite numerous enquiries, I had been unsuccessful in locating a source for it. Thwarted, I had decided to make my own.

"I am attempting to replicate a powder I saw in India," I temporised. "If I am successful, the powder will require no flame. It will be sensitive enough to ignite itself upon impact." Plum's eyes widened in horror.

"Damnation, Julia, you will blow up the building! And Mrs. Lawson dislikes you quite enough already," he added, a trifle nastily, I thought.

I bent to my work. "Mrs. Lawson would dislike any wife of Brisbane's. She had too many years of keeping house for him and preparing his puddings and starching his shirts. Her dislike of me is simple feminine jealousy."

"Never mind the fact that you have created a thoroughly mephitic atmosphere here," Plum argued. "Or perhaps it is the fact that you keep blowing out the windows of her house."

"How you exaggerate! I only cracked the first lot and the smoke damage is scarcely noticeable since the painters have been in. As far as the south window, it is due to arrive tomorrow. Besides, that explosion was hardly my fault. Brisbane did not explain to me that sulphur is quite so volatile."

"He is a madman," Plum muttered.

I pierced him with a glance. "Then we are both of us mad, as well. We work with him," I reminded him. "Why are you here?"

Plum snorted. "A happy welcome from my own sister."

"We are a family of ten, Plum. A visit from a sibling is hardly a state occasion."

"You are in a vile mood today. Perhaps I should go and come again when you have sweetened your tongue."

I carefully measured out a few grains of my newly formulated black powder. "Or perhaps you should simply tell me why you are here."

He gave another sigh. "I need to consult with your lord and master about the case he has set me. He wants me to woo the Earl of Mortlake's daughter with an eye to discovering if she is the culprit in the theft of Lady Mortlake's emeralds."

I straightened, intrigued in spite of myself. "That is absurd. Felicity Mortlake is a thoroughly nice girl with no possible motive to stealing her stepmother's emeralds. I am sure she will be vindicated by your efforts."

"That may be, but in the meantime, I have to secure for myself an invitation to their country seat to make a pretense of an ardent suitor. This would have been far easier during the season," he complained.

"Can you put the thing off?" I asked, wiping the powder from my hands with a dampened rag.

"Not likely. The emeralds are still missing, and Brisbane said Mortlake is getting impatient. Nothing has been proved of Felicity, but until his lordship knows something for certain, he cannot be assured of her innocence or guilt. One feels rather sorry for him. Of course, one ought rather to feel sorry for me. Felicity Mortlake detests me," he said, pulling a woeful face.

I felt a smile tugging at my lips. "Yes, I know." I remembered well the time she upended a bowl of punch over Plum's head in a Mayfair ballroom. Not his finest moment, but very possibly hers.

I bent again to my experiment. "The French now have a smokeless gunpowder," I mused, sulking a little, "and yet I still cannot manage to perfect this wretched stuff."

Plum edged towards the door. "You do not mean to light that," he said as I took up a match.

"Naturally. How else will I know if I am successful? You needn't worry," I soothed. "I have taken precautions this time," I added, gesturing towards the heavy apron I had tied over my oldest gown. I had already ruined three rather expensive ensembles with my experiments and had finally accepted the fact that fashion must give way to practicality when scientific method was employed.

"I am not thinking of your clothes," he protested, his voice rising a little as I struck the match and the phosphorus at the tip flared into life.

"If you are nervous, then wait outside. Brisbane will return shortly," I said.

"Brisbane has returned now," came the familiar deep voice from the doorway.

I looked up. "Brisbane!" I cried happily. And dropped the match.

The fact that the resulting explosion broke only one window did nothing to ameliorate my disgrace. Brisbane put out the fire wordlessly—or at least I think it was wordlessly. The explosion had left a distinct ringing in my ears. His mouth may have moved, but I heard nothing of what he might have said until we returned to our home in Brook Street that evening. Brisbane had ordered dinner served upon trays in our bedchamber, and I was glad of it. A long and fragrantly steamy bath had removed most of the traces of soot from my person, and as I approached the table, I realised I was voraciously hungry.

"Ooh! Oysters—and grouse!" I exclaimed, taking a plate from Brisbane. I settled myself happily, and it was some minutes before I noticed Brisbane was not eating.

"Aren't you hungry, dearest?"

"I had a late luncheon at the club," he said, but I was not deceived. He plucked a bit of meat from one of the birds and tossed it towards his devoted white lurcher, Rook. For so enormous a dog, he ate daintily, licking every bit of grease from his lips when he was finished with the morsel.

I laid down my fork. "I know you are not angry or you would be shouting still. What troubles you?"

He passed a hand over his eyes, and I felt a flicker of alarm lest one of his terrible migraines be upon him. But when he opened his eyes, they were clear and fathomlessly black and focused intently upon me.

"I simply do not know what to do with you," he said. For an instant, I felt sorry for him.

"Four explosions in a month's time are a bit excessive," I conceded.

"Five," he corrected. "You forgot the house party at Lord Riverton's estate."

"Oh, would you call that an explosion? I should have called it a detonation." I picked up my fork again. If we were going to retread the same ground in this argument, I might as well enjoy my meal. "The oysters are most excellent. Pity about Cook giving notice in order to live in the country. We shall never find another half so skilled with shellfish."

Brisbane was not distracted by my domestic chatter. "Regardless. We must do something about your penchant for blowing things up, my lady."

The fact that Brisbane used my title was an indication of his agitated state of mind. He never used it in conversation, preferring instead to employ little endearments, some of which were calculated to bring a blush to my cheek.

He poured out the wine and took a deep draught of it, then loosened his neckcloth, an act of dinner table impropriety that would have affronted most other wives, but which I strongly encouraged. Brisbane had a very handsome throat.

I applied myself to the grouse again. "It is the same dilemma that always afflicts us," I pointed out. "I want to be involved in your work. You permit it—against your better judgement—and somehow it all becomes vastly more complicated than you expected. Really, I do not know why it should surprise you anymore." After four cases together, including unmasking the murderer of my first husband, it seemed ludicrous that Brisbane could ever think our association would be simple.

He sighed deeply. "The difficulty is that I seem entirely unable to persuade you that dangers exist in the world. You are more careless of your personal safety than any woman I have ever met."

Considering how many times I had directly approached murderers with accusations of their crimes, I could hardly fault Brisbane for thinking me feckless.

I put a hand to his arm. "You understand I do not mean to be difficult, dearest. It is simply a problem of enthusiasm. I find myself caught up in the moment and lose sight of the consequences."

His witch-black eyes narrowed dangerously. "Then we must find you another enthusiasm."

I knew that half-lidded look of old, and I crossed my arms over my chest, determined not to permit myself to be seduced from the discussion at hand. Brisbane was adept at luring me out of difficult moods with a demonstration of his marital affections. Afterward, I seldom remembered what we had been discussing, a neat trick which often provided him a tidy way out of a thorny situation. But not this time, I promised myself.

I tore my glance from the expanse of olive-brown throat and met his gaze with my own unyielding one.

"We cannot spend the whole of our marriage having the same argument, although I realise there are one or two issues which remain to be settled," I conceded.

We had been married some fifteen months, but our honeymoon had been one of long duration. We had returned to London several weeks past. Since then, we had found a house to let and moved many of his possessions from his bachelor rooms in Chapel Street and mine from the tiny country house on my father's estate in Sussex. We had hired staff, ordered wallpaper, purchased furniture and bored ourselves silly in the process. We wanted *work,* worthwhile occupation, cases to solve, puzzles to unravel. He had retained his flat in Chapel Street as consulting rooms and space for experiments with an eye to keeping our professional endeavours separate from our private lives, but I was growing restless. He had already tidied away three major cases since our return, and I had been given nothing more engaging to solve than the mystery of why the laundress applied sufficient starch to only five of the seven shirts he sent out.

"But you promised to let me take part in your work," I reminded him. "I am doing my best to learn as much as I can to make you a good partner." I hated the pleading note that had crept into my voice. I stifled it with a bit of bread roll as he considered my words.

"I know you have," he said at length. "No one could have worked harder or with greater enthusiasm," he conceded, his lips twitching slightly as he held back a smile.

"And that is why I think it is time you embarked upon your first investigation."

"Brisbane!" I shot to my feet, upsetting the little table, and in an instant I was on his lap, showering him with kisses. Rook took advantage of the situation to browse amongst the litter of china and food. He dragged away a grouse to gnaw upon, but I did not scold him. I was far too happy as I pressed my lips to Brisbane's cheek. "Do you mean it?"

"I do," he said, somewhat hoarsely. "Plum must pursue the Mortlake girl, and I want you to go with him. You are acquainted with the family. It will seem more natural if you are there. And Lord Mortlake suspects the theft of the emeralds to be a feminine crime. You will be invaluable to Plum as a finder-out of ladies' secrets."

I ought to have been thoroughly annoyed with him that he considered me fit only for winkling out backstairs gossip, but I was too happy to care. At last, Brisbane had accepted me as a partner in the fullest sense of the word.

"You will not regret it," I promised him. "I shall recover the emeralds and unmask the villain for Lord Mortlake."

"I shall hold you to that," he murmured, pressing his mouth to the delicate pulse that fluttered at my neck. Dinner was forgot after that, and some time later, as I drifted off to sleep, Brisbane's heavily muscled arm draped over me, I mused on how successfully we were learning to combine marriage with business. It wanted only a little patience and a little understanding, I told myself smugly. I had proven myself to him, and he had full faith in my abilities to assist in an investigation.

I ought to have known better.

Things had already begun to unravel the next morning. I hurried down to breakfast in high spirits, brimming with plans for my time at the Mortlakes'. I could hardly wait to discuss them with Brisbane over a delectable meal in our pretty breakfast room. With robin's-egg-blue walls and thick velvet draperies hung at long windows that overlooked the back garden, it made a calm and pleasant room to begin one's day. Only the enormous cage that housed our raven, Grim, struck an incongruous note, but I was very fond of the fellow, and he in turn was very fond of the titbits I passed along.

I descended to the hall just as our butler emerged from the green baize door separating the kitchens from the rest of the house.

"Good morning, Aquinas."

"My lady," he returned with a bow from the neck. Even carrying a rack of toast, he managed a grave dignity.

"How is the hiring coming along? Have you found a replacement for Cook yet?" Aquinas had been with me for years, first as butler at Grey House during my previous marriage, and later as my own personal retainer. My faith in him—and my boredom with domestic arrangements—was immense. I had left the staffing of the new house entirely in his hands, instructing him to use Mrs. Potter's, one of London's most fashionable agencies, to supply us. The results had been middling at best.

"I have engaged a replacement for Cook, and she has prepared breakfast," he informed me with a little moue of distaste at the slightly burnt toast in the rack.

I raised my brows. "I have never known you to bring burnt toast to the table, Aquinas. I gather this is not her first attempt?"

"Fourth," he said tightly, "and this was by far the best. I did not wish to delay you or Mr. Brisbane by pressing the matter further, but I will speak with her directly breakfast is over. I have also taken the liberty of engaging another chambermaid in light of Mr. Eglamour March's arrival."

I went quite still at the mention of my brother. "Mr. Eglamour?" Eglamour was Plum's Christian name and one that was never used except by the staff and polite society.

"Mr. Brisbane informed me yesterday that Mr. Eglamour March will be taking up residence here shortly. I thought perhaps the Chinese Room would do nicely for him as it has its own dressing room. I also thought the southern light would be quite suitable should he care to pursue his painting."

Southern light indeed, I thought with pursed lips. As the fourth—and therefore almost entirely useless—son of an earl, Plum had amused himself with art before taking up detection, and privately I thought him quite talented. But neither of those pursuits called for him to live under my roof.

I plucked the toast rack out of Aquinas' hands. "I will take this in, if you don't mind. I should like to have word with Mr. Brisbane."

Aquinas withdrew to fetch the tea and I girded myself for battle. I did not have long to engage. One look at my face when I entered the breakfast room and Brisbane threw up his hands.

"I know. It is not ideal. He did not like to tell you, but Plum has had a falling out with your father."

A little of the wind ebbed out of my sails then. I put the toast rack onto the table and went to open Grim's cage. He gave me a polite bob of the head.

"Good morning," he said in his odd little voice. I returned the greeting, and Grim dropped to the floor to pace the room, peering into corners and making his morning inspection. I broke up a piece of toast for him and put it

onto a saucer on the floor before helping myself. I turned to
Brisbane. "They have quarrelled over his role in your business, I presume?"

Brisbane nodded. "His lordship does not find the endeavour suitable to one of Plum's elevated birth," he said lightly,
but I wondered if he felt the sting of Father's disapproval. It
was terribly ungrateful of Father, really. Brisbane had saved
his life upon one occasion and the family honour more
times than I could count.

"I did warn you he would be difficult," I murmured.
"Particularly just now. Portia says he has been feuding terribly with Auld Lachy." Father's quarrels with his hermit had
become so heated Homer could have written an epic poem
upon the subject. It had not helped matters when I put it
to Father that it was an absurd notion to keep one's hermit
in town in the first place. But it was no more than Father
ought to have expected. He had hired Auld Lachy from a
newspaper advertisement, and as I had reminded him, one
ought never to hire a hermit without proper references.

I took up a knife and a piece of toast and began to scrape
off the burnt bits. Grim had studiously ignored his. I dol-
loped a bit of quince jam onto his saucer and he bobbed
his head happily. "That's for me," he said, before applying
himself to tearing into his breakfast. He had none of Rook's
dainty ways when it came to food. I added some jam to my
own sad, sooty piece of toast and resumed the theme of the
conversation.

"The thing you must remember about Father is that he is
the most terrible hypocrite. He reared us all with his Radical ideals, and yet he does not actually believe them, at least
not as they apply to his children."

"He gave his blessing to our union," Brisbane pointed
out calmly.

I gave him a fond smile. "Father doesn't care overmuch what the girls do so long as we are happy and don't make too much of a scandal. It is his sons he frets about. Between Bellmont's turning out Tory and Valerius practicing medicine, he feels the disapppointment of his heirs keenly."

Poor Father had not had an easy time of it with his sons. For the most part, those who had married had married well, but his eldest and the heir to the earldom—Viscount Bellmont—was a force for the Tories. The youngest, Valerius, had taken up as a consulting physician, and Lysander and Plum dabbled in the arts. Only Benedick who ran the Home Farm at the family seat in Sussex was a source of pride and comfort to him. Father admired Brisbane's dash and cleverness, but their relationship was a prickly one, with Father blowing hot then cold, and Brisbane always maintaining a courteous—if advisable—distance.

I bit into my toast, chewing thoughtfully. "And I suspect it was your ducal connections that allayed any doubts he might have had. He really is the most frightful snob, the poor darling."

Brisbane's elderly great-uncle was the Duke of Aberdour, a connection that served to ameliorate the fact that his mother had been a Gypsy fortune-teller and his father— well, the less said about him, the better.

I went on. "But Father's disapproval is not the issue at hand. Why is Plum moving in with us? There is the small bedchamber in the consulting rooms in Chapel Street. He can stay there," I suggested. Grim quorked impatiently for another piece of toast and I obeyed.

Brisbane picked up his newspaper. "I am afraid that won't do. Monk is using the room at present."

I sighed at the mention of Monk. Once Brisbane's tutor and later his batman—a connection I still meant to explore, as neither of them would ever speak of their time in the army—Monk served as Brisbane's right-hand during investigations. He had taken a liking to me upon our first meeting. Since then, our relationship had been coolly polite. I had supplanted his role as Brisbane's confidant and I think he felt the loss of their former closeness sharply. It was entirely supposition on my part, for the subject was never discussed, but Monk had made a habit of absenting himself as much as possible and treating me with detached cordiality when our meeting was unavoidable.

Brisbane had an uncanny ability to intuit my thoughts at times. "He will come round," he said, his voice gentle. I gave him a weak smile.

"I hope so. It is quite lowering enough that Mrs. Lawson has decided to hate me."

Brisbane did not dispute the point, and I made a mental note to be more discreet during my visits to Chapel Street. I really had made life very difficult for Mrs. Lawson with my experiments, and it would not do to alienate everyone from Brisbane's bachelor days.

"Well, Aquinas said he will put Plum in the Chinese Room and he has already engaged another maid, so I suppose it is a *fait accompli*. Although," I added, brightening, "I do not see why he could not take the attics in Chapel Street." Upon our return from abroad, we had taken over the floor above Brisbane's rooms. It was admirable space for storage, but could easily be fitted out for Plum's comfort, and the place would be far larger than what we could offer him.

"Impossible," Brisbane said, folding his newspaper with a snap. "I have plans for the attics."

"But, Brisbane, really—"

He rose and dropped a kiss to the top of my head. "I

thought it would make the perfect space for you to pursue photography. In fact, the equipment is due to arrive whilst you are at the Mortlakes'. By the time the case is concluded and you return to town, you will have your own photographic studio complete with darkroom."

"Brisbane!" I flung my arms about his neck for the second time in as many days. "You astonish me. I have not mentioned photography in weeks." I had been intrigued by the work of a lady photographer we had met during our last investigation and had longed for a camera of my own. I admired the ease with which it combined both science and art, and with my extensive family I knew I should never lack for subjects or inspiration.

He kissed me firmly. "Yes, well, I knew you would enjoy it, and I think it will prove quite useful during investigations to have our own means of taking photographs. If you have a talent for it, it may well provide you with a part of the business that is entirely your own."

I was dazzled at the notion of having something that was both useful and completely mine. I could contribute now, really contribute, and I promised myself that I would succeed. I had applied myself diligently to the other subjects Brisbane had set me, but that would be nothing to my study of photography. I would earn my position in the agency, I vowed, and so delirious was I at the prospect, I scarcely listened as he went on.

"There will be workmen about, partitioning off the space for the darkroom and fitting tables and shelves and whatnot, so you will want to keep clear of the place today. When you return from the country, you can make a proper inventory and if there is anything I have missed out, you can order it."

I said nothing for a moment. I rose to survey the dishes

on the sideboard and found them distinctly uninspiring. I took a kidney for Grim, as they were a special treat, but the rest of the dishes did not tempt me. I placed the kidney on Grim's saucer and clucked to him. He trotted to it and applied himself greedily. I ran a finger down his silky dark head, studying the flash of green in the depths of his black feathers. "When do Plum and I leave for the country, dearest?"

"The Mortlakes are hosting a house party beginning tomorrow. The country house is just in Middlesex. Take the late-afternoon train out of Victoria Station, and you should easily arrive at Mortlake's estate by teatime. Does that suit?"

I turned back to stare into those guileless, handsome black eyes and smiled widely. "Of course, but if I am to leave tomorrow, I must shop! I will likely be quite late to dinner tonight. And I must call in on Portia before I go."

He kissed the top of my head again and left, and as he quit the room, I could not help feeling the relief rolling from him in waves. Aquinas entered then with a pot of tea.

"Mr. Brisbane has left then, my lady?"

"He has," I said, musing quietly. Aquinas puttered for a moment, returning Grim to his cage and tidying up the dishes upon the sideboard.

"The eggs are watery and the porridge was a lump," I told him. "Give the new cook another day, and if she does not improve, you must return to Mrs. Potter's and find us another," I instructed.

"She has already given notice," he informed me.

"What notice? She only started this morning."

"She means to leave by luncheon today."

"She has given us three hours' notice?"

"It would appear so, my lady."

I sighed heavily. "What was the trouble with this one?"

"She was frightened of the new stove."

I suppressed the urge to snort. The stove had been an extravagance, the latest in domestic technology and Brisbane had insisted upon it. He adored gadgetry of any kind, and as soon as he had clapped eyes upon the great rusting monstrosity in the kitchen, he had demanded it be ripped out and replaced with the very newest and most expensive model. The difficulty was that most cooks were an old-fashioned lot and did not care for change. For a woman trained to prepare meals upon a coal or wood fire, cooking upon a gas stove was a terrifying proposition. I flapped a hand at Aquinas. "I will leave it to you to send to Mrs. Potter's for another. I have much to do today."

"Very good, my lady."

I turned my past two conversations with Brisbane over carefully in my mind, then directed Aquinas to find my maid.

"Send Morag to me, would you? I must discuss the packing list with her."

"For the trip to the country? Very good, my lady."

"Not at all," I said, holding up my cup for more tea and baring my teeth in a smile. "I have absolutely no intention of going to the country."

The
SECOND CHAPTER

If it be a man's work, I'll do it.
—*King Lear*

That afternoon, my errands accomplished, I took refuge in my sister Portia's town house. She gave me tea and brought out her newly adopted daughter for me to see. The infant, Jane, was carried by her very competent Indian nurse who had come from Darjeeling with us, and I greeted Nanny Stone warmly. Of course, her real name was nothing like Stone, but she had been delighted with all things English, and had put off her beautiful silken saris and her lovely Hindi name in favour of a black bombazine gown with a starched pinafore and the appellation of Nanny Stone. She had mastered the fundamentals of English before leaving her native land, but she had applied herself diligently to perfecting it by engaging anyone who would speak to her in lengthy conversations. The result was a curious mixture of interesting grammar and street slang, spoken in her lovely lilting accent.

She had dressed the baby in emerald-green, an inspired choice against the child's fluffy halo of ginger hair. The baby clutched a coral teething ring in one plump fist and drooled excessively as the nurse held her out.

I returned the smile, albeit with an effort. "I don't think I will take her just now, Nanny. She seems a bit moist."

Nanny Stone plucked a handkerchief from her pocket and began to wipe at the child, crooning some soft cradlesong.

"Nanny, I think her gums are paining her again. Perhaps a bit more of the oil of clove?" Portia suggested.

What followed was a painfully dull debate on the merits of oil of clove for a toothache as compared to Nanny's native remedies, and in the end Nanny prevailed, bearing her charge off to the nursery to apply some mixture of her own devising.

When they had gone, Portia fixed me with a reproachful glance. "She is your goddaughter, Julia. You will have to hold her sometime."

I clucked my tongue. "I am very well aware she is my goddaughter. If you will recall, I gave her a lovely set of Apostle spoons to mark the occasion. Now, she is a love, Portia, and I am very fond of her, but you must admit, she is a very damp child. There is always something moist about her mouth or her nose or other places," I added primly. She glowered, and I hurried on. "I am just not terribly comfortable with babies. Perhaps when she is a bit older and I can take her to the shops or the theatre," I said brightly.

Portia gave me a little push and we settled in to her morning room to discuss my husband's duplicity.

"You really think he means to get rid of you?" she asked, eyes wide. Portia loved few things in life so much as a good bit of gossip. She curled onto the sofa with her ancient pug, Mr. Pugglesworth, a flatulent old lapdog who ought to have been dead at least five years past.

"For a few days, at least. Plum is entirely capable of

managing the Mortlake case on his own," I added with a meaningful look. Plum was a handsome fellow, and when he exerted himself, the most charming of our brothers. Wooing a young lady, even one as ill-disposed towards him as Lady Felicity Mortlake, would be child's play to him. "No, Brisbane had some other purpose in putting me out of London. And not just out of London," I told her, drawing down my brows significantly. "He is trying to keep me away from Chapel Street altogether."

Portia looked at me reprovingly. "One cannot entirely blame him, dearest. You have attempted to burn down the place on at least three separate occasions."

"Four," I corrected, thinking of the previous day. "And I know I could master the self-igniting black powder if I had enough time."

"But you think Brisbane had another reason for wanting to be rid of you," she said, leading me gently back to the subject at hand.

"Hmm? Yes. He was quite artful about it, but he most definitely indicated that I should not visit the consulting rooms before I left town."

"Because there was something there he did not want you to see?" she hazarded.

"Someone," I corrected. Quickly, I related to her my activities that afternoon. I had stationed myself in a nondescript hackney cab on Park Street with a careful view to anyone who approached the consulting rooms from Park Lane. Some two hours into my watch, I had seen something—some*one*—most unexpected.

"Bellmont!" Portia cried. Her colour was high and her eyes bright, and I was glad of it. She had suffered the tragic loss of her dearest companion earlier in the year, and the child, Jane, had come to her as a result of this death.

Unexpected motherhood and the loss of her beloved had been difficult burdens, and I was happy to see her so peaceful within herself that she could be engaged in my little problems.

"Yes, dearest. And I put it to you, what business could our eldest brother possibly have with my husband?" Bellmont had made his disapproval in the match clear. Brisbane's livelihood touched too near the bone of being in trade, and Bellmont, while perfectly cordial, had never behaved with anything like true warmth towards my husband. But then, Bellmont was not known to show warmth towards anyone in particular. He adored his wife, Adelaide, but we often snickered in the family that the extent of their physical warmth was a yearly handshake. How they managed to beget a family of six was a question to twist the sharpest wits. He was a creature of politics and propriety, devoted to his own ideals and wildly at odds with the eccentricity for which our family was famed. It was often said that the expression "mad as a March hare" was coined at the antics of our forebears, whose heraldic badge was a hare. Bellmont did everything in his power to distance himself from that reputation.

"Perhaps blood will out," Portia suggested wickedly. "What if he has got himself a dancing girl and wants Brisbane to destroy the evidence before Adelaide gets word of it!"

I snickered. "Lord Salisbury, more like. Bellmont is far more concerned with the Prime Minister's opinion than his wife's." Since Lord Salisbury's last rise to power, Bellmont had assumed a significant role in the government, often introducing legislation in the Commons crafted to further his mentor's policies.

"Oh!" Portia sat up quickly, disturbing the dog. "Hush,

Puggy," she soothed as he gave an irritable growl. "Mummy didn't mean it." She turned to me. "Perhaps Virgilia is being pursued by a questionable sort."

I blinked at the mention of Bellmont's eldest daughter. "Virgilia came out two years ago. Is she still on the loose? I rather thought Bellmont would have arranged something for her by now."

"You know Bellmont has a blind spot where she is concerned." Puggy emitted a foul noise, followed hard by an even fouler odour, but Portia ignored him. "He has grown quite sentimental of late about Gilly. He has been very worried about an attachment she has formed with Lord Fairbrother's heir. He promised if she made no formal arrangements with the lad, he would consider the match."

I lifted a brow. "The season ended three months ago. Has he really prevented her from entering into an engagement? I must credit him with greater powers of persuasion than I thought."

Portia shrugged. "Gilly has always been his favourite, I suspect because she resembles Mother." I said nothing. Our mother had died in childbed with our youngest brother when I was very small. I did not remember her at all; I carried only the vaguest recollection of the rustle of yellow skirts and the scent of lemon verbena. But Portia remembered more, and sometimes, when she fell silent and brooding, I knew she was thinking of our mother, who had laughed and danced and left us far too soon. As the eldest, Bellmont would have remembered her better than any. He had been almost grown at her death, and I sometimes thought he had felt it most keenly.

"All the more reason for him to forbid the match entirely if he truly objects to the Fairbrother boy. What is wrong with the fellow?"

Portia gave me a little smile. "He is a devoted follower of Mr. Gladstone." We laughed aloud then to think of our priggish elder brother forced to spend the rest of his natural life with a son-in-law who was entirely committed to the Liberal cause. Bellmont loathed Gladstone, not the least because Sir William had been a frequent visitor to our house during our formative years. Our devoted Aunt Hermia had been so moved by Gladstone's work with prostitutes that she had formed her own Whitechapel house of reform for teaching ladies of the night the domestic trades. Most of our ladies' maids had come from her refuge, including my own Morag. I ought to have applied to Aunt Hermia to help me staff my new home, but one reformed prostitute in my employ was quite my limit.

"Poor Bellmont," I said at last. "Still, I wonder if he would stoop to asking Brisbane to ferret out something unsavoury to keep poor Gilly from an engagement."

"If there is something unsavoury about the fellow, Bellmont has a right to know it," Portia pointed out rather primly. I stared at her. Since becoming a mother, her own priggish tendencies, once entirely smothered, were coming occasionally to the fore.

"Yes, but I hope he has not taken it in his head to ask Brisbane to create some fiction of impropriety to prevent the marriage."

"Would Brisbane do such a thing?"

"Of course not!" I returned hotly. "Brisbane has a greater sense of integrity than any man I have ever known, including any of our family."

"Then you have nothing to worry about," she said, her voice honey smooth. Portia was convinced, but I was not. Something about the set of his shoulders as he walked away from Chapel Street told me something was very wrong with our eldest brother. His usual arrogance had been taken down a bit, and the aristocratic set of his chin—quite natural in a man who was heir to an earldom of seven hundred years' duration—had softened. Was it merely the thought of losing his beloved daughter to a political opponent that gnawed at him? Or did he wrestle with something greater?

I meant to find out. I turned to Portia. "In any event, you must see that it is impossible for me to go away. I have to know what Bellmont is about."

"Why?" she demanded. She wore a mantle of calm as easily as any Renaissance Madonna, and I suppressed a sigh of impatience at her newfound serenity.

"Because either Bellmont is in trouble or Brisbane is," I told her with some heat.

"Brisbane? What sort of trouble? And why would he look to Bellmont for aid?"

I spread my hands. "I do not know. But if Brisbane were in some sort of trouble, his first inclination, his very first, would be to see me safely out of the way. You know how annoying he is upon the point of my personal safety." The issue was one—the only one, in fact—that caused dissension in our marriage, but it was a common refrain. "And once I was safely out of the way, he might well turn to Bellmont. Our brother is superbly connected, one of the most trusted men in government, and he has the ear of the Prime Minister. One snap of the fingers from Lord Salisbury, and whatever trouble Brisbane might have found himself in goes away." I snapped my fingers for emphasis, rousing Puggy who promptly flatulated again.

"True," Portia said, somewhat reluctantly. "But I cannot imagine a situation Brisbane couldn't extricate himself from. The man is as clever and elusive as a cat," she added, and I knew she meant it as a compliment.

"Yes, but even cats need more than one life," I reminded her. "And this particular cat now has a partner to look after him." I took a deep breath and lifted my chin. Whatever difficulty beset my husband, I was determined to see it through by his side, offering whatever aid and succour I could.

I fixed my sister with a deliberate look. "And that is why I have formed a plan..."

I arrived home to find Brisbane busily engaged in a project that required a pair of workmen wearing leather aprons, endless spools of wires and significant alterations to the cupboard under the stairs.

"Brisbane?"

He backed out of the cupboard, shooting his cuffs. "You are rather earlier than I expected. I had hoped to present you with a surprise."

He gave me a bland smile and I narrowed my eyes in suspicion. I had reason to be cautious of his surprises, I reflected.

"What is this?" I asked, collecting the workmen and their wires with a sweep of my arm.

"A telephone," Brisbane informed me.

I stared, blinking hard. "A telephone? To what purpose?"

"To the purpose of being able to speak upon it," he explained with exaggerated patience.

"Yes, but to whom? In order to speak upon the telephone, one must know someone else with a telephone."

"We do." He wore an air of satisfaction. "I am having a second one installed in Chapel Street. We shall be able to communicate with the consulting rooms from here and vice versa."

"We are paying for two telephones?" I asked, *sotto voce*. I had no wish to quarrel with Brisbane, particularly over money, and most particularly in front of workmen. Still, the expense was staggering. "Whatever would possess you?"

"It will be extremely convenient for my work," he replied smoothly. "I am surprised you are not more enthusiastic, my dear. I should have thought the notion that we could speak with one another at any time would have appealed to you."

"Of course it does," I told him in full sincerity. "I was simply taken by surprise. It does seem a rather complicated enterprise."

"Not at all," he assured me. "In fact, Bellmont has had a device for some weeks and says it is quite the most useful invention."

"Bellmont?" My pulses quickened. "Have you spoken with him recently?"

Brisbane was skilled at cards, and with a gambler's sense of timing, he did not pause for an instant. He merely lifted one broad shoulder into a shrug. "Not since the last dinner at March House. But Bellmont and I spoke at length about it then. Surely you heard us. And you were supposed to ask your Aunt Hermia to give you the recipe for the persimmon sauce she served with the duck that night. It was particularly good."

Brisbane's lie had taken the warmth out of the room. I felt a chill seep into my bones, and when I spoke, it was through lips stiff with cold. "I am afraid I forgot. I will send a message to March House to ask her for it. We will have it when I return from the country," I added, twisting my lips into a semblance of a smile. "I must see if Morag has finished the packing if I am to leave tomorrow," I told him, turning towards the stairs.

"Pity Lord Mortlake doesn't have one of these," he said, nodding to the device being fixed to the wall. "I would have been able to speak to you even in the country."

I silently blessed the fact that the expense of telephones had kept most of our acquaintances from their use. The last thing I needed was Brisbane telephoning the Mortlake country house only to find I had never arrived.

I gave him a brilliant, deceitful smile. "A pity indeed, my love."

The next morning, I dispatched my trunk and Morag to the country with very specific instructions.

"It will never work," she warned me. "That Lady Mortlake might have less sense than a rabbit, but even she will notice a missing guest."

"Not if you do precisely as I have ordered," I retorted. "It is very simple, really. I have already left a note for my brother that I mean to take the early train. He is a late riser, and by the time he reads the note, the early train will have already departed with you and my trunk. When you arrive at the Mortlake house, it will be far earlier than expected. They will be at sixes and sevens," I continued. "You have only to request my trunk be sent to my room and explain that I had a headache from the train and wished to walk in the garden before I saw anyone."

Morag was listening closely, the tip of her tongue caught between her teeth. But disapproval lurked at the back of her gaze, and I hurried on. "You will say that my headache has not improved, and you will make my excuses tonight at dinner. I am unwell and wish to see no one as I mean to retire early. I have already written a note of apology to Lady Mortlake, which you will send down when the dinner gong is sounded. It explains that I am dreadfully sorry but I am simply too ill to meet with anyone, and that I am quite certain the fresh country air will revive me by breakfast."

"And when it doesn't? What then? Shall I tell them you've gone for a walk and fallen in the carp pond?" she asked nastily.

I took her firmly by the elbow. "This is not for me," I hissed at her. "This is for Mr. Brisbane, of whom I need not remind you, you are inordinately fond."

I struck a nerve there. Morag, with her common ways and her flinty heart, had formed an attachment to Brisbane. Perhaps it was the shared link of Scottish blood—or perhaps it was simply that he was a very easy man to idolize—but Morag adored him. She insisted upon referring to him as the master and had taken it upon herself to do his mending, as well as my own. I had little doubt she liked him more than she did me, and the disloyalty rankled, but only a bit. The truth was she had been somewhat easier to live with since Brisbane had entered our lives. At least she was now occasionally in a tractable mood.

"Very well," she said, rubbing at her arm. "I will do it, but only for the master. Still, it is a pretty state of affairs when a lady must lie to her own husband."

She gave me a look of injured reproof and I pushed her. "Do not be absurd. I am not betraying him. But I fear he may be in trouble, and he will not confide in me. I must discover the truth on my own, and then I will be in a position to help him."

To my astonishment, tears sprang to her eyes. She dashed them away with the back of her hand and before I could prepare myself, she dropped a kiss to my cheek. "Forgive me, my lady. I ought not to have thought you would ever be disloyal to the master."

"Disloyal!" I scrubbed at my cheek. "Morag, could you possibly have a lower opinion of me?"

"Well, you did mean to sneak about like a common trollop," she pointed out. "How was I to know you had no plans to meet a lover?"

She adopted an expression of wounded indignation and would have kissed me again, but I waved her off. "Oh, leave it," I snapped at her. "I should have thought that after so many years together, you would know me better."

Morag raised her chin with a sniff. "You've no call to be so high and mighty with me, my lady. Many a finer lady than you has been tempted from the path of righteousness."

I narrowed my eyes at her. "Have you been reading improving tracts again? I told you I will not have Evangelicalism in my house. You are free to practise whatever religion you like, but I will not be preached at like a Sunday mission," I warned her.

She patted my hand. "I shall pray for you anyway, my lady. I shall ask God to give you a humble heart."

I suppressed an oath and handed her the note I had prepared for Lady Mortlake. "Take this and do exactly as I have said. I will send further instructions by telegram when I have plotted my next move."

Morag tucked the note into her sleeve and gave me an exaggerated wink. "I am your man," she promised. "Where will you be whilst I am pretending to attend you at the Mortlakes'?"

"I shall be staying with Lady Bettiscombe," I informed her. Portia had agreed to supply me with a bolthole and any other necessities I should require.

"And what shall you give me to ensure I do not relate

that information to Mr. Brisbane or Mr. Plum should they ask it of me?"

I squawked at her. "You cannot seriously think you can extort money from me to purchase your silence!"

She gave me a calm, slow-lidded blink. "It might be worth rather a lot to your plans to keep me silent, and I think it is not the job of a lady's maid to enter into intrigues."

I smothered a bit of profanity I had learned from Brisbane and rummaged in my reticule. "Five pounds. That is all, and for that, you will persuade everyone—*everyone*—that I am rusticating in the country."

I brandished the note in front of her, and her eyes lit with avarice. "Oh, yes, my lady! I will make them all believe it, even if I have to lie to the queen herself," she promised.

"Good." She reached for the banknote and I held it just out of reach. At the last moment, I tore it sharply in half and gave one of the halves to her.

"What bloody use is this?" she demanded.

"Do not swear," I told her. "Aunt Hermia would be most disappointed if I told her you still spoke like a guttersnipe."

"If you don't want me to swear, don't steal my bloody money," she returned bitterly.

I tucked the other half of the note into my reticule.

"You may have the other half when the task is completed to my satisfaction. If you exchange both halves at the bank, they will give you a crisp new banknote in its place," I informed her. She brightened.

"I suppose that's all right then," she conceded. "Mind you don't lose the other half."

"Shall I give it to the Tower guards to look after with the Crown Jewels?" I asked.

She waggled a finger at me. "I shall speak to God about that tongue of yours, as well."

"Do, Morag, I beg you."

The THIRD CHAPTER

I had the gift, and arrived at the technique
That called up spirits from the vasty deep...

—*"The Witch of Endor"* Anthony Hecht

With my maid and my trunk safely dispatched to the country and my web of lies coming along nicely, I took myself off to my sister's house on foot, approaching through the back garden. I thought to make an unobtrusive entrance, but when I arrived, I found the entire household standing outside, admiring a cow. A man stood at the head, holding its halter and nudging its nose towards a box of hay.

Portia waved me over to where she stood with Jane the Younger and Nanny Stone.

"Isn't she divine?" Portia crooned.

I sighed. "Yes, she is quite the loveliest baby," I assured her, although truth be told, she had the rather unformed look of most children that age, and I suspected she would be much handsomer in another year or two.

"Not the baby," she sniffed. "The cow."

I turned to where the pretty little Jersey was being

brushed as it munched a mouthful of fresh hay. "Yes, delightful. Why, precisely, do you have a cow in London?"

"For the baby, of course. Jane the Younger will require milk in a few months, and I mean to be ready. She cannot have city milk," she informed me with the lofty air of certainty I had observed in most new mothers. "City milk is poison."

I said nothing. Portia could be rabid upon the subject of the infant's health and I had learned the hard way not to offer an opinion on any matter that touched the baby unless it concurred with hers in every particular. In this case, I could not entirely fault her. Adulterated milk had been discovered in some of the best shops, much of it little better than chalky water and full of nasty things. It was difficult to believe that in a city as grand as London we should resort to keeping cows in the garden to feed children, but I suppose the greater evil was that not everyone could afford to do so.

I studied the animal a moment. It was a sound, sturdy-looking beast, with velvety brown eyes and a soft brown coat. It paused occasionally to give a contented moo, and in response, Jane the Younger gurgled.

"Well, congratulations, my dear," I told her. "You have just acquired the largest pet in the City."

We both subsided into giggles then, and Portia passed the baby off to Nanny Stone and escorted me to my room for the night. I had brought with me only a carpetbag, but the contents had been carefully selected. Her eyes widened as she watched me extract the garments, a short wig and a set of false whiskers.

"Julia! You cannot possibly go about London dressed like that," she objected, lifting one garment with her fingertips.

"Leave it be! You will wrinkle it, and I will have you know I am very particular about the state of my collars," I added with an arch smile.

But Portia refused to see the humour in the situation. "Julia, those are men's clothes. You cannot wear them."

"I cannot wear anything else," I corrected. "If I am to sleuth the streets of London undetected, I can hardly go as myself, nor can I take my carriage. It is recognisable. I must take a hansom at night, and that means I must travel *incognita*."

"Is it *'incognita'* if you are disguised as a boy? Perhaps it should be *'incognito'*?" she wondered aloud.

"Do not be pedantic. I knew this costume would prove useful," I exulted. "That is why I ordered it made up some weeks ago. I have been waiting for the chance to wear it."

I had ordered the garments when I had commissioned a new riding habit from Brisbane's tailor, using an excellent bottle of port as an inducement to his discretion upon the point. He was well-accustomed to ladies ordering their country attire from his establishment, but the request for a city suit and evening costume had thrown him only a little off his mettle. "Ah, for amateur theatricals, no doubt," he had said with a grave look, and I had smiled widely to convey my agreement.

In a manner of speaking, I was engaging in an amateur theatrical, I told myself. I was certainly pretending to be someone I was not. I had last adopted masculine disguise during my first investigation with Brisbane, and the results had not been entirely satisfactory. But this time, I had ordered the garments cut in a very specific fashion, determined to conceal my feminine form and suggest an altogether more masculine silhouette. And I had taken the precaution of ordering moustaches, a rather slender arrangement fashioned from a lock of my own dark chestnut hair. The moustaches did not match the plain brown wig perfectly, but I was inordinately pleased with the effect, certain that not even Brisbane would be able to penetrate my disguise.

I spent the rest of the day in my room, finding it difficult to settle to anything in particular. I skimmed the newspapers, ate a few chocolates and attempted to read Lady Anne Blunt's very excellent book, *The Bedouin Tribes of the Euphrates*. At length, Portia had a tray sent up with dinner, but I found myself far too excited to eat. I rang for the tray to be cleared and applied myself to my disguise. I observed, not for the first time, that gentlemen's attire was both oddly liberating and strangely constricting. The freedom from corsets was delicious, but I found the tightness of the trousers disconcerting, and when Portia came to pass judgement, she shook her head.

"They are quite fitted," she pronounced. "You cannot take off the coat at any point, or you will be instantly known for a woman."

I tugged on the coat. "Better?"

She gestured for me to turn in a slow circle. "Yes, although you must do something about your hands. No one will ever believe those are the hands of a young man."

I pulled on gloves and took up my hat, striking a pose. "Now?"

Portia pursed her lips. "It will not stand the closest inspection, but since you mean to go out at night, I think it will do. But why did you chose formal evening dress? Surely you do not intend to travel in polite circles?"

I shrugged. "I may have no choice. Everything depends upon where Brisbane is bound. If I am in a plain town suit, I cannot follow, but if I am in evening attire, I might just gain entrée. At worst, I can pretend to be an inebriated young buck on the Town."

She hesitated. "It seemed a very great joke at first, but I am not at ease. The last time you did this, you took Valerius. Could you not ask one of our brothers to accompany you? Or perhaps Aquinas. He is entirely loyal."

I nibbled at my lip, catching a few hairs of the moustaches. I plucked them out and wiped them on my trousers. "I cannot ask any of our brothers. They are as peremptory as Brisbane. Although I do wish I had thought of Aquinas," I admitted. "He would have been the perfect conspirator, but it is too late now. Besides, I am not certain I could afford it," I added, thinking of the five-pound bribe I had promised Morag.

I tugged the hat lower upon my head and flung a white silk scarf about my neck, just covering my chin. I collected a newspaper in case I grew bored during my surveillance and tipped my hat with a flourish. "Wish me luck."

Portia linked smallest fingers with me and I was off, slipping out of the house on quiet feet. Too quiet, I reminded myself. Men walked as if they owned the earth, and I should have to walk the same. I slowed my pace, my heels striking hard against the pavement. On the corner, the lamplighter had just scaled his ladder. After a moment's work, a comforting glow shone from the lamp. I smiled, and the lamplighter touched his cap.

"A cab for you, madam? There's a hansom just coming now."

I cursed softly, then called up to him. "What betrayed me?"

He gave me a broad smile. "A gentleman would never smile at a lamplighter. But the effect is not bad. For a moment, you had me quite deceived," he reassured me.

I sighed and gave him a wave before hailing the hansom. Struck with a sudden inspiration, I adopted a thick French accent to address the driver. It was a point of national pride for Englishmen to consider Frenchmen womanly and effeminate, and it occurred to me that I could manage a far better job of impersonating a Frenchman than an English fellow.

"Where to, me lad?" he asked, but not unkindly. I hesitated. Brisbane could be departing from either our home or the consulting rooms, but I could not be certain which. On a hunch, I called out our home address in Brook Street. Whatever business Brisbane was about, he would most likely have gone home to bathe and dress for the evening and shave for the second time. His beard was far too heavy to permit him to go out for the evening without secondary ablutions.

I jumped lightly into the hansom, beginning to enjoy myself. I instructed the driver that I meant to hire him for the night. He demurred until we settled on an extortionate rate for his services, at which point he was my man. He threw himself into our surveillance with an admirable enthusiasm, holding the hansom at some distance from the house itself, but still near enough I could see the comings and goings. I think he thought me involved in a romantic intrigue, for I heard several mutterings about Continentals and their wicked ways, but I ignored him, preferring to keep a close watch upon my house instead.

And while I watched, I discovered an interesting fact—surveillance was the dullest activity imaginable. I had not been there a quarter of an hour before I was prodding myself awake, but my evening was not in vain. Some half an hour after we arrived, I saw Brisbane emerge, elegantly attired in his customary evening garments of sharp black and white and carrying a black silk scarf. Just as he emerged, another hansom happened by, or perhaps Brisbane had arranged for its arrival, for he stepped directly from the kerb to the carriage without a break in his stride, tucking the scarf over his shirtfront as he moved. I rapped upon the roof of my own carriage to alert the driver, and after a few moments, we followed discreetly behind.

My man was a marvel, for he never permitted Brisbane's hansom out of his sight, but neither did he draw near enough to bring attention to us. He held the cab at a distance as Brisbane alighted in front of an imposing old house on a respectable if not fashionable street. A lamplighter had been here, as well, and by squinting, I could just make out the sign, marked in imposing letters. *The Spirit Club.*

There came a low whistle from the hansom driver and I put my head through the trap. "I know. Give me a minute." I banged the trap back down and sat for a moment, thinking furiously. I knew I had encountered the name of this particular club recently, very recently, in fact. I scrabbled through the newspaper until I found the notice I sought.

The Spirit Club hosts the acclaimed French medium, Madame Séraphine for an indefinite engagement. Ladies may consult with Madame during the Ladies' Séance held every afternoon at four o'clock. Gentlemen will be welcomed for the evening sessions, held at eight and ten o'clock. Places must be secured by prior arrangement.

I ought to have known. When Spiritualism had become fashionable, several dozen such clubs had sprung up around London like so many toadstools after an autumn rain. Usually they were maintained with a tiny staff and a resident medium to hold sessions for paying clients. Depending upon the talents of the particular medium, the sessions might involve a séance or automatic writing or some other sort of spiritual manifestations. Some clients went purely for the purpose of entertainment, viewing the mediums as little better than fortune-tellers. Others went from desperation, and it was sometimes the most surprising people who turned to Spiritualism to give them comfort or answer their questions. Sometimes perfectly rational men of business became so dependent upon their medium of choice that they refused to stir a step with regard to their investments without the advice of the spirits. Engagements could not be announced, children could not be named, houses could not be purchased until the spirits had been consulted.

For my part, I found the entire notion of Spiritualism baffling. It was not so much that I felt it impossible the spirits could revisit this life as I thought it vastly disappointing they should want to. If the afterlife could promise no greater entertainment than visiting a club of clammy-handed strangers, then what pleasure was there to be had in being dead?

I blessed the instinct that had caused me to kit myself out as a man, but puffed a sigh of irritation when I realised that without prior arrangement, I could hardly expect to gain entrée into the club.

Still, nothing ventured, nothing gained, I told myself brightly, and I dropped to the pavement. I tossed a substantial amount of money to my driver with instructions to wait some distance farther down the street, then made my way to the Spirit Club. There was no sign of Brisbane, and I realised that he had disappeared as I was tearing through the newspaper for information. I had broken the cardinal rule of surveillance and taken my eyes from my subject, I thought with a stab of annoyance. But the Spirit Club was the only likely destination for him, I decided, and taking the bull firmly by the horns, I rang the bell and waited. After a long moment, an impossibly tall, impossibly thin gentleman opened the door. He had a lugubrious face and a sepulchral manner.

"May I help you?" He gave me a forbidding glance, and I knew instinctively that I should have to put on a very good performance indeed to gain entrance to the club.

I coughed and pitched my voice as low as I could as I adopted an air of *bonhomie*. "Ah, *bonsoir,* my friend. I come to see the great medium—Madame Séraphine!" I cried in my Continental accent. I swept him a low, theatrical bow.

The lugubrious expression did not flicker. "Have you an appointment?"

"Ah, no, alas! I have only just this day arrived from France, you understand." I smiled a conspiratorial smile, inviting him to smile with me.

Still, the face remained impassively correct. "Have you a card?"

I felt my heart drop into my throat. How I could have been so stupid as to forget such an essential component of a gentleman's wardrobe was beyond me. I did not deserve to be a detective, I thought bitterly.

The porter noted my dismay and took a step forward as if to usher me from the premises. But I had come too far to be turned back.

I flung out my arms. "I should have, but the devils at the station, they pick my pockets! My card case, my notecase, these things they take from me!" I cried. "It is a disgrace that they steal from me, the Comte de Roselende, the great-nephew of the Emperor!"

Napoléon III had been deposed for the better part of two decades, but an innate snobbery lurked within most butlers and porters, and I depended upon it. "I am here in England to visit my beloved great-aunt, the Empress Eugénie," I pressed on. "She lives in Hampshire, you know."

This much was true. The Empress lived in quiet retirement in Farmborough, and had once taken tea with my father. It was a particularly brilliant stroke of inspiration as it was well-known that the Empress had once hosted the famous medium Daniel Douglas Home who had conjured the spectre of her father. I watched closely, to see if my connections with royalty swayed the porter at all, but he seemed unmoved.

"I am sorry, Monsieur le Comte, but without a prior appointment, I cannot admit you to the Spirit Club," he intoned sadly. He made to shut the door upon me, but just then a woman appeared, her plain face alight with interest.

"Monsieur le Comte?" she asked, coming forward to put a hand to the porter's sleeve as she peered closely at me. "You are a Frenchman?"

Her own accent was smoothly modulated, perhaps from long travels out of her native land, for I detected French as her native tongue, but touched with a bit of German and a hint of Russian in her vowels.

"*Oui, mademoiselle!* St. John Malachy LaPlante, the Comte de Roselende, at your service." I sprang forward to press a kiss to her hand, praying my moustaches would not choose that moment to desert me. But they held fast, and I released the little hand to study the lady herself. She was dressed plainly, and it occurred to me that I had erred grievously in paying her such lavish attentions.

But she merely ducked her head, blushing. "You are very kind," she murmured in English for the porter's benefit. "My sister will be very happy to find a place for you."

"Ah, you are the sister of the great Madame Séraphine!" I proclaimed grandly.

She gave me a shy, gentle smile. "Yes, I am Agathe LeBrun.

Please, come in. You will be our special guest. Beekman, let the gentleman pass."

The porter, Beekman, stepped aside, not entirely pleased at the development. I smiled broadly at him as I passed and followed the kindly Agathe as she conducted me down a dimly lit corridor. She stopped at a closed door and inclined her head. "This is where the gentlemen gather before the séance. Please sign the guestbook and make yourself comfortable. There are cigars and whisky."

I pretended to shudder and she gave me a look of approbation. "I understand," she mumured in French. "Whisky is so unsubtle, is it not? I will see if I can find something more palatable for you."

"You must not exercise yourself on my behalf," I protested.

She ducked her head again, glancing up at me, a thin line of worry creasing her brow. I put her at somewhat older than my thirty-three years, perhaps half a dozen years my senior, and her plain face would have been more attractive had she not worn an expression of perpetual harassment.

"I wonder if you are troubled, monsieur," she said softly.

I started, then forced myself to relax as I realised how clever the arrangement was. Doubtless she was meant to extract information from me in the guise of a simple conversation—information that would be conveyed to her sister for use in the séance. The opening gambit was such that could have been used upon anyone at all, and I marvelled at its simplicity.

"It is kind of you to notice," I murmured back. "Money troubles. It is for this reason that I come to England."

Her expression sharpened then, and I knew I had said the wrong thing. My entrée had doubtless been because I had neatly dropped the Empress' name into conversation. The notion that I was rich and well-connected—and therefore could prove valuable to Madame Séraphine—was my only attractiveness. I hastened to reclaim it.

"Of course, I have expectations, *excellent* expectations," I confessed. "But I am a little short at present. I would like to know how long I am expected to wait for my hopes to be realised."

I tried to adopt a suitable expression, but I found it difficult. How did one manage to convey respectable avarice?

It must have worked, for her features relaxed again into faint worry, and she dropped a curtsey. "I understand, monsieur. May I take your hat? Please make yourself comfortable. The séance will begin in a moment."

I handed over my hat and she gestured towards the door, leaving me to do the honours as she disappeared back down the darkened hall. I took a deep breath and steeled myself before opening the door. By the window stood an older gentleman of rigid posture and decidedly military bearing. His clothes were costly enough, but his shoulders sported a light dusting of white from his unwashed hair, and his chin was imperfectly shaven. He stared out the window at nothing, for the garden was shrouded in blackness, and I suspected he stood there as a stratagem to avoid conversation.

In contrast to him was a second gentleman, who occupied himself with the whisky and a gasogene. He was sleekly polished, with a veneer of good breeding that I suspected was precisely that—a veneer. His lips were thin and cruel and his brow high and sharply modeled. He put me in mind of a bird of prey, and he eyed me dismissively as I entered. The third gentleman looked a bit less certain of himself, a trifle rougher in his dress and decorum, and only he gave me a smile as I entered. He was dressed in an evening suit that I guessed to be second-hand, and his bright ginger hair had been slicked down with a heavy hand.

I nodded politely towards them all and made my way to the guestbook, where I took up the pen and signed with a flourish. Just as I finished the last scrolling vowel of *Roselende,* the door opened, and I gave a start. For one heart-stilling instant, I thought it was Plum, but instantly I saw my mistake. Like the newcomer, Plum was an elegant fellow, but I daresay if the pair of them had been placed side by side, few eyes would have fallen first upon my brother. They were of a size, both being tall and well-made, and both of them had green eyes and brown hair shading to the exact hue of polished chestnuts. But Plum lacked this fellow's predatory grace, and there was something resolute about the set of this gentleman's jaw, as if he seldom gave quarter or asked for it. His eyes flicked briefly around the room, lingering only a fraction longer upon me than the rest of the company. He inclined his head and advanced to where I stood next to the guestbook. I stepped back sharply and held out the pen.

"Thank you," he murmured in a pleasant drawling baritone. I flicked my eyes to the page as he scrawled his signature with a flourish.

Sir Morgan Fielding. I had heard the name once or twice in society gossip, but I did not know him, and I relaxed a little as I realised he doubtless did not know me, either.

He replaced the pen, and although he did not look at me, he must have been aware of my scrutiny, for his shapely mouth curved into a slow smile, and I felt a blush beginning to creep up my cheeks.

Hastily, I turned away and picked up the latest copy of *Punch.* I flicked unseeing through the pages, grateful when the door opened to admit another visitor. To my surprise, this one was a woman, thickly veiled and silent. She was dressed in unrelieved black, at least twenty years out of date, and the severity of her costume was a trifle forbidding. She moved well, but it was impossible to place her age. She might have been twenty or forty or anywhere between, for she was slender enough and her step was light. She approached the guestbook, but before she could sign, the door opened again and Agathe LeBrun appeared in the doorway.

"It is time," she intoned, and to my surprise, I found myself shivering. I wondered briefly where Brisbane was, but I trotted along obediently as Agathe herded us out.

The military gentleman cast a quick look at the veiled lady and grumbled at Agathe. "I thought this was a gentlemen's only session," he began.

Agathe shrugged. "Madame makes exceptions when it suits her. This lady has come several times to commune with the spirit of her dead child, and it is not the practise of Madame Séraphine to turn away those in need of her services."

"Still, I do not like it," he said, his mouth mulish.

"The lady's presence means there will be seven at the table. It is a most auspicious number for Madame."

He opened his mouth to argue, but Agathe turned with a snap of her skirts and beckoned for us to follow. The veiled lady inclined her head towards the military fellow to show she bore him no ill will. He gave a harrumph and strode off behind Agathe. As he passed me, I caught a whiff of old dust and unwashed flesh and wrinkled my nose. The sleek and hawkish gentleman who had stood by the whisky offered the veiled lady his arm and she took it. The rest of us fell in line like a crocodile of children just out of the nursery.

Agathe led us down a long, narrow corridor, off which

opened several rooms set aside for various purposes. Small signs directed vistors. *Automatic Writing Room. Lecture Hall. Summoning Room. Room of Special Examinations.* It all sounded faintly alarming, and instinctively I crept nearer to the fellow in front of me. The ginger-haired young man gave me a sharp look, and I fell back again, muttering an apology in French.

The walls of the corridor were very dark and the lighting almost nonexistent, lending an otherworldly effect. Over it all, I detected the thick floral scent of incense, the smoky fumes of funeral flowers burnt to ash. It did not seem to disturb the others, but I found it increasingly difficult to breathe, and my head grew light and oddly disconnected from my body.

At last, we came to the final door in the corridor, marked *Séance,* and Agathe stood by to let us enter. As we passed her in turn, she gave each of us a meaningful look. The general was first, and he rummaged in his pockets, producing a bit of money, which he pressed into her palm. She murmured her thanks and the rest of us followed suit. I had no idea what the expected donation might be, so I handed over a guinea as I entered the room, and it must have been acceptable, for Agathe nodded and said softly, "Monsieur le Comte is very generous."

The chamber was of modest size, the walls hung with black, and illuminated by a single lamp near the door. A heavy round table, also draped in black, stood in the centre of the room, and about it were ranged a series of chairs. The black hangings were velvet, dull and weighty, and the room felt oppressive. More of the thick aroma hung in the air, and a small brazier smoked upon the cold hearth. There were no paintings or decorations of any sort, only the web of unrelieved black, robbing the room of all light and movement, and a single clock upon the mantel. The timepiece was a strange affair of black enamel with a figure of Death looming over the clock's face and gesturing to it with his scythe. I supposed it was meant to warn us of the fleeting nature of time, but the hands never moved, and I shivered at the ghoulishness of it and turned my attention to the rest of the room.

At the opposite end from the door stood a cupboard of sorts, and I realised with a start that it was a spirit cabinet, a place for manifesting souls that did not rest. It was some seven feet high but quite narrow and only some two or three feet deep. A heavy velvet curtain closed it off from the rest of the room, and I wondered what mysteries it concealed. Would Madame claim it was a portal to the other side, a ghostly no-man's land of disembodied voices and spirits that could not sleep? I felt a quickening of my pulse, a sudden longing to be quit of the place. But before I could act upon it, we were instructed to take any chairs save the one in the centre, and we seated ourselves quickly. As near as I could tell, the chair in the centre was the same as the rest, but my suspicions had been raised. I took the chair next to it, the ginger-haired man on my other side, whilst the chair opposite mine was taken by the handsome latecomer, Sir Morgan. On either side of him sat the other gentlemen, and the veiled lady took the chair across from that reserved for the medium.

We had been seated only a moment when Agathe appeared again in the doorway, now wearing a black shawl over her plain gown, and proclaimed, "Honoured guests, I present your guide to the spirit world, Madame Séraphine!"

There was a moment's pause—to heighten the anticipation, I had no doubt—and then a figure materialised behind her. As she moved forward, I saw that she was slender and delicately boned, but she gave the impression of great force, as if a much larger and more imposing person had come into the room. It was a trick of personality, I supposed, and I believe it would have been impossible to ignore her even in a crowded ballroom. In this small space, she commanded our attention. She was dressed in black robes, and as she walked, I saw that the robes were embroidered with various arcane signs and symbols. Her hair, thick and black and perhaps assisted by the hairdresser's arts, flowed freely down her back, and her eyes were heavily ringed with kohl. They gleamed in the dim light of the room, locking briefly upon each of us with a sort of knowing that touched my spine with a shiver.

As she reached the table, she raised her arms as if in benediction, and her small white hands floated upwards in the air like doves. "My friends," she intoned in a sweet, light voice. "I thank you for coming, and I ask the Spirit that covers us all to bless you."

Her voice rang with sincerity, and I wondered precisely how much of a fraud she was, for I had begun to suspect Brisbane had been engaged to unmask her, although precisely where he was at that moment, I could not imagine. I knew he had done such work a few times in the past, always at the behest of families who worried that the ancestral fortunes were being squandered upon charlatans by a gullible relation. I was convinced he had set out upon such work again, and I was vastly irritated that I had followed him upon an errand that clearly had nothing to do with Bellmont. I should have to continue to trail him if I meant to uncover his connection there, and that would mean a rather late night. I stifled a yawn.

Agathe turned down the lamp by the door, leaving us in

almost complete darkness with only a pale glow of ghostly blue where the jet still flickered. The door opened once, and in the dim glow from the corridor, I saw Agathe leave, closing the door behind her to plunge us once more into gloom. Arranged about the table in our black evening clothes, we were little more than a collection of disembodied heads nodding in the shadows.

"Join hands," the medium commanded sharply, and I started in my chair. She offered me one of her hands, and I took it, joining with the ginger-haired man on the other side. He gripped my hand tightly, and I wondered for an instant if he noticed that mine was smaller than it ought to have been. But he showed no sign of interest in me whatsoever. His eyes were fixed firmly upon Madame Séraphine as she began the séance.

"My friends, you have come tonight to hear messages from the spirit world. I promise you shall. But I must warn you. I cannot summon spirits who do not wish to come, and I cannot promise that each of you will receive a message. The discarnates will not manifest before those who do not believe. If you doubt, you must leave now and never return." She paused, piercing each of us with that dark, magnetic gaze, made all the more dramatic by her heavy use of kohl. Then she bowed her head. "Very well. We will begin." She settled herself more comfortably in her chair and closed her eyes. "Spirits of the world beyond, I now part the veil for your return and summon you to come forth and bring us news from the other realm."

She was silent a long moment, then suddenly, just as I began to grow bored, I felt her hand tighten upon mine. A deep humming seemed to emanate from her chest. It grew louder and louder, and finally she spoke, but in a voice entirely unlike the one she had used before. It was deep and husky, the voice of a man, but it came from her throat, of that I was certain.

"I wish to speak."

Madame Séraphine gave a deep shudder and spoke in her own voice by way of reply. "I see you. What is your message? To whom do you wish to speak?"

"I will speak to the general."

A muffled cry came from the military man.

"Speak on, spirit."

"I forgive." The general gave another cry, then mastered himself.

"You forgive, spirit?"

"Yes. I forgive. I have passed on. The general must release himself of his burdens. It was our destiny to die."

I suppressed a sigh. No doubt Agathe had determined the general's rank when he secured his place at the séance. Any military man of his age and rank would have seen battle, and any commander would have seen men fall and questioned himself after. It would take no great imagination upon the part of the medium to guess that such a thing would weigh heavily, even years after.

Madame continued the extraordinary two-handed conversation. "What is your name, spirit? Give your name to the general that he may know you."

The voice was fainter now. *"Sim—Sim,"* came the distant reply. The voice paused, and the moment stretched out, the anticipation mounting.

"Simpson?" cried the general.

"Simpson," the spirit finished, almost inaudibly. *"Farewell!"*

Madame spoke. "I have nothing more from Simpson. He has vanished in a burst of light, the light of the Spirit's love. He has gone to the other side now, and will not speak again."

The general subsided into a series of noisy snuffling sounds, and I marvelled. A general would command a goodly number of men. It was an excellent guess that one of them might bear the surname Simpson or Simmons or any of a dozen other variations. Or perhaps it had not been a guess at all. If the general had made his appointment with a few days' notice, Madame Séraphine would have had more than enough time to investigate his record of service. The newspapers detailed all of the trials and tribulations of the army. It would have been the work of a few hours to find something that would have touched a tender spot with the general, even to find a name. The logic of this was inescapable, but I had to admire her performance. The delivery was impeccable. The two halves of the conversation had been seamless, very nearly overlapping at one point, and when she meant to convey the spirit's withdrawal, she had given the impression of such impassable distance, of a veil dropping over to conceal the worlds between. It was superbly done, and I had little doubt she would have made an excellent actress had she chosen to tread the boards.

The general at last lapsed into sniffles again, and Madame passed on.

"Some new spirit has come forth. Speak, spirit!" Again a dramatic pause, and then a new voice, this one high and girlish.

"*Papa!*"

The tall, sour gentleman gave a start. "Honoria?"

"*Yes, Papa! I come to watch over you all. I am at peace.*" The gentleman cleared his throat hard, and I smothered another sigh. It was all too maudlin for words. But I do not know what else I might have expected. Those who consulted mediums always did so because their dead did not rest easily.

They looked for forgiveness, for absolution, and Madame gave it them.

"Honoria, I must know. Did you compromise yourself with your sister's fiancé? Did you take your own life?"

I blinked in surprise, but the bluntness of the questions did not throw Madame from her purpose. The high, girlish voice continued. *"I am beyond such things, Papa. It is so beautiful here, I cannot think of where I have come from."* It was a clever answer, neatly skirting the question.

But the father was not satisfied. "Honoria, do not witter on. I must know if you betrayed your sister's faith and if you took your life. Your mother insisted we bury you in the family plot, but by God, I will have you removed if you disgraced us," he thundered. Whatever sympathy I might have felt towards this miserable parent was smothered with that last bit of cruelty. I could well imagine him as a father—intolerant, impatient, unforgiving—and I was rather glad poor Honoria was done with him.

Madame Séraphine must have felt the same, for she cut in, still employing Honoria's voice, but lit with a new fire.

"Enough, Papa! In the spirit world I am perfected, and you have no power here. Leave me be and mend your unkindness lest you fail to join me here."

He gasped and closed his mouth with a sharp snap of the jaws. Next to me, the ginger-haired young man gave a snort—of suppressed laughter, I suspected. I wondered if the spirits had a message for him, but Madame's head suddenly dropped forward.

"I have a message from a dark lady. Will you speak aloud, spirit?" She paused and cocked her head, as if listening intently. "She will not. She begs that I will speak for her. She says that all things will come right in the end. But one must act with generosity of spirit to achieve one's aim. She is very close now, so close to understanding. She needs only a little encouragement from one who sits at this table." Madame gave a little start forward, her eyes still closed. "She is withdrawing behind the veil and I have nothing more from her." Madame settled back into her chair again.

"Speak to me, spirits," she intoned in her own voice. A long moment passed, a very long moment, in fact, and I felt a prickle at the back of my neck, as if the hairs had stood right on end. The atmosphere was eerie, and I felt in that moment as if anything at all might happen.

I turned to Madame, whose grip upon my hand tightened. She began to rock back and forth, the humming rising once more from her chest. She bent forward at the waist, as if she were sick, but the humming never faltered. It gave way to a low moaning, her head turning from side to side, and suddenly, horribly, out of her mouth came a filmy white substance.

"Ectoplasm!" cried the general.

The white substance hovered in the air, glowing a little in the darkness. There was a sudden terrible shudder from Madame, and the ectoplasm vanished. "The spirits call upon you to believe and to speak of what you have seen this night!" she pronounced. She opened her eyes and fixed them upon each of us in turn. "You must speak the truth and say that you have seen the world beyond the veil, that Madame Séraphine has communicated with the dead. That is all, the spirits have gone."

With that, she dropped our hands and rose, drooping as if exhausted. Agathe materialised and took her sister's arm, supporting her from the room. At the door, she turned back.

"It has been a difficult evening for Madame and she suffers from exhaustion. If you wish to come again, Madame will be receiving the spirits tomorrow night. She bids you adieu with her blessings and those of the spirits."

Madame lifted a pale, trembling hand, and they were gone. The lady and gentlemen at the table rose, doubtless as startled by Madame's sudden departure as they had been by what they had seen. The veiled lady took her leave immediately, and I was not surprised. The general had been less than cordial to her, and she might not have wanted to linger in his company. For his part, the general daubed at his eyes with a handkerchief as he left the room, followed hard upon by Honoria's father. The ginger-haired young man made to leave just as the handsome fellow stepped to the door. What followed was a pantomime of exaggerated politeness as the ginger-haired younger man moved aside. The handsome fellow then paused to check his watch and pat his pockets for his cigarette case as the ginger-haired young man cooled his heels, clearly regretting his own good manners as he made his way through the door at last. I followed him, wondering where I should next look for Brisbane. Just as I reached the door, hands, hard and unyielding, clamped about my mouth and upper arm and I was dragged backwards into the spirit cabinet. The velvet curtain fell, entombing me with my assailant in the stuffy darkness.

The
FOURTH CHAPTER

Glendower: I can call spirits from the vasty deep.
Hotspur: Why, so can I, or so can any man.
But will they come when you do call them?

—*Henry IV, Part One*

I would have cried out, but his hand was fast over my mouth, his body pressing hard against mine as we wedged into the narrow cabinet. He bent to my ear, whispering harshly.

"I knew there was one chance in a thousand I was going to get you safely out of town, but this is entirely too much, Julia. I ought to take you home, strip off that ridiculous costume and beat you senseless." I wriggled against him and Brisbane clamped his hand tighter. "Unless that is an invitation, keep still. Agathe will return in a moment and she must think you have gone with the others."

I prodded his hand, and to his credit, he trusted me enough to remove it. We waited in silence then, although I could feel the slow, rhythmic thunder of his heartbeat, and I knew he could feel the lighter, faster beat of mine. There was a brief rustling in the room, a muttering of French under the breath, and then a decisive bang as the outer door closed. We were alone.

I could not see him, but I could feel the heat emanating from his body, and I knew he was shatteringly angry. I rose on tiptoe and put my lips to his ear.

"I had no choice," I began.

He shied back. "Your moustaches are tickling me," he said coldly. Without preamble, he reached down and tore them from my lip.

"Ow!" I began to remonstrate with him, but he put his hand to my mouth again.

"Hush!" he rasped into my ear. "This cabinet is a passageway. It leads to Madame's private quarters."

I was confused. If Brisbane meant to expose her, why not do so during the séance itself, when she was bringing forth ectoplasm? Why wait until she was alone in the privacy of her own rooms?

I raised my brows at him, and even though we were in darkness, he must have sensed my curiosity. "I do not care about her medium's tricks," he explained. "Altogether bigger game is afoot here."

I felt a dull thud of dismay. He was on the trail of something more important and I had ruined it by blundering in. I touched his hand and he removed it.

"I am sorry," I whispered. "I thought you were in some sort of trouble. I came to help."

I felt him cant his head sideways in the darkness. "You thought I was in trouble?"

I nodded. I felt him begin to tremble in my arms, and it was only after a long moment that I realised he was laughing, great silent belly laughs that he was having difficulty suppressing.

"You may amuse yourself at my expense, Brisbane, but I did come to help," I returned.

He wiped at his eyes, and when his lips grazed my ear, I felt the anger in him had ebbed. "I have no doubt of that. You aren't wearing any more moustaches, are you? I got them all?"

I felt my upper lip, still tender from where he had wrenched them from me. "I am myself again. Why?"

"Because I cannot kiss you properly with those absurd things glued to your lip."

"Oh," I murmured. *"Oh."*

He did not release me for some minutes, and when he did, it occurred to me that I ought to make him angry more often if this was the result.

"Ought we not continue your investigation?" I asked as I tucked my shirt back into my trousers. "We cannot stay here all night."

"We might," he offered, his voice thick in the darkness. "It occurs to me there are distinct advantages to your not wearing a corset."

I smoothed my waistcoat. "I was rather proud of this disguise and my arrangements to elude you," I told him, studiously ignoring his importunate hands.

"It was very well done," he conceded. "How did you manage to get out of the house party?"

"I bribed Morag with five pounds," I told him. "How did you discover me?"

"I bribed her with ten."

I smothered an oath and Brisbane bent once more to my ear. "I must press on. Draw yourself up as tightly against the wall as you can so I can move past you."

I did as he bade me, making myself as small and flat as possible. It was a very snug fit, and I was not at all certain he would manage it, but he slid at last to the other side of me and turned back.

"I am making my way to the end of the passage and I dare not leave you behind. You will follow hard upon my heels, and you will make no sound. Beekman should be in the cellars drinking off the best of the port, but I do not wish to take any chances. Understood?"

By way of reply, I gripped the back of his coat and he gave a small grunt of approval. I felt his hands pass over the joining between the back and side walls and the back wall sprang open as if obeying a conjurer's commands. I felt a rush of cooler air as we moved into a slightly larger passageway beyond and the panel slid closed behind us, clicking neatly into place.

Some distance ahead, a faint glow showed the way, and I continued to grip Brisbane's coat as he moved forward. After a moment, I saw that the light came from the top of a steep flight of stairs that twisted once upon itself. The hidden stair was so narrow Brisbane was forced to climb sideways, leading with one shoulder. At the top, we found another small passageway that seemed to end abruptly at a wall.

Overhead, a single dim electric bulb cast its feeble light, throwing harsh shadows and putting Brisbane's face into diabolical relief. He pointed to the wall.

"Behind this is a looking-glass in Madame's boudoir," he mouthed against my ear. I did not ask him how he knew. He stepped forward and touched another hidden mechanism. The panel yielded but did not swing open, and I saw that this was to our advantage as Brisbane was able to slide one finger into the gap and ease it aside just enough to put an eye to the opening. I slipped below him to see for myself and immediately he clamped a large hand to my neck to hold me still. He could not speak then, but I knew to expect a lecture once we had quit the place.

I could see the merest sliver of the Madame's room, but what I saw did not surprise me. It was furnished in more of the same heavy theatricality of the chambers on the main floor, with the addition of several bouquets of flowers, doubtless from her admirers and clients. There was a second looking-glass, smaller than the one we crouched behind, and Madame sat before it, combing out her long dark locks. Agathe scurried about the room, sometimes visible to us, sometimes not, attempting to bring order to the room. She began by tidying up lengths of very fine muslin, placing them into a box with a series of curious rods and other accoutrements of the spiritualist's arts. I noted trumpets and armfuls of scarlet roses fashioned of silk. Most surprising of all was a little bottle that Agathe uncorked. Suddenly, the whole bottle seemed to glow with an unearthly luminosity, pale gold and heavenly. She gave a nod of satisfaction and placed it into the box with the other things. After she finished gathering the medium's tools, she busied herself collecting discarded clothes and papers, chattering in French all the while.

"It was a very poor show tonight, I think. You did not produce any apports or speak with your spirit guide. You did not even let me blow breath upon their necks or touch them!"

Madame seemed not to listen as Agathe chattered on.

"You should not have spoken in such a fashion to Sir Henry! He is a valuable client and he will not wish to come again when you have scolded him like a little child," she complained.

Madame waved a languid hand. "It matters not to me. What care I for pences and pounds?" She took up a jar of expensive-looking skin crème and began to apply it to her hands with slow, methodical strokes.

Agathe gave a snort of derision. "You will care very much when we cannot pay the butcher! Always it is the same. Always you with your head in the clouds, and me with my feet upon the ground."

Madame massaged in the crème, paying close attention to her décolletage, lifting her chin this way and that as she stared at her own reflection. "Is that a wrinkle starting there, do you think? No, just a shadow. God, the trouble one takes to stay young!" She gave a sigh and regarded her sister in the looking-glass. "Oh, stop fretting! Sir Henry deserved it, Agathe. He is no friend to our kind. He has no romance in his soul, no understanding."

"He has money," Agathe pointed out sourly. She bundled the clothes into the wardrobe and tamped the papers into a neat stack and handed them to Madame.

The lady drew a slender chain from her bodice. At the end dangled a key, and she used it to unlock a coffer standing upon her dressing table. She placed the papers neatly inside, then relocked the box and replaced the key as Agathe continued to tidy the room. She opened a box and removed a length of cobweb-fine French muslin. It was the whitest muslin I had ever seen, and so light, a spider might have felt at home upon it.

"For the next session," she said, handing the stuff to Madame. I suppressed a gasp as I realised I had just discovered the source of Madame's ectoplasm.

"And mind you draw it out more slowly next time," Agathe scolded. "You rushed the moment during the last session and it was not as dramatic as it ought to have been. Now, you have just enough time to eat something before the next séance. You must keep up your strength."

There was a wistfulness in her voice then, a note of pleading, and I saw that they were bound by strong emotion. I
wondered if the bickering between them was simply the
result of being too much in one another's pockets.

Madame smiled at her. "You take good care of me,
Agathe, sometimes against your will, I think."

Agathe pierced her with a look. "How can you say such a
thing to me? Have I not been devoted to you?"

Madame sighed. "Of course you have. But you do not
trust me. Always with the lectures and the harsh words, as
if I were a child to be scolded when it is I who will be the
making of us!"

Agathe tightened her mouth further still, but the disapproval was writ upon her face. Madame gave a harsh little
laugh.

"I know you do not approve. But this time it will be
different, Agathe." Her dark eyes fixed again upon her
own reflection and she touched her face, as if to trace lines
that would soon be visible. "This may be my last chance
to secure my future, *our* future," she said, her eyes burning brilliantly. She spoke slowly, her voice pitched low, as
if more to herself than her sister. "Security, Agathe. At last.
For both of us. You must trust me." Her eyes flew once
more to her sister's, but Agathe would not meet her gaze.

"And still you will not tell me anything? I must learn of
your affairs by eavesdropping like a maid?"

Madame laughed again. "I know you too well to think
you would approve, Agathe! Oh, do not look so stricken.
Once my plans come to fruition, I can tell you everything
and you will see that all shall be well. Soon we will live
like queens! Now, run down and set us a table in the supper
room. I will be down in a moment."

Agathe did as she was ordered and a moment later, after

scenting herself heavily from a flacon on the dressing table, Madame trailed along. I counted to one hundred as Brisbane eased himself out of the hidden passageway. He crossed the room in quick, silent strides, drawing his lockpicks from his pocket as he moved. The casket was open before I reached his side, and he rifled quickly through the papers before swearing almost inaudibly. He put them back as he had found them and then replaced the lid and locked it again, a skill that required extreme dexterity and experience. I kept watch whilst he searched the rest of the room, so neatly that even the eagle-eyed Agathe would not suspect it. He rapped softly for hidden panels, searched under carpets and the undersides of drawers. He felt along the back of the smaller looking-glass and inside the springs of the recamier sofa. He even stuck an arm up the chimney, but he turned up nothing, and since I did not know what we were searching for, I was of little help. The most I could do was keep a sharp ear cocked for a sound upon the stairs, and after perhaps half an hour, I heard it. I waved frantically at Brisbane, but he calmly replaced the carpet over the floorboard he had been testing and grabbed my hand, whirling me into the hidden passageway just as the door opened.

Madame entered, followed hard by a pleading Agathe. "What is it? You must let me call a doctor!"

Madame was doubled over in pain, scarcely able to walk. Her complexion was pale and her brow beaded with sweat. She fell upon the recamier sofa, drawing her knees to her chest and moaning softly. "Oh, what have I eaten? What has done this to me? I am so cold, Agathe!"

Agathe fluttered around her sister, wringing her hands. "I am sending for the doctor," she repeated. Madame gave no sign that she heard her. She shivered and shuddered with convulsions. Agathe snatched up a robe and covered her sister with it before fleeing from the room, calling out to Beekman the porter as she ran. She was gone a long time, or perhaps it just seemed so as we crouched there in the hidden passageway. Madame was sick, comprehensively so, and there was no basin at hand. She did not seem to know or care, and when she began to moan, great gasping moans, I rose as if to go to her. Brisbane's hand held me fast, gripping mine so hard I thought surely the bones must crack. I looked up and he gave a sharp shake of the head, his black hair tumbling over his brow. I moved to push past him, for Madame was in deadly distress now, but Brisbane would have none of it.

Without a sound, he reached down, looping one strong arm around my chest to hold me fast against him. When he spoke, his lips against my ear, his voice was a harsh whisper. "We can do nothing but watch." I made to resist, but he tightened his grasp. I watched then, his hand hard against my mouth, stifling my little cries of horror, as Madame's life ebbed away. She was dying and there was nothing that could be done for her. It happened slowly, as if in a dream, and I knew that I should remember each of those terrible minutes for as long as I should live. I saw her writhe and cry out, and I watched her fall silent as she slipped into the coma, the sleep of death. And I witnessed Agathe, bursting in with the doctor to find her there, the light of life completely extinguished.

Madame was not beautiful in death. Her eyes were only half-closed and her mouth was slack and stained with sick, and I saw it all through the veil of unshed tears. I saw Agathe fall to the floor, sobbing into her sister's skirts, and I saw the doctor searching fruitlessly for a pulse. I saw him close Madame's eyes and drape a shawl over her face, and I saw him draw Agathe from the room, consoling the grief-stricken woman.

When they had gone, Brisbane hauled me roughly to my feet and shoved me along the passageway, back the way we had come. I stumbled down the stairs, and if he had not had hold of my collar, I would have fallen heavily. But he pulled me to my feet and when we reached the spirit cabinet, he paused. With his thumbs, he wiped at my cheeks.

"You must bear up, Julia," he said. "This next bit is the most dangerous. I will do everything I can to get you out of here safely, but you must follow my orders instantly and without question."

I nodded and he eased a finger through the velvet drape to peer through. He ducked back immediately, shaking his head to signify that someone was in the room. He motioned for us to go back the way we had come. We slipped into Madame's room, and I kept my eyes studiously averted from the draped figure on the sofa. Brisbane tried the door, swearing softly.

"Locked. From the outside."

"Pick it!" I ordered. I had no desire to spend the night trapped in a room with a fresh corpse.

He shook his head. "No time. They might return at any minute. There's no help for it. We must take the window."

He moved directly to the window, easing aside the heavy velvet drapes. There was a small bit of coping outside, surely not enough to support him, but he opened the window and flung a leg over the sill, testing the stone with the tip of his boot.

"Brisbane! You're mad. You will be dashed to the stones below," I warned him.

He fixed me with a quelling look. "Instantly and without

question," he reminded me. "Now, climb onto my back and hold tight. You might want to close your eyes."

I did as he suggested, clinging to him with all of my might and never once daring to look down. To my astonishment, he did not descend when we quit Madame's room. He went *up,* climbing the wall until he reached the mansard roof above. He ducked his head and gestured for me to climb over him. My limbs trembled, but I did as he commanded, finding myself atop the roof of the Spirit Club. Alone. I threw myself at the edge of the roof to see what Brisbane was about, and to my horror, realised that he was climbing back down to secure the window and remove all traces of our departure. I huddled on the roof, too numb even to pray, shivering in the cool night air as my head swam from the height. There was a sliver of a moon, and I kept my eyes fixed upon that as I waited. At last, he sprang onto the rooftop, dropping lightly to his feet.

"Oof," was the noise he made as I flung myself at him.

"Brisbane, you are never to do such a thing again," I commanded. "You frightened me half to death. It was far too dangerous and I forbid it. Do you hear me? I *forbid* it."

I was babbling, but to his credit, he merely enfolded me in his arms and held me close to him for a moment. "I had no choice," he murmured. I burrowed closer, borrowing his warmth, until he patted me gently upon my posterior. "We must go."

He took my hand and led me to the edge of the roof. A narrow gap divided this house from the next, and Brisbane leapt lightly, holding out his hand for me to follow after.

"Madness," I muttered. "I do not have a head for heights."

Brisbane gestured impatiently. "I have seen you stare down murderers. If you think I will permit you to turn

missish now, you are quite mistaken. Now, jump!" There
was no mistaking the authority in his tone, but still I
hesitated.

"Julia, if you do not jump by the time I count to five, I
will come back and throw you across. One. Two."

I jumped. Being dashed to death on the street below was
preferable to any punishment Brisbane might think to apply,
I decided. And at the next house, he only had to count to
one before I leapt. By the third, I was crossing side by side
with him, although I still felt a trifle giddy at the height.
Thus we proceeded down the street, walking softly over
rooftops. It was too early for the servants to be settled into
their attic beds for the night, but we took no chances. To
my astonishment, I began to rather enjoy myself. I would
not let myself think on the horror of Madame's death, but
in this moment, I was a real part of Brisbane's investigation,
a true partner in detection, and I almost laughed aloud as
a sharp river breeze caught at my wig and snatched it off,
loosening my hair from the pins.

Just then we came to the end of the last house, and I realised what I ought to have seen before—there was no easy
way down. I peered over the edge of the roof far down to
the cobbles of the darkened street.

"Brisbane? What now?"

He motioned for me to climb onto his back again and
I did so, squeezing my eyes shut once more and cursing
myself for a fool for ever thinking this might be enjoyable.

He proceeded slowly, but as we descended, it became
clear that it was a much more difficult thing for him to
make his way down with me attached to him like a monkey
than it had been to climb up. The momentum alone should
have torn him from the wall, and I saw the effort it cost

him to keep us safe as the muscles of his shoulders and arms corded tightly.

At last, we reached a small bit of coping and I was able to slide from his back as he held on to a piece of ironwork. I gulped in great draughts of fresh air—or what passed for fresh air in London—and pondered our next move.

Suddenly, Brisbane reached out and grasped me high up on the arm and swung me free of the wall. My boot tips brushed the stone, and I stifled a scream as I looked up into his eyes.

"Trust me?" he challenged. There was a grim purpose there, but something more, some animal vitality that the evening's adventure had roused in him. He was a man thoroughly within his element.

"I trust you," I vowed.

And then he dropped me.

The
FIFTH CHAPTER

You tread upon my patience.

—Henry IV, Part One

Before I had a chance to scream out in surprise, I landed upon a soft pile of wool, newly shorn and smelling warmly of lanolin and bound for the mill in a wagon. A second later, Brisbane landed almost directly on top of me, crushing me down into the soft wool beneath.

"Brisbane, that is the second time in our acquaintance that you have done such a foul thing. And you are crushing the breath out of me. Remove yourself," I remarked coolly, attempting to recover my *sangfroid*. I knew his little trick was to get back a bit of his own after I had bungled my way into his investigation, and I took it with good grace. I deserved far worse, if I was honest.

He slanted me a smile. "Oh, I think the situation offers up some very interesting possibilities."

I shoved hard against his shoulder and he heaved a sigh before levering himself off of me. "Pity," he murmured, and I felt my own lips twitching in response. He rolled away and we spent the next quarter of an hour lying very quietly and collecting our breath. I longed to ask him a thousand questions, but just when I opened my mouth his eyes sharpened and he rose, pulling me hastily to my knees.

"Quickly. The cart is preparing to slow down for an omnibus. Wait, now, just until it stops. Here we are then, over the side," he ordered, pushing my backside until I obeyed, landing solidly on the cobbles with Brisbane hard after.

"Where are we?" I demanded. We were on a street wholly unfamiliar to me and rather unsavoury in appearance. A gin palace stood upon the corner, the doors thrown open to night air. Raucous laughter and the tinny music of an elderly piano filled the air along with the stench of raw sewage in the gutters. I wrinkled my nose as Brisbane rose and dusted himself, taking in the surroundings. I realised what a sight we must present, for Brisbane was clearly a gentleman dressed in the forefront of fashion in an unfashionable part of town, and I, without my hat and moustaches, was undeniably a woman pretending to be something she was not.

A creature of the night crept from a doorway, offering some unspeakable service and Brisbane grabbed my wrist. "Let us go, and quickly," he muttered under his breath.

We hurried into the nearest alley, a narrow street thick with shadows. Against my will, I thought of the vicious murderer who had terrorised the East End during the previous year. He had never been apprehended, and just because the murders had ceased was no guarantee they would not be resumed.

I clung to Brisbane's hand as we moved silently through the shadows. His head swung left and then right, carefully assessing the situation at all times. Suddenly, he lifted his head like a pointer and thrust me behind him. An instant later, a villainous fellow materialised in front of us. His accent was so thick I could scarcely understand him, but it was quite apparent that he was demanding our money, and when he brandished his cudgel, he grinned broadly at the pair of us.

Brisbane swore fluently, and I made no attempt to remonstrate with him. I had long since given up on civilising his choice of oaths when he was in a temper.

He gave a deep sigh and slid out of his coat, handing it to me. "Keep it out of the fray, would you? I just this week had it from my tailor."

He unpinned his cuffs and turned back his sleeves with the same casual grace I saw him use every night when he disrobed. He loosened his neckcloth and folded it tidily into his pocket, and only then did he turn back to the fellow and gave a little gesture of impatience. "Come on then."

"I do wish you had not done that," I muttered, for as the fellow came forward I could see he was far larger than I had first anticipated. He was unkempt and had misplaced a few of his teeth. When he smiled, there were noticeable gaps where the teeth ought to have been, and he smiled rather too often for my comfort. The effect was one of a leering jack-o'-lantern, and I shuddered. But I knew better than to say a word, and I simply held Brisbane's coat, creasing the fabric irreparably in my clammy fingers.

The ruffian came at him quickly, anticipating a hard left to the jaw would take Brisbane by surprise and drop him instantly. But he had seen Brisbane's clothes and taken him for a creature of the city, a soft, useless gentleman who had never raised his fists except in the boxing ring against another of his own kind.

He did not know Brisbane. Elegant as a matador, Brisbane stepped neatly aside, avoiding the blow, and at the last moment, pivoted and swung his right elbow up sharply into the fellow's jaw, using the villain's own momentum to throw him to the ground.

The ruffian rose quickly and threw himself forward, head down like a bull's, barrelling directly for Brisbane's torso. He flung his arms out wide, as if to forestall any thought that Brisbane might have of stepping aside again. This time, Brisbane grabbed each of the fellow's shoulders as he came in and flung himself backwards, hitting the villain squarely upon the chin with the hardest part of his knee. The fellow dropped to his knees, and Brisbane turned hard upon his heel to deliver a nasty right directly behind the ruffian's ear. He dropped like a stone, instantly unconscious, and bleeding freely from his ear.

Just then another miscreant slithered from the shadows.

"'Ere now, what did you do, Little Ned?"

This fellow was somewhat smaller, but his weapon was significantly more impressive, an Italian stiletto, long of blade and polished to a wicked gleam that shone in the dim light of the alley.

Brisbane sighed. "How considerate of you all to take it in turns." Before the other fellow had quite got himself prepared, Brisbane moved, slapping the blade of the stiletto between his palms and twisting sharply upwards sending it clattering out of sight. The fellow's eyes rolled in fright, and I almost felt sorry for him.

He lunged forward and Brisbane countered, clasping him about the neck even as the miscreant's hands reached for his throat. They remained locked for a short moment, nose to nose, until Brisbane closed one hand about the fellow's wrist and gave another sharp twist. I heard the bone snap and the scream that came after. I daresay if the fellow had been clever, he would have left it there and the matter would have ended. But he lunged for Brisbane instead, and at that close a distance, he had little chance. He lashed out with his uninjured hand, and Brisbane neatly dodged the blow. Quick as a serpent, he put out his hand and closed it about the fellow's windpipe. The villain clawed at the air with his free hand, his eyes rolling even more wildly than before, and just as they went completely white, Brisbane dropped him.

"Is he dead?" I demanded.

Brisbane snorted. "Not by half. Merely a touch of asphyxia and a broken wrist. And I will remind you, my dear, he did attempt to stab me."

Brisbane stepped back over the fallen men to retrieve his coat. He shrugged into it and took a five-pound note from his case, dropped it on the smaller of the pair, and before I could speak, he took my arm and we began to walk, very fast indeed.

"That was not terribly sporting," I remarked when we had gone a safe distance and were certain we were not being followed.

He stared at me in frank astonishment. "Sporting? Julia, there is nothing sporting about a street fight. The rule is to drop the other fellow as fast as possible and by any means possible."

"I meant the money. You know he will be robbed before he wakes," I chided him.

He frowned. "It was strategic. Five pounds was a fair price for getting any lingering villains to quarrel amongst themselves for the money rather than chase us. Now, be quiet. I am trying to deduce precisely where we are."

I did as he instructed, attempting to bring some order to my hair as he simply stood and closed his eyes. I knew he would not attempt to determine our position by landmarks, but was retracing our journey in his mind, calling forth his excellent sense of direction and his intimate knowledge of the city to establish our whereabouts.

"I have it," he said after a moment. There was no mistaking the satisfaction in his voice, and I thought again that this was a man deeply content with his lot in life.

He took my hand and set off at a rapid pace, almost too rapid, and I had cause then to be grateful that I was wearing a comfortable pair of boots as I scurried in his wake. To my surprise, we plunged even deeper into the shadowy stews of London, nipping in and out of dirty alleys and narrow streets, dodging both the occasional patrolling bobby and importunate prostitute. At last, we emerged into a more respectable street, where I suddenly remembered my hansom.

"Brisbane! We must go back. I haven't dismissed my driver. He will still be waiting for me," I said, tugging at his hand. It remained clamped hard upon my wrist.

"I will dismiss him. You are going home, *directly* home," he said through clenched teeth, and I knew the easy camaraderie we had shared during our adventure was finished. Now the danger was past, Brisbane was giving way to his temper, and I suspected the ensuing scene would not be a pleasant one.

I sighed and continued to trot along behind until we reached our own garden. We entered through the back gate, cutting through the darkness until we came to the back door. Brisbane rapped sharply, and I was not surprised to find Aquinas standing at the ready, lamp in hand.

He opened the door, bowing low. "Sir, my lady."

To his credit, he did not so much as blink at my attire.

Brisbane did not turn loose of me yet. "Have Lady Julia's things arrived?"

"Yes, sir. Morag arrived back less than an hour past, and

Lady Bettiscombe has sent along Lady Julia's carpetbag with her compliments."

I smothered a sigh. Apparently none of my conspirators could stand against Brisbane.

"Excellent," Brisbane said. "I will see Lady Julia to her room and then I am going out again. You need not wait up, Aquinas. And I should mention that Lady Julia will not be accompanying me," he added coldly.

Aquinas bowed again. "Yes, sir. And if she should attempt to?"

I crossed my arms. "Brisbane, really! You've no need to talk about me as if I were not here."

Aquinas kept an enquiring look fixed upon Brisbane, who flicked me a quelling glance.

"If my lady so much as opens the door to her bedchamber, you have my permission to use force to restrain her."

"Brisbane! Aquinas, ignore him. He does not mean it," I assured him.

Brisbane rounded on me, and I saw the rage, barely restrained within him. "Do. Not. Try. Me," he managed through gritted teeth.

Before I could reply, he stalked past Aquinas, dragging me along and up the stairs until we reached the bedchamber. Morag was there, laying out my nightdress.

"Out," Brisbane ordered. It was a mark of his bad temper that he should speak to her so. He was usually gentle as a lamb with Morag, treating her with better courtesy than he did most society ladies. She started, dropping my nightdress onto the floor.

"Judas," I muttered as she bent to retrieve it. She put her tongue out at me as she fled, banging the door sharply behind her.

Brisbane towed me as far as the bed, where he dropped

me as if I weighed no more than a feather. I blinked up at him and he braced his hands upon the bedposts, clenching so hard his knuckles turned white and I heard the bones cracking.

He leaned forward, the crescent-moon scar on his cheekbone standing out in livid relief against the smooth olive of his skin. I had never seen his eyes so fathomlessly dark, so implacable. Usually Brisbane's temper was cold, his rages controlled, but this night, he burned with it, the heat of his anger fairly radiated from him, scorching me where I sat.

"I do not know where to begin," he ground out. "I have never lifted a hand to you in anger, but you must know what it is costing me not to beat you within an inch of your life."

"Brisbane," I began, my tone deliberately soothing.

I reached a hand and he shied as if I had burned him. "Do not think to wheedle me. I have been soft with you, Julia. I have looked past deeds other men would have whipped you for and I have laughed. I have allowed you to take chances that might well have got you killed, and this is the coin with which you choose to repay me."

"Do not say that," I protested. "I have taken every precaution to preserve my safety. And the chances I take are nothing compared to the risks you collect! And do not attempt to turn this back upon me when you have lied to me," I flung.

It was a hit, a palpable one, for he rocked back. "What do you mean?"

"My brother called upon you, and you gave me a lie when I asked if you had seen him. You cannot deplore my subterfuges when you force me to employ them," I explained calmly. It was a gambit only. I pretended to coolness so he could not see how deeply his emotion had affected me. If he had pressed his anger just a moment further, my poise would have deserted me, of that I had no doubt. I had no skill for anger. My father was a gentle soul, whose occasional bad moods were something his children laughed about. My previous husband had given me a taste of violence and I had found it completely unnerved me. Until this moment, Brisbane's rages were something that excited me. To arouse passion, of any sort, in a man like Brisbane felt like an accomplishment.

But this was no accomplishment, I realised as I saw the naked anguish in his eyes. He dropped his hands from the bedposts.

"I gave him my word," he said simply, each word bitten off sharply.

"I have no doubt of it, and it is to your credit that you kept it. But I am no child to be cossetted and protected from everything that is dark and dangerous. If you cannot tell me the truth, at least own that you cannot and do not lie to me! I would not have liked it if you had told me you were bound to silence, but I would have respected it."

Derision twisted his lip. "Now who gives a lie? You would have done precisely the same as you did tonight if I had given you half an answer. Do not deny it."

I nibbled at my lip. He was, of course, correct. If I had known he was investigating on behalf of Bellmont, it would have made no difference. I would have acted the same as when I believed Brisbane himself was in danger.

"Perhaps you are correct," I conceded.

"Perhaps?" One brow arched in enquiry. I did not rise to it. I merely dropped my head and contemplated the toes of my boots.

"I did not mean to frighten you," I said softly. "I never

imagined things would go so far. I only thought to follow you and be at hand if you had need of me."

He cocked his head. "Because you believed I was in trouble."

"A point which caused you no end of amusement when we were in the materialising cabinet," I pointed out.

"It does not seem quite so funny now," he commented. "But that was before that stupid French charlatan got herself killed."

He was calmer now, the heat of his anger cooling just a bit. I ventured a question.

"Why could nothing be done for her? It was so dreadful just watching her die."

He fixed me with a curious look, and I saw something there that told me his anger was not quite so cool as I thought.

"You found that dreadful, and yet you still question my wisdom in excluding you from such things? I have seen a thousand uglier deeds than that, my dear, and I carry memories that would turn the sanity of any man. Yet still you defy me."

"I do not know what to say." I spread my hands. "The situation was not at all what I expected, but neither I think was it entirely to your expectations," I ventured carefully. "You did not look to Madame to be murdered tonight."

"But I knew it was a possibility," he said evenly.

"And you could not prevent it?" Too late, I heard the note of horrified accusation in my voice.

He stared at me a long minute, his emotions now carefully held in check, his expression as neutral as a chess king.

"Some people do not deserve to be saved," he replied.

I said nothing, for there was nothing to say.

After a moment, he roused himself and shot his cuffs. "I am going out. You will remain here. I want your word upon it."

There was no purpose in fighting with him. I was thoroughly exhausted, in mind and body. I wanted nothing more than a hot bath and my bed.

"You have it."

He regarded me closely. "If you break it, I will keep you here by force the next time, if I have to tie you to the bed myself."

I did not think even for a moment that he might have been jesting. I licked my lips and nodded. He did not kiss me goodbye, but crossed the room, pausing with his hand upon the knob.

"I am surprised at you," he added as a parting shot. "You have seen someone die of aconite poisoning once before. Did you not recognise the symptoms?"

He did not wait for a reply. He left, and to his credit, he did not lock me in. He did not have to. I lay on the bed, utterly spent, considering all that we had said and done that night. It did not make for a very edifying inventory, I realised. We had been cruel to each other, each of us lashing out from our own fears until we drew blood from the other. Brisbane's last remark was particularly barbed. My first husband had died as a result of aconite poisoning, and although it was unkind of him to point it out, he was correct. I ought to have seen it.

Madame had been lavishly sick shortly after eating. She had the same pallor as Edward had, the same convulsions. But I wondered. Many poisons could create a similar effect, some of them quite accidentally administered. Was there a chance Madame had met with her fate unintentionally? But Brisbane had been certain she had been killed with a purpose, and his remark that she did not deserve to live had not been delivered apropos of nothing. He had been uncharacteristically vicious in his speech, but not his thinking. He would have had a good reason for his opinion of Madame, but I had seen nothing in her séance or her conversation with her sister to indicate what evil she might entertain.

Of course, pondering Madame's fatal evening meant I could avoid thinking of Brisbane and how badly I had blundered once again. I had meant to discover the truth about Bellmont's call upon Brisbane, and instead I had muddled my way into something else entirely. It was not the first time I had pushed my way into his world, and not the first time I had made him shatteringly angry in doing so. The trouble, I believed, had its roots in our respective pasts. I came from a family too much in each other's pockets. We Marches were forthright, emotional, feckless and impulsive. We also loved to talk. There was not a thought or deed that went unremarked amongst us. Secrets were short-lived in our family. We made a life's work of interfering in each other's business, and then telling the others about it, and with ten children, there was always much to tell.

Brisbane's upbringing could not have been more different. He was an unwanted child, half Gypsy, half Scot, got in the heat of a passionate and tempestuous marriage that had not even lasted until his birth. His mother had died in gaol, accused of heinous crimes and crying down curses upon her accusers. His father was best unspoken of. His aristocratic Scottish family would not so much as acknowledge he had existed. His name had been struck from the family Bible, and Brisbane himself hovered on the edge of both worlds. He was neither fish nor fowl, for his Gypsy kin felt him too much a Scot, his Scottish family considered him a wild and savage Gypsy brat.

He had brought himself up, leaving his mother before he was ten and living upon his wits since then. He had achieved respectability by his own merit and wealth from his own accomplishments. He had built a life for himself that was larger than any his family could have given him. He was a man in a thousand, ten thousand, for I had never met another like him, and only Brisbane with his passion and his maddening ways could have tempted me again to marriage. I adored him in ways that frightened me, and the notion that frightened me the most was that Brisbane would come to regret marrying me. He had lived so long upon his own that the act of trust was a difficult one for him to master. He had his associates and friends—the redoubtable Monk, the gentle Dr. Bent, and now, perhaps, my brother Plum. His former mistress and my dear friend, Hortense de Bellefleur, was another. That he was capable of love was undoubted. That he could live with it was another matter entirely.

I made up my mind to call upon Hortense at the earliest opportunity and slid into an uneasy sleep, only to rouse as soon as Brisbane returned. I spied from the face of the clock that it was past two.

"Brisbane?" I called softly.

He sat heavily on the edge of the bed. I had turned the fire down before going to sleep, and only the softest glow from the hearth lit the room. His face was thrown into shadowed relief, and I could see his features only in turn. He pulled off one boot and dropped it to the floor.

"The death has been reported to the authorities. There will be a postmortem and an inquest." The second boot fell.

"Good," I said fervently. "Even if she was dreadful, her sister deserves to know what happened."

He said nothing as he stripped off his clothes, draping them over the chair by the hearth. He was, as ever, casual about his nudity, but the sight of him never failed to distract me completely. My first husband had been pale and slender, like a statue of a youthful prince, waiting for his throne. Brisbane was a king through and through, a man fully in possession of his powers, and I watched the play of shadow over his sleek muscles. He slid under the bedclothes, and to my relief, reached an arm to me. I rolled close, pillowing my head upon the hard curve of his shoulder as his arm came around me.

"I am sorry," I murmured.

"I know. I ought not to have threatened to beat you," he returned. He pressed a kiss to my hair.

"I just cannot bear to be kept out of your life," I said into the dark.

He gave a sigh. "Julia, you daft woman. When will you understand? You are my life."

It cost him something to say it, for Brisbane's declarations were always a thing of pain to him, wrenched by some force, as if he were Samson, giving up his strength a lock at a time with his words.

I said nothing, pressing closer and easing myself on top of him. We were silent, but in our silence was desperation, feverish and sharp, and when we spent ourselves and lay, damp and exhausted in each other's arms, we were silent still.

The SIXTH CHAPTER

Rest, rest, perturb'd spirit.
—*Hamlet*

The next morning, Brisbane was up and gone before I descended to breakfast. Aquinas entered with tea and toast as I helped myself to eggs from the sideboard. As a very superior butler, he made no allusion to events of the previous evening. It fell to me to raise the subject we were so carefully avoiding.

"I do hope the rest of the staff were not disturbed by our arrival last night," I began.

Aquinas poured out the tea and tidied up the various pots of jam and honey. "Not at all, my lady."

"Hmm. Did they happen to notice anything amiss?"

Aquinas gave me a kindly smile. "It is beneath the dignity of a member of staff to notice or remark upon the activities of the family," he reminded me.

I took a piece of toast, crumbling it in my fingers. "I suppose. I should hate for the new members of staff to think that such goings on are typical of this house."

Aquinas' lips thinned a little as he folded Brisbane's newspaper. I dropped the toast. "Oh, very well. You'd best prepare them that such things are entirely typical. That the mistress will occasionally dress in boy's clothes, that the master has been known to disguise himself as a pedlar or a beggarwoman, that we keep ravens in the morning room and that from time to time, we are menaced by murderers and thieves and blackmailers and villains of every description," I said, flinging up my hands in exasperation.

"I have already done so, my lady," he informed me. "And I have hired the staff at a premium to accommodate the inconvenience."

"Oh, well done," I murmured. "Are we fully staffed then?"

"All but the tweeny," he acknowledged. "She gave notice yesterday on account of the telephone device that has been installed under the stairs. She thinks it an ungodly and heathenish apparatus and will not remain in a house where one is in use."

I snorted. "Any other domestic troubles? Have we a new cook yet?"

"I am assured by Mrs. Potter that a new cook will be in residence by this afternoon. We are also lacking a valet for the master, although Mr. Brisbane is quite gracious about my own efforts in that capacity."

Aquinas had been acting as valet to Brisbane for some weeks, although it was not entirely fair to expect him to continue to do so. The duties of a butler were onerous at times, particularly in our establishment, and Brisbane could be exacting about his clothes. Of course, he also managed perfectly well by himself without a valet when necessity demanded it. On our honeymoon, he had availed himself of hotel valets and shipboard stewards to see to his clothes, but I had seen him just as impeccably turned out whilst camping at an archaeological site in Turkey or pursuing a murderer in the Himalayas as in any London ballroom.

Aquinas went on. "Furthermore, Mr. Brisbane and I discussed the matter this morning, and I suggested a pair of footmen for messages and carrying packages, with the notion that one or both could serve as valets as needed."

"And he was amenable?" I asked.

Aquinas whisked away invisible crumbs from the tablecloth. "Not at first. He pointed out that he is accustomed to living rather more simply, and did not immediately grasp all of the advantages to keeping a pair of footmen on staff."

"Advantages?"

Aquinas took up the empty pan of eggs and retreated as far as the door, giving me a smile that was almost, but not entirely, correct. "As it is the custom for fashionable ladies of rank to take a footman with them upon leaving the house, I pointed out to Mr. Brisbane that it would be far easier to ensure your ladyship's safety with a footman in attendance at all times."

I gave a squawk of protest. "Aquinas, tell me you did not!"

He straightened himself to his full—if diminutive—height. "I do not think that my lady fully comprehends the depth of regard in which she is held by every member of this establishment," he said firmly. "Her safety and comfort are our highest duty."

With that, he took his leave, and I could not scold him. I knew Aquinas was deeply affected whenever he resorted to addressing me in the third person. Besides, I mused as I crunched into a piece of toast, it was rather better to have one's husband and staff devoted to one's safety than the opposite, but I could not like the feeling that I was being slowly bound up in chains. Velvet chains, but chains to be sure.

After a hasty breakfast, I summoned Morag and the town coach and made my way to the house of my dear friend, Hortense de Bellefleur, in the pretty little neighbourhood of St. John's Wood. Her elderly maid, Terese, admitted me and carried Morag off to the kitchens for a good gossip. Hortense—Fleur to her friends—rose and greeted me with alacrity.

"Julia!" she cried, her lilting French accent rendering my name something lovelier than it usually sounded in English. "How happy I am to see you."

I went to her and kissed her cheeks, feeling suddenly ashamed of myself. I had not seen her in such an intimate setting in far too long. Our friendship had been a prickly one. I had come to terms with the fact that she had once, many years ago, been Brisbane's mistress, and I knew their friendship was nothing more than a deep affection on both sides. She was almost twenty years his elder, and the attraction had been easy enough to understand. She had been a glamorous widow, a lady of the world, both exciting and kindly for a very youthful Brisbane. She had cared for him when his migraines bedevilled him, and she was one of the few, the very few, who knew the story of where he had come from and how he had made his way in the world.

No, I had learned to look past her *affaire* with my husband in his youth. It was her liaison with my father that had raised my hackles. They had met when I was convalescing at my father's house after nearly losing my life at the conclusion of the investigation into my husband's murder. To my astonishment, they had struck up an immediate friendship, and then something more. By the time I had returned from a six-month sojourn in Italy, she had become his paramour. The relationship was a terribly discreet one, but the family were still scandalised. Fleur had made her way in life as little better than a courtesan, taking up with men of power and influence and wealth. Some of them she had married, some of them she had merely entertained. The difference between Fleur and a true professional was that she always fell in love with her admirers, my father included. Ultimately, their relationship drifted, and as a result, I found my own relationship with her had regained some of its previous warmth. We resumed our correspondence throughout my travels, and I had looked forward to each of her chatty, engaging letters.

But they were no substitute for the genuine pleasure of her company, and as she hugged me to her, I felt a surge of the old affection take hold.

"My dear girl," she said, drawing back, and I saw her beautiful eyes were bright with unshed tears. "Sit! I will have Terese bring a pot of chocolate and it will be like the old days."

Guilt lanced me then. I had been uncomfortable with her connection to my father, and I had used that as a pretext for cooling my friendship with her. But I had missed her terribly, and apparently the feeling was mutual. I ought to have overlooked it, I scolded myself. I ought to have done more to support her. She was my friend, and although the house in St. John's Wood was pretty and comfortable, it struck me that it must sometimes be lonely, for Fleur's company was beyond the pale for respectable society ladies.

"That would be lovely," I told her truthfully, and we chatted of trivial things until Terese appeared with the pot of chocolate and a plate of dainty feather biscuits.

When we were alone, Fleur poured out with graceful

gestures, and permitted me to sip deeply from the cup before she took up her needlework. She had taken to doing whitework to pass the time, and I marvelled at her deft and graceful stitches, so precise and very nearly impossible to see rendered as they were in white silk on a background of white linen. I admired her latest creation and we chatted for a few moments of inconsequential things.

Then, her eyes upon her work, she said gently, "Nicholas was here this morning."

I flicked her a look of surprise. "Was he indeed?"

She continued to stitch, her hands never varying in their slow, precise rhythm. "I want you to know I would never keep such thing a secret from you, nor would he want me to. He loves you quite devotedly."

I set down my cup with a resounding crack. "Fleur, I have never, *would* never, suspect you of resuming your attachment to Brisbane. You shared something twenty years ago, but you have both grown far beyond that. And you are two of the most loyal people I know. Your affection for me would prevent either of you ever from acting upon any such impulse."

The lovely face diffused into a smile. "I am so glad you know this! You are very right. My passion for Nicholas burned itself out very quickly. We were too different, or perhaps too much alike. I never knew. I only knew that the physical attraction we held for one another did not endure. Only the affection remained. For me, he is like a son now. Well, perhaps not a son. A nephew," she added with a generous smile.

That she could speak of such things without blushing I put down to her French blood. She was the only person in Brisbane's life who referred to him by his Christian name, and it struck me then that any other woman might have been jealous. For my part, I was glad for what he had shared with Fleur. She had been the first woman to offer him un- fettered affection. It pained me to think of how solitary his life had been before he had met her, and how little feminine kindness he had known before their *liaison*.

"Of course," she went on, "his attachment to you is en- tirely different. I think the physical passions will be quite enduring with the two of you."

"Fleur, really," I murmured.

She gave a little laugh, the light peal of silvery bells. "I have embarrassed you—how pretty you are when you blush! But I am too much a woman of the world not to know a man entirely enthralled when I see it. You have bewitched him, my dear. And I congratulate you. It is not easy to keep a man of that mettle. I have tried," she said ruefully, and I knew she was not talking of Brisbane.

"My father," I guessed.

She gave a little shrug and put on a brave smile. "Hector is a magnificent man. But it was not to be," she said lightly.

I shuddered slightly to hear my father described so, but I was glad she had appreciated his better qualities, if only for a little while. "I am sorry that he broke off the connection," I offered. "Perhaps he is out of the habit of romance. It has been so long since my mother died."

It was a sorry excuse, but the best I could offer her. Sit- ting in her exquisite, sunlit morning room, surrounded by her elegance and her warmth, it seemed impossible to me that he could have been so stupid as to cast off her affec- tions. But then, my father had never been renowned for doing the sensible thing, I mused with some irritation.

She shrugged again and let the comment pass. "Nicholas is worried about you."

I sighed. "I am worried about him. That is why I have

come. I wonder sometimes if we did not make a terrible mistake in our marriage."

She cocked her head to the side. "Why do you say such a thing? You love him, he loves you. These are the only facts which matter."

"I wish it were as simple as that." I spread my hands. "I want so badly to be part of his life, his real life—his work. And he promised I could help him with investigations if I applied myself to certain studies. I have done so, and I have proven in the past that I can be useful, to a surprising degree at times. And yet still he fights me, conceals things from me. He forces me to blunder about in secret, a far more dangerous approach," I pointed out, warming to my theme, "and then he is enraged when I do. There is no winning with him."

"It is not a contest, Julia," she reminded me gently. "It is a marriage! La, what a time of it you will have together if the pair of you cannot understand this." She clucked her tongue, and I looked at her through narrowed eyes.

"Did you give Brisbane the same advice?"

"Of course! I tell you both that you must not accuse the other of being less than honest when you yourself have been deceitful."

"Deceitful!" I sat up very straight, my back stiff with outrage.

She arched a brow at me. "Do you not find it deceitful to pretend to be a boy so you can skulk around the city, following your husband about his business?"

I dropped my eyes. "Oh. He told you about that."

"He did. And he confessed that he lied to you when you asked about his meeting with your brother, Lord Bellmont. I told him this was equally unacceptable and wholly stupid."

"You did not tell Brisbane he was stupid," I said, blinking hard at her.

"I did. And I will say the same to you. You are a stupid woman if you cannot put love above everything else." I opened my mouth to protest, but she raised her voice, something I had never heard her do in the whole of our acquaintance. "Love is the only thing that lasts, Julia, the only thing that matters. And both of you are trying to throw it away with both hands because you are proud and stubborn. For all your differences, you are too much alike, the pair of you. But you are lucky, so lucky and you are too blind to see it! This man, this magnificent man, offers you love and you take it and say, 'Give me more, give me respect!' And he does the same to you, saying to this beautiful woman, 'Your love is not enough, I want your obedience, as well!' Why cannot love be enough for the both of you? It is more than some of us have or will ever have again," she finished on a sob, and to my astonishment, she broke into a fit of weeping.

Even that was gracefully done, I mused as I went to embrace her. Her tears slid slowly down her cheeks, and her nose never turned pink. She daubed lightly at her eyes, and begged my forgiveness.

"I do not know what you must think of me," she murmured.

"You are overcome," I told her. "I did not think to ask if you had troubles of your own, and yet here we come, loading ours upon you. It was too much, and I am sorry for it."

I held her then, and she patted my arm, and when she spoke, her voice was older and calm. "I am right, you know. It is only the love that matters. And one day you will know it, too."

The SEVENTH CHAPTER

O, where will ye gang to and where will ye sleep,
Against the night begins?
My bed is made wi'cauld sorrows,
My sheets are lined wi'sins.

—*"The Witch-Mother"* Algernon Charles Swinburne

After Fleur dried her tears, I encouraged her to talk, but the moment had passed, and she confided nothing. I do not know what thwarted liaison prompted her outburst of emotion, but clearly she had been disappointed in love once more, and I cursed the fool who had crushed her tender hopes. She had given me much to think on, and I pondered it as I took myself to Chapel Street, where I found Brisbane in his consulting rooms sitting at his desk and holding a flaming coal in his bare hands.

"Brisbane!" I shrieked. I darted around, looking for something—anything—to extinguish the flames, but he merely rose with maddening calmness and dropped the coal into the fire.

He held up his hands. "No harm done," he assured me.

I stared at him, open-mouthed. "That was a vile trick."

"I did not realise you were coming in," he pointed out.

He went to the table where I had been conducting my experiments with black powder and rummaged in the bottles until he found a solvent. He took up a rag and began to work the stuff over his hands. "Easy enough to apply, but the very devil to remove," he muttered.

"What is it?" I crept close enough to see that he had been quite correct. There was no mark upon his skin.

"A formula I found in a conjurer's book. It requires precise amounts of camphor, aquavitae, an ounce of quicksilver and another of liquid styrax shaken all together and spread upon the hands. It forms a barrier for the skin and protects it from the fire. Rather effective, I think."

He was entirely too pleased with himself.

"Is that what you've been doing whilst I was out? Parlour tricks for conjurers?"

He shrugged. "Tinkering helps me to think. I started by making a bottle of spirit water, but I got bored of it."

"Spirit water?"

"The stuff that Agathe was packing away last night. It looks unearthly, but it's the merest child's play to make so long as you have enough matches."

He said nothing for a moment, letting me work it out for myself.

"Phosphorous!" I exclaimed. "Oh, that is clever. What do they do? Soak the matches?"

"The match heads," he corrected. "Quite a lot of them in a rather small bottle. The whole mess is left to steep until the phosphorous has been leached out. Then it's strained and rebottled and corked up. It takes only a bit of air inside the bottle to achieve that glowing effect."

"So simple and so devious," I mused.

"Yes, well, that sums up the whole of the medium's bag of tricks, doesn't it? Simple and devious."

I canted my head. "Do you believe in none of them? Do you think them all frauds and charlatans?"

"Have you ever been to a séance before?"

"No, but we children spent one summer trying to conjure the ghost of Shakespeare."

He lifted a brow as he scrubbed at a particularly stubborn spot upon his hand. "I am sure you had an excellent reason for doing so."

"Father was in an excessively bad mood. We thought a chat with Shakespeare might knock him right out of it."

"And did it?"

"No," I said, feeling myself colour slightly. "We made such a nuisance of ourselves by tipping tables that Father banned us from dabbling in Spiritualism altogether. I think what really infuriated him was when Benedick broke the nose off his favourite bust of Shakespeare when he went behind it to throw his voice."

"And you have just proven my point. You did not conjure a spirit. You manufactured one. It is the same with professionals. Mediums are frauds and charlatans with a child's collection of tricks to fool the unwary. There is nothing authentic or genuinely occult about any of them."

"Perhaps," I said. I stripped off my gloves and set aside my hat as he finished cleaning his hands. "I have been to see Fleur," I announced, taking the chair opposite his desk. He opened his mouth and I stopped him with an upraised hand. "I did not follow you. I intended to see her first thing this morning, and she told me you had already been. She said she gave you some advice, the same advice she gave me."

"That love is all that matters?" he hazarded, his black eyes gleaming as he came to sit at the desk.

"Yes. And I have come to make a proposal. If we mean

this marriage to work, to really work, we must make a pact to move forward in perfect honesty."

He regarded me thoughtfully. "In all matters?"

"Of course," I replied in an even voice, but the truth was, my hands were shaking. If he did not agree, I could not imagine how we were to proceed in this marriage. It would disintegrate around us.

"Very well," he said briskly. "I do not much care for your new hat."

"Brisbane," I began in a strangled voice. "Be serious."

"I am quite serious. The brim is too wide and it hits my nose when I try to kiss you."

"Brisbane," I said again, and this time he took note of the tone, for he sat forward, his manner now perfectly sober.

"I know. I will always look to protect you, Julia. It is in my bones, as it is with any man, that to love a woman, he must keep her safe. You cannot change that."

"I do not look to change that," I told him. "But we agreed to a marriage of partners, and if you do not realise that the urge to protect one's loved ones speaks to women, as well, then you have much to learn."

He started. "You wish to protect me?"

"Why else would I have gone to the trouble of kitting myself up as a boy and haring around London in a hired cab? I was afraid you needed help, and I wanted to be that help." I did not mention my overweening curiosity to learn the nature of whatever secret bound him to Bellmont. My inquisitiveness had often been a point of contention between us, and the less said upon that subject, the better.

He sat back, shaking his head. "I thought you were joking last night. You told me you were there to protect me, and I did not believe you were serious."

"Deadly serious," I told him grimly. "I would face any danger for you, risk any foe. You must know that by now."

He hesitated. It was unlike Brisbane to be at a loss for words, and when he spoke, the words came slowly, as if he were understanding them for the first time.

"Then I have misjudged you. I have expected you to put aside feelings I have justified in myself, feelings I could never separate from myself because they are a part of me. And that was wrong."

I stared, open-mouthed. "Was that an apology?"

"Very near," he acknowledged with a ghost of a smile.

"I will accept it," I said quickly.

"So, my gallant wife," he said, clearing his throat. "If we are to proceed in honesty, then I will tell you when your skills are unsuited to an investigation and you will accept it?"

"Agreed, so long as you make a fair assessment of my skills and the investigation and do not permit yourself to be blinded by your inclination to protect."

He tightened his jaw, but gave a short nod. "Agreed. In that case, I must tell you precisely why I went to see Madame Séraphine."

I sat forward eagerly, my blood beating hard at the thought that at last I had made him understand me, at long last I was about to become a full partner in his work, sharing every risk, every danger, standing at his side.

"Tell me everything," I urged.

"Very well. I went to see Madame because I was commissioned to do so at the urging of Lord Bellmont."

I blinked at him in surprise. "You were not there to unmask Madame as a fraud? You were there for Bellmont? What connection does he have to Madame? Did Adelaide visit her for a consultation and offer too great a donation?

Or did Virgilia take up with a gentleman too much devoted to the tricks of a charlatan?" I felt giddy with excitement at the possibilities.

And then I noticed his expression. Brisbane was regarding me with something like pity, but he did not hesitate this time. Like a physician lancing a wound, he plunged straight in.

"Madame Séraphine was his mistress."

"Oh."

I rose and began to pace the room. I had always found it a vastly interesting place, reflecting as it did Brisbane's past as well as his passions. It was littered with the souvenirs of his travels, some fine antiques, some trifles, but all of it representative of the man himself, from the camel saddle in the corner to the tiny knot of calico blessed by a Gypsy seeress. I saw none of it as I paced. My vision seemed clouded and there was a buzzing in my head as I tried to make sense of what Brisbane had just told me. To his credit, he said nothing. He held his silence until I was ready to speak.

"He confessed it?" I asked finally.

He nodded. "Yesterday, when he called upon me. He needed my help, and to secure it he had to tell me the full story."

I gave a short, bitter laugh as I reached the end of the room. "My God, that must have cost him. Bellmont—the paragon of virtue! And did it surprise you to find that his halo was tarnished?"

"Not so much as it surprises you, I think," he said gently.

I stopped and swung round to face him. "You expected this of him?"

He lifted one heavy shoulder in a shrug. "Expected it? No. But Bellmont is not the first fellow to champion standards of behaviour even he cannot attain, and he will not be the last. He is a man, after all."

I moved to the chair where I had sat and gripped the back of it so hard I thought surely the wood must splinter in my hands.

"You defend him?" The words were heavy as stones, dropped into the silence.

"I understand him," he corrected. "For years, he has wrapped himself in the mantle of propriety, permitting himself few diversions from his work. His children are growing up, his wife is growing older. He seeks escape."

"From Adelaide?"

"From himself. Bellmont will not see forty again, and sometimes that knowledge is painful for a man. He has no other source of excitement in his life, and when Madame Séraphine sought him out, he was flattered."

"She sought him out?" For some unaccountable reason, I felt a tiny flicker of relief that he had not gone in search of such entertainment himself.

"She did. And in such a calculated fashion that Bellmont was entirely taken in by her. She was introduced by a mutual acquaintance and presented herself as a lady in distress, in need of wise counsel."

"Nothing would appeal to him more," I reflected. Bellmont did so enjoy telling others what to do.

"Indeed. The lady knew her prey. She set a precise and perfect snare for him. She flattered his vanity, bringing him along slowly. And when she judged the moment to be ripe, she threw herself at him."

"And Bellmont caught her," I added with some bitterness.

Brisbane bowed his head. "There was never a moment

they were together that he did not regret his actions or feel the hypocrisy of them."

I blinked. "Surely do you do not believe that? He must have taken pleasure in her company, felt himself justified somehow in lying with this woman who was not his wife."

Brisbane shrugged again. "I am merely repeating what Bellmont told me. He must dress the matter up as best he can so he can face himself in his shaving glass each morning. The truth is a bit more sordid, I have no doubt. He did confess that certain difficulties have presented themselves in his relations with Adelaide that did not manifest with Madame Séraphine."

I moved to the front of the chair and sank into it, covering my face with my hands. "He was unmanned with Adelaide? Little wonder he took up with Madame! If he could see himself virile once more with her—"

"I realise these revelations are painful to you, my dear. Do you wish to withdraw your participation in this particular investigation?" The question was offered up in a silky voice, and it was a seductive one. Two minutes in and already I had learned things I would have given a great deal not to know. But I had come too far to retreat, and I flung up my head and fixed Brisbane with a determined eye.

"How long did the liaison last?" I demanded crisply.

"Two months," he replied, and I fancied I saw a gleam of admiration in his gaze. "During that time, he was sufficiently indiscreet as to write letters to the lady."

I groaned. "Of all the stupid, senseless, idiotic things to do! By God, when Bellmont decides to show himself a March, he does it with a full measure of the family recklessness."

Brisbane's lips moved as if he were smothering a smile. "Your words, my love. Not mine."

I resisted the urge to put out my tongue to him. "I presume you were searching for the letters last night?"

"I was. Bellmont has come to his senses and broken off his *affaire* with the lady, but she has declined his request for the return of the letters. He fears she might have planned to keep them for some indiscreet purpose."

"Blackmail!" I sat forward, scarcely breathing.

Brisbane gave a slow nod. "Precisely. One of those letters leaked to the press could be disastrous for Bellmont's political hopes, to say nothing of his marriage and the future attachments of his children. He is in a particularly untenable position, and the only recourse for him was to engage someone to retrieve the letters by stealth."

"So he asked you to steal the letters from Madame," I murmured.

"Oh, he did not ask me. It was more in the nature of a command. He thought he could hire me," Brisbane supplied.

I smothered another groan. "And you refused him."

He gave me a bland smile. "I am engaged at present with a few more pressing cases. I was forced to decline to be employed by his lordship." I winced. I was not surprised that Bellmont had blundered by offering him money, and I was not surprised that Brisbane had politely refused.

"You made him ask you to do it as a favour," I guessed.

Some primitive satisfaction shone in his eyes. "I pointed out to him that as a private enquiry agent, my time was my own and I had every right to refuse his trade. But as his brother-in-law, if he asked me nicely, I could hardly say no."

I goggled, open-mouthed. "If he asked you *nicely?*"

"I made him say 'please,'" Brisbane informed me, smiling. There was nothing genial or pleasant about that smile. It was the smile of a predator contemplating its prey, and I knew Bellmont had paid dearly for every snub he had offered my husband.

"I cannot fault you for it," I said upon a sigh. "Heaven knows he has shown often enough that he considers himself your superior, and you would have been less than human if you had not taken some great satisfaction in the situation."

"Oh, tremendous," Brisbane acknowledged freely. "But I also told him I would do my best, and it rankles that I left the Spirit Club without the letters."

"Because of me?" I hazarded.

"Only partly. You slowed me down, but it was Madame's death that put paid to my efforts. I ought to have had the entire second séance to finish searching her rooms."

I began to think aloud. "I found it curious that she did not complete the first séance. Remember what Agathe said to her? She remarked that there was no conjuring of her spirit guide, no opportunity for Agathe to blow upon the guests' necks."

"Again proving my point that they were frauds," Brisbane said.

I considered my next words carefully. "I understand that you do not believe in Madame Séraphine's powers, but do you not suppose that somewhere in the world, even one medium may be authentic?"

"I have no reason to believe it."

"You have every reason," I said quietly. "You have yourself."

The handsome mouth thinned. "If you are referring to my own rather freakish abilities, I wish you would not. Besides, they are not the same. Madame and her ilk claim to conjure the spirits of those who have died. What happens to me is nothing of the sort."

He fell silent then, a tiny muscle in his jaw jumping as he sat, his eyes fixed upon his hands.

"Both defy rational explanation," I began.

He cut me short with an impatient gesture. "I do not wish to speak of it now."

I sighed. "All right then. Let us talk about the Spirit Club. We shall have to make enquiries. We must know the identity of the owner and whether the management of the club rests in the same hands."

"The management is not involved in Madame's death," he said swiftly.

I blinked. "How can you possibly know that?"

His gaze held mine. "Because I had occasion to investigate the place once before. The owner is entirely above such things. I can tell you no more."

I puffed out a sigh of irritation, but before I could launch into an attack, Brisbane held up a hand.

"I can tell you no more. Now, I know we promised to deal truthfully with one another, and it is the truth that I cannot divulge the details of what I know. You must leave it there."

"Very well. Keep your secrets, but it is a bit of sophistry not to tell me. You have a Jesuitical mind, Brisbane."

He bared his teeth in a wolfish smile. "Thank you, my love."

"It was *not* a compliment."

"I have already told you more than I ought about Bellmont's affairs, but as you were there, I could hardly avoid giving you a full explanation," he pointed out.

"Will you tell him you have told me?"

Brisbane flicked a glance to the clock upon the mantel. "Tell him yourself. I believe he is arriving even now."

The EIGHTH CHAPTER

I see my reputation is at stake.

—*Troilus and Cressida*

Just then there was a tap at the door and Mrs. Lawson entered at Brisbane's bidding.

"Lord Bellmont to see you, sir," she intoned formally. She gave me a disapproving look. "I did not realise you were here, *my lady*." She always made a point of stressing my title as if she could not entirely believe I deserved it. "Shall you require tea?"

I gave her a gracious smile. "Thank you, but no, Mrs. Lawson. If my brother requires refreshment, I suspect he will want something rather more bracing than tea."

She drew herself up and gave a sniff. "It is eleven o'clock in the morning, my lady."

"Thank you, that is all, Mrs. Lawson," Brisbane said, delivering the dismissal with a smile of such charm that Mrs. Lawson simpered on her way out the door.

"Honestly, Brisbane," I told him. "It is simply revolting the way they fawn upon you."

"Whom?"

"Mrs. Lawson, Morag. I daresay the new cook will be next."

He gave me no retort, for the door opened again and there was Bellmont. My brother looked surprised to see me, but no mere surprise could account for his extreme pallor and the dark shadows beneath his eyes. He had suffered a shock, and from the newspaper clutched under his arm, I could guess what it was.

He covered his dismay at seeing me with a greeting that was barely polite.

"Julia, my dear, an unexpected pleasure. I trust you are in good health?" he enquired, but his eyes darted from me to Brisbane, imploring.

"I am well, Monty, but I think you are not. Let me pour you a glass of whisky."

He blinked rapidly, but did not demur. I had thought I would be angry with him, and in some measure, I was. I was outraged on Adelaide's behalf, on behalf of the children. But to my surprise, I found I was rather sorrier for Bellmont. Our father had warned me once that Bellmont would find his middle years difficult ones. He was too ambitious, too rigid. He had not the March talent for living easily with his own faults. He was no friend to his own shortcomings. The rest of us were willows, bending easily with the wind. Bellmont was a stout oak, strong and straight, too unyielding to tempests. He would stand or he would break, there was no ground in between.

I poured him out the glass of whisky and handed it to him without a word. He looked up at me, and the little bit of colour in his face faded right away.

"My God, you know," he whispered. He drained off the whisky and pointed a finger of accusation at Brisbane.

"I trusted you, but now I see what your word as a gentleman is truly worth."

I put a hand to Bellmont's sleeve. "He did not tell me, at least not until I followed him to the Spirit Club and joined him in searching Madame Séraphine's rooms."

"You searched her rooms?" He swung round to Brisbane. "I do not know whether to take a horsewhip to you on my own behalf or my sister's! What do you mean permitting her to accompany you?"

Brisbane had not moved. He merely gave Bellmont a slow, steady stare. But I knew Brisbane too well not to see the coiled tension in him, and if Bellmont had made a move towards him, Brisbane would have dropped him as easily as he had the ruffian in the street the night before.

I hurried to settle my brother. "Bellmont, collect yourself. You will not threaten my husband under his own roof when he was out doing your bidding last night."

Brisbane stirred himself then. "I do not require your protection, Julia," he said in a low, dangerous voice.

"I am well aware of it," I told him through clenched teeth. "I am trying to protect Bellmont."

Bellmont whirled at me. "I do not require protection from the likes of him!"

I smothered the urge to stamp my foot. Brisbane was showing remarkable restraint under the circumstances, but I fancied I saw cracks in the veneer of his control. I could not know which of my brother's barbs might strike a blow that Brisbane found impossible to resist, and I for one, did not want to see the result.

I turned on my brother. "Bellmont, do not be a fool. I have seen Brisbane with sword, horsewhip, his fists and a pistol, and I can assure you that if you push him so much as an inch further you will have cause to see it, too, and I have no wish to clean up the blood. Mrs. Lawson hates me quite enough already without the carpets being ruined. Now sit down." I adopted a schoolmistressy tone and pushed at his shoulders. *"Sit down."* To his credit, he obeyed and I hastened to put another whisky in his hands. For some of my brothers, that would have been kindling to the fire, but not Bellmont. Good liquor always made him quieter, and Brisbane stocked only the best.

"Now let us discuss the matter peacefully," I proposed. "Yes, Bellmont, I do know why Brisbane was sent to Madame's last night, and I admit I intruded upon his work for reasons that need not concern you. He apprehended me inside the Spirit Club before he had an opportunity to search the rooms alone. He had no choice but to bring me along lest I be discovered by someone else."

I paused, letting Bellmont digest this bit of information. He said nothing, merely sipped at his drink, and I continued on. "Brisbane and I were able to search Madame's boudoir, but discovered nothing pertaining to you. Unfortunately, she returned earlier than expected from her supper and we were forced to hide ourselves in a secret passage."

"A secret passage?" His tongue slipped ever so slightly upon the words, and I knew the whisky was beginning to have an effect.

"From Madame's boudoir to the materialising cabinet in the séance room," I informed him. "No doubt she employed it during her more dramatic séances, but we found it quite useful for our purposes last night. In fact," I paused again, darting a glance to Brisbane's impassive face, "we were there when Madame succumbed to some malady and died in her boudoir."

Bellmont groaned and dropped the whisky glass, spilling the last drops upon the carpet. I sighed. Mrs. Lawson would doubtless blame me for that. After a moment, Bell-mont lifted his head.

"I read the notice in the papers and thought they must have got it wrong. How could she be dead?"

I thought I detected a slight lament for his *inamorata,* and the notion that Bellmont might mourn her caused the slender threads of my sympathy to snap.

"Well, she is, and in a rather nasty fashion, too. Brisbane thinks she was murdered."

Bellmont gripped the arms of the chair as if to anchor himself to the earth. "Do not say it," he implored Brisbane.

But Brisbane gave him a cold nod. "Indeed. It seems impossible to me she was not."

"But who? Why?" Bellmont asked, his voice rising.

Brisbane shrugged. "Another discarded lover?" He did not bother to hide his disdain. "She had any number of such gentlemen. Any one of you might have done away with her."

"Any one of *us?*" Bellmont's voice rose higher still. "You accuse me?"

Brisbane gave him a wintry smile. "I merely point out the possibility."

Bellmont rose and made his way to the door on unsteady legs. "I will see you in hell," he ground out, pointing at Brisbane. He left, banging the door so hard behind him that the framed map of Damascus on the wall fell, shattering the glass.

I turned to Brisbane. "I do hope you are proud of yourself," I said, my tone repressive.

He gave me a brilliant smile. "Oh, quite."

I took up the chair Bellmont had recently vacated and studied my husband. "What now?"

He steepled his hands, thinking. "We wait."

I bristled with impatience. "Surely not. There must be something we can do."

"Such as?"

"We could gain entry once more to the Spirit Club, search Madame's apartments with real thoroughness. We could find Bellmont's letters," I pressed.

"There may be nothing left to find. She may have had a change of heart and destroyed the letters. She may have given them to a friend or consigned them to her bank or her solicitor for safekeeping," he pointed out. "And even if she did conceal them somewhere in the Spirit Club, how precisely do you expect me to retrieve them in the midst of an official investigation into her death?"

"I have seen you accomplish far more demanding tasks," I returned with some irritation. I suspected Bellmont's recent nastiness had prompted Brisbane to be difficult.

"Julia, be reasonable. It is not worth the chance of apprehension just on the possibility that the letters are at the club. If I knew they were there, that might—*might*—be different. But the risks I take in my business are calculated ones, and this is too great."

I cocked my head at him. "You are a professional enquiry agent. Surely the authorities would merely send you off with a flea in your ear if they discovered you."

He leaned forward, piercing me with those fathomless black eyes. "If I am discovered, I will be taken up for theft and sentenced to hard labour."

My lips went quite dry and I found it difficult to breathe. "Hard labour? You cannot be serious."

"Deadly, I am afraid," he returned with the ghost of a smile.

"All this time, I thought you had some sort of arrangement with the authorities," I murmured. "You have handed over murderers and jewel thieves and blackmailers to them. You must be in league together."

He gave a short, mirthless laugh. "Would you be in league with someone who regularly showed you up? I will grant you, one or two of the inspectors are well-enough disposed towards me, but the vast majority would be very pleased to bring me up on any charges at all. If I let them take me in the act of stealing a dead woman's property, I might as well choose my own cell in Newgate."

"Don't," I begged. "I had no notion. I thought all of you worked together to see that justice was accomplished."

"They are bound by the law," he reminded me. "I have rather less respect for that institution, and I have made no secret of it."

I struggled to make sense of what he said. "So last night, when we were concealed at Madame's, if we had been discovered—"

"I would have found a way out of that," he assured me.

"But when we were scrambling over rooftops and you were brawling in the streets, surely that was not legal."

"I may have broken one or two minor laws," he admitted.

I shook my head. "Little wonder you were so angry."

He said nothing for a long moment whilst I studied my hands. "I owe you an apology. I have pushed too hard to be included in your world, and you are entirely right. I have no notion of the difficulties, the dangers. It never once occurred to me that you might be gaoled for no more than pursuing your occupation."

He rose and came around the desk, pulling me to my feet. "I am careful," he promised. "Very careful."

I hid my face in the shoulder of his coat. "You cannot

be careful enough. I think I would like it very much if you gave up this line of work altogether."

I felt him stiffen in my arms, then relax as he pressed a kiss to my head. "You know that isn't possible."

"Yes, but I can wish."

"You knew what I was when you married me."

"No, I did not. I had a very different idea altogether," I told him. "I knew you pursued villains of all descriptions, but I never realised how entirely alone you are. I always thought the police would rescue you if you needed it."

There was a rumble of laughter from his chest, and I rubbed my cheek against him. "You think I need rescuing?"

"It is possible," I persisted.

"Well, perhaps now you will reconsider your efforts to join me in my work," he said, his lips in my hair.

I pushed away from him. "Reconsider? When I have just this minute discovered how much you really need me?"

His eyes narrowed sharply. "Need you?"

"Brisbane, I am even more determined to assist you. You require a partner, and I am she."

"God help me," he groaned.

"Julia, stop distracting Brisbane. We have work," came an irritable voice from the door. I rose on tiptoe to look over Brisbane's shoulder. Plum arrived just as I was declaring my intentions to Brisbane, and he fixed me with a resentful stare.

"Hello, Plum," I said, settling a bright smile upon my lips. "You are come back early. Did you enjoy your stay at Mortlake's estate?"

He banged the door shut behind him, dropping his bags upon the floor. "In point of fact, I did not. And it is entirely your fault."

Brisbane resumed his seat behind the desk, and I detected from his expression that he was rather glad of the interruption. I made up my mind to raise the subject again later, and turned my attention to my brother.

"Did you not recover the emeralds?"

"Oh, I found them, all right. And turned them over to Lord Mortlake, who was not best pleased."

I was genuinely curious now. "Did he not appreciate your efforts?"

"You could hardly expect him to, since he was the one who engineered the theft in the first place!" Plum went to the whisky decanter and poured out a hefty measure. I sighed. At this rate, we should have to order more spirits and quickly.

"Lord Mortlake himself stole them?"

"The jewels were heavily insured," Brisbane explained.

"You knew he stole them?" Plum's handsome face flushed with anger. "Why the devil didn't you tell me?"

"Because I had no proof. It might have been anyone in the house. Lord Mortlake was merely the likeliest candidate in my estimation." Brisbane kept his voice even in the face of Plum's irritation. "I discovered that the policy was only written two months ago—the first time the Mortlake emeralds have ever been insured. It seemed entirely logical that Lord Mortlake himself was the culprit and had only engaged me as a ruse to pacify the insurance company."

"But why suggest the thief was his own daughter?" I questioned. "That was a stroke of cruelty."

Brisbane shrugged. "If I had to guess, I would say because she was an excellent scapegoat should Plum get lucky and find the emeralds. No one would expect him to turn his own daughter in to the authorities. It would be settled as a private family matter. Where did you find them?"

"There is a monstrous old humidor in Lord Mort-lake's study. The emeralds were inside, stuffed in an old stocking."

"Perhaps one of Lady Mortlake's?" Brisbane suggested.

Plum gave a nod. "I suppose Lady Mortlake herself might have done the deed. She came to the marriage with nothing, and if he is ruined, their sons' inheritance will be lost. I suspect his losses must have been greater than he let on." I quirked a brow at him and he explained. "Gaming tables. Mortlake favours large bets on losing hands. He's an exceptionally poor player, but he does love to gamble."

I sniffed some satisfaction in his demeanour. "You played with him, and won, I would wager."

He gave me a slow, lazy smile that I would have sworn he learnt from Brisbane. "Rather a lot, as it happens. I suppose it was the insurance company's money."

"Which they will want back as soon as they discover the emeralds are returned, unless Lord Mortlake means to keep it secret," I surmised.

"Not a chance," Plum related proudly. "I handed them back to him in the middle of the ballroom. Lady Mortlake even presented me with a token of her gratitude in the form of a kiss upon the cheek."

I seized the opportunity to needle him a little. "And Lady Felicity? Was she suitably impressed?"

He curled a lip. "She missed it entirely. I saw her for five minutes when I first arrived and then she took to her bed with a sick headache. She never made it down to the ball at all, although she did thank me quite handsomely this morning."

"You kissed her!" I crowed.

The blush deepened to almost apoplectic levels. "I am a

gentleman," he reminded me with some heat. "I would never impugn a lady's reputation by speaking of such things."

I waved a hand. "Nevertheless, you kissed her. And enjoyed it, unless I am mistaken."

"Julia Desdemona, shut your mouth," he said through gritted teeth.

Brisbane knew better than to interfere in our family quarrels. He occupied himself with his penknife whilst we squabbled.

"If you had such a lovely time with the lady, why are you so put out with me?" I enquired. "I was not even present."

"Precisely. And your absence was extremely difficult to explain—difficult to the point of awkwardness. The Mortlakes think we are quite uncivil."

"But surely you must have struck a point in our favour with the return of the emeralds."

Plum's hands were fisted at his sides. "Not enough to undo the damage of your appalling rudeness in not showing up for the house party."

"Except with Lady Felicity. She must not have minded," I said sweetly. Plum started forward until Brisbane rose smoothly to his feet. He said nothing, but the mere fact that he had seen fit to rise stopped Plum in his tracks.

"How you can endure her is beyond me." Plum pointed a finger at me. He could turn nasty more quickly than any of my brothers, but I was genuinely happy for him. He had suffered too long at the hands of an unrequited passion. He deserved a little happiness, although it seemed to me he would have his hands full, convincing the Mortlakes to accept him as a suitor to Lady Felicity.

"She has her redeeming qualities," Brisbane assured him.

I bristled. "Redeeming qualities indeed! Back to the matter at hand. What will become of the Mortlakes now?"

"Ruination," Brisbane guessed, resuming his chair. "Mortlake will have to return the funds to the insurance company or be charged with fraud."

"But he does not have the money, not if he used it to settle his gaming debts," I argued. "And he cannot sell the estate. It is entailed with the title."

"He has properties in town. He will see nothing like their true worth if he means to sell quickly, but he has enough to cover his losses," Brisbane explained.

"They will be ruined socially," Plum said, sinking into the chair next to mine. He clutched at his hair. "I did not think. When I gave those jewels back to him, I did not imagine I would be the instrument of ruin for his entire family. They will be driven from society."

"There, there," I soothed, patting his arm. "We will think of something."

Brisbane slanted me a curious look. "What precisely will we think of?"

"Some way to restore the Mortlake reputation."

"Julia, there is no way to recover it," Plum argued. "I handed back the jewels in the most public way. The insurers will hear of it, and Lord Mortlake will be forced to put his town properties up for sale to cover the payment. Society will speculate and put the worst possible construction upon the matter. They will whisper and gossip and chatter about Lord Mortlake, and his family will be disgraced."

Before I could respond, there came a tap at the door and Mrs. Lawson entered, brimming with disapproval. She ignored me and went straight to Brisbane.

"A lady to see you, sir. Here is her card."

She handed over the calling card and Brisbane's brows rose at the sight of it. "Indeed? Send her up, please. And I think the lady might like tea."

Mrs. Lawson bustled out, pursing her lips, but as soon as Brisbane passed me the calling card I understood her displeasure. Mrs. Lawson never liked it when unmarried ladies called upon Brisbane without an escort. She thought it indecent.

I handed the card to Plum. "It seems you will have a chance to apologise to the lady herself," I observed.

His colour rose. "Lady Felicity is here?" Unconsciously he smoothed his turquoise striped waistcoat and shot his cuffs.

A moment later, Felicity entered wearing a pale blue costume of last year's mode. It might have made a charming effect were it not for the furrow upon her white brow. She looked distracted, and at the sight of Plum her colour rose.

"Mr. March! I did not know for certain that you would be here. I am so glad," she burst out. Then, recovering herself, she bit her lip prettily. "I mean, Mr. Brisbane, thank you for seeing me without prior arrangement. Lady Julia, how nice to see you again. It has been quite a long time, I think."

Brisbane, who had risen from behind his desk, bowed from the neck, and I went to shake her hand. "Lady Felicity, what an unexpected pleasure. Do sit. Brisbane has ordered tea, and we can have a nice chat whilst we wait."

Plum had started forward to shake hands, but then thought better of it, and resumed his chair with a little less than his usual grace.

Felicity took the chair next to his and perched on the edge, twisting a handkerchief in her gloved hands. On a good day, Felicity's looks might have been described as arresting. This was not a good day. She was blonde, but darkly so, with sooty lashes and brows framing startling blue eyes. Her skin was good, but she had the sort of pale complexion that could look sickly if she were tired or worried, both of which appeared to be the case at present. There were soft violet shadows under her eyes, but the blue gaze was steady and unflinching as she looked from my husband to my brother.

"I have come to thank you," she said simply.

Brisbane quirked a brow. "Indeed?"

If Plum was thinking of the rather more intimate demonstration of her gratitude she had given him, he was gentleman enough not to betray it.

"Yes," she went on earnestly, collecting me with her gaze. "You see, I have been very worried about Father. It is no secret that we have not got along very well since Mama died," she said, her expression touched with wistfulness. "The new Lady Mortlake was my governess when Mama was alive. He married her within the year, and I am afraid I was not as understanding as I ought to have been. And then when the boys came along," she broke off, giving a hard sniff, and I felt my heart go out to her. To have lost her mother would have been difficult enough; to be thrust into the heart of her father's new family would have been unendurable.

She touched her nose with her handkerchief and went on. "The match has not always been a happy one. They put up a good front in public, and Father is very glad to have an heir at last," she added with a self-deprecating little smile, "but he is unhappy. I can see it. And it breaks my heart. I wish that he could confide in me, but it is too much to ask. So we seldom speak, and when we do, it always seems to end in cross words."

I could not imagine such a thing. My own father was the most maddening man I had ever met, but I could not imagine any quarrel so great it would divide us.

Lady Felicity went on. "The unhappiness in his marriage causes him to gamble—with disastrous results. There is very little money left, and Father is always haring off on schemes to restore the family fortunes. The trouble is that his hands are tied by the entailment. He cannot sell the house or the jewels or the paintings, nothing of real value. I fear he struck upon this latest bit of foolishness out of desperation, and I am so very grateful to you, to you both," she said, darting a glance from Brisbane to Plum, "that the scandal of it will not become public."

Doubt shaded her voice, and I realised the real reason for her visit. She might have intended to thank Brisbane and Plum, but she also craved reassurance that her father would not be made a laughingstock. She wanted to secure our discretion, and on this point, I hastened to reassure her.

"Be at ease, Lady Felicity. No one will know of what transpired. I presume the other guests merely thought the emeralds mislaid?"

"Yes," she said. "They were very happy the emeralds had been found. I do not think they guessed for a moment that Father had been so foolish."

"Then all will soon be forgot," I promised her.

"Not entirely," Brisbane put in softly.

Lady Felicity's head jerked up as if he had struck her. "What do you mean?"

His voice was deliberately gentle, but there was no soft way to deliver the blow. "We were discussing this very point when you arrived, Lady Felicity. It will soon become apparent that your father has lost his fortune. It simply will not be possible for him to conceal it."

She looked from him to me, to Plum, and back again, the colour ebbing slowly from her face. "Ruin," she murmured.

"There can be no hope for any of us. The boys will have no education and I will have no dowry."

"Something must be done," Plum said with surprising fierceness.

"What?" she demanded, her eyes shimmering with unshed tears. "How will the boys manage if they are never properly educated? And what man will have me with no money?"

The demand hovered sharply in the air between them, and I thought of our youngest brother's impetuous proposal of marriage to a girl he barely knew. It had been rejected, mercifully, but if Plum proved equally irrational, Lady Felicity might well accept him. I held my breath as Plum spoke.

"Something must be done," he murmured again.

Lady Felicity looked away quickly, embarrassed, I think, and we fell silent for a moment as she collected herself.

"We were talking earlier of the London properties," I began. "Lord Mortlake does own rather a lot of real estate in town."

"A public sale would expose the loss of his fortune," Brisbane reminded me.

"Not if the properties are sold privately," I corrected.

Brisbane canted his head at me. "Come again?"

I folded my hands in my lap. "It is very simple, my love. You are responsible for Lord Mortlake's ruin."

"I?" He fairly choked upon the word, and Felicity gasped aloud.

"You," I repeated with some firmness. "Plum is in your employ and was acting as your agent when he discovered the emeralds and presented them publicly to Lord Mortlake."

"That is entirely beside the point," Brisbane began, but I carried on as if I had not heard him.

"What Lord Mortlake did was very wrong. But his entire

family should not be made to pay for it. Lady Mortlake has a pack of young sons, whose inheritance must not be stripped away from them. And Lady Felicity must have her marriage portion. Surely you do not wish to be responsible for the ruination of an entire family of quite innocent and very nice people?"

Felicity put up her hands. "No, really, Lady Julia! They were simply acting for the best, and I am grateful. How much worse would this affair be if Father were prosecuted for defrauding the insurers? You must not lay the blame at their feet."

I smiled at her. "Do not trouble yourself, my dear. They must accept that there are consequences to their actions."

Brisbane was shaking his head, dazed. "This cannot possibly be made to be my fault."

"Yours and Plum's," I corrected. "He ought to have had more discretion than to hand over the jewels so indiscreetly." I shot my brother a repressive look. "Really, Plum. What were you thinking?"

He gaped at me, then at Brisbane. "She cannot be serious."

"You have known her longer than I," Brisbane returned bitterly. "You ought to be accustomed to it by now."

"Gentlemen," I recalled them, "we were speaking of the Mortlakes. Now, Lord Mortlake has been very foolish indeed, but I think we all agree his family must not be made to pay the price for his silliness."

"Silliness? Julia, the man has committed a serious crime," Plum put in. He darted a look at Felicity and flushed painfully. She looked at the handkerchief in her hands and would not meet his gaze.

I waved a hand again. "We have all done stupid things

from time to time," I reminded him. "But luckily for Lord Mortlake, he has us to retrieve the situation."

Brisbane levelled his gaze at me. "I know I will regret this, very likely for the rest of my life, but precisely *how* do you intend we should retrieve the situation?"

"We will buy Lord Mortlake's London properties."

Felicity jumped like a scalded cat and Plum choked, but Brisbane merely sat in perfect stillness.

Felicity recovered her wits first. "Lady Julia, you cannot mean it," she said, just as Plum spluttered, "Julia, you are jesting."

"Not a bit of it. The three of us will contribute the funds and we will purchase his properties privately. It is not a bad investment," I added. "Most of them could be let for income with the exception of the Belgravia house. The family will have to remain there to avoid gossip. We might expect a peppercorn rent for it, just until Lord Mortlake manages to retrench his finances. The other properties we could sell at a tidy profit. Although," I put in, frowning, "it occurs to me that Plum might like to keep the property in Golden Square. It is a very fine house and would suit him well should he choose to take a wife in due course."

"A wife?" Plum choked again, this time so deeply that I was forced to strike him hard several times upon the back before he recovered. Lady Felicity looked deeply embarrassed, but her breathing had quickened and she darted a glance at Plum from beneath her lashes.

"You seem quite determined," Brisbane said to me at last.

"I am. Each of us has contributed to Lord Mortlake's predicament, and we ought to help him out of it. He really is a decent fellow, you know. He has been a member of Father's

Shakespearean society for decades. Father would want us to help him."

"What Father would want is bloody well not the point!" Plum spluttered.

I clucked at him. "Language, Plum. And it is the point." I turned to Brisbane. "You have held forth many times upon the subject of justice, my dear. I know it is the principle that guides your every action. If we destroy Lord Mortlake for a momentary weakness and in doing so ruin his entire family, where is the justice in that?"

Brisbane knew I had the right of him. He did not answer my question. He merely folded his arms over his chest and posed one of his own. "And—begging your pardon, Lady Felicity—if we save him, he might just as easily go off and do it again. Who will save him then?"

Felicity leaned forward towards me, her expression earnestly sweet. "Mr. Brisbane is quite right. It is entirely possible that Father will do something foolish again. You cannot be expected to rescue us a second time."

I pondered this a moment, then brightened. "We will give him the chance to save himself! We will have him sign a statement, a confession of sorts that he instigated this, and shall assure him that should he ever gamble again, we will proceed directly to the authorities with the evidence."

"That is blackmail!" Plum exclaimed.

I furrowed my brow. "Really? I thought it was extortion. Brisbane, you will have to explain the difference one of these days."

"It is practical," Felicity said slowly. "And it isn't as though Father has many alternatives left."

Brisbane covered his face with his hands for a long moment, then dropped them, and to my astonishment, he was smiling. "One woman in a thousand," he murmured.

He cleared his throat. "Very well, wife. You, Plum and I will put up equal shares and purchase the Mortlake town properties. I will summon Mortlake this afternoon to explain the situation and offer us up as his saviours."

I would have flown to him to offer my thanks, but the presence of Plum and Lady Felicity was rather chilling in that regard. Instead, I blew him a kiss and hoped that would suffice as both a thanks and a promise.

Lady Felicity sat, shaking her head as if to clear away a waking dream. "I cannot believe it is all going to come right. I feel as if I have just walked through a whirlwind."

"The Marches tend to have that effect," Brisbane agreed. "You will grow accustomed to it in time."

Mrs. Lawson appeared then with the tea tray and it took ages to pour and hand round the sandwiches and cakes, but I noticed as I offered Lady Felicity her cup, she was still pleasantly pink from Brisbane's last remark. The implication that her association with the Marches might be one of long duration had clearly made her very happy. She was conversing softly with Plum, their heads close together, his so dark, hers so fair. They made a pretty picture, and I saw a sudden smile soften her features. She was rather smitten with my brother, I decided, and for Plum's part, he seemed cautiously attracted. I wanted him happy. His heart had been broken long enough over a woman he could not have, and if he could make up his mind to love Felicity Mortlake, matters might indeed come right in the end.

The

NINTH CHAPTER

Yea, though I die, the scandal will survive.

—*"The Rape of Lucrece"*

A few days later, Brisbane and I were enjoying a most delicious breakfast courtesy of our new cook. I gave a contented sigh at the properly shirred eggs and even spooned one into a saucer for Rook. He lapped delicately at it, and from over my shoulder Grim made a threatening quork.

"Oh, very well. What about a nice bit of kedgeree?" I asked, preparing a small dish for him. He bobbed his head happily when I put the bowl into his cage. "Breakfast," he said in his reedy little voice. I left him to it and resumed my chair just as Brisbane gave an exclamation, leaning forward swiftly in his chair as he focused intently upon his newspaper.

"Brisbane?"

He lowered the newspaper, a feline smile playing about his lips, and handed it to me.

It was not difficult to discover what had captured his interest. The inquest into Madame's death had made the newspapers. I skimmed the piece, brief as it was, and gave a gasp.

"It was just as you said. Aconite poisoning."

"Keep reading," he instructed, serving himself another plate of eggs and devilled kidneys. The new cook was proving rather too skilled, I thought. If Brisbane continued to eat so heartily, he soon would find himself paying a visit to his tailor.

I surveyed the rest of the article until I came to the conclusion. "Accidental death! They have returned a verdict of accidental death," I said, brandishing the newspaper. "Do you think it accidental?"

"Not bloody likely." His expression was grim. "It is entirely too coincidental that a woman such as Madame, who collected lovers and kept mementoes of her *affaires,* should have died accidentally."

I pursed my lips. "It says here that the Spirit Club's cook is an elderly fellow and mistook the root of *aconitum napellus* for a horseradish. He has cataracts. It is supposed that the greengrocer's boy, who brought the produce, must have inadvertently delivered the wrong root."

But Brisbane was not to be swayed. "I do not like coincidences. Besides, it is only a theory that the cook mistook the horseradish root. There was none left to test. It had been thrown out and the dish scoured by the time investigators thought to ask after it. A kitchen mishap is merely the simplest explanation, and a damned lazy one, in this case. And the greengrocer's boy makes far too convenient a scapegoat. He swore under oath that the horseradish root was a proper horseradish root. His employer swore to the same, a man with forty years' experience with vegetables. And yet the police are perfectly content to accept this nursery story about mistaken roots instead of pursuing *where* the aconite came from."

I put the paper aside and stirred my tea thoughtfully. "No one traced the root. If the greengrocer and his lad are telling the truth, the boy delivered horseradish, not aconite. So where did the aconite itself originate?" I sat back. "An interesting question, to be sure, and one that no one seems to be asking. I presume you believe the greengrocer is correct."

"I do."

"So you think the verdict in error. Do you mean to investigate?"

"I detect a note of disapproval, my sweet. You want me to leave it alone?"

I struggled to give voice to my thoughts. "It is simply that Madame is dead, and for better or worse, there is a verdict in the case. Her poor sister, Mademoiselle Agathe, has an answer—whether it is the correct one or not—and we do not know that it isn't," I reminded him. "There has not been a breath of trouble as far as Bellmont is concerned since Madame's death."

"That we know of," he corrected.

"True. I daresay his last visit was so contentious that he might well hesitate to turn to you again, even if the devil himself were at his heels. Still, I saw Aunt Hermia yesterday and she mentioned that she had dinner with Bellmont the day before and his spirits were better than she had seen in some time. He has never been good at concealing his feelings. I think he has begun to put this entire unsavoury episode behind him. And perhaps you were right. Perhaps Madame did destroy the letters. She would not be the first woman to keep a memento of a love affair and then change her mind."

Brisbane gave me the courtesy of thinking over his reply

and for a moment, said nothing. "You make perfect sense, my dear. But I cannot shake the feeling that there is more afoot here than a simple kitchen mishap."

"Perhaps there is," I conceded. "Perhaps she was murdered. But it does not touch upon my brother. Whatever evils Bellmont may contemplate, I assure you murdering his mistress is not among them," I added with some tartness.

Brisbane regarded me thoughtfully. "You are a very loyal woman, Julia. I often wonder what would happen if you were forced to choose between your family and me."

I started, spilling my tea. "Brisbane, what an extraordinary thing to say!"

The tea smeared the headlines about Madame's inquest, blurring the words. "And yet you do not know the answer," he said softly.

I dropped the sodden mess of tea-soaked newspaper. "Yes, I do, you great fool. You *are* my family."

"I am glad to hear you say it," he told me, and though I waited for some smile or other sign of levity, I saw that he was deadly serious.

"Brisbane, you are even more enigmatic than usual this morning. What are you about?"

He shook himself, as if throwing off a reverie that made him melancholy and gave me a humourless smile. "Nothing, my dear."

He rose and pressed a kiss to my brow. "I am off to my consulting rooms. I will take your excellent advice and leave this," he said, nodding towards the ruined newspaper. "For now."

He left me then, and I sat for a while, pondering the strange conversation that had just passed between us.

Before I could reach any firm conclusions, Plum appeared, dressed in one of his customary dashing ensembles—a town suit with an emerald-and-pink-striped waistcoat and a violet silk neckcloth. He always took great pains with his *toilette,* but he had grown even more attentive to his appearance since he had begun to spend time with Lady Felicity. They had met, carefully chaperoned, for the theatre and the occasional walk in the park, and matters seemed to be moving along—with glacial slowness, to be sure, but forward at least.

"Good morning, Julia." He helped himself to the hot dishes on the sideboard and cast a glance at the pile of wet newspapers.

"What happened here?"

"Hmm? Oh, I was clumsy. I am sorry, the paper is quite ruined."

I waited for an outburst of temper, for Plum loved nothing better than to read the paper thoroughly over breakfast, but he merely shrugged.

"No matter. You can tell me any news of importance."

His spirits were unnaturally high, and I leapt to the logical conclusion.

"I take it you saw Lady Felicity last night?"

He gave me a smug smile. "I did."

"I do hope she is more appreciative of our efforts than her father." If my tone was waspish, I could not help it. Contrary to my expectations, Lord Mortlake had not been at all pleased at the solution we had presented to his troubles. He had been outraged by the statement Brisbane had given him to sign and almost apoplectic at the notion of selling his town properties. But he crumbled at the round figure we offered and had finally agreed to sell us his properties at very fair prices, reimbursing the insurance company and giving him the opportunity to retrench and salvage his family name.

Plum helped himself at the sideboard. "She regrets his attitude, but she still takes a rather more pragmatic view of the situation than Lord Mortlake. She is happy to keep the matter from the papers and her father's reputation unsullied."

"Excellent." I pressed him no further. I knew the attachment to Lady Felicity was tender and new, and I also knew that nothing could kill a romance in its cradle as fast as sisterly intervention.

I bade him a good morning, and as I left the breakfast room, Aquinas approached.

"If you have a moment, my lady, I should like to present the new staff for your approval."

"New staff? Have we more besides the cook?"

"I have engaged a pair of footmen I think will fit in quite nicely with the establishment. Would you care to meet them, my lady?"

"I suppose now is as good a time as any." Our changes in staff had become so frequent that I had instructed Aquinas only to present them in batches once a week rather than piecemeal. It had saved a considerable amount of time.

Aquinas hurried off, and in a very few minutes he returned with the three newest members of the household. The cook removed her apron and thrust it behind her. Her hair was mousy brown, and she had watery, rather protruberant eyes.

"Welcome to our home. I hope you do not mind if we simply call you Cook. It's rather a tradition with my staff. I must compliment you on the wonderful food you have been sending up. Quite delicious, and we're all terribly pleased."

She ducked her head and mumbled something inaudible to Aquinas.

He stepped forward. "Cook is Swiss and uncertain of

her English, my lady. She says she is happy to have given satisfaction."

"Oh, I didn't realise. Well, how very exclusive we are to have a Continental cook." I addressed her in Italian then, thanking her again, and she gave me a look of confusion.

"Not that part of Switzerland," Aquinas murmured.

"Oh, I see." I switched to German, and the cook brightened immediately. I thanked her for the excellent breakfast, and she seemed very pleased with my compliments. I gave her permission to return to her baking, and she bobbed a clumsy curtsey to me before fleeing back to her kitchens. I turned my attention to the remaining pair.

It was their first morning in service and they had been breakfasting belowstairs and showing off their new livery. I had chosen it myself and was rather proud of it—smart black tailcoats with waistcoats of striped black and pewter. The trousers had a narrow piping of scarlet and the effect was dashing, or would have been with a pair of matching six-footers. Aquinas had proven himself an original in his choice of footmen, for it was the custom to engage footmen in pairs as close to one another in appearance as possible. A set of identical twins would have been a coup beyond measure, but even young men with similar build, good shoulders, excellent calves and superior height would have been the thing.

The pair that presented themselves to me looked more suited to the stews than a drawing room. They were of wildly variant heights, the taller having long limbs and a particularly graceful neck and a head of shining silver-blond hair. The shorter of the two had a great barrel chest and a nose that looked as if it had been broken. Twice.

I summoned a smile. "Welcome to our employ. Mr. Brisbane and I do hope you will be happy with us."

I put out my hand to shake theirs, and the shorter of the two nearly crushed it in his great paw. The taller gave me a gentler, but still thoroughly brutal handshake. I winced only a little.

"Tell me, I am curious as to your previous employment." I turned to the taller of the two. "Where have you worked before?"

The tall fellow darted a glance at Aquinas, then swiftly back at me. "At a club in St. James Street."

I regarded him a moment, then put the same question to the other. He gave me a nod. "What he said," came the gruff reply.

I stepped back and looked them over again. "Aquinas," I began, setting a deliberate smile upon my lips, "I know I have not Mr. Brisbane's experience of the world, but one thing I do know is what a footman should look like. Neither of these men has ever so much as seen a suit of livery before, much less been engaged by one of the St. James Street clubs."

Aquinas began to protest, but I held up a hand. "Really, Aquinas, you ought to have known better. The St. James Street clubs are the most fashionable in London. They employ only the most experienced, most exclusive staff in the city. They do not engage men who look as if they have just lost a prizefight."

"Here, now, my lady, I have never lost a fight," protested the shorter of the pair. "I am undefeated, I am."

I narrowed my gaze at him. "You are a prizefighter?"

He drew himself up to his rather diminutive height and gave me a broad smile, revealing a pair of missing teeth and an enormous one that seemed to be made of solid gold.

"I am. Bert Pigeon, at yer service, my lady." He swept me a low bow.

I looked to the other. "And you? What is your talent?"

He gave me a languid glance. "I am a cracksman, my lady, and the best pistol shot in all of Surrey and sometimes Kent."

Aquinas began to speak again and once more I held up a hand. "You did not find these men, Aquinas. Brisbane did."

"That he did," Bert Pigeon said proudly. "And a finer man to work for you'll not find in all of London. He's a proper gentleman he is, and he saved me from the hangman's noose and I'll not forget it." He pitched his voice lower. "There was some bother with some jewels, but we will not speak of it," he added with a wink.

"And you? Did Brisbane save you, as well?" I asked the taller fellow.

He shifted a little. "Mr. Brisbane might have intervened in a matter that could have caused me some trouble," he acknowledged. He cleared his throat. "Bert and I formed a professional partnership that was ill-fated."

"And jewels were involved?"

He gave a graceful nod. "They were, my lady."

"You were stealing them." It was not a question. I knew the answer.

Bert Pigeon's expression was pained. "Well, that is a blunt way of putting the matter, but I do admit we had an eye to liberating one or two items when Mr. Brisbane apprehended us and put it to us that it was perhaps not the best of schemes."

My head was swimming, and I took a deep breath, striving for patience. "Whose jewels?"

The taller fellow blinked. "Beg pardon, my lady?"

"Whose jewels?" I persisted. "If I am to have two jewel

thieves in my employ, I want to know what your intentions were."

They exchanged wary glances.

"Well," Bert Pigeon began uncomfortably, "I suppose you might say they were Her Majesty's, although I like to think of them as belonging to all of us as it were."

I blinked at him. "You were attempting to steal the Crown Jewels?"

"Aye, my lady."

"From the Tower?"

"Aye, my lady."

"How close were you to success?" I demanded.

They exchanged glances again, this time with a touch of pride. "I held the Koh-i-Noor in my hands," Bert Pigeon said, raising his blunt chin.

I turned to Aquinas. "I really ought to have a vinaigrette for moments like this."

"Shall I fetch one, my lady?" he asked, eager for something—*anything*—to do.

"No, I think I shall recover." I turned to the pair. "I can only surmise that my husband had his reasons for engaging you, and I trust him completely. I would, however, like to remind you quite firmly, that any and all felonious activities are strongly discouraged from this point on."

They nodded sharply. I turned to the shorter of the two. "It is the custom to address footmen by their Christian names, but I cannot have a footman called Bert. You will be Pigeon in the house."

He nodded briskly. "That suits me fine, my lady."

I pressed my lips together, trying not to think of the perfectly turned out and impeccably mannered servants that other people managed to employ. "And you, I do not believe I heard your name."

"Swanson, my lady, although since Bert and I took up partnership, folk usually call me Swan."

I looked from one to the other. "Very well. Pigeon and Swan. Welcome to our employ."

I hesitated, a sudden suspicion dawning. "Pigeon, how did you break your nose?"

He gave me another of his broad smiles. "Ah, that would be Mr. Brisbane, my lady. I did require a bit of persuasion to give up the Crown Jewels."

"Of course you did," I said faintly. "Of course you did."

Accompanied by a rather conspicuous Pigeon, Morag, Swan and I went to pay a call upon my sister, collecting a fresh newspaper along the way. In spite of my admonitions to Brisbane about leaving Madame's death well-enough alone, I wanted to see what the more sensationalist newspapers might have to say upon the subject. Brisbane always read the *Times,* but I wanted something a little more colourful, so I instructed Pigeon to purchase a copy of the *Illustrated Daily News.* It described the inquest of Madame in lurid detail, complete with some rather fine sketches of the affair. Unlike the *Times,* this periodical featured a great deal of speculation, including some unsavoury information about Madame's work as a medium and her penchant for wellplaced lovers.

"Blast," I muttered as I perused the article. To read the *Times,* one would suppose the business over and done with, but the journalist—if one could call him such—from this paper clearly wished to prolong the affair. I skipped to the byline, noting the name—Peter Sullivan—and put the newspaper aside. Doubtless Mr. Sullivan and his proprietors hoped to sell newspapers and were sensationalising the situation for profit, but I hoped they would find bigger game to hunt and quickly, for Bellmont's sake.

I discarded the newspaper before I reached Portia's, but I might have known she would have already read the full account for herself. I had not seen her since I had left her house the night of the séance. I was a trifle put out with her for giving me up to Brisbane so easily, so I had not called upon her. I had merely sent word to her that I had followed Brisbane as far as the Spirit Club and learned nothing of importance regarding either my husband or our brother. Whether she believed that or not was another matter. She fairly pounced as soon as I arrived, pausing only to blink in astonishment at my footmen before whisking me off to her morning room for a private tête-à-tête.

"I shan't even ask where you found those two. You look as if you are trailing about town with the remnants of a circus. Now, I haven't seen you for far too long. Tell me everything you discovered about Bellmont," she instructed.

I folded my hands in my lap and adopted a guileless expression. "No mystery at all, I'm afraid," I said smoothly. "Bellmont's call at Brisbane's consulting rooms was simply by way of being a family visit. Brisbane wanted to install a telephone at our house and meant for it to be a surprise. That is why he lied about Bellmont calling at his rooms in Chapel Street."

Portia pulled a face. "I call that distinctly disappointing. And Bellmont was not involved in the matter at the Spirit Club at all?"

"Apparently not. Brisbane was there to unmask Madame Séraphine as a charlatan, but she died before he had the chance. So, no great revelations to be had."

"Oh, that is disappointing! I should love to think of Bellmont entangled in some bit of naughtiness," Portia said, falling into gales of laughter.

If my own laughter was subdued, she did not seem to notice. I was immensely relieved at having put her off the scent, and to ensure that she stayed off it, I offered up another tasty morsel of family gossip and related to her the facts of Plum's burgeoning attachment to Felicity Mortlake.

Portia was agog, and we spent a companionable visit chattering about our various friends and relations, and by the time I had left, I resolved to put the mysteries of the Spirit Club entirely behind us.

And so the matter of Madame Séraphine's mysterious death seemed to fade away. Over the next week, I busied myself with my new photographic equipment, establishing a proper studio in the attics at Chapel Street, and spending nearly every waking moment intent upon the craft. I was enthralled by the process, which perfectly married the scientific and the artistic, particularly as I had never thought of myself as an artist before. My sole attempt at sculpture had ended in tears, and all of my watercolours resembled muddy bogs. But behind the lens, something dynamic came to the fore and I felt as if I were really seeing the world for the first time. I was at home in that studio, whether suffocating under the heavy drape behind the camera or working with the nasty chemicals required to fix and develop the images. There were noxious smells from the solutions and draughts from the windows left open to ventilate them, but I did not mind.

I experimented with light and shadow, learning how the merest shift from one to the other can highlight a face or throw it into relief. I took endless photographs of Plum and

Monk and Morag, and even Mrs. Lawson was upon occasion persuaded to sit for me. At first I had costumed my subjects as many lady photographers did. The fashion was to present classical subjects from literature or mythology, to illustrate ancient tales with modern faces. But I found I preferred nothing so much as the naked emotion of a sitter's true feelings revealed upon the features. Perhaps it was a disastrous sitting with Morag garbed as Boadicea that persuaded me, but in the end, I put aside the costumes and the props and began to photograph people as I saw them—not as I wanted them to be, not as they wanted themselves to be, but as they were.

To Mrs. Lawson's outrage, I began to photograph all sorts of people whose paths crossed mine, from duchesses to coster boys directly from the gutter. I made no effort to clean them up. I wanted them as they were, gritty and real, London come to life in a thousand faces. I photographed Pigeon and Swan. I photographed my sister with her babe, and I even photographed Auld Lachy, the irritable Scottish hermit living in Father's garden. On one memorable occasion, I heard the muffin bell and ran downstairs to persuade the muffin man to sit for me, promising to buy all of his wares if he would oblige me.

For this last, Mrs. Lawson lodged a formal complaint with Brisbane, threatening to turn us out of the house entirely. Brisbane offered Mrs. Lawson a substantial bonus, and I continued happily in my newest endeavour. I plagued Brisbane only marginally less to let me partipate in his investigations, and upon one or two occasions, provided him some assistance in photographing evidence he wished to preserve. Matters between us settled to an easy routine, and I found myself relaxing into marriage. Each afternoon I descended from my studio to take tea with Brisbane, as cosy and companionable as any married couple, and I did not fail to notice that Brisbane himself seemed easier. He consulted me upon cases without prompting, and I offered my perspective without pushing myself forward to share in the physical dangers of his work. It became more of a partnership, I thought, a refuge for both of us, and I allowed myself to be happy.

And so it was that I had quite forgot the matter of Madame's death. I had seen little of Bellmont, but he and Brisbane had apparently mended their quarrel, for as I descended to tea one afternoon, I found him in Brisbane's rooms.

"Monty! I did not know you were coming. Brisbane, have you rung for Mrs. Lawson to tell her we will be three for tea?" I asked brightly.

But one look at Bellmont's face told me this was not to be a peaceful family visit. He was slumped in a chair, his complexion waxy and pale, clutching a letter in his hands. I sank into the chair next to him and put out my hand.

He seized it, his expression aghast. "Good God, Julia, what have you been doing? Your hands are utterly ruined."

"I have been at work in my darkroom. The chemicals turn the skin black."

He dropped the hand with a little moue of distaste. "You look common. Is there no remedy?"

"I hear cyanide of potassium works rather well, but it has a tendency to be fatal," I replied tartly. "And haven't you more important things to worry yourself over just now? Like the blackmail note in your hand?"

Wordlessly, he handed it over, and I saw that his hand trembled slightly. The hunted look had come back into his eyes.

The letter was concise, as such things often are. It explained that the sender was in possession of certain papers that would destroy Bellmont if he did not arrange payment for a particular sum. I lifted my head to Brisbane.

"There are no directions for payment."

Brisbane was thoughtful. "Such demands seldom include details with the first communication. The sender wants Bellmont in a state of anxiety so that when the details are conveyed, he will act. This is merely the first."

"The first for the rest of my life," Bellmont put in bitterly. He pierced Brisbane with his gaze. "What do you advise?"

Brisbane gave a slow-lidded blink. "I advise you to have the sum in readiness. When the next demand comes, pay it."

"Pay it!" Bellmont's face flushed dull red and he started forward in his chair. "You must be mad."

Brisbane endeavoured to explain. "You have nothing to work with here, only a single sheet of paper of the sort that may be purchased at any stationer's in London. The postmark tells us nothing save that it was posted in London, which gives us over four million suspects. There are no telltale watermarks upon the page, no distinctive perfumes. There are no peculiarities of syntax or grammar to give us a hint as to the blackmailer's identity, and there is nothing to learn from the handwriting save that these smudges here indicate the individual wrote with the left hand in order to disguise the writing and throw you from the scent. So," he concluded, "we have a right-handed blackmailer who lives in London and has the means to purchase the cheapest of all possible paper."

"But you must know something else," Bellmont insisted. "The person must be close to Madame to have her papers."

"Not necessarily. Madame may have sent them to anyone of her acquaintance, a friend, a banker, a man of affairs."

"Surely a banker would not attempt to blackmail a member of Parliament," I put in.

Brisbane slanted me a curious look. "You have never met the sort of bankers I have dealt with," he observed. "In any event, Madame could have given her papers to anyone at all, including any member of the Spirit Club, her family, even her other lovers." He paused a moment and Bellmont sucked in his breath sharply. Brisbane went on. "Or she may not have given them to anyone. She may have hidden them and they were discovered after her death. They could have been secured for safekeeping and some chambermaid may have helped herself."

"I hardly think a chambermaid would be sufficiently intelligent to orchestrate a blackmail scheme," Bellmont objected.

Brisbane smiled thinly at the sarcasm. "No, but a police inspector might. Madame's rooms were searched along with the rest of the Spirit Club. Any one of a dozen police officers or their superiors could have found the papers and decided to make use of them. I hear a police pension is not what it ought to be," he finished blandly.

Bellmont looked at him with barely concealed contempt. "I shall never forget how singularly difficult you have been during this business."

I put a hand to my brother's sleeve. "Bellmont, he is only attempting to prepare you for the worst." But another thought had come to me, one I wished to discuss only with my husband. I rose briskly and put an end to the conversation. "You must leave it with us, Monty. Go and get the funds together and when you receive another note, you must bring it to us at once. In the meantime, we will begin to work on the likeliest sources for this new outrage."

Bellmont did not like being brushed aside, but he

eventually left, and I resumed my seat, only to find Brisbane's eyes resting thoughtfully upon me. I gave him a reproving glance.

"You might have made that easier for him."

"Yes, I might have," he agreed. "But I saw no point. He is demanding the earth and he cannot have it. He is still the same arrogant, entitled, overbearing fellow he always was. It will do him good to cool his heels."

"I do not say you are wrong about him," I said with some primness, "but you should be a trifle more considerate of his difficulties in future. This entire affair has shaken him badly."

Brisbane snorted. "My dear wife, your brother and his mentor, Salisbury, have embarked upon a scheme to augment the navy by some twenty-one million pounds. If he cannot manage his nerves over a simple spot of blackmail, how can he possibly hope to keep Germany in check?"

I sighed. Brisbane had strongly opposed the Naval Defence Act, and some of the more acrimonious exchanges he and Bellmont had had in the past struck precisely upon the point that Bellmont felt it necessary to spend millions of pounds shoring up the navy against German aggression whilst Brisbane maintained it would only lead to an escalation of German and French military spending. The entire question left me cold, but they had argued contentiously upon the matter, and Bellmont had been less than gracious when Parliament finally passed the act and building had begun.

"Politics aside," I said firmly, "we are family and we must do what we can to unmask the villain who threatens him."

Brisbane narrowed his gaze. "You have a thought upon

the matter. I saw your eyes light up just before you threw Bellmont out."

I repressed the urge to explain that I had not actually thrown Bellmont out. "It may be nothing at all, but I had a sort of inspiration, a flash of intuition."

To my astonishment, Brisbane leaned closer over his desk. "Go on."

"Well, I am sure you will think it quite absurd, but it did occur to me that when I read the account of Madame's inquest in the *Illustrated Daily News,* it seemed rather too detailed, too precise, as if the reporter had actually been at the Spirit Club."

Brisbane shrugged. "I daresay he would have gone to get a feel for the place and attended another medium's séance."

I shook my head. "No, I don't think so. There was something familiar in his writing, as if he knew his subject quite well, intimately almost."

"You think he might have been another lover of hers?" Brisbane's gaze sharpened.

"I don't know. But he might well know something about Madame's associates, someone whom she might have trusted with her papers and who would not scruple to use them."

"And she might have trusted the reporter himself with the papers," Brisbane pointed out.

I blinked. "You mean, he might be the villain? Good heavens, I thought the press were above that sort of thing."

Brisbane gave me a pitying smile. "In my experience, no one is above that sort of thing."

The
TENTH CHAPTER

Sit by my side
And let the world slip.

—*The Taming of the Shrew*

Unfortunately, after several pleasant days of marital accord, a quarrel of substantial proportions ensued, and we found ourselves covering old territory again. I pressed every advantage I had, and in the end, Brisbane agreed that I could investigate the Spirit Club. We had decided that until Bellmont received more information, our only leads were the club itself and the reporter. I pointed out, with inescapable logic, that we could cover twice the ground in half the time if we divided the investigation, and in the end, Brisbane was forced to concede the point. He left to investigate the reporter and make casual enquiries at his clubs, for it occurred to both of us that Bellmont might well be one of many gentlemen being persecuted. The sum in question was sizeable, and it might prove difficult for some to raise on short notice. Any whisper of sudden financial worries would be sure to reach the clubs. I was to pay a call upon Mademoiselle Agathe and use her as an instrument to discover all I

could about the workings of the Spirit Club. It was an eq-
uitable division, and one that made me entirely happy, for
it was the first time Brisbane had given his approval to my
direct involvement in a case.

I dressed carefully in a striking and expensive costume of
dark red silk trimmed with black *passementerie,* calculating
that Agathe might be swayed to gossip by the combination
of fashionable clothes and my title. I had not thought of a
proper pretext for calling upon her, and as I made my way
to the club, it suddenly occurred to me that she might have
taken up residence elsewhere. With her sister's death, there
was nothing to keep her at the Spirit Club, and I thumped
the seat of the carriage in disgust. Well, there was nothing
for it. I would simply have to demand her new address if she
had taken herself off, and as I alighted from the carriage, I
set a smile upon my lips. Pigeon darted ahead to rap smartly
upon the door, and the porter, Beekman, seemed startled to
see him, swinging his glance between the two of us.

"Thank you, Pigeon, that will be all," I said with a note
of finality. He hurried back to the carriage with a backwards glance at the club, and I wondered if Brisbane had
ordered him to be particularly watchful. I turned to the
porter with my winsome smile.

"Good afternoon. I am looking for Mademoiselle Agathe
LeBrun, the sister of the late Madame Séraphine."

He gave a gruff cough. "Mademoiselle Agathe is in session."

I started in surprise. "In session? Mademoiselle is holding
a séance?"

"She is." His gaze turned suspicious. "Isn't that why you've
come?"

"Yes," I hastened to assure him. I cast wildly for a plausible excuse for my confusion. "I thought she gave only private readings."

He stepped backwards. "You can wait. In there," he added with a nod of his head towards the antechamber where we had gathered before the séance the night of Madame's death. It was entirely the same as the last time I had seen it, from the Spiritualist publications to the open guestbook lying upon the table.

Suddenly, I was seized with an idea. I scrabbled hastily in my reticule for a pencil and my notebook and turned the pages of the guestbook until I reached the date of the séance. It was the work of a moment to transcribe the names into my notebook, and when I was finished, I stuffed the notebook and pencil back into my reticule and took up a magazine and an expression of studied nonchalance. I had not long to wait. I had just begun a rather fascinating article about spirit photography when Mademoiselle Agathe entered, wearing the same embroidered black robe her sister had worn.

"You asked for me?" she enquired. There was an anxious furrow between her eyes, as if she had not thrown off the mantle of the lesser yet, and as she slipped out of her robe, I saw that she wore the same dull gown she had worn upon my first occasion at the Spirit Club.

"I did. I am Lady Julia Brisbane," I informed her. "You may be acquainted with my father, the Earl March. He is very interested in all matter of Spiritualist subjects," I added in a well-bred murmur. It was a lie, of course. The only interest Father would have had in Spiritualism would be in conjuring the ghost of Shakespeare. But his title seldom failed to open doors, and at the sound of it, Agathe's expression sharpened slightly.

"I have not had the honour," she told me, "but welcome to the Spirit Club. What can I do for you, my lady?"

"I wanted to speak with you about Madame Séraphine."

The dark eyes clouded with tears. "Oh. Did you know my sister?"

I temporised. "I had not the pleasure of meeting her formally, but I do know several people who attended her sessions. They were quite overcome."

Her mouth curved and she put out a hand as if to touch mine, then thought better of it. "You are very kind, madame."

"I see that you are holding sessions, as well."

She shook her head. "I have nothing like her talent, but the management is very insistent that her contract be fulfilled. I am doing my best with my wretched skills."

"I am sure you are very talented," I soothed.

Agathe gave me a shy smile. "Would you care to take some refreshment, my lady? This parlour is not very comfortable, but I could take you upstairs and ring for some cordial."

I agreed with alacrity, and in a very few moments we were cosily ensconced in Madame's boudoir, sipping a fruited cordial. I tried not to think about Madame as I seated myself on the recamier, but I did shudder ever so slightly as I remembered her lolling there, her eyes half-closed, quite dead. There was a drape of some silken fabric over the sofa, doubtless to hide the stains, I thought nastily.

"This was my sister's room," Agathe said suddenly. "She died here."

I gave her a look pregnant with sympathy. "What a dreadful loss for you. You have my deepest condolences, mademoiselle."

She sipped at her cordial. "The inquest says that the

death was accidental. A bit of poisonous root mistaken for horseradish."

"A terrible tragedy," I commented.

"Inexcusable," she returned harshly. "To cut down my beautiful sister in her prime and with such a stupid mistake! It is unbearable."

"You were very close." The comment was a lure, designed to coax reminiscences from her, and it was successful. The words came thick and fast, tales of their impoverished upbringing in a farming village in France, of their time in an orphanage, and how Madame's abilities and clever ways had extricated them. Agathe talked of their travels and their life together, speaking quickly, as if she knew that she must outpace the pain of her memories. Theirs had been a life of daring, of chances seized and opportunities made. They had crafted an existence for themselves that was adventuresome and intrepid, and always Madame had been the leader, the driving force behind their resolve. And as she spoke, the customary mask of control slipped, and I saw what I think few others had seen.

"I shall not know how to begin to live without her," Agathe finished, succumbing at last to emotion. She buried her face in her handkerchief, but when she lifted her head, she had dried her tears and once more mastered her feelings. "Forgive me, madame, but you have been so kind to listen. No one else wants to know. The management of the club, they are concerned only with money. The clients want only answers. Only you have looked at me and seen the grieving sister."

I said nothing, but merely inclined my head in silent sympathy. She hesitated, and then leaned closer, her lips parted. For an instant, I thought she was about to reveal something, but then her mouth closed and she said nothing.

I leaned closer myself, tempting confidences. "You seem troubled. Is there something beyond the loss of your sister? You may tell me."

She hesitated, perched on the edge of a precipice, but she would not fall.

I prodded again, gently still. "It sometimes is good to unburden oneself."

She gave a short, sharp laugh. "Unburden? What do you know of my burdens?"

"Nothing," I returned boldly. "But I would like to help."

She gave me a cool stare, and I returned it, unflinching. At last a smile curved her lips. "I wonder if you mean that," she murmured.

I said nothing, and she seemed to be deliberating something within herself. At last, she made up her mind and drew a small box from her pocket.

"Very well. I will give you something to remember this meeting by."

She opened the box and tipped the contents into her palm. I suppressed a gasp. A single button lay there. The button was jewelled, the facets sparkling up at me in invitation. I reached for it almost against my will. There was something repellent about the tiny jewel. It was Teutonic in origin, dark yellow, a strange and menacing sort of colour, and it was overlaid on the top facet with a bit of black enamel worked in the shape of an eagle bearing a shield upon its chest. The shield was quartered in black and white, a most distinctive piece indeed.

"Very interesting," I murmured, determined to conceal my excitement. I turned it over, but there were no identifying marks upon the button itself, and I made to hand it back to Agathe, almost against my will.

As if she sensed my reluctance, Agatha refused to take it, shaking her head firmly. "I do not want it," she said fiercely. "Take it away with you."

Obediently, I tucked it into my reticule.

"Do you understand what I have given you?" she asked, tipping her head as she regarded me. "No, I thought not."

"It is a pretty trinket," I temporised.

She laughed again, a mirthless sound in that small room where death had stood. "It is more than a trinket. If I should die, that button will point the way to my murderer."

"Mademoiselle! You fear a murderer?"

She shrugged. "I cannot say. Sometimes bad things happen because the good God makes it so. And sometimes the devil's hand is at work instead. But that button belonged to someone close to my sister, someone who had her full trust, fuller than mine," she added bitterly.

"A lover?" I guessed.

"A conspirator," Agathe corrected. "Séraphine thought to secure our future with her machinations. It is possible her death was an accident. But it is also possible that she over-played her hand. One must be careful in playing games of chance with the devil."

At this, she went off in gales of laughter, and it was a long moment before she sobered. I endeavoured to retrieve the thread of the conversation.

"Mademoiselle, if you are in fear of your life, I can help you."

She regarded me with pitying eyes, and it was the pity of a cat for a mouse locked between its paws. "My poor Lady Julia, you only mean to help, and I talk in riddles. But I can tell you nothing more. Only keep the button. One day it may have secrets to tell."

I longed to ask her about the last séance, but I dared not.

If she pondered the guests that night too closely, she might note the resemblance between myself and the Comte de Roselende, a risk I dared not take. I rose then. "I think I had best be going now. Thank you for the cordial and for the conversation, mademoiselle."

She nodded, a cruel smile playing about her lips. "It was my pleasure, my lady. But you have not communicated with the spirits yet. Was that not why you have come?"

"Perhaps another time."

"Very well," she said, guiding me to the door. "But I should tell you that when you come next, there is a woman who wishes to speak to you. She is wearing yellow and there is a smell of *vervain*, verbena you call it. She says her name is Charlotte. Do you know such a person?"

My hand stilled upon the doorknob. My mind whipped back a quarter of a century to the last time I saw my mother, dressed head to toe in yellow, her favourite colour. She was laughing and she crushed me to her, for Mama never did things by halves and her hugs were meant to be felt. The scent of her verbena perfume still clung to my hair when they came to tell me she had died, and some months later, when the stone had been carved at her grave, I traced the letters with my finger, my first lesson in literacy. *C-H-A-R-L-O-T-T-E.*

I turned back to Agathe. "I am afraid not, mademoiselle."

"I am sorry," she said, bowing her head. "My mistake."

I left her then, and I did not look back.

The encounter with Mademoiselle Agathe had left me deeply shaken. I was jubilant to have found a real clue as to Madame's possible killer—and even more pleased to have found a suspect besides Bellmont to offer up to my husband.

But I was plagued by questions, most notably regarding Agathe's parting remarks about my mother. Her voice and demeanour had altered considerably, her aspect quite flat and unaware. I had no doubt that if I had spoken to her, she would not have heard me. I had read of such mediums and the tests to which they were put by sceptics. I knew that once in a trance, many had been subjected to flames and needles being passed under their skin, to pinching and bruising, all in the name of rational enquiry. And many of them had been exposed as frauds.

But occasionally, just occasionally, one had demonstrated complete unawareness and in such a state had delivered messages of things that could not possibly have been known. Was Mademoiselle Agathe such? Did she have true Spiritualist gifts?

I turned the questions over in my mind until I reached Brisbane's rooms. He was out, leaving me to prowl his rooms restlessly until at last, just as I was prepared to leave a note for him, he appeared.

"Hello, my dearest," I greeted him, pressing a kiss to his cheek. "Any luck?"

He gave me a swift glance. "None, but I see you have been far more diligent. Tell me."

I dropped the button into his hand. "This belonged to a conspirator who was plotting with Madame Séraphine. I think Agathe believes the owner of this button may have had a hand in her sister's death."

I made to take the button back, but Brisbane's hand closed swiftly around it.

"I will pursue this line of enquiry, my dear. Thank you."

I felt a thrust of annoyance at having my clue usurped. I put out my hand. "I think I will have my button back."

He merely stared at me, his fist closed over the button.

I paused, allowing the anticipation to heighten between us as I formed my next reply. "I should be permitted to pursue the enquiry. I found the button, and furthermore, I am aware of its significance. That button is a link between Madame and *a member of the German Imperial family.*"

In the years I had known Brisbane, I had never seen him so entirely dumbfounded as he was in that moment.

"You recognised it?"

"Of course. It bears the badge of the Sigmaringen-Hohenzollerns, the cadet branch of the German Imperial family. It was devised by the kaiser himself when Germany was still called Prussia."

He shook his head. "I know I will regret asking, but how can you possibly know that?"

"As children, when we were naughty, one of our governesses used to set us to copying out pages of the *Almanach de Gotha,*" I added. "My favourite bits were always the parts about the heraldic badges."

"How is it that you remember an entry you have not seen for two dozen years?"

I primmed my mouth. "I was naughty rather often. I must have copied that particular entry ten times. So, it is, in fact, an excellent clue. I cannot think why you are so grim."

"I have no love for Germans," he said flatly.

I was surprised. I had never heard Brisbane speak so dismissively of any particular group, and his antipathy roused my curiosity.

"Brisbane."

His handsome mouth thinned. "Under Prussian law, any Gypsy over the age of eighteen can be hanged."

I blinked at him. "For what crimes?"

"Breathing," he said coldly.

I felt a chill as I considered the implications. "That is horrifying."

"That is Germany. At least it was. One hopes the kaiser will be more tolerant in his policies, but it isn't likely, not with his mother in disgrace."

Kaiser Wilhelm's mother, our own Princess Victoria, was a liberal and forward-thinking sort of royal. Unfortunately, the family she married into was not. She and her husband had been effectively excluded from the rearing of their son, and his sympathies were firmly entrenched with the most reactionary bastions of German patriotism. So deeply embedded was his suspicion of his English mother that, upon his father's death, the kaiser had ordered his mother's house searched for papers that might incriminate her as a traitor to Germany. There seemed little hope that any of her influence might be reflected in his reign. Only those who served Germany's greater interests would be tolerated, and Gypsies certainly did not fit the bill.

I hastened to change the subject to something less thorny. "Well, then tell me what you have discovered at the clubs."

Brisbane steepled his fingers under his chin, his ill temper past. "You will be happy to know there isn't even a tittle about Mortlake. He seems to have dodged ruination quite nicely."

"I am glad to know it."

"As for Mr. Sullivan, I met with a bit of resistance there. Mr. Froggitt, the editor of the *Illustrated Daily News,* was not terribly forthcoming. He could only tell me that Sullivan is a fellow who works freelance, not an employee of the newspaper. He sends in his stories and the editor runs them. He keeps no office at the newspaper, and the editor has no means of contacting him."

I gave a start. "That is curious. How does the fellow receive assignments?"

"The editor sends a runner to a particular coffeehouse each afternoon at four o'clock. If the fellow is there, he receives his assignment. If not, the editor merely passes it along. An unconventional arrangement, but the editor is pleased enough with the work, he is content to leave it so."

"Did you learn anything else?"

"Only that the fellow is American and has ginger hair."

"Ginger hair?" My mind hurtled back to Madame's last séance. There had been a slight young man with ginger hair and whiskers in attendance, I remembered. I had nearly stepped on his heels as we made our way into the séance room and, once there, I had taken the chair next to him.

I mentioned the coincidence to Brisbane. "I recall him," my husband assured me. "And tomorrow I mean to pay a call at four o'clock to a certain coffeehouse to see if we have our man."

"*We* mean to pay a call," I corrected him.

Brisbane's only reply was a groan.

In the end, I did not accompany him. Brisbane, with a great deal more patience than he usually exhibited, explained that in this particular neighbourhood a lady of any variety, much less one of some means and dressed fashionably, would attract far too much attention and doubtless scare our man away. Naturally, I offered to don my masculine garb, which won me a rather fluent bout of profanity from Brisbane, but good sense prevailed and I grudgingly agreed to remain at home. Brisbane promised to reveal all to me as soon as possible, and so I spent the better part of the afternoon sitting in the airless cupboard under the stairs waiting for the shrill summons of the telephone.

At last, sometime after five o'clock, it came and I pounced upon it. After the usual preliminaries with the operator, Brisbane came on the line, speaking to me from his rooms in Chapel Street.

"Brisbane! Tell me everything!" I ordered.

There was an exclamation of pain and then, after a long moment, my husband's voice. "Do not shout, Julia. It is not necessary."

"Are you sure? Can you hear me properly?" I stared at the device suspiciously. It seemed counterintuitive that one could speak normally and still be heard down the wire.

"For God's sake, *I hear you!*" he roared.

I winced. "Goodness, Brisbane, there is no call to howl at me. I can hear you perfectly."

"Good," he said, his voice oddly tight as if he were grinding out the word through clenched teeth.

"Now, what of our American?"

"He appeared after some delay, but spied me through the window. As soon as he caught sight of me, he ran, and I followed him for some distance before I lost him."

I thought rapidly. "But if he ran at the sight of you, that means he must know you! How?"

Brisbane's jaw was set. "He has written one or two stories about previous cases of mine. I recognised the byline."

"Did you recognise him?"

"He was indeed the ginger-haired fellow who sat next to you at the séance."

"Oh, well done!" I cried.

"Julia," Brisbane growled again.

"I am sorry," I whispered. "But this is really excellent. It means we have a firm lead on this American fellow, particularly since he ran from you. He wouldn't have done so if he had nothing to fear."

"Yes, but we have lost him with precious little means of tracking him down. He won't show his face at that coffee-house again." I paused so long he thought the connection broken. "Julia? Are you still there?"

"I am here," I said finally. "Brisbane, you just said 'we.' You said we lost him with little means of tracking him down."

"No, I didn't."

"Yes, you did!" I persisted. "You have begun to think of me as a partner, whether you like it or not."

"I cannot hear you, Julia. I think the connection is faulty."

"The connection is fine, you impossible man!"

But it was too late. He had disengaged.

That night after dinner we sat comfortably in our draw-ing room and considered our next move as Brisbane pre-pared his hookah pipe. He fiddled with coals and the tarry black bits of hashish as I went into the details of my visit with Mademoiselle Agathe. I took the first deep draught of the heady smoke as he told me again of the chase the fleet-footed American had led him on, and how the fellow had craftily dodged into the train station just as a train was arriving, using the arrival to cloak his disappearance from Brisbane.

I pondered a moment, then sat up quickly—too quickly, in fact. The smoke made my head swim. "It makes no sense."

"What doesn't, my love?"

"The ginger-haired fellow is a reporter of the most vulgar sort. He writes for a lurid newspaper and revels in the lowest manner of details. He spied you through the window and *then he fled*. It makes no sense whatsoever. You are one of the foremost private enquiry agents in London, son-in-law to an earl and brother-in-law to one of the Opposition's leaders. You might have given him a treasure trove of information for a story! Instead, he took to his heels and fled as if the very hounds of hell were after him."

"Thank you for that charming image of me," Brisbane said drily. He took a long draught from the pipe, blowing out the smoke into a series of delicate rings.

"Brisbane, think of it. He did not behave as a proper reporter ought to behave. Why?"

Brisbane said nothing, and I continued on, warming to my theme. "How could I have been so blind? How could *you* have been so blind? The police never questioned the guests of the séance, Madame's last public session. They never interviewed them or it would have been in the newspapers. They never made an effort to find me. If they had wanted to speak with the Comte de Roselende, they would have circulated a description and placed advertisements in the newspapers, and yet there was no mention at all. And no mention of the guests was ever put forward at the inquest. They focused solely on the kitchens, blaming an elderly cook's poor eyesight."

Brisbane stirred himself lazily. "Your point, my dear?"

"My point is that any one of us might have murdered Madame. The murder hinged upon one thing, the substitution of an aconite root for a horseradish. It has been done before. The two are not unalike. But one doesn't make up horseradish at the last minute. It might be done at any time. Any one of us might have disguised ourselves as a greengrocer's lad and slipped down to the kitchen with the fatal root and done the deed without the cook ever noticing at all."

"Including the general? In full evening dress and bald as

a new egg? You think he might have been mistaken for a kitchen boy?"

I pursed my lips. "Perhaps not, but he might have adopted a disguise, any of the guests might have. Or," I added, my excitement rising, "the murderer might have brought a servant from home—a kitchen boy or a hall boy. It would have been easy enough to give him the deadly specimen and instruct him where to leave it. Servants of guests are always entertained in the kitchen. What could be more natural?"

"And you think a murderer clever enough to use this method would have put himself into the power of a kitchen boy? He would have just opened himself up to blackmail." Brisbane blew out another puff of smoke, this one sinuous as a serpent curling above his head.

"If the boy ever realised what he had done," I argued. "Kitchen boys are the lowest of the low. They are not educated. They do not read newspapers. They do not question their betters. Imagine it, an illiterate urchin instructed by his master to do this one thing, perhaps his master presents it as a joke or a merry prank. The boy is given a coin to spend on whatever he likes and the only caveat is that he must not tell anyone because it's his master's secret jest. He would do it in an instant, I tell you, and spend his coin on a pint of beer and that would be the end of it. He would never realise what he had done, and his master is entirely in the clear."

I sat back, feeling entirely happy with my hypothesis. Until Brisbane pricked my balloon.

"And if his master is taken up for murder? What if the boy had been detected or his master had been found out? How does the master explain it away when there is a witness to his crime?"

I nibbled at my lip, then brightened. "Easily! He simply

has the boy killed, although this time, I think the master would do the deed himself. Far better to tie up this loose end with his own hands rather than letting himself in for more of the same trouble later. If it were me, I think I should drug him, tie him in a sack weighted with stones and fling him into the Thames. No blood in the parlour."

Brisbane stared at me, open-mouthed, then shut his jaws with a decided snap upon the mouthpiece of the pipe to take a sharp puff. "That is the most cold-blooded thing I have ever heard you say."

"Murderers are cold-blooded. If he would not scruple to kill Madame, why would he stop at the murder of a kitchen boy? Once the impossible has been done, it becomes possible always," I pointed out.

Brisbane shook his head. "It is a credible theory, I grant you, but there is still no evidence of murder. The inquest verdict was accidental, and although the blackmail note to Bellmont suggests more nefarious things afoot, we cannot say definitively that the lady was murdered," Brisbane reminded me. "The blackmailer might simply be a creature of opportunity, seizing the chance to make some easy money."

I considered this, then dismissed it. "No, I think Madame was murdered, and by someone at that séance."

Brisbane canted his head and gave me a predatory smile. "Would you care to wager upon the point?"

"That is highly unprofessional," I said primly. "Fifty pounds?"

"One hundred," he countered. "One hundred pounds to you if Madame was murdered by someone at that séance."

I rose and went to him, offering my hand. "Shall we seal the wager?"

He put aside his pipe. He took my hand and pulled me down hard onto his lap. "Yes, but that is not precisely how I had in mind."

The
ELEVENTH CHAPTER

Be patient, for the world is broad and wide.
—*Romeo and Juliet*

The next morning, I ran Brisbane to ground with a new thought. He was in his study, scrutinising the button. "There must be a list somewhere, a registry of sorts of the gentlemen who have been given the right by the kaiser to wear that particular emblem," I remarked, taking the button to study it more closely.

"And their retainers?" he asked swiftly. "The Queen of England's guards and servants wear her badge. What of the kaiser's? If he gives that wretched eagle only to men of his family, the list is manageable. But if he extends the courtesy to his closest aides, to men who have served at the court in Berlin, it is an entirely different matter. We might be looking for a very elusive needle in a Teutonic haystack."

His expression was grim, and I set a bright smile on my lips. "Never mind that now. What are your plans for the day?"

"Plum and I are off to Richmond. Lady Riverton has been robbed of some rather valuable silver. She suspects the butler, but hers is the fourth such complaint I've had in the last three months. I suspect a ring of thieves is abroad in Richmond. I shall endeavour to apprehend them myself or try to persuade her to turn the matter over to the police."

"You must be careful," I admonished. "You and Plum both." He reached for the latest copy of the *Journal of Psychology* then, and I slipped the button into my pocket and said nothing more.

With Brisbane safely out of the way in Richmond, I was free to pursue my own investigations, and if they were not conducted with his knowledge, at least I consoled myself that they ought to have been. Really, what woman of character and spirit would lie down in the face of a wager of that size and not do her utmost to win?

I retrieved my list of the guests at the séance and locked myself in the study for an hour to prepare my plan of attack. There had been three names inscribed legibly in the guest-book besides mine. The veiled lady, alas, had come too late to sign, but Agathe had vouched for her as a legitimate client and therefore she was of no use to us. General Fortescue signed in a bold hand, while Sir Henry Eddington had a crabbed signature with a pinched look to it very like his mouth. Sir Morgan Fielding, I recalled, had an elegant hand, penning his name with economical good taste.

I used the newspapers and Debrett's to supply much of the details I required, and a bit of discreet gossip with Morag took care of the rest. I coached her carefully on my expectations, taking her into my confidence only so far as was absolutely necessary for her cooperation. Of course, it cost me another five-pound note to secure her participation, but once she had the note in hand, she was more than agreeable. I dressed carefully in a flattering costume of emerald-green, the gown and reticule trimmed in peacock feathers. I forced Morag to harness herself into her best black, a stiff bombazine affair that very nearly stood on its own accord. Swan was waiting in the hall as we took our leave, and he sprang to attend us. With his extremely tall and thin frame, his striped livery made him resemble nothing so much as an insect, albeit an elegant and exotic one. But he ushered us into the town coach and leapt nimbly to his seat just as the driver pulled away.

It was a short journey to the Bloomsbury house of General Fortescue, our first call of the day. Swan took my card and rang the bell, and a very few minutes later I was ensconced in the general's stuffy morning room. In spite of its name, it offered no comforts. The morning sun did not illluminate this gloomy room, nor had a fire been lit. The tables had not been recently dusted, either, I observed, and the blinds still shuttered the windows. There was an unpleasant odour in the room, a warm mustiness that told me neither the gentleman nor his possessions was particularly well cared for.

In all, it was the home of a man sunk in gloom, and when the general appeared, nothing about him altered my opinion. This man who had once been accustomed to commanding thousands of men, had been reduced to something rather pitiable. He had made an attempt at shaving, but rough patches of white whiskers still dotted his chin, and his uniform—once pristine and festooned with bright medals—now hung shapelessly, the medals dark with tarnish.

He greeted me civilly enough, and I applied myself to acting my part, but all the while I thought of Morag, and wondered if she was up to the task I had set her.

"General, how very kind of you to receive me," I said sweetly. He peered at me from beetling white brows.

"Do I know you?" he demanded, but his gruff demeanour was nothing like the bellicose man he was once reputed to have been.

"I think we have not been formally introduced. I am the daughter of the Earl March."

His expression darkened. "That Radical?"

"And the sister to Lord Bellmont," I hastened to add.

Those were the magic words, for his expression lightened at once. "Ah, yes, Lord Bellmont, capital fellow. I very nearly had his vote for bringing corporal punishment back into the ranks. In the end, he voted against it, but he considered it very carefully."

I coughed slightly. "Yes, well, I am sure it grieved him very much not to have been able to vote for such a fine piece of legislation. After all, one cannot have too much discipline in the ranks, I always say."

"Do you, by God? That is good to hear. Not many ladies understand that," he added, giving me a look of thoughtful appreciation. "Would you like a drink, my dear?"

"Oh, yes. Tea would be lovely—" I began, but when I saw where he was bound, I amended the remark instantly. "But a bit of something stronger would be much appreciated."

He poured a hefty measure of gin into two smeary glasses and presented me with one of them. "A stiffener," he said, giving me a broad wink.

I sipped at the vile fluid, trying manfully not to choke. "Very refreshing," I said finally. It was cheap stuff and tasted rather like my Uncle Leonato's shaving lotion smelled.

But the general did not seem to notice. He had quaffed half the glass before we settled to a cosy chat.

"I have come because I have taken up the study of photography and I am particularly interested in the subject of spirit photography. Your name was mentioned to me as a person of some great knowledge upon the subject."

He preened a little, the liquor clearly blunting his defences. "Well, I do have some experience. It's very easy for a woman to get taken in by some of the charlatans, you understand. Yours is the gullible gender. No fault of your own," he hastened to assure me. "It is how God made you, and glad we are of it. But you haven't the brains to think rationally."

"Haven't we?" I asked weakly.

"Not a bit of it. You must rely upon us to discover the frauds and the mountebanks."

"And those who are not frauds," I prompted. "Could you discover those, as well?"

His eyes grew rheumy and thoughtful then, glazed with memories. "Only once have I ever known a true medium. You might have photographed her, but she is dead and gone, my girl."

"What a pity! She was the genuine article then? A person who could commune with the dead?"

"That she could. She spoke with their voices, voices I have not heard in decades. She found them, though, God rest her soul!" He broke off then and took a healthy swallow of the nasty stuff.

"She sounds a remarkable woman. I am sorry not to have known her," I urged. "Did she bring you messages from the beyond?"

He gave a great sniff, and to my horror, I saw a fat tear rolling down his reddened nose. "She did. She spoke in their voices, the voices of those brave lads who fell. She found them, and they used her as their instrument to speak to me, their commander, one last time. Good boys, they were, and they loved me like a father."

He seemed more intent upon convincing himself than me, and I thought with some pity of how heavily the burden of those dead men must weigh upon his aging shoulders.

"Did you call upon her often?"

His eyelids were drooping beneath the extraordinary brows, and he recalled himself with a jerk. "What? Erm, yes, rather. I saw her from time to time. It helped to keep the dreams at bay."

His head bobbed a little, and I knew I had only a short time left. "What dreams, General?"

"Dreams of the boys, they come to me, dripping gore and pointing fingers. But that's not real. Madame said they understood. They forgive…"

His head fell heavily onto his chest and the empty glass rolled from his hand. He gave a deep, snoring exhalation, and I rose to see myself out. Swan collected Morag from the kitchens, and in a very few minutes we were on our way. I took several deep breaths of bracing London air to clear my head.

"So?" I prodded Morag. "What did you learn?"

She shook her head. "No kitchen boy in service there, nor has there been. Only an old army cook and a sad little scullery maid. Bored to sobs, they are. The old fellow drinks his dinner most days now."

"Keep a respectful tongue, Morag. The old fellow is a highly decorated general," I reminded her tartly. My disappointment made me waspish. I was so certain of success, and I had rather liked the general for a villain in spite of my defence of him to Morag. He was precisely the sort of military man I abhorred—arrogant, unyielding and entirely too sure of himself.

Or was he? The dreams he mentioned seemed to indicate his conscience did not rest easily. He was tormented by the ghosts of dead men, good young men he had ordered to their graves. His desperate visits to Madame had won him some measure of peace from their accusations, and in that light, it seemed entirely unlikely that he would have had anything to do with her death. He had had an actual need of her dark consolations, I reflected, and would no more have done her harm than he would have worn her petticoats. He had apparently gone steadily downhill since her death, and I wondered if he had thought to avail himself of Agathe's services as a substitute.

I took the little notebook from my reticule and pencilled a line through his name.

"Next is Sir Henry Eddington," I noted with some distaste. I had not cared for Sir Henry's attitude towards his dead daughter, and I suspected I should not like him any better on closer acquaintance. He owned a sizeable mansion in Kensington, very near the park, and shortly after I presented myself I was shown into his study by a maid who looked faintly terrorised. I had the notion that Sir Henry acted the martinet with his family and staff, and prepared myself accordingly.

Unlike General Fortescue, Sir Henry clearly had a mania for order. Every angle in his study was a square one, with books and papers rigidly positioned, and even the chairs placed at precise distances from one another. Not a speck of dust or smear of furniture polish marred the icy perfection of the room. Even the curtains at his windows hung at attention.

When the maid ushered me in, Sir Henry rose from behind his desk, clearly annoyed at the interruption but enough of a man of business to hold his irritation in abeyance until he knew the nature of my errand. Debrett's and the society columns had revealed that he was the second son of a minor baronet from Derbyshire who had made his own fortune after an indifferent education. Reading between the lines, it was easy to surmise that he had been embittered by his experiences, frustrated that his family fortunes had been too reduced to permit him to live as he believed he ought. He had quarrelled with every member of his family, save his rather downtrodden wife and daughters. They had long since given up any pretence at defiance.

Except perhaps for the curious Honoria, I marked. I set a gracious smile upon my lips and advanced. Doubtless he anticipated I was collecting for some improving organisation and about to make a call upon his purse. I could already see the refusal rising to his lips and hurried to disarm him.

"Sir Henry, it is so good of you to see me," I said, giving him my hand. He looked as if he did not quite know what to do with it. He dropped my hand and gestured for me to sit, more out of propriety than any real desire for my company, I fancied. I perched on the edge of my chair, not entirely surprised to find it excessively uncomfortable. I had a notion that Sir Henry was not inclined to desire his callers to linger.

He glanced at the card the maid had carried in upon my arrival. "Lady Julia Brisbane. Your brother is Lord Bellmont, is he not? He put me in the way of a rather good investment last spring. Foundries," he commented. I suppressed a sour smile. Bellmont must have been very certain of the Naval Defence Act passing if he was recommending investments on the strength of it.

"How nice. It is always best if these things stay between people who really understand them," I said, pitching my voice low, as if I did not wish to be overheard. "Sir Henry, I come to throw myself upon your mercy. I should like some advice."

He blinked, and a pale pink stain stole over his complexion. I realised he was flushed with satisfaction, and it occurred to me that this particular enquiry might be far easier than expected.

"You see, I find myself in need of guidance, from the other side, as it were."

The colour ebbed instantly, and his face was white as old paper. "The other side?"

"Yes, we do not like to speak of it outside the family, but as you are a gentleman of such discretion and good judgement, I felt it was worth the trouble of consulting you." I took on the air of one confiding a great secret. "My first husband, Sir Edward Grey, died rather suddenly a few years ago. He did not have sufficient time before his passing to divulge the secret of where he had cached the Grey Pearls, a rather extraordinary set of jewels passed down in his family for several generations." It was a lie, of course; the pearls had been resting comfortably in a bank vault when Edward died. "I find myself in rather extreme need at present," I confessed. I paused a moment and lifted a handkerchief to my eye. Sir Henry was unmoved by the gesture, and I dropped the handkerchief at once to proceed with my narrative. "I have tried everything, but I am growing desperate. I thought perhaps a medium might be able to make contact with Edward and persuade him to give up his hiding place."

Sir Henry's gaze narrowed tightly. "And why do you come to me?"

"I have heard that you have experience in such matters."

He leaned forward over the desk, and when he spoke,

flecks of spittle decorated his papers. "Mediums are nothing but charlatans and frauds, every last one of them."

I started at the venom in his voice. "You really think so?"

"I know it," he told me, warming himself upon his righteousness. "I have investigated half a dozen and none of them has given me a proper answer to the questions I put to them."

"Honoria, of course," I murmured.

The colour began to rise again. "What do you know of my daughter?"

"Only that it was a tragedy, such a terrible burden for a loving and stalwart father to bear."

The flattery may have been thick as treacle, but he lapped it up. "Well, yes. I was always a good father to my children, even if they were girls. But Honoria had no proper pride. There were questions left behind when she died, and no medium has ever been able to answer them to my satisfaction."

"How very awful for you to have suffered such a loss," I said, larding my voice with sympathy. But I had erred.

Sir Henry rose, his colour ebbing once more, leaving an aspect so flat, so devoid of emotion, I wondered if he was entirely human.

"Honoria's death was not a loss, my lady. The only loss was to my good name, and she cast that aside with both hands." A bitter note leached into his tone, and his lips twisted a little. "She was difficult, even as a child. Nothing I did seemed to make a difference. No correction amended her course, no punishment, however stern diverted her from her wildness."

"Stern?" I asked, not entirely certain I wanted him to elaborate.

He shrugged. "You know the old saying. 'A dog, a woman, a walnut tree, the better ye beat them the better they be.' Not Honoria," he added with real resentment. "If she had been a boy, such spirit would have been more understandable. No more acceptable, of course, but one could have at least comprehended it. But a girl is only useful so long as she is tractable. If she cannot be bent and broken to the proper role, how is she to bring honour to herself and her family?"

I suspected the question was rhetorical, and I was glad of it. I did not trust myself to answer him.

If he thought my lack of reponse curious, he dismissed it, doubtless because I was merely a useless female, I thought with some irritation. He rose and inclined his head with the barest attempt at politeness. "Now, if there is nothing more…"

It was dismissal, and I took it with good grace. I gathered up Morag and waited for her report in the carriage. She shook her head. "A French chef with his nose very high in the air, I must say," she related. "And a pair of kitchen maids and a scullery maid. No boys at all, save the hall boy."

"Aha!" I cried. "Now we are on the scent. Perhaps we have our boy at last."

"Mayhap if you are looking for a black fellow," Morag replied sourly, "because this one is the colour of night. I couldn't even see him in the shadows until he smiled. Fair scared me half to death, he did."

"Morag, your provincialism is showing. Do shut up," I ordered.

I sat back on the seat, muttering a curse under my breath. The first promising lead and it was dashed already. "What a poisonous man. I hate to say it, but I suppose that is another fellow we must cross off our list. Sir Henry shows no love for the profession, but neither has he any reason to kill Madame. I forgot to ask if he had seen her more than the one time, but I doubt it. And strange that such a pragmatic fellow should have consulted mediums at all," I mused aloud.

"That's the face he shows to the world," Morag commented. "It may not be the face he sees in the shaving glass each morning."

I considered that Brisbane had made a similar remark and regarded her thoughtfully. "Morag, for all your daftness, you are occasionally terribly wise."

"I have my moments, my lady. I have my moments."

The
TWELFTH CHAPTER

Be thou as chaste as ice, as pure as snow,
thou shalt not escape calumny.

—*Hamlet*

The third house was a stylish town house in St. John's Wood, rather near to Hortense de Bellefleur's pretty home. This town house was the abode of Sir Morgan Fielding, youngest son of the Earl of Dundrennan. He had been knighted for his services to the Crown—something about translating Chinese poetry into English, which I had to read twice to believe. It seemed an absurd thing for which to receive the accolade, but there it was. He received me in his writing room, a stunning little room that seemed designed to cater to every comfort in very modern ways. It borrowed heavily from William Morris, but with a dash of something quite new. There was a handsome tiled Swedish stove in the corner for warmth, and a set of excellent Japanese woodcuts on the walls. A screen covered in a lush Bohemian silk stood in front of the windows, diffusing the light from the garden and giving the air an otherworldly feeling. An elegant an-

tique fruitwood tea caddy stood in solitary splendour before
it, as much an object of art as utility.

"Your home is lovely," I told him quite truthfully.

He beamed his pleasure, and I remembered that in the
half-light of the Spirit Club, I had almost mistaken him
for Plum. There was something similar in the set of the
eyes, perhaps, or the extraordinary cheekbones. Over his
more conventional garments, he was wearing a robe of
heavy bronze silk, embroidered with designs I could not
quite place. "From Tashkent," he said, guessing my question. "And the décor is of my own design. I am an aesthete,
my lady. I find I cannot write unless I am inspired, and I am
not inspired by ugliness."

He waved me to a rather bizarre and sinuous chair of various iron bits welded together. I regarded the thing doubt-
fully, then lowered myself onto it, surprised to find it quite
comfortable.

"I designed the chair to conform to the contours of the
female body," he noted, and although such a remark would
have been entirely inappropriate from most gentlemen, from
him it was somehow inoffensive. There was something arch
and playful about him, by turns challenging and charming.
I imagined his conquests were legion.

"So," he said, settling into his own chair with an air of
mischief, "you are the dashing Lady Julia. I have heard of
you."

"Have you? From whom?"

He waved a languid hand, but his gaze was frankly admiring. "Various circles. And I am quite fond of your sister,
Portia. If she could bring herself to become attached to a
gentleman, I would offer for her tomorrow."

I grinned at him. "She is rather wonderful, isn't she?"

"A paragon amongst women, although," he added, skimming my form with a critical eye, "I think you may well be challenging her for the title of most marvelous March. Tell me, my lovely Lady Julia, does your husband know you've come to see me?"

"Do you know Brisbane?"

He gave me a slanted smile. "Our paths have crossed. I find him quite the most terrifying man I have ever met. And that alone will ensure I treat you with every courtesy whilst you are my guest," he added with an exaggerated bow from the neck. "I think we ought to be cosy. We must have tea."

He clapped his hands and a servant appeared, an East-Indian fellow with a saffron-yellow turban and a tea tray. The cups were Chinese, fashioned of thinnest porcelain and without handles. The tea itself was green and so delicate the flavour of it seemed to dissolve on my tongue into nothingness. To my surprise, the tea caddy was not simply an object of beauty to be admired. Sir Morgan unlocked it with great ceremony and spooned out the fragile green leaves. To complement the tea, there was a plate of dainty little almond biscuits. It made a refreshing change from the usual groaning tea tray laden with sandwiches, tarts, cakes, bread and butter and scones. Sir Morgan poured out and presented me with an almond crescent. I studied him as he moved, his gestures entirely graceful, his manners almost studiedly effete. He worked hard to give the impression of delicacy, but his shoulders were solidly set and there was something resolute about him, something that suggested he was a person who could be trusted.

As if he sensed my scrutiny, he turned his head so the light fell perfectly upon his profile. It was an excellent profile, I noted, and the dark green of his eyes was arresting.

His handsomely shaped mouth curved up into a smile,

and when he turned to me, I realised he was exerting the full power of his charm quite deliberately for my benefit.

"So do you see the family resemblance?" he asked.

I blinked at him. "Family resemblance?"

The smile deepened. "To you, of course. Didn't you know I was a March?"

I gaped at Sir Morgan and in doing so, nearly choked myself on the pretty little almond biscuit. He hurried to refill my cup of tea as he apologised profusely.

"I am sorry, my dear. I ought not to have sprung it on you so abruptly."

I gulped half the cup of steaming green tea while I tried to make sense of it.

"You are a March. You mean, Father…" I could not bring myself to say the words.

"Oh, heavens no!" he assured me, waving his hands. "No, no. I am not your brother, dear lady. I am your cousin. Your Uncle Benvolio's child."

"But you are the son of the Earl of Dundrennan," I protested.

"Officially," he corrected. "My dear mother was a bit freer with her charms than she ought to have been. My eldest brother and the second son belong to my father, of course. It would never have done for her to threaten the earldom with illegitimate heirs, but after Lucas and Neddy were born, Mama and Father went their separate ways. They had an understanding of sorts. Mama would not kick up a fuss about Father's peccadilloes, and he would acknowledge all of her bastards as his own children. Rather tidy."

"All of her bastards? How many—" I broke off. There was simply no way to phrase it politely.

"Seven, altogether."

"Oh, my. And were any of the others Marches, as well?"

"Goodness, no. Benvolio was simply a passing fancy. They met up just the one time at a house party and nine months later I was born. A bit of bad timing, I suppose," he added thoughtfully.

I took a long sip of the tea, composing my thoughts. Sir Morgan wore his bastardy easily, with no sense of shame or impropriety. And why should he? I asked myself. The deeds belonged to his parents. It was really nothing to do with him at all.

"Did your mother tell you about Uncle Benvolio?"

"Oh, yes. It's tradition, you see. On our thirteenth birthdays, Mama takes us for nice luncheon at the Langham Hotel and reveals our real parentage. Mine was a bit of a letdown, if I am honest. My elder sister is the bastard fruit of the Duke of Scilly, and the next child dear Mama got from the Bishop of Barnstaple. Having the younger brother of the Earl March for a father is not quite so impressive."

"You seem to know rather a lot about us," I remarked.

He smiled again, and I noted that for all his confidence and ease, there was a touch of melancholy to his smile.

"I used to see the lot of you from time to time in town, and I was so envious of you all. Watching you walk through the park was like watching the circus come to town, a riot of colour and noise and excitement. I felt as if I had my nose pressed to the glass of a sweetshop window, and never got to come in."

"You would have been most welcome," I assured him. "At last count, I have forty-three first cousins. What's one more?"

The smile turned arch. "I do not expect you to recognise the connection in society, dear lady."

"Does Portia?" I nibbled at the almond biscuit. It was quite tasty now that I was not choking upon it, I thought.

"No, I haven't told her."

"But you told me. Why?"

He shrugged. "It amused me. And I know you want to ask me about Madame Séraphine. It seemed best if you understood that I have nothing at all to hide."

I smothered the urge to choke again and took another sip of tea. "How do you know I want to ask about Madame?"

He gave me a pitying look. "My dear lady, your exploits are notorious. You like murder, and the only murder I have been attached to is Madame's."

"Madame's death was officially ruled an accident," I reminded him.

He snorted, a gesture I often made, and I was startled at the resemblance between us. "Officially. But I have my doubts."

"Had you attended many of her séances?"

"Half a dozen," he replied promptly. "She was a fraud, of course, but a delicious one."

"If you thought her a fraud, why did you attend so many?"

He flicked a glance to the narrow writing desk in the corner. It was littered with sheets of closely scribbled foolscap.

"I am writing a novel and the main character is a medium. I was using her for a character study."

"Did she know it?"

"Oh, yes. I was quite honest with her about my intentions. She only laughed. She thought it a very great challenge. She meant to change my mind and make a believer of me. From time to time she invited me up to her boudoir to take tea. She was really quite lovely. The only fly in the ointment was the dragon at the door, Agathe."

"Agathe?" I widened my eyes to give him the impression

that I was not *au courant* with the inhabitants of the Spirit
Club. It seemed best to conceal what little I did know, although I could not have said precisely why.

"Madame's sister, poor drab Agathe LeBrun. Séraphine
was a bird of brilliant plumage. Agathe is a wren. She
guarded Madame's privacy most diligently. I think she had
an idea that I was a wastrel and only out for what I could
get."

"Were you?"

To his eternal credit, Sir Morgan laughed. "Bless you,
no. I make a comfortable living from my writing, and dear
Mama's father was the Duke of Esherton. His title was entailed through the direct male line only, and he had no sons
after him. He was so furious that none of his daughters'
boys could inherit the title that he left us all of his money.
My poor cousin has the dukedom and no means of supporting it, whilst we have all the cash. A pity for him, but there
it is."

I drew the conversation back to the matter at hand. "Was
Madame helpful to you in your work?"

Sir Morgan fell serious for a moment, and his usual arch,
laughing manner sobered. "Not entirely. I am not quite
happy with the character I have created based upon her. I
needed another month's study and then I could have really
got her. She was an elusive sort, full of secrets and change-
able as the very devil. One minute, she would be warm
and generous, the next she would pout over something entirely trivial and I would spend the entire evening making
amends. Very curious and most vexing," he informed me.

Just then a figure moved in the corner, and I started.

"Good heavens, what a peculiar cat!"

The feline in question had emerged from a fanciful little
house of Chinese design with a fluted pagoda roof and

heavily lacquered walls. I had seen such elaborate houses before—Puggy slept in a tiny French château—but I had never seen such a cat. Its fur was short and the colour of Saharan sands, shading to sable-dark paws and a velvety mask surrounding piercing blue eyes. It walked with the haughty grace of an emperor.

"A Siamese," Sir Morgan informed me. "They once roamed the sacred temples of Siam."

The cat tiptoed near to me, lifting its aristocratic little nose and twitching it in my direction. I noticed then that she—for I could see now that the creature was demonstrably female—had a kink in her tail. She peered up at me with a squint, which I found rather endearing. The flaw seemed to ameliorate her haughtiness a bit.

"I see you have noticed the idiosyncrasies of the breed," Sir Morgan observed. "Siamese are particularly prized by the royal family and it is said that the kink is to hold in place the jewelled rings presented them by their royal masters."

"And the squint?" She came closer still, touching her nose to the feathered trim of my reticle.

"Legend says one of the breed was charged with guarding a valuable vase that was of special importance to the king. The cat took the charge to heart and wrapped its tail tightly about the vase and stared at it, peering so closely that every Siamese after was born with a kinked tail and crossed eyes."

"A charming story," I murmured as she lifted a pretty paw to bat at the feathers.

"The king thought so," Sir Morgan said with a smile. "The king commissioned me to set the story in verse and was so pleased with the result he made me a gift of her."

Deftly, she teased one of the feathers free and darted after it. Sir Morgan gave an exclamation of dismay. "My dear lady, I do apologise. I am afraid peacock feathers are one of her dearest temptations. You must permit me to make reparation for Nin's larceny."

I flapped a hand. "Think nothing of it. I bought armfuls of the stuff in India, and I keep peacocks in the country. I can always replace it."

"You are too gracious," he said. "Not every lady would be quite so tolerant of her misbehaviour."

"I have a raven at home, as well as a lurcher. I am quite accustomed to destructive pets," I assured him. "Her name is lovely. Is it Siamese?"

"Nin? It is. Her real name is Sin, which is Siamese for 'money.' The king thought it a great joke because he gave her to me in lieu of a cash prize for the poem. But I thought Nin had a slightly less alarming sound. It means 'sapphire.'"

"After her eyes," I said, noting again the brilliant blue hue.

Just then she left off toying with the feather and came near to me again. She sat upon my hem, stretched up on her haunches and put a dainty paw to my lap.

Sir Morgan sat forward. "Nin, leave off."

"It's quite all right," I assured him. "She is only being friendly."

"But she never does that," he said with some astonishment. "She is a friendly cat, but her demonstrations of real affection are usually confined to me. I am afraid it seems I have a rival for her regard."

I put a fingertip to her paw, stroking the silken fur. She purred then, a loud, rumbling purr that sounded very like the engine of the motorcar Brisbane had been agitating to purchase.

"Extraordinary," Sir Morgan said softly.

I sat back a little, which Nin must have viewed as an invitation, for she leapt up into my lap, as lightly as an acrobat. She straightened, then touched her brow to mine, nuzzling against my face, and just as quickly as she had come she was gone again, leaping off my lap and collecting her feathered trophy. She trotted away, the feather waving over her head like a sultan's plume.

Sir Morgan and I exchanged glances of amazement. "I have never known her to do such a thing. She must like you very much indeed."

"I am honoured," I told him, and I was rather surprised to find that I meant it. She was a lovely creature, and the interlude had been well worth the price of a peacock feather.

I made an effort to retrieve the subject we had been pursuing before Nin's appearance.

"Will you be able to finish the book?"

He lifted one shoulder in a theatrical shrug. "Perhaps. I hope to, but if I cannot, I might turn the subject into an epic poem instead, something Byronic. Pity, really, as I think it would make a far better novel, but if I cannot capture the essence of Madame, I will have no choice."

We settled in for a cosy gossip then, consuming two more pots of green tea and several more plates of biscuits. He was charming company, and I enjoyed myself thoroughly until the clock—a pretty affair of quite good *chinoiserie*—struck the hour.

"Good Lord," I cried. "Is it really so late? I must fly."

He kissed me on both cheeks and urged me to come again.

"If only for Nin's sake. And now that we are known to one another, I will know you better," he proclaimed. I agreed and took my leave of him, returning to the carriage with a sour Morag.

"What ails you?" I demanded.

She pursed her lips. "That heathen fellow served me green tea. *Green*. As if that's a proper colour for a person's tea," she groused.

"And did you discover anything of interest from him?"

She flapped an irritable hand. "He didn't say two words to me, he didn't. But there was a charwoman come to clean and she told me plenty."

"Go on," I said, but I dearly wished she would not. I had felt an instant affinity for my newfound cousin, and I would not like to think he had any hand in Madame's murder.

"The heathen what wears a turban, he waits upon his master as valet and majordomo," she informed me. "He brews up the tea on a spirit lamp and the biscuits are brought in, as are all the master's meals. There's a charwoman for the heavy work and the valet fellow to look after the master personally. All of the meals are sent in and the laundry sent out. Very economical."

"Very economical indeed, for a fellow who claims to have a great deal of money," I mused. "Brisbane must make enquiries about that and see if he is as solvent as he claims. So that's the end of it? No boys kept to run errands or shine shoes?"

"Not a one. I asked about the errands and the char said the master gives her a coin or two extra to do for him or she finds any passing lad. There's none attached permanently to the house."

"Blast," I muttered.

I contemplated the list of séance guests in my notebook. As much as I would have liked to have found a gentleman with a definitive motive and a kitchen boy in service, I had crossed all of the men from my list, even Sir Morgan. Further investigation would be necessary for each of them, but I strongly believed that each of them either would have wished to keep Madame alive or would have been indifferent to her death. None of them had had a sufficient motive to bring it about, including Sir Morgan. His urbane demeanour had slipped momentarily when we had discussed his book, and I had seen real anguish there as he described his efforts to capture Madame's character in words. More time with her would certainly have suited his purposes, just as it would have the General. Only Sir Henry had been finished with her, but he had been finished with half a dozen other mediums and no one had reported a rash of murders against the mediums of London. No, he had taken his irritability home and exercised it upon his daughters and that had been the end of it, I was certain.

I clucked my tongue, wondering what I had missed. I put the matter aside and ordered the coach to take us home.

I did not see Brisbane that evening, for he was still engaged upon the case in Richmond until very early in the morning, and over breakfast I took the opportunity to begin to relate to him my activities of the previous day. I told him about my interviews with the general and Sir Henry, as well as Morag's discoveries—or lack of. His expression grew blacker and blacker as I spoke, and I hurried the matter along by telling him merely that I had learned nothing of significance from my last call and left it at that.

Brisbane shook his head, and I thought I detected a new silver hair in the inky depths. "I ought to lock you in your room," he commented finally.

"But then you would never have learned all that I had discovered yesterday," I reminded him. I tried very hard to keep the note of triumph from my voice, but I fear I failed.

"Very true," he agreed. "Of course, I am not the only

one who knows what you were about," he added, tossing the *London Illustrated Daily News* onto my lap.

I skimmed through the newspaper, and several pages in and below the fold but still quite prominent, I found it—a sketch of me dashing from my carriage to a town house. I looked positively hoydenish, skirts flying, hairpins rattling to the ground, as keen as any hound on the scent of a hare. Ahead of me, a cadaverous Swan rapped on the front door, and behind me, a distraught and rather slatternly looking Morag bent to gather my pins.

I swore softly, and Brisbane did not correct me. "But how—" I began, and broke off as I saw the byline.

"Our ginger-haired American friend." I swore again, and Brisbane nodded towards the newspaper.

"Sullivan was very thorough. He followed you from here to Portia's house and then to your first two calls. I don't suppose it occurred to you to look to take precautions to see if you were being followed?"

"Of course not!" I snapped. "Would it have occurred to you? Do not answer that. If it had, you would have warned me. You cannot fault me here."

"No," he acknowledged. "That would be unjust. But I find it curious just the same."

"What?"

"Sullivan took great pains to follow you, and yet I left the house before you. I am the enquiry agent. Why did he choose to pursue you?"

My mouth felt suddenly dry as I skimmed the blurry text. "He does not connect my calls with Madame, but he makes it quite clear I called upon each of those men in the course of an investigation."

"The implication is rather nasty," Brisbane agreed.

We fell to silence then, a terrible silence and the weight

of it nearly crushed me. Just when I thought I could bear it no longer, I heard a faint ringing sound, shrill and accusing for all its faintness. After a long moment, Aquinas appeared in the doorway, his expression apologetic.

"The telephone for you, my lady. It is the Earl March."

I swore yet again and Aquinas pretended not to hear. I rose slowly and made my way around the table, wondering when Father had managed to have a telephone installed at March House. Just as I passed Brisbane, his hand shot out to clamp hard upon my wrist. He turned his head slowly, piercing me with that implacable black gaze. "Do not think this is finished," he said, and the awful calm in his voice was worse than any anger might have been.

I walked to the telephone with the lagging steps of a doomed queen making her way to the block. I could hear Father raging before I even picked up the earpiece.

"Father," I said brightly. "I did not realise you had installed a telephone."

"Of course I have! If it is good enough for that damned upstart the Duke of Marlborough, it's bloody good enough for the Earl March," he shouted.

It required a great deal of hubris to refer to a duke with a title of some two hundred years' duration as an upstart, but I had no chance to raise the point. He launched himself into a tirade against my appearance in the newspaper, permitting me not the slightest word. I let him continue, for there was no possible way of stemming the tide of his ire, and after a quarter of an hour, he ended with an order. I was to come to March House immediately.

"Yes, Father," I murmured. He ranted again for another half an hour before cutting the connection abruptly. I collected Morag and called for the coach, and to my astonishment, Brisbane was already seated inside, waiting for me.

"You are coming with me to March House?" I asked, my throat tight with gratitude that I should not have to face the ordeal alone.

"Only to make sure there is something left of you for my turn," he ground out through clenched teeth.

"I do not see why you should be so angry. We did agree to work together," I reminded him.

"We did not agree that you should expose yourself unnecessarily to public speculation and physical danger," he riposted.

I opened my mouth to argue, but he held up a hand. "We will discuss this after his lordship has had a turn at you."

He said nothing more for the duration of the trip, and I sulked in the corner, sniffing occasionally into my handkerchief. It was not a strategem. Tears did not work upon Brisbane any more than they did my Father. But it gave me something to do while we rode along in our speaking silence.

We arrived far too quickly at March House, and there seemed to be a pall over the place. The butler, Hoots, opened the door and shook his head mournfully at me. "Oh, my lady," he murmured, and I felt my temper beginning to rise.

"Yes, I know," I snapped. "Where is he?"

"In the garden," he said, gesturing beyond the staircase to the garden door as if I had not lived in that house for the whole of my life before marrying Edward. I stormed past him, flinging open the garden doors. I had hoped to catch Father off guard, throw him a little from his planned attack, but my diversion had no effect whatsoever. Father was already engaged in a battle with his hermit. I reached them just as Auld Lachy was brandishing an enormous seashell. With his green robes and long white beard and hair, he looked like Neptune's slightly mad brother. It was the tea cosy upon his head that rather spoilt the effect.

"Hello, Lachy. That's a pretty shell you have there," I said politely.

"Do not take his side," Father ordered. "I will deal with you in a minute."

"Aye, you would tell the poor lass to hold her tongue!" Lachy shouted. "You know she would agree with me. A seashell grotto is much to be preferred to a fernery. A fernery! Have you ever heard a thing so ridiculous?" He turned to me, and I spread my hands and gave him a bland smile as I found a place to sit. It looked as though matters might drag on for a bit.

Brisbane discreetly seated himself some little distance away on a painted toadstool. Lachy fashioned garden furniture out of stumps, and this one was one of his best. He shaped and painted them in fanciful designs. My own seat was a great snail with a curiously stern expression.

Lachy looked from me to Brisbane. "Are we to have a tea party then? I am a hermit. That means I want solitude, not a mess of people trailing through my garden as if it were Victoria Station!"

"Your garden!" Father started towards him, his complexion reddening by the moment. "This garden, and everything in it, belongs to me. And if choose to put a fernery in it, I will bloody well do so."

Lachy crossed his arms over his chest. "The hermitage falls within my purview. It is in the contract."

"Don't you even think about lecturing me upon the contract, you impossible Scottish insect. I wrote it," Father raged.

"And all improvements must be approved by me," Lachy returned coolly.

Father snapped his jaw shut, which I knew meant—as did Lachy—that the hermit had carried the day. I was rather happy for Lachy; after all, a fernery is usually an exercise in boredom, but I was keenly aware that Father's ire would be fully directed at me as a result. Triumphant, Lachy tactfully withdrew to his hut, cradling his seashell like an infant.

As if on cue, Father swung around and began to lecture, fluently and with one or two obscure Shakespearean references thrown in for good measure. I heard about the proud name of the Marches being dragged through the mud, the unspeakable constructions that could be put on my actions, the infamy I had called down upon my ancestors. This last was a bit much considering what infamy my ancestors had accomplished in their own time.

"You forgot about the sharpness of a serpent's tooth," I put in sulkily.

"Do not speak!" my father thundered, setting off on another round of vituperation.

I hazarded a look round at Brisbane. "Are you going to say anything?"

Brisbane crossed one leg lazily over the other, flicking an imaginary piece of lint from his trousers. "I think he is doing quite well without me."

"I did not mean for you to help him, I meant to defend me," I said, huffing slightly in my indignation.

"Do not turn around," my father ordered. "I am not finished with you."

The curious thing about Father was that he had two types of tempers. The first was quick to catch, like very dry kindling held to a flame. It burst, burnt itself out and was finished with very little to show for it. It also happened so frequently that most of us children had learned to ignore it entirely. We had discovered that by waiting a quarter of an hour, we could avoid engaging at all when he was in such a mood because it would have passed, quick as a summer storm.

But the second variety was altogether different. It required every mite of his innate theatricality, causing him to pace and rage, holding forth upon our shortcomings like some sort of tragic actor soliloquising the doom of all mankind. These rages were epic, lasting hours if he was not diverted, and occasionally ending with disinheritance. The only consolation was that he always felt so wretched for losing his temper that within hours he would repent and reinstate our allowance and usually send along a nice present.

I had little hope of that this time. He carried on for so long I began to get a little hungry. I had not had much breakfast, and he really had gone on an unconscionable period of time. Just as I pondered the wisdom of ringing for Hoots to bring sandwiches, Father recalled himself.

"And that is why you really are the most shockingly misbehaved March in seven generations," he concluded, drawing himself up with all the nobility of his position. My only consolation was that in his rage, he had not thought to ask precisely *why* I was engaged upon those calls. I had already made up my mind to shield Bellmont if the situation demanded, but I was immensely relieved it had not come to that.

I tried to look suitably contrite. "I do apologise, Father. I had no idea there was a reporter following me. I was only trying to assist Brisbane."

It was the wrong thing to say, and I knew it as soon as the words came out of my mouth. I nearly bit my own tongue with wishing to call them back, but there was no help for it.

Father swung round to Brisbane, "And as for you—"

Brisbane rose with his customary indolent grace. "With all due respect, your lordship, this interview is finished. Julia is your daughter, and you have a father's care for her, and that is why I permitted you to have your say. I am under no such obligation for myself. Come, Julia."

"If it were not for you, my daughter would not be the subject of scandal!" he roared.

"Father, really, Brisbane didn't mean—"

"No," Brisbane cut in smoothly, "you were content for her to moulder away in a marriage to a man who contemplated violence against her."

Father went suddenly quite white, and then burst out. "How dare you throw Edward Grey at my feet! I did not know what he truly was."

"Brisbane, that's quite enough. Father did not mean—"

I turned from one to the other, watching helplessly as they advanced towards each other, these two men whom I had loved better than any in all the world, tearing at each other like animals.

Father raised a hand, and his finger shook as he pointed to the garden door. "Get out. Leave my house and do not ever come back. You have already cost me three of my children. I will give you no more."

Brisbane turned on his heel and walked to the garden door, departing in perfect silence. He never once turned to see if I would follow him, but then there was never a question that I would.

I looked at my father and spread my hands helplessly. "I do not know if I can mend this."

He said nothing, and I did not wait for him to do so.

Just then, Auld Lachy poked his head out of his hut. "You are a singularly histrionic family," he pronounced. "I blame aristocratic inbreeding. Only an inbred would want a fernery."

Father turned to blast him as I ran after Brisbane. I caught up to him just as he reached the front door, grabbing his hand. He did not look at me, but when he took mine, he crushed it so hard that I felt the marks of my rings for some days after.

"You ought not to have said such things," I told him when we had gained the relative privacy of the carriage. Morag turned her face to the window and pretended not to listen, but I could see she had her ears out on stalks, collecting every word.

"He ought to have protected you from that marriage," Brisbane said tightly.

"Father did not know. None of us did. Do you think I would have married Edward had I known what he would become?" I demanded. "It was his illness made him so."

"And the minute he so much as looked at you with violence in his mind, your father should have taken you home. It was his duty."

"I never told him," I confessed.

Brisbane swung his head round to pin me with a glance. "Never?"

"Not in so many words. I was ashamed. I did not know how to speak of it, to anyone. Father knew there was trouble between us, but he did not know the nature of it."

"He should have made it his business to discover it," Brisbane said savagely, and I realised how shatteringly angry he was still.

I ventured an unspeakable question. "Are you so angry with Father for not protecting me then because you feel you have failed to protect me now?"

The gaze he settled upon me was so baleful that I felt an instant sympathy with the victims of Medusa. Being turned to stone would have been a relief in that moment, but I knew I had struck a nerve, and so did Brisbane.

"Do not ask me that again," he warned. "Besides, you will have no more chances to be unprotected. From this moment on, you do not stir a foot outside our house but that I am with you."

I stared at him. "Brisbane, you cannot mean that."

"Try me."

The
THIRTEENTH CHAPTER

I have done nothing but in care of thee,
Of thee my dear one, thee my daughter.

—*The Tempest*

That evening, Brisbane took me to Portia's, and I counted myself fortunate for even that small concession. He had business to attend to, but he was magnanimous enough to agree that I might dine at my sister's provided he accompany me there and I promised not to leave the house until he collected me.

"What if the house catches fire?" I demanded. "I shall have to leave it then."

The grinding of his teeth was the only response, and I could not blame him. It was a childish remark and unworthy of me, but I put it down to the distress of being at odds with Father with whom I had seldom, if ever, seriously quarrelled. I was deeply upset that he had not only taken my own peccadillo so much to heart but that he blamed Brisbane for it. The question of how to reconcile two such stubborn and proud men occupied me for the better part of the day, and when I was not pondering that, I was wondering why Brisbane's temper had not fully erupted. The answer finally occurred to me when we were in the carriage on the way to Portia's.

"I know you spared me a lecture because you know how wretched I feel after that scene with Father. It was very kind of you. I will be better tomorrow," I promised. "You can rail at me then."

He handed me his handkerchief and—to my astonishment—gathered me close. "Your chin is wobbling. It was a nice effort, though."

"I really am trying to be very strong, but Father and I have never fought like that." I gave a hard sniff, dabbing at my eyes.

"It will come right in the end."

"Will you scold me then?" I asked in a still, small voice. Beneath my cheek, I felt his chest rise and fall in a deep sigh.

"No. It was my own fault for not keeping a better eye upon you. You are curious as a monkey and brave as a lancer and the combination may well be the death of me."

I punched him lightly upon the thigh. "I cannot like being compared to a monkey. But a lancer is rather flattering. Thank you."

I reached up to press a kiss to his cheek. "Do not be too angry with Father. He did not mean it, not really."

"Angry? I feel rather sorry for him. We are kindred spirits," he observed with a wry twist of his mouth.

"How so?"

"We both of us suffer because you will not understand how utterly essential you are to our happiness."

I stared at him, but he was looking out the carriage window to the darkened streets. "You take risks," he went on in a tight voice, "unacceptable risks, and threats and warnings will not dissuade you. We cannot protect you from yourself, and that is the greatest danger."

"I do not mean to be difficult," I protested.

He gave a short, dry laugh. "I think you honestly believe that. But you have battered down the last of my defences, my dear. I have nothing left to hold you at bay. So you must prepare yourself. In the coming days, you will learn things you would rather not, things from which I cannot shield you any longer."

"Brisbane, you're frightening me."

"Good," he responded grimly. "It is the fear that will keep you alive." There was no time to ask more. We had arrived.

Brisbane declined to eat with us, pleading an engagement related to the ending of the Richmond case, but Plum appeared just in time for the fish course and I fixed him with a suspicious eye.

"Oughtn't you to be with Brisbane, tying up the loose ends in Richmond?"

"Brisbane said he could settle Richmond alone," he said, his expression a study in blandness.

"Feathers. He sent you to watch over me."

Plum cocked his fez to a more rakish angle. "What if he did? It gave me a chance to dine with my two favourite sisters. Ooh, is that crab?"

He applied himself to the fish course and we talked of various things for the rest of the meal. Or rather, Portia talked—almost entirely about the baby—and Plum and I listened.

After the sweet course was cleared, we withdrew to the drawing room for tea and spirits, and Nanny Stone appeared, dressed in severe black bombazine and carrying the infant Jane.

"It is time, my lady," she said to Portia. She settled Jane the Younger into Portia's lap and took herself off with an air of satisfaction.

"What was all that about?" Plum asked.

Portia primmed her mouth. "Nanny Stone has apparently been chatting with the other nannies in the park. She has discovered that it is customary to have one evening off per fortnight and has decided to take it. And Sunday afternoons."

"Good God, don't tell me the nannies of London are *organising*," Plum put in waggishly. "Do you think they will strike like the dockworkers?"

I rolled my eyes at Plum. "Those poor fellows have only just gone back to work. It is far too soon to jest about it." The dockworkers had spent five weeks on strike in order to protest their abhorrent working conditions. Before them had been the gasworkers and before them the match-girls. It seemed all of London was protesting something, and I for one seldom read the accounts in the newspapers anymore. Their stories were simply too awful to contemplate, and I knew Portia felt the same.

"Of course the nannies are not organising," Portia snapped. "It is simply that Nanny Stone is entitled to some private time and we mutually decided that she should be employed under the same terms as other nannies."

It was unlike Portia to be so prickly, and as I stared at her furrowing brow, a terrible suspicion began to creep over me.

"Portia, dearest, have you ever actually been alone with the baby before?"

She muttered something unintelligible and I poked at her knee.

"Very well! No. I have never actually been alone with her. I do not know what the trouble is. I adore her, of course. I am her mother. But infants are difficult and I am not entirely certain of what needs be done when."

"Of course not," I soothed. "We all know how much you adore her. That is not even a matter for discussion. But most mothers have many months to prepare for motherhood. Yours was a more sudden attachment."

"Precisely," she said, her brow relaxing a little. The child squirmed in her arms, and Portia slid her smallest finger into the baby's mouth. Jane the Younger began to suckle greedily.

"I know it looks awful, but she's bringing out a tooth," Portia apologised. "She likes it when I rub at her gums."

"See there? You do know how to take care of her. Doesn't she, Plum?" I demanded, fixing him with a piercing stare.

"What? Erm, yes, of course. Lovely mother, one of the best," he put in hastily.

"There now. Even Plum sees it. And we will be here this evening should you need moral support," I promised.

Portia had just shot me a grateful smile when the door fairly flew back on its hinges to reveal our youngest brother, Valerius. He entered like a whirlwind, tossing off his overcoat and kissing his sisters. He gave a nod to Plum and threw himself onto a sofa.

"Julia, what the devil did you do to set Father off? I went to dine with him and he was savaging a plate of ortolans."

One could always tell the state of Father's temper by his table manners. If he was feeling upset, he liked nothing better than to apply himself to something he could tear into rather brutally—something like a plate of ortolans. I felt a pang of pity for the little songbirds, then reminded myself better them than me.

"I am surprised you have not heard the full story," I said, plucking at an arrangement of flowers upon the low table.

"Julia has gone and got herself in the newspaper," Portia supplied.

Val's eyebrows rose. "Really? I don't think one of the March ladies has done that since Aunt Tamora rode her horse into the House of Lords as a protest against fox-hunting."

I pulled a face at him. "Don't be absurd. Bee was written up in every paper in London when she was caught smoking at a garden party at Buckingham Palace with the Earl of Bowes-Ruthven's heir." We fell silent a moment, musing on our second-eldest sister and her eventful coming-out. The queen had not been at all amused, and Bee had found herself struck from every guest list in society, which had rather been the point. She was already besotted with a reclusive Arthurian scholar and had made up her mind to avoid the formality of a season by becoming notorious at the first possible opportunity.

"Didn't Father disinherit her for that?" Val asked. He had still been in the nursery when Bee achieved her aims and scarcely remembered her. Her marriage had taken her off to Cornwall and she seldom came to town.

"Yes, but only until he realised Bowes-Ruthven's heir had tried something most ungentlemanly behind the potted palms. Then Father was outraged Bee hadn't struck the fellow," Portia supplied.

"It was the talk of the season, as I recall," Plum went on. "Father challenged the pup to a duel. The queen got wind of it and boxed Father's ears for even suggesting it.

She's quite fond of the old goat. Didn't they share a drawing master when they were children or some such?"

"Dancing master," I corrected.

We were all laughing by then, imagining our scapegrace elderly father learning to waltz with the future queen in his arms. In spite of her reputation for primness, the queen did appreciate a good joke, and she always said that Hector March was the liveliest boy she ever knew. She ordered the Bowes-Ruthven heir to apologise and the matter was settled without bloodshed after Father made a tremendous donation to one of her pet charities. It had been quite the scandal at the time, and I suppressed a pang of irritation that what was sauce for the goose was so seldom sauce for the gander, even in our outrageous family.

"This will pass," Portia assured me, correctly assessing my mood.

"Of course it will," Plum added. "You're just feeling gloomy because you are Father's favourite and you aren't accustomed to feeling the full weight of his displeasure."

"I am not his favourite!" I protested. "If he has a favourite, it is Val. Val is the baby, and besides, none of the rest of us would have got our way if we had wanted to study medicine. Clearly Val is his pet."

Val spluttered into his cup of tea. "I most certainly am not. He cut me off four times and I still am not permitted to live at March House. He hates that I make my livelihood with my own two hands as much as he hates the fact that Bellmont has ended up a Tory. At least I know our eldest brother is no competition for the title of favourite," he jested.

The remark cut too near the bone. Without thinking, I leapt to his defence. "Bellmont is not so awful. He has given Adelaide and the children a very comfortable home for these many years. His constituency are very fond of him, too. They have returned him every election since he was twenty-two. He has been in service to them and to his country for the whole of his adult life, with little thanks and less affection. We have made him the butt of our jokes and sniggered at him behind his back, and we ought to be ashamed of ourselves."

I broke off to find my siblings staring at me in astonishment. Plum had paused with a muffin halfway to his mouth, Portia was open-mouthed, and even Jane the Younger was regarding me with something akin to reproach.

"Good God, Julia, it was just a joke. And since when have you been such a devotee of Bellmont's? He used to play your nerves as much as anyone's," Val managed.

"He still does," I admitted, smoothing my skirts. "It's just that we so often make him the butt of our jests that I think we forget he does have some good qualities." I broke off again. I had said too much already, and any more of this spirited rebuttal would only lead to further questions. I had surprised myself. Bellmont had irritated me so thoroughly and so often that I did not realise I harboured such affection for him. I wondered if it would pass.

I hurried on. "But perhaps you are right, Val. You are not Father's favourite. I think it must be Plum. I would lay money upon it."

Plum snorted. "I have done nothing with my life except execute some painfully mediocre art and take up employment as an enquiry agent. I am in his black books as much as Julia at present. No, his favourite is most certainly Portia."

Portia blinked. "You must be joking. He fussed at me for quite quarter of an hour last week because I would not sell him my cow. Julia is decidedly the favourite."

"But you have the baby," I retorted. It was a palpable hit.

Father doted upon all of his grandchildren, showing not a particle of difference in his affections for Portia's adopted daughter as he did for those born to his own children. As if on cue, Jane the Younger began to stretch and fuss a little.

"Poor little mite," Plum said. "Does she need to be dandled on Uncle Plummy's knee?" Plum's devotion to babies was a trifle unnerving. He was the one uncle who always delighted in them as infants, proving surprisingly adept at soothing tempers and bringing up wind. But his attentions were short-lived. Once they were able to walk and eat meat, he lost interest entirely. Fortunately, with so many sisters and sisters-in-law constantly producing children, there was never a shortage of wee ones for him to cuddle.

Portia passed the baby to Plum, who cradled her expertly, and we spent a very pleasant half an hour engaged in domesticity. Portia poured out tea and Val toasted muffins upon the hearth while I slathered them in butter and handed them round. Plum amused the baby with verses of nonsense, calling forth delighted coos of laughter, and for that short while, I forgot Madame and the séance and the scandal I had wrought with my own two hands.

Just as I rang for more muffins there was a commotion in the hall, and the four of us turned expectant eyes towards the door. A moment of breathless silence, and then the door opened to reveal a thoroughly unexpected sight.

"Lady Felicity!" I cried.

She stood, hesitating in the doorway, turning appealing eyes to Portia.

"I am so sorry to intrude. I did not know where else to go."

Plum made to stand and suddenly realised he was still holding the infant Jane.

"Oh, do not disturb yourself!" she said, shrinking back

a little. She was very clearly distressed, and it was equally apparent that whatever trouble beset her had come quickly. She was dressed formally, in a gown of primrose-coloured silk, a vile choice for so pale a blonde, but the cut was good—if a year out of date—and the fabric expensive. She was pleating the silk with her gloved fingers, very nearly shredding the stuff, and I think it was that small gesture of uncertainty that roused Portia's sympathies.

She rose and went to Felicity. "Come and sit by the fire. It is cool this evening and you have come out without a wrap."

"Oh, I had a cloak, but your butler took it," Felicity corrected. "I did not think he was going to admit me, so I slipped out of it and ran to the first room where I saw a light under the door."

"Very clever of you," Portia said soothingly. "But there was no call for such theatrics. Granger knows to send in every card."

"But I came away without my cards," Felicity demurred. She let Portia guide her to a chair near the fire. Valerius had straightened his posture to something more upright now that we were no longer a family party, and Plum was still suspended in an awkward half-crouch, holding Jane the Younger at a precarious angle until she gave a roar of disapproval and he righted himself.

Portia poured out a cup of tea for Felicity and added a healthy dollop of whisky. The girl took it and drank deeply. She gave a heaving cough and her face went white then red. "Oh, spirits," she said breathlessly.

"Whisky is restorative," Portia told her firmly. And after a moment of sipping, this time more cautiously, Felicity did look greatly recovered from her distress.

"You're very kind," she murmured as Portia pressed another cup upon her.

"We are, naturally, delighted to see you, but to what do we owe the pleasure of your call, Lady Felicity?" I asked.

She put her cup onto the saucer with a sharp click and placed the saucer upon the table. Then she folded her hands in her lap and said, quite calmly, "I have run away from home."

The room went very still, and for an instant there was no sound save the popping of the gas fire and a breathy sigh from Jane the Younger.

It was Portia who recovered her tongue first. "And you came here? How kind of you to permit us to help you." Her tone was perfectly serious, but Felicity's lips twitched, and I realised she was on the verge of hysterical laughter.

"Oh, Lady Bettiscombe, I am sorry! I went first to Brook Street. I thought to find Lady Julia or Mr. March," she said with a nod to each of us, "but they were not at home, and Lady Julia's butler was kind enough to tell me where they had gone. I had no thought save finding them and throwing myself upon their mercies."

I darted a look at Plum, but he kept his eyes firmly fixed upon the infant in his lap. "What precisely can we do for you, Lady Felicity?"

She began to pleat her silk again, folding the fabric between her fingers this way and that, creasing it irreparably.

"I thought you might suggest a haven for me," she said with admirable frankness. "I am afraid I did not think this out very well. It was only after I left my father's house that I realised I had no decisive plan of action. And then I thought of Mr. March and it occurred to me that the ladies of your family—" she broke off here, stumbling a little over her words "—well, that is to say, the March ladies—"

"Get into enough trouble that the men in our family ought to know how to get them out?" Valerius guessed.

To her credit, Felicity flushed deeply and gave me an apologetic look. "I did see the newspaper this morning."

I flapped a hand. "Do not worry about giving offence, my dear. I daresay you are quite right. Now, what precisely is your situation? Have you left home for good? Have you any money?"

"Julia!" Plum's voice was a strangled hiss. I had no doubt he would have liked to have shouted at me, but concern for the baby on his lap prevented him.

I shrugged. "We must know the facts if we are to help Lady Felicity formulate a plan. So, I ask again, what are the facts? Have you broken irreparably with your family?"

"Irreparably," she said stoutly. "My father revealed his true character to me this evening, and I will not be sheltered under the roof of such a man, not even for a single night more."

I hazarded another glance at Plum, but he was still ignoring me. I wondered if Felicity had discovered some new duplicity in her father with regards to his finances. But that was a business matter, and many ladies turned a blind eye to the business dealings, however dubious, of their menfolk. Was it something that touched Felicity directly then?

My suppositions must have been writ upon my face, for Felicity lifted her chin and looked me directly in the eye, her own gaze calm as a millpond. "My father wished me to marry where I do not love and cannot esteem simply for his own financial advantage."

"How dreadful," I murmured, but I was deeply conscious of Plum's abruptly stiffened posture. So was the baby. She roared again, and Portia clucked at him.

"If you are going to flinch, give her back. I do not want her shouting down the house."

Plum gave her a nasty look and soothed the baby. I glanced at Felicity to find her eyes lingering upon the pair of them, her expression soft.

"So the breach is irreparable," I said, guiding her back to the subject at hand.

"Indeed. I will marry where I wish, or not at all," she said firmly.

"As you should. Now, in the meanwhile, you must have a roof over your head and food upon your plate."

I paused and she had the grace to colour slightly. "I do have some means. My mother left me an annuity. Father cannot touch it, and the funds are paid me directly by the bank. I can keep myself."

"Excellent. A woman should always be able to keep herself," I said roundly. "But even if we think you should be able to do so, society does not. If you take a house alone, you will be cut off from all polite society and any chance of a marriage you might like to make for yourself one day. You must live with someone respectable," I finished. "Have you any elderly female relations?"

"None." Her voice had lost some of its crispness, as if she had only just begun to realise the magnitude of what she had done.

For a quarter of an hour, we put up names, suggesting various ladies of our acquaintance who might take Felicity in and rejecting them just as quickly. At each barrier, Felicity's spirits seemed to sink a little lower, until she finally fell into a reverie, staring at the flames. When she spoke, her voice was distant.

"It's absurd, this time we live in. A woman is Queen of England, mistress of all our destinies, and yet as a spinster I cannot so much as take a house with my own money without society destroying me for it," she said, and every word was laced with bitterness.

"It is absurd," Portia agreed. "But it is the truth, and it is also true that only the veneer of respectability need be maintained."

Felicity looked up. "What do you mean?"

Portia smoothed her skirts. "I mean, that you ought to come and live here. I am neither society's most discreet nor most conservative member, but I am a member nonetheless. Your reputation would not be ruined completely if you lived here, at least the damage would be far less than what you would suffer if you lived alone. What say you?"

I opened my mouth to object, but Felicity had flushed deeply, her eyes suddenly shimmering with unshed tears. "Do you mean it, Lady Bettiscombe?"

"Of course I mean it," Portia assured her. "I live alone, save for the staff and the baby, and I have far too many rooms here. You can come and go as you please until such time as you choose to make other arrangements."

"There are no proper words to express my gratitude," Felicity murmured. "I will of course pay something towards the household expenses."

"Yes, well. We will quarrel about that tomorrow," Portia said with a gentle smile. She looked to Plum and nodded towards Jane the Younger. The little beauty's lids were drooping fast, and her pretty rosebud mouth was slack.

"Give her over, Plum. I must see her to bed."

Plum rose and waved Portia off. "I will see her tucked up and tell the upstairs maid to have a listen should she cry out."

Felicity jumped to her feet. "Oh, no, let me!" She held out her arms. "I have four younger brothers. I am an old hand at helping with the babies, and I should so like to be helpful whilst I am here."

Plum obediently handed over the sleeping child. Felicity turned anxious eyes to Portia. "I hope I have not over-stepped myself. My stepmother always said that small children can be so very demanding, and I want to be able to contribute. You have been so kind."

Portia gave her a gracious nod. "Not at all. Plum will show you the way." She watched them leave with a specula-tive gleam in her eyes and I waggled a finger at her.

"You are playing at being Cupid," I accused.

"What if I am?" she demanded. "The girl is rather smit-ten, and so is Plum. If they are thrown together a little, they might come to like each other quite well. Or they will discover that they do not suit. It is always better to know."

"It is," I agreed. "If it came to it, I would have taken her, you know. You needn't have inconvenienced yourself."

"This house is too big," she said simply. "It echoes some-times." I knew she was thinking of her beloved lost com-panion, Jane, then. I did not press the point.

A few moments later, Plum returned with the news that Felicity was still with the child, singing lullabies. I suspected she wanted to give us a chance to speak privately, and I commended her discretion. Almost immediately, the four of us fell again to discussing my predicament.

"I cannot understand why Father is so terribly upset," Val put in. "Julia engaged in some rather unladylike behaviour in calling upon those gentlemen with only her maid, but that is really quite tame compared to what Marches usually get up to," he said with a touching display of loyalty to me. I smiled at him fondly.

"It isn't what she did," Portia explained, using her patient elder sister tone. "It is that she was careless enough to do it

in front of a reporter. Father has a horror of the sensationalist press, and this *Illustrated Daily News* is the absolute worst.
They always put the most awful construction upon things
without ever saying anything truly actionable. Believe me,
he would be far less upset if Julia had been written up in the
Times."

"It is more than that," Plum offered. "I think he is genuinely quite terrified for her. Dashing about on such esca-
pades leaves her open to assault by any villain. This reporter
was bent only on embarrassment, but he was apparently
quite close to her for the better part of an entire day. He
might have harmed her at any time."

A slight shudder ran through me, and for the first time,
I began to truly understand the danger I had faced. I felt
faintly violated, now I thought about it properly.

"I think he's angrier with Brisbane," Val added. "Feels he
ought to have done a better job of protecting her."

Plum snorted. "A full regiment of Beefeaters couldn't
protect Julia. She is entirely reckless."

"I say, that's uncalled for," I said, sulking a little, but Plum
was not entirely wrong, although I would never give him
the satisfaction of admitting it. "Besides, Father is the one
who encouraged me to take up a hobby during my widow-
hood. It is his fault for not specifying what sort of hobby."

"I think he meant something along the lines of beekeep-
ing or betting on horses," Portia offered. "I think I suggested gymnastics to you, did I not?"

I put out my tongue. "I like investigating. And I am
rather good at it." Although, I reflected darkly, I had not yet
managed to extricate our eldest brother from what might
prove to be a disastrous situation. I thought of his children
then, the pretty Virgilia and dear Orlando, Bellmont's eldest
boy, newly married and made a father just this past winter.

Bellmont's first grandchild had been born in Yorkshire to much merrymaking—a fourth-generation March heir to secure the family name. Yet one more life to be shattered if Bellmont's *liaison* came to light, I thought with a pang.

"You are woolgathering," Portia said gently. "Where did you go?"

I summoned a smile. "Nowhere, dearest. Just building castles in Spain and thinking on what a lovely family we have."

Portia looked from me to the handsome faces of our two brothers and smiled back. "We do, don't we?"

Buoyed by my evening with my family, I was in much better spirits when Brisbane collected me. His evening had proven very satisfactory, as well, ending in the collection of a hefty fee for resolving the matter, and we entered our house to find the telephone ringing away in the cupboard under the stairs.

Brisbane waved off Aquinas and answered it himself. He summoned me to come to the instrument almost immediately.

I took it as reluctantly as if it were a snake.

"Yes? To whom am I speaking?"

"Who else has a telephone?" my father demanded, apparently still in a prickly mood. "It's Mary, Queen of Scots."

"Good evening, Father," I said as politely as I could manage.

"Yes, well, I thought you ought to know. There won't be any more fuss with that *Illustrated Daily Dungpile* that published that story about you."

"Really? How can you be sure?"

"Because I bought the bloody thing this afternoon."

The

FOURTEENTH CHAPTER

Choose the darkest part o' the grove,
Such as ghosts at noon-day love.

—*"A Spell"* John Dryden

The next day, true to his word, Brisbane took me with him
to visit his tailor, a rather sober gentleman called Stokes.
Mr. Stokes had personally overseen the cut of Brisbane's
clothes for half a dozen years, and it was a measure of his
personal regard for Brisbane that he did so, for Mr. Stokes
was a man who could not be bought. In fact, he could very
often not even be found. His rooms were on Bond Street,
but discreetly situated, with no sign to betray their whereabouts. Like the queen, he flew a standard to indicate when
he was in residence, and clients of his establishment knew
better than to try the door when the flag was absent. He
bestowed his attentions only upon gentlemen he felt were
stylish enough to carry off his clothes to their best effect,
and no amount of money would induce him to personally
fit a gentleman who lacked the necessary aplomb or the
required references. I had taken it as a high compliment
when he had agreed to make my own riding habit and the

masculine disguise I had adopted during my investigation, and as he cast a critical eye over my costume, I was pleased to see approbation along with the appraisal.

"Well done. The stance of the jacket might be a fraction higher, but the pairing of dove-grey with cerise was an inspired choice and the set of that sleeve is inordinately fine."

Brisbane cocked a brow at me. "High praise indeed. I knew Stokes for two years before he complimented me once."

"And only then because you were wearing one of my coats," Mr. Stokes put in with a surprisingly waggish gleam in his eye. For all his soberness, Mr. Stokes was an engaging fellow, and we had a comfortable chat while Brisbane was being fit for a new city suit.

"He ought to have something for the country whilst we are here," I observed. "I think that black tweed with the dash of green in the weave is just the thing."

Mr. Stokes admired my excellent taste and offered me a glass of carnation ratafia. "It is a very old-fashioned sort of libation, but ladies seem to enjoy it," he explained. I had not heard of anyone drinking carnation ratafia since my grandmother's time. It was a pretty concoction—sugared brandy that had been steeped with carnation petals and spices—and for a ladylike drink, it was terribly powerful. It could fell a grown man in three glasses.

But I was eager to enjoy a convivial moment with Mr. Stokes, so I accepted. It soon became apparent that Mr. Stokes enjoyed ratafia as much as the ladies. He went so far as to open a tin of wine biscuits and we chatted and munched as various assistants trotted to and fro with samples and fabrics for Brisbane's new suits.

"I wonder," I said after we had established something of a genial rapport. "I came across a most unusual button, and it occurred to me that you must know all the most exclusive haberdashers in London and perhaps you had seen the like of it before."

He preened a little, as I had expected he would, but when I dropped the button into his palm, he took on the serious air of a scholar examining a rare specimen.

"German, of course, although one ought to be precise and say Prussian," he murmured. "An hereditary order for members of the Sigmaringen branch of the Hohenzollern dynasty."

All of which Brisbane and I already knew. I prodded further. "Is it possible to tell anything else from this button? I wondered if the kaiser might permit members of his household to wear them or perhaps the regiment assigned to his personal service."

"Oh, I shouldn't think so," Mr. Stokes assured me. "This is most definitely a costly piece with exquisite attention to detail. It would have been made for members of the order itself. Something in a similar style out of stamped metal would have done for the retainers."

I thanked him and made to return the button to my reticule, but he hesitated.

"Yes, Mr. Stokes? Is there something more?"

He shook his head thoughtfully. "I cannot say. Something about this button disturbs me, but I cannot tell you what it is. May I keep it?"

I hesitated and he hurried on. "Only for a day or so, and only to discover what else I can tell you about this particular item. I presume the matter touches upon Mr. Brisbane's work?" he asked, *sotto voce.*

I nodded and he laid a finger over his lips. "Fear not, my lady. I am silent as an oyster. A tailor must be, you know."

"Really?"

He gave a short, dry cough that I realised was supposed to be a laugh. "Of course! It would not do at all if I could not keep a confidence. No gentleman wishes it to be known that he pads his shoulders or wears a corset."

"You have clients who wear corsets?" I leaned closer, inviting confidences.

Mr. Stokes, warm and forthcoming as a result of the ratafia, nonetheless retained his discretion. He merely laughed again and wagged his finger at me. "Now, that would be telling!" No amount of coaxing could win even so much as a hint from him, and I felt better about leaving the button in his hands. At least until I told Brisbane once we had settled ourselves into our carriage.

He stared at me in stupefaction. "You left our one solid clue with my tailor?"

"He seemed to think he could help."

Brisbane thrust his fingers into his hair, disarranging it wildly. "I brought you with me because you cannot be trusted on your own, and in the five minutes I was out of your company, you managed to lose the only clue we had."

I flapped a hand at him. "I do not see what the fuss is about. We had deduced as much as we could from the button. Mr. Stokes believes he can discover additional information. Besides, I have not lost the clue," I corrected. "I put it to work for us."

Brisbane subsided against the seat. "I surrender. There is no point in even getting angry anymore."

"I am glad you see it," I returned. "Now, direct the driver to Simpson's and I will buy you a plate of roast beef to sweeten your temper."

"I am not hungry."

"No, but you are grinding your back teeth together. You at least ought to give them some meat to chew on."

A leisurely luncheon did put Brisbane in better spirits. He always enjoyed the quiet luxurious calm of Simpson's, and we were given our usual table, discreetly hidden from the rest of the room by a large palm. By the time the waiter had rolled up the silver trolley to carve the great haunch of good Scottish roast beef, Brisbane was admitting—albeit grudgingly—that it had been a rather good idea to give the button to Stokes, and as he spooned up the last of the cream from his apple tart, he actually smiled again.

"Where do we go from here, my lord and master?" I gave him a wide-eyed glance from under my lashes that I hoped would beguile him.

"Have you something in your eye?" he demanded. "You're blinking as if you have a cinder."

"It was meant to be enchanting," I told him.

"Well, it is absurd, and thoroughly unnecessary. You are quite enchanting enough without playing the coquette."

"Do you mean that you do not like me tractable and sweet?" I asked, pursing my lips at him.

"Christ, no. I want you just as you are, maddening and bedevilling and curious as a cat."

"I am glad to hear you say it. Sometimes I wonder if you haven't changed your mind about me. I know I am rather more trouble than I am worth," I told him.

He fixed me with a ferocious stare. "Never say that. Haven't I given you cause enough by now to know that I am completely and irrevocably in love with you?"

"It is quite nice to hear it, particularly when things have been so disordered as they have been lately."

By way of reply, he kissed me. The rest of the patrons

could not see us, but the waiter gave a discreet cough, and I pulled away.

"Brisbane," I whispered, "I have caused quite enough scandal for one week."

He behaved himself then, and over tea he became expansive on the subject of the investigation.

"I have Monk making enquiries on the financial situation of our gentlemen guests from the séance. I respect your assessment of them," he hastened to assure me, "but I want to be quite certain that none of them is in dire straits enough to warrant turning to blackmail."

"And in the meanwhile?"

"The blackmail note."

"I thought the blackmail note was a nonstarter."

He fished into his pocket and retrieved a new note, one I had not yet seen. I caught my breath as I read it. "Five thousand pounds to Highgate Cemetery at midnight."

"Suitably theatrical," Brisbane observed drily.

"At the Circle of Lebanon," I continued. My mouth suddenly felt as if it were stuffed with cotton wool. "The Circle of Lebanon is where Edward is buried." My first husband had insisted upon the most fashionable address in London even in death.

"I do not like this, Brisbane. There is no significance to that location for Bellmont. It holds meaning for *me*. And the note says you are to make the delivery, not Bellmont. Why?"

Brisbane lifted one shoulder in a shrug. "We are brothers-in-law, and the blackmailer knows—or has at least surmised—that Bellmont has consulted me upon the matter. It makes sense, really. I deal with such things quite regularly in my profession. Bellmont does not. He is far likelier to do something needlessly stupid like try to lie in wait and take the money back. I am a professional."

It did make sense, but I would not be persuaded. "I do not like this. There is something quite nasty and quite specifically directed at you, at *us*."

"Precisely. And that is exactly why you are coming with me."

"I cannot have heard you correctly. You have preached at me about my safety almost since our first meeting. You cannot seriously mean to take me to a meeting with a blackmailer that seems deliberately designed to make a victim of me."

Brisbane sat back in his chair with the air of a man who is deeply satisfied.

"You are quite correct in your assessment, my love. The blackmailer means to draw me into Bellmont's business. If he was not certain that Bellmont had consulted me, this would have sealed it. The very pointed reference to the grave of your first husband brings you squarely into the middle of the situation. A normal, rational, sane man who cares about the safety of his wife would lock her in the house before setting off for Highgate Cemetery. But, thanks to my long association with you and your family, I am no longer normal or rational or sane. I am composed of desperation and instinct and nothing more," he finished.

I narrowed my gaze. "I do not believe it."

"Believe what you will, my pet. That note was cleverly crafted to ensure that I leave you safely at home, for reasons that are not entirely clear to me yet. Perhaps the blackmailer seeks to muddy the waters. Perhaps he seeks an opportunity to attack." I gave a start, but Brisbane continued smoothly on. "In any event, we will not oblige him. You will kit yourself out in that absurd masculine costume and by ten o'clock we will be en route to Highgate to see what may be seen."

I sat with my hands folded in my lap, quietly digesting all Brisbane had said. This was precisely what I had wanted for so long, a partnership, real involvement in his investigations. And now that I had it, I was not entirely sure it suited me. What, I wondered, had I got myself into?

It was a question I was to ask myself a dozen times more before the night was through. According to Brisbane's instructions, I garbed myself in my suit of men's clothing, although this time I had no wig. It was only necessary to preserve the illusion from a distance, he assured me, so that anyone who might be watching our house would believe Brisbane had left in the company of a gentleman friend. Plum, who still did not know Bellmont's troubles, had been dispatched upon an errand connected to another case, and the rest of the household had been sent to bed. Only Aquinas knew what we were about, and he lit us through the morning room to the garden door. In silence, he latched it behind us and left a lamp burning in the window to light our way.

A faint glimmer of moonlight illuminated our path, and I trailed behind, stepping neatly in Brisbane's footsteps to make certain I did not stumble over an errant rock or twisting root.

After a moment, we came to the garden wall and slipped through the gate, closing it noiselessly behind us. It was a mark of his attention to detail that Brisbane kept the gate oiled at all times.

We cut round and emerged into Cock Yard and thence to Davie Street, where we hailed a hackney. I would have preferred the lighter and swifter hansom, but Brisbane elected to make use of the privacy the hackney offered. Concealment was to our advantage, and as we settled inside, Brisbane quickly doused the lamps. We rode in silence to Highgate, alighting a little distance away in order to make our entrance on foot. It was not until we reached the gates that it occurred to me they would be locked. I muttered a curse, but Brisbane was not discomfitted by such an eventuality. He laced his fingers into a cradle and told me to step up and vault myself over the high stone wall.

"Are you sincerely mad?" I hissed. "Pick the lock!"

"It would take far too long and make enough noise to wake the dead. Have I taught you nothing?" Now that he mentioned it, I did recall some lecture to the effect when he was first teaching me to pick locks. The tools required would have been enormous, never mind the fact that it would look terribly suspicious if he were discovered crouching over the lock. No, it would have to be over the wall, and quickly.

I placed my foot where he indicated and after one or two false starts, managed to land atop the wall. "Oof," was the noise I made as I hit hard. "Be careful. There is broken glass here," I told him. It had doubtless been laid to discourage this very activity, but luckily there was little of it where we had chosen to cross.

In an instant, Brisbane was beside me, and then he was down again, on the other side and motioning impatiently for me to join him. I closed my eyes and threw myself down, knowing he would catch me. When he set me on my feet, his lips grazed my ear.

"From here on, no more talking," he instructed. And I nodded to show I understood.

We moved slowly forward, and it seemed we walked for an age. Highgate was an enormous place, comprised of many different walks and gardens, each packed with crypts and monuments. Weeping angels jostled with crosses and heraldic badges and woeful statues. It might have been beautiful, in a terrible and melancholy way, were it not for the errand we were bent upon and the rising fog. For fog had begun to creep through the stones, swirling at our feet and obscuring the path.

Brisbane noted it and gave a short nod, indicating he was pleased. The fog would give us a bit more protection from prying eyes, and he was careful as he moved not to disturb it more than necessary. Perhaps it was something learnt in his Gypsy boyhood, for I saw how a quick motion could cause the fog to swirl and eddy, betraying one's presence. But Brisbane moved with the litheness of a cat, fitting himself to the fog as it passed over the dew-soaked grass.

I followed as noiselessly as I could, and in due course we reached the Circle of Lebanon. I had not seen it in some years, not since Brisbane and I had discovered the identity of Edward's murderer. I had visited once to lay my flowers and my ghosts at the same time, and I had not come back. That part of my life was finished and done with, and I could not fathom why it had been raked up again.

The Circle of Lebanon was a crescent of stone crypts, overshadowed by an enormous cedar of Lebanon which spread its dark branches against the pale moonlight, blotting out all but the faintest trace of silver. The crypts were deeply shadowed, but some little distance away stood a solitary chapel on its own. The door of this was open, and a light glowed from within.

With a gesture, Brisbane indicated for me to stand behind him as he made his way to the chapel. It was an achingly slow process, with each step requiring a pause as he listened intently in the dark. There was no sound, not even wind in the trees, for the night was still and it felt as if the stones themselves were waiting with bated breath.

At last, he reached the chapel door. He stooped to grasp a handful of pebbles, and after a moment's contemplation, he threw them hard inside the chapel, steeling himself for a response. There was none—only the fog, shifting as it rose, and the warm, beckoning glow of the torch. We remained there, poised at the open door, for an eternity before Brisbane signalled that we were to move again. When we did move, he was diligent in keeping me behind him, darting his glance swiftly around to peer into the darkness and make certain we were not followed.

He hurried me into the chapel, and it took but a moment to realise we were entirely alone. It was a very small chapel and filled with narrow wooden pews and a metal table that I quickly realised was a bier of sorts. There was no space for a villain to hide. The only sign of life came from the flickering torch that had been placed in a bracket by the door. Brisbane nodded towards it and I took it up in my hands. As the light shifted, we both looked to the bier. Upon it lay a small white envelope. As one, we moved to the bier to retrieve it. I held the torch up and put out my hand.

As I did so, there was a great grinding creak and the floor suddenly gave way beneath us. Instantly, Brisbane flung out his hand to grab my wrist, and for the space of a heartbeat I teetered between the hard strength of my husband and the yawning nothingness that had opened up behind me. Brisbane pulled sharply and I fell against him, clinging to his arm as I watched our progress. We were descending slowly into some black abyss whose depths we could not see. I watched the crypt above us moving further out of reach. As unnerving as the crypt had been, it now seemed to be a place of safety, a refuge against whatever horrors lurked below. At last, the floor settled into place, and a quick glance above showed we had come down some thirty feet or so.

"What the devil?" I demanded, for it seemed we had descended to the very bowels of hell. We were in a sort of vaulted chamber, and I realised that the floor of the chapel above was not precisely a floor at all, but rather a platform attached to a pulley system with wheels and gears and enormous chains. I stared in disbelief. "What is this place?"

Brisbane looked about us, assessing the situation. "I have not been inside one of these in years. It is a private crypt, built to secure the dead against graverobbers."

"Graverobbers!" I peered into the gloom around us. By the light of the torch, I could make out a series of iron cages, and beyond the bars I saw shelves fitted to the wall. Upon each of them rested a coffin. The air was thick with damp and decay and the smell of wet stone. I wondered if I fancied the sickly sweet scent of human putrefaction.

"These tombs were very popular when graverobbing was in its heyday, but they fell out of fashion half a century ago," he informed me. "The platform was for lowering the coffins and then the graveyard workers would shift the coffin to a trolley and wheel it to the proper cage to be locked safely away."

"How do you know about such places?" I asked, rubbing my arms with a shiver. I was not cold. At least, not yet. But fear prickled my skin.

"I lived in one when I first came to London," he said absently.

I stared at this charnel house and shook my head. I could not have heard him correctly. "You lived in one?"

"Yes. It was better than the streets. Shelter from the rain and plenty of space and lots of peace and quiet."

I broke my heart over the picture of him as a child of ten, alone in this vast city and living off scraps he stole and sleeping in such a place as this. But Brisbane was not conscious of my emotion. He stepped off of the platform to inspect the pulley system, peering intently at the gears. I held the torch close, glad to turn my attention to something other than the mouldering corpses around us.

Brisbane was rather a long time, poking about various bits of the elderly hydraulic machinery, and finally he rose, wiping his hands with his handkerchief, his face a picture of disgust. "Jammed. Irretrievably so, no doubt by the blackmailer."

"But it worked a moment ago," I protested. I liked to think of myself as stalwart as any Englishwoman, but spending the night in a crypt was not my preferred form of entertainment.

"It has been rigged, and rather cleverly so, to descend when someone stepped on the platform. But the combined body weight that triggered the descent also broke the rod that held the bloody thing together."

"Can you fix it?"

"Certainly. Let me fetch my tools from the ironmongery."

I pulled a face. "Don't be prickly, Brisbane. I wondered if you could contrive a temporary solution, just enough to see us safely back up to the chapel."

He shook his head. "Not anything I would trust your life or my weight to."

"There must be another way out. We will find it." It seemed a reasonable enough assumption, but Brisbane was shaking his head again.

"That was rather the point of these places, my dear. A single way in or out. No point of access for a graverobber, except the way we descended, and the crypt above would have been locked save during a funeral."

"You mean, we are trapped here?" My voice rose slightly, and I knew I had to get hold of myself lest I give way to hysteria. I squared my shoulders and looked Brisbane directly in the eye. "I do not accept that."

"Accept it or not, it is a fact."

"Your saying it is a fact does not make it a fact," I parried. I took the torch and began to investigate.

"Julia, what are you doing?"

"I am finding a way out. Would you care to help me?"

"We do not require a way out. This tomb is not sealed, so we shall not lack for fresh air. The flaring of your torch tells us that much. It is damp, but not overly cold, so we are in no danger of hypothermia, merely discomfort. Bellmont knows where we have come. When we cannot be found tomorrow morning, he will come to Highgate."

"And how will he know we are *here* in this particular place?" I demanded. "Do you expect the blackmailer will have left a helpful torch burning outside or a banner reading, 'This way, please'? If he has anything approaching common sense, he will have doused the other torch and locked the crypt behind him, leaving no trace that the place has even been opened in the last half a century. And even if Bellmont does come, how will he explain that he knew we were here? He will be exposed, as surely as if he did not pay the blackmail," I argued.

Brisbane's brow furrowed. "That is a curious point. If the blackmailer truly wanted money, why did he leave without it?" He patted the pocket where five thousand pounds lay tidily wrapped in brown paper.

"Maybe he means to come back. When we're dead," I

whispered in a suitably sepulchral voice. "It is no crime to steal from a dead man."

"Yes, in point of fact, it is. And I do not believe the blackmailer has lured us here to entomb us like the Mistletoe Bride," he retorted.

"Do you have a better explanation?"

"Not at the moment," he admitted. "But it is always a mistake to theorise without enough information."

I rolled my eyes at him and continued to investigate. The chamber was enormous, much larger than I had first supposed, and within it was a warren of cages, each securely locked and hung with an iron plaque bearing a family name. Some of the cages held only a coffin or two, but others were stuffed, the dead layered upon the dead, and it struck me as faintly obscene.

"It looks like a wine cellar for the dead," I muttered. Brisbane, for all his nonchalance, had taken up the search with me, and together we covered every inch of that vile place, tapping upon stones and examining seams in the walls for any hint of a second entrance.

As we searched, I noticed his breathing changed. It became heavier, and he paused once or twice, his eyes fixed upon nothing in particular. There was a glassiness to his stare that I did not like, and at one point, his lips moved soundlessly.

I touched his face, surprised to find it cold as death. "Brisbane, what is it?"

He shook his head slowly, his eyes never meeting mine but instead fixed upon some point in the distance. "Something is happening," he murmured in a faraway voice.

"To you? Brisbane, are you ill? Speak to me," I demanded. The terrible stillness did not abate, and his flesh seemed to cool even further at my touch. If I were given to fancies, I might have thought he was somehow slipping away from me, although he stood upon his own feet, tall and strong as ever. Only, his spirit seemed distant, and my mouth went dry as a desert as I suddenly realised what was happening.

"Are you having a vision?"

His eyes widened, and he continued to stare unblinking at the stone wall in front of him.

"I must get you out of here," I muttered. I shoved hard at him, but he did not blink. I tugged his hair, I pinched him—hard enough to leave a mark—but he did not respond. Desperation welled within me, and I murmured an apology as I drew back my hand and struck him hard across the face, once then twice.

He rocked back on his heels and his eyes slowly focused upon my face.

"Something bad is happening," he ground out through clenched jaws. "We must get home."

I grabbed his hand and hurried us back to the platform and its ominous, unworkable gears. I had no idea how long he would remain lucid before slipping away again, and I knew I must act quickly.

I stared up the vertical length of chain as it rose through the gloom to the shadowy height of a ceiling I could barely see, and I knew what I must do.

"Brisbane, I am going to climb the chain and go for help. I will get you out of here," I promised. If he heard me, he did not respond. He clutched at his head and sank to his knees.

"Brisbane!" I cried. I knelt beside him, torn. I knew I had to go to find assistance, but it cleaved my heart to leave him alone in this place.

He looked at me with a stranger's eyes. "Go," he ordered, and his voice was something less than human.

Without hesitation, I stripped off my coat and rolled up my sleeves and put my boot to the chain. I would have sworn all the way up the chain, except that I had no breath. My dislike of heights, coupled with the difficulties of climbing the chain, made it impossible for me to do anything other than focus all of my attention on the links in front of me. Slowly, painfully, I climbed. Each time I set my foot into a link, each time I clasped my hands around the rusting iron, I bit back a scream of pain and fear. I dared not look down; I dared less to look up. I was afraid that if I saw how far I had yet to go, I would lose first my hope and then my grip.

So I climbed, onward and upward, long agonising minutes, until at last I found myself peering over the edge of the chapel floor. Suddenly, I felt paralysed, completely uncertain of how to proceed. I had climbed the chain, but I had not considered how to manage the last bit. I considered it for a long moment, until I felt the sweat seeping from my hands. The chain was slippery in my palms, and to my horror, I found my grip beginning to fail.

"You have one chance, Julia Brisbane," I told myself firmly. "And this is no different than mounting a horse." With a great shout, I flung myself up and over the edge, landing hard upon one hip. I almost sobbed in relief, so happy was I to be done with that purgatorial climb. I lay for several minutes, slightly dazed, and when I rolled back over, I gave a shriek.

"Brisbane!"

He had climbed up behind me, and so intent had I been upon my own ascent that I had never noticed. He vaulted from the chain to the crypt floor, but his movements were stiff and slow, and I took his hand as I led the way from the crypt.

We emerged cautiously into the cool night air. I breathed great lungfuls of the stuff; it was intoxicating after the dank atmosphere of the crypts.

We made our way through the cemetery, picking our path carefully through the stones. The fog had thickened to a dense white blanket, sending gauzy fingers through the trees and amplifying sounds strangely. There was the scampering of small nocturnal creatures and the call of a late nightingale, but that was all, and we soon found ourselves at the gate. Once more we went over the wall, and in a very short time, hailed a hackney and directed it to take us home.

He collapsed against me once inside the carriage, and I held him close, knowing that he suffered torments when the visions were upon him. He fought them so bitterly that the usual result was a migraine of a particular vicious variety. This time, something of the vision had forced its way through, and the result left him disoriented and exhausted. I, too, was conscious of a deep fatigue, bone-tired after our ordeal and longing for a hot bath and my bed. I must have dozed off as we rode, for the next thing I knew, Brisbane had roused himself, and I heard his voice, still distant and strange.

"Julia," he said, as if the word was unfamiliar to him.

"I am here," I promised, rubbing the sleep from my eyes.

"What is it?"

The hackney drew to a stop just as Brisbane pointed.

"The house is on fire."

The FIFTEENTH CHAPTER

Let us make an honourable retreat.

—*As You Like It*

The rest of that night passed as a grim dream. The women of the staff were herded to the back of the garden, huddled together in their nightdresses, whilst the men gave every aid to the fire brigade in putting out the fire. It was not so bad as we had thought, for it was only the very corner of the house that had caught, and the place suffered far more from the smoke than actual flames. The morning room was in ruins, but the service passage had been spared, as had the kitchens and domestic offices. Even Aquinas' pantry had little damage, and it was Aquinas, in his nightcap and a very dapper striped dressing gown, who organised the staff and retrieved Rook and Grim.

With the extinguishing of the fire, Brisbane seemed to have recovered himself, although his colour was deathly pale and his eyes still slid occasionally out of focus, as though he saw things from a faraway place.

We were assembled in the garden with the various staff

and pets when Brisbane took Aquinas aside. "Who rang the fire bell?"

"I did," Aquinas related. "I was wakeful and thought I would read for a while. Just as I sat up to put on the lamp, I smelled something peculiar. I traced the odour to the morning room, where I found the fire."

"How do you think it began?" Brisbane put in.

Aquinas replied promptly. "The lamp in the morning room window ignited the carpet."

Brisbane seized upon this like a dog with a bone. "The carpet? Not the draperies?"

"No, sir."

"So the lamp was overturned," Brisbane reasoned.

"It appeared to be so." Aquinas' expression was perfectly correct. I put my hand to his arm.

"I know you have said nothing so as not to alarm the staff. Do not speak of this to the fire brigade. We will let them think it an accident."

"Very well, my lady," Aquinas said, bowing from the neck. He moved off, and I turned to Brisbane. "We will have to give him a rise in salary for this. Everyone will think it his fault and we cannot correct the impression that this was an accident." I sighed. "I was such a fool. When we arrived, I really did think that monstrous new kitchen stove caught fire."

"A bit too coincidental on the same night we were trapped in a crypt, don't you think?" His voice still held a stranger's coolness, but he gave me a ghost of his usual smile.

"And you don't believe in coincidences," I finished. "But why set fire to the house when the blackmailer already had us in his power?"

"Because he did not realise he had us. He thought he

had me," Brisbane explained. I had seldom seen him so somber. "He wrote such a note that I would be compelled to go myself rather than permit Bellmont to go. But perhaps the blackmailer does not realise I insisted upon taking you with me. He knows I am bound for Highgate, but believes you to be alone in the house. It was an opportunity and he took it."

I set my teacup down with a decided crack. "You really think the blackmailer believed I was here?"

"He may have *wanted* you here," Brisbane said slowly.

My mouth felt unpleasant then, and I realised the bitter taste upon my tongue was fear.

"But who? Why?"

"That is what I mean to find out."

It was my own fault for underestimating him. I had thought after such an ordeal as spending the night in a crypt and having one's house set on fire, Brisbane would have required a bit of rest. I ought to have known better.

The fire had not been out half an hour before he ordered me to put a few things into a carpetbag.

"We are leaving?" I said, mystified. The rest of the house had been largely undamaged and I craved nothing so much as my own bed.

"I think we ought to stay away from the house for a few days."

"You believe the blackmailer might try again?"

"I do not know what I believe, and that is the damnable part of it. There is a pattern here, an explanation, only I cannot see it." I heard the frustration lacing his voice, and I knew how much it must have infuriated him not to have answers.

"I think it an excellent notion," I informed him. "You

needn't look so surprised. I do not argue with you about everything."

He smiled. "No. But I think you will be surprised at where we are bound."

"I presumed Portia's. Or Father's. He is still prickly with me, but he would never turn us away if we needed shelter."

"Neither of those will do. They are entirely too expected, and Portia has the safety of the baby to consider. Besides that, both of those town houses have staff. We do not yet know whom we can trust, and the fewer people who know where we are, the better."

"Where can we go that we will be hidden away and protected?"

The smile deepened. "The Gypsy camp on Hampstead Heath."

Preparations to leave for the Gypsy camp were remarkably few. I dressed in a walking suit of country tweeds with a tidy blouse and stout boots. Brisbane permitted me one small carpetbag of miscellany, which I packed myself in order to avoid involving Morag.

"The staff are in no danger," he assured me. "We will make a production of leaving and setting out for the station. Anyone watching will think I am packing you off to the country."

We left the house that evening, the two of us and Rook. It was early, after darkness had fallen but before the slender moon had risen. Brisbane had concluded that there was every possibility we might be followed, and so he created a circuitous route for us across London. We changed carriages four times, often alighting swiftly from one to cross the street and take another heading the opposite direction.

Once at the station, we hurried in as if we feared we were about to miss a train, only to lose ourselves in the crowd on the platform and dodge out a side door where still another conveyance awaited. This was a grubby cab driven by a disreputable-looking villain, whose clothes stank of gin and whose vehicle was nearly rusted through. The driver's face was heavily muffled from the nose down, and his cap was pulled low over his brow. He hunched in his seat and waved us in with a gesture of irritation, as if he resented the promise of actual work since it deprived him of his time to drink.

I hesitated to climb into the cab, but the driver turned and gave me a broad wink.

"Monk!" I cried softly. He made a show of taking a pull from his flask and whipped up the horse, driving away at a brisk trot. I felt infinitely better for being in Monk's capable hands. I knew there was no one Brisbane would rather have at his back at such a time, and I settled in for the ride with rising spirits.

It took a long while to reach Hampstead Heath, and it felt as if we covered half of London. The night was fair, for the fog of the previous night had been blown away by a brisk wind that stank of London itself as we climbed out of the streets; but as we rose towards the heath it changed. Here it smelled of late roses and oak leaves and the peculiar green odour of pond water. And when I caught the scent of campfires, I knew we were near. At the edge of the heath, Monk drew up in a discreet copse and turned to Brisbane.

"I kept a close eye. No one followed."

"Excellent, Monk." He put a hand to his majordomo and Monk clasped it.

"I will return tomorrow with news," he promised. He inclined his head towards me as Brisbane handed me down from the cab. "Take care, my lady," he said softly, touching his hand to his hat.

"Thank you, Monk," I called. We did not wait for him to leave, but crept through the copse and onto a path leading higher on the heath. Brisbane knew his way, for he had often camped here as a boy, and he moved swiftly through the darkness, guiding me ever closer to the camp.

The glow of the campfires beckoned us closer, but as we came near, the horses, pegged out on their lines, whickered softly, and a pair of savage-looking dogs began to bark an alarm. Brisbane gave a rough command and they subsided at once, ducking their heads. Just then an enormous fellow with great moustaches rose from his seat near the fire and called a challenge into the darkness.

Brisbane stepped from the shadows, giving a sharp, distinctive whistle, something like the cry of a fox. The fellow gave an answering whistle, and his face split into a tremendous smile, baring great white teeth as he laughed.

I looked at Brisbane, who flicked me a glance. "It's how Gypsies identify each other in the dark. Each tribe has its own whistle. Rather useful at a distance, as well," he added as the enormous Rom beckoned us in, chattering quickly to his companions, sketching broad gestures of welcome.

He reached out and embraced Brisbane, nearly crushing him in his meaty arms. They conversed a moment in Romany and I saw Brisbane's face go quite still suddenly and he swore, in English, not his native tongue.

"What is it?" I prodded, coming forward to take his arm. As I did so, the enormous Gypsy caught sight of me and began declaiming loudly. He grasped me by the hand and then swung me into a crushing embrace.

"Welcome, lady," he said in careful English.

"My cousin, Wee Geordie," Brisbane informed me.

"Oh, indeed? How do you do?" I said politely.

The giant Wee Geordie embraced me again with a hearty laugh. Then he began to speak rapidly again to Brisbane, and the word I heard several times was *puridai*.

It is said that the Gypsy tongue is so wild and so beautiful that its witchcraft once dragged down the moon when it came near just to listen. I knew I could have happily listened to the pair of them talk all night, for the language had all of the dark lilting beauty of Italian. But I could see Brisbane's expression deepening to a scowl each time Wee Geordie repeated the word *puridai*.

"What does that mean?" I asked Brisbane.

He frowned. "It means this whole affair just became vastly more complicated."

"What is *puridai*?"

"Wee Geordie is referring to the female leader of the clan. He is more than willing to give us shelter, but permission must come from the *puridai* herself."

Wee Geordie beckoned us to follow him and as we trotted along, I pressed Brisbane with more questions.

"Why does this woman have to grant permission?"

"Because it's the Roma way. I am in disgrace because of my marriage."

I squawked in outrage. "Your marriage? Whyever so?"

"A Roma girl who marries outside the tribe can never bring her husband in. He won't be accepted. But a Roma male can usually do so without difficulty."

"Then I do not see the problem."

Brisbane slanted me a look. "I am not fully a Rom. I am only half-blood. And when I chose to live apart, the family did not take it well. Out of respect, I ought to have got permission to marry you."

"Permission?" I spluttered. "What is wrong with me?

I am the daughter of a belted earl whose title bears seven hundred years' worth of history. I have more money than I could possibly spend in an entire lifetime and my god-mother is the Princess of Wales."

Brisbane stopped and laid a quieting finger over my lips. "You are not a Rom. It was a sign of disrespect that I did not go to the *puridai* to inform her."

I huffed, partially in my efforts to keep up with Wee Geordie's tremendous stride and partially out of annoyance.

"I have half a mind to tell this woman what she can do with her permission," I said darkly.

Brisbane gave a smothered groan. "For the love of God, do not speak. Just smile and say nothing and let me handle this."

I grumbled a bit more, but we had drawn near to a large, brightly painted caravan, a *vardo* in their language. Screening the open door was a sort of curtain that had been fashioned of beads, I thought, although I realised as we came near that the beads were bones. Small, white bones that clicked and clacked in the breeze. A campfire was burning brightly in front of the *vardo* and on the steps was a small bundle of clothing. To my astonishment, Wee Geordie addressed a few words to the bundle; it struggled and eventually rose to its feet. It was a woman, so small and so old, she looked to be made of withered leather. But in the proud line of her nose and the arch of her brow, I saw that she had once been very handsome indeed. A heavy circlet of gold coins sat upon her snow-white hair, and the plait of it fell to her waist, festooned with more gold coins, as was the hem of her full skirts. Still more coins loaded her wrists and ears, and I saw that for the Roma, this was a woman of great wealth who clearly commanded power and respect.

She looked at Brisbane a long moment, then her eyes went to me. I was not tall, but she scarcely reached my shoulder. She said nothing, but merely studied me, smoking a long clay pipe as she contemplated.

Brisbane did not break the silence. He knew the ways of his mother's people, and he accorded the lady the respect her position demanded. She turned again to him and said something. I caught the word *poshrat,* the Romany term for a half-breed, but she said it with a twinkle in her eye, and I realised with a start that she held some affection for Brisbane.

He bent swiftly to her hand and raised it to his lips, pressing a kiss to the leathery paw. I had never seen him perform so courtly a gesture, but he executed it with perfect gravity. The tribal elder cuffed him fondly and lifted her chin, muttering something as she looked at me. It was a command of sorts, for Brisbane beckoned me forward.

He intoned something in Romany to the woman. She nodded and gestured for me to come closer still. I obeyed and she scrutinised me from head to foot, as I had often seen my father do when buying a horse.

My fraying temper threatened to snap, and I rolled my eyes towards Brisbane. "Does she mean to welcome me or to buy me?"

Before Brisbane could respond, the old woman opened her mouth and gave a wheezy cackle. Her breath was warm upon my face and smelled of apples.

"When did you marry, girl?" she asked me.

"The summer of last year. Midsummer Day," I told her.

This must have satisfied her, for to my astonishment, she reached forward and pulled me down to kiss my brow. Then she kissed me upon either cheek.

I looked to Brisbane, who was staring at me in palpable

relief. I saw a bead of perspiration at his temple and realised how very anxious he had been for the lady's acceptance.

She rattled off a few sentences in Romany and Brisbane came forward to finish the introductions. "The day is an auspicious one for Roma marriages and she is pleased. Julia, the *puridai* welcomes you as her guest."

I smiled widely at her to show my pleasure and she gave me a grave inclination of the head, as regal as any mediaeval queen granting a boon to a peasant.

"What am I to call her?" I asked.

She gave another cackle and said, "You may call me Granny Bones, child."

"Granny Bones?"

She nodded, taking a deep inhalation from her pipe. "I tell fortunes, child. Some use the leaves, some the cards. I cast the knucklebones of the sheep, as pagan priests once did for the emperors in Rome."

I thought of the times I had had my fortune told in the tea leaves and shuddered. Tasseomancy had proven a little too accurate for my taste.

"How interesting," I said politely.

She gave me an enigmatic look. "You do not think so yet, but you will. The bones never lie."

I started, but she only laughed again, that rusty squeezebox laugh and turned to enter the caravan beckoning for us to follow.

I turned to Brisbane. "She is quite a character. And she seems very fond of you."

His mouth twitched ever so slightly. "She ought to be. She is my grandmother."

It took me the better part of the evening to reconcile this small, wholly Gypsy woman with my sophisticated husband.

But as we talked, his urbanity slipped away a little, and he grew more expansive, gesturing widely and speaking the lilting Romany tongue with fluency and passion. I had met two of his Rom relations, but it had never occurred to me that his grandmother might still be alive. When she slipped out for a moment, I took the opportunity to chide him.

"Why did you never tell me?"

He shrugged. "Granny and I never got on particularly well after I ran away. She was upset when I left the tribe. She wanted me to marry a girl of her choosing and breed horses. I knew I could never live that life. I wanted nothing to do with any of it, the horses, the travelling, the fortune-telling…" His voice trailed off. We seldom spoke of his second sight or the terrible migraines that came when he refused to permit himself to slip into a trance. I sometimes thought the cure was worse than the sickness, for as awful as his visions were, the pain he suffered and the drugs he took to numb it were often just as vile. He had left the Roma to escape himself, and here he was, just past forty and back again, welcomed into the fold with open arms. I was not surprised to detect an air of satisfaction in him. Brisbane might have cast off the Romany ways, but Gypsy blood flowed in his veins, and blood will always tell.

"I have seen her half a dozen times over the years," he went on. "She has never formally forgiven me."

"Until tonight?" I prompted.

"No, not even now," he corrected. "Granny is an opportunist. There is something she wants or she would not be half so nice as she is at present."

I scolded him. "That sweet old woman? How can you say such a thing?"

"Because I know her," he returned in some exasperation. "If she were introduced to the Prince of Wales, she would curtsey to the floor and pick his pocket at the same time. No, Granny wants something."

I pursed my lips and declined to hear any more on the subject of Granny's larcenous ways.

She returned then, bearing plates of food, and the rich, savoury scent of it reminded me that I had not eaten much that day. There was a juicy bone for Rook and a meat stew for the rest of us with hunks of warm bread spread heavily with goose fat and salted. I ate heartily, sopping up the gravy from the stew with bread until every scrap was gone. Granny watched, nodding with a smile, and she said something in Romany to Brisbane, who had also cleaned his plate.

"What was that?" I asked, wishing there had been second helpings.

"She is impressed. Not many *gorgios* enjoy *hotchiwitchi*," he told me.

I knew *gorgio* was their term for an English person, but I was puzzled at the second word. *"Hotchiwitchi?"*

Granny Bones gave me a wide smile. "Hedgehog."

"Oh, dear," I murmured, surpressing a tiny burp.

"You like more?" she asked.

"No, no. I am quite full," I assured her, patting my belly.

She nodded. "Is good to be have a full belly." I remembered then how often her people went hungry. I imagined it was difficult enough to always find sufficient food, but that was not the only trouble that beset them. It was still legal for an Englishman to turn out a Gypsy cookpot to make certain they were not cooking infants. It was an absurd law, and the injustice of it burned within me. They were unique to be sure, and they did not hold the same views on property or the same values, but some things were universal.

They loved their children and wanted food to eat and a safe place to sleep. We were not so very different.

I turned to Granny. "It is indeed very good to have a full belly. Thank you for sharing your meal with us."

She inclined her head again with that peculiarly gracious air and then rose. "Time to bed."

Brisbane and I followed her outside, where she gave him quick instructions. *"Ava,"* he told her, the Romany word for agreement, and she returned to the caravan, emerging after a moment with a length of canvas and a few sticks, along with several quilts and a feather pillow. She waved and went back inside, banging the door tightly behind her by way of good-night.

"What now?" I asked Brisbane.

"Now, we camp," he informed me. Around us the rest of the camp had settled in to sleep. The fires had burned low, and in the distance, I heard the croon of a lullaby. I sat upon the steps of the *vardo* with Rook as Brisbane worked swiftly.

First, he moved the fire several feet from where Granny had built it. He shoveled a thin layer of dirt over the hot earth left behind and then pitched the tent atop it. The quilts were fashioned into a mattress of sorts, holding in the warmth of the earth. I removed my boots and my coat, wriggling into the small tent. Brisbane had saved us one quilt to draw over ourselves, and I was astonished at how warm and cosy a bed he had made for us. He whistled to Rook, who came and lay across the opening of the tent as we settled inside.

"It is very nearly as comfortable as our bed at home," I told Brisbane sleepily.

He drew me close, pillowing my head upon his shoulder. I realised then that he had kept the feather pillow for himself. I did not mind. There are few finer cushions than the well-muscled shoulder of one's beloved, and I curled into his chest, falling deeply into sleep. It was not until later that I learned that Brisbane lay awake the whole of the night, one hand wrapped around my back, the other gripping a loaded revolver as he peered into the night.

The SIXTEENTH CHAPTER

Nature teaches beasts to know their friends.
—*Coriolanus*

I awoke early the next morning, cold and stiff as a corpse. The romance of a Gypsy bed palled swiftly, and it took several minutes before I managed to persuade all of my limbs to function properly. Brisbane had already bestirred himself and presented me with a steaming tin mug of bitter tea. I drank it down, grateful to cup my hands around the warmth of it.

"What is your plan?" I asked him. He looked every inch the Gypsy this morning, his black locks tumbled over his brow, his shirt open at the throat and the sleeves rolled back to reveal his strong forearms. It was a rather arresting picture, and it occurred to me—not for the first time—that if Brisbane had lived half a century earlier he might well have given Byron cause for jealousy.

Brisbane sipped at his tea. "There is a line of enquiry I wanted to pursue regarding Madame's past."

"When do we leave?" I demanded, my mind dashing

ahead to the question of how to make myself presentable for society with the limited means of ablutions at hand.

"We don't. The information I want might well be here in the camp."

"But I thought we were here for our safety."

He gave me a quick grin. "Two birds with a single stone. You said Agathe revealed to you that she and Madame worked in a travelling show on the Continent. Only later did it occur to me that world is a very small one."

"You mean, they were Gypsies? But your family work as hop pickers and horse traders. They are not circus folk."

"The fellow I have in mind is. He married my cousin and brought his bears with him."

"Bears! We slept in a camp with bears," I said slowly, trying to remember if I had heard any suspicious growls in the night.

"Tame bears," Brisbane assured me. "Ludo is a member of the *ursari*. They are a clan with special talents with the bears. They capture them as cubs, teach them to dance and do tricks. Ludo had a falling out with his brother and took his bears from the travelling show and came to London. He met my cousin and married her and the bears came, too. Come," he said, rising and taking my hand. "I will introduce you."

I insisted upon taking a few minutes to attend to my appearance. There was no call to be untidy even if were only going to meet bears, and as soon as I had sorted myself, we were on our way. Brisbane pointed sharply at Rook, and the dog sat with an air of resignation to await our return.

"The bears won't like him," Brisbane explained as we walked. The camp awoke slowly, I saw, for the campfires were just being stoked into life by yawning women and their husbands were emerging from tents, scratching their bellies and cuffing their children with affectionate smiles. The smell of woodsmoke and the contents of the cooking pots hung heavily in the air, and I heard the thin whine of a violin as an old man tuned his fiddle.

There was no sign of Granny Bones or Wee Geordie, but the others stared with frank curiosity as we passed, and one or two called a greeting to Brisbane. He replied with quick fluency, and very shortly we presented ourselves at the far edge of the camp at a brightly painted *vardo* parked some little distance from the others. Behind it were a pair of stout cages, and at the bottom of each was curled a small brown bear, sound asleep and snoring gently.

"Ludo says they must sleep apart from the rest of the camp because the bears like a bit of privacy," Brisbane told me as we approached. An aggressively bosomy woman with enormous hips stood at the fire, stirring a pot that hung over the flames. She looked up at Brisbane and froze. A long moment passed and then she dropped her spoon into the fire and fairly hurdled the pot to get to Brisbane. I would not have expected a woman so large could move so swiftly, but in the blink of an eye she had gathered him up into an embrace so ferocious I thought his spine would crack. She was chattering excitedly in Romany—at least I believed she was, for she was missing several teeth and the result was softly slurred vowels that might have belonged to any one of a dozen languages.

Brisbane patted her shoulder and she put him down, kissing him soundly on both cheeks, then slapping each one hard. Without waiting for a response, she hurried off, calling loudly to Ludo.

I raised a brow at Brisbane, who looked rather pale after the experience. "That is Lala, a very distant cousin."

"She seems very fond of you," I observed.

"Yes, well, Granny Bones tried to arrange a marriage between us when we were children."

I tipped my head to the side. "I cannot see it. To begin, she looks ten years your elder."

"Two," he corrected. "And that was her objection."

"Do you mean Lala refused you?"

He cleared his throat. "She did. I was ten and she was twelve. Lala thought I was too much of a child for her. Shortly after that, I ran away and the following year she married Ludo."

"At thirteen?" I barely suppressed a screech of surprise.

Brisbane shrugged. "It is not unusual for the people." It was a sign of their pride that the Roma referred to themselves as "the people." It was also a sign that Brisbane was slipping, at least partly, back into his early ways as a Rom.

"So your grandmother wanted you to marry at ten?"

"No, and that was Lala's problem. I would not have been permitted to marry until I was sixteen or seventeen. Lala did not want to wait for me."

"And so she threw you over? For a man who dances with bears?"

I could scarcely contain my mirth and Brisbane gave me a darkling look. "You are enjoying this a trifle too much."

"You say she was pretty as a girl?"

"Extremely." He bit off each syllable sharply. "But a lifetime of travelling and eleven children have a way of leaving their mark."

"Eleven children?"

Brisbane did not reply. He did not have to, for at that moment, the door of the *vardo* opened and the entire brood erupted, shouting and jumping and falling over one another to greet Brisbane. Their mother controlled them as best she could, which is to say not at all, and came to shake my hand, bearing in her arms her newest child, an infant of some two years, whose mouth and nose were in desperate need of washing.

She took my hand and pumped it as if she were hoping to strike water, all the while chattering swiftly in Romany. I understood none of it save the sentiment, which was "welcome." Just then, one of the little bears roused itself and began to make a fuss, and a small man emerged from the *vardo,* rubbing his eyes and buttoning his shirt. He only managed half the buttons and the rest hung open, revealing a chest almost as furry as one of his bears.

"Who comes and disturbs my bears?" he demanded in mock seriousness.

Brisbane extricated himself from most of the children— one still clung, limpetlike to his leg—and moved to embrace the man.

"Ludo!"

"Nicky!"

They exchanged greetings and eventually the child was pried from Brisbane's leg and the others were shooed away, except the one in Lala's arms. She beckoned us into the *vardo* and locked the door upon the rest of the children.

She turned to give me a smile. "My mother will give them breakfast," she assured me, and she waved me to take a seat at the small table.

The *vardo,* like most others of its kind, was as cleverly fitted as a ship, with everything neatly contained and the most made of every square inch. This one had a cunning little table with a board at either side to serve as benches. A wide bed stretched the back width of the caravan, and various other piles of bedding had been formed into pallets for the children. The smell of warm sleep and unwashed bodies still hung in the air, but it was comfortable enough, and I settled in to hear what Ludo could tell us.

"It is a long time," he said to Brisbane, who nodded slowly.

"The years have been good to you and Lala. You have been blessed with many fine children," Brisbane began, and I realised there was a formula to be followed, courtesies that must be observed. It was odd to think that a Gypsy camp might have protocol as strict as that of the royal court, but the proprieties must be observed and Brisbane spent half an hour asking after various relations and friends.

As the men talked—in English for my benefit—Lala bustled about her tiny home, making tea and feeding the youngest child, which she did with an air of complete casualness, thrusting the infant under her blouse without preamble. The child seemed lost for a moment and I worried it might smother, but it must have found what it wanted, for I heard a contented sigh and mother and child seemed to relax.

By then the conversation had turned to the matter at hand, and I made myself attentive.

"You know that to earn my living, I ask questions," Brisbane began.

"You solve problems for the *gorgios*," Ludo said proudly. He smiled broadly at me to show he meant no offence, and I returned the smile to assure him none had been taken.

"Yes," Brisbane said. "I solve problems. And the one I am solving now involves a medium called Madame Séraphine. She used to tell fortunes in a travelling show with her sister. Do you remember such a woman?"

Ludo stretched himself, scratching his chin as he thought. "A Frenchwoman?" Brisbane nodded and Ludo continued to think. He closed his eyes and sat very still, for so long I began to think he had fallen asleep. But just when I darted Brisbane a look to see if he ought to wake Ludo, the fellow opened his eyes and snapped his fingers. "In Bavaria. I spent a little time with a travelling show that had a fortune-teller, also a Frenchwoman. She made very little money as I recall. No one much liked her. But her sister—" He broke off to give a soundless whistle. "She was a beauty and free with it, she was."

I glanced at Lala, but she and the baby were still basking in a haze of contentment. If she minded hearing about her husband's youthful peccadilloes, she gave no sign of it.

"But her name was not Séraphine," Ludo continued. "She was called something else. I cannot think of it. I remember them well. The winter had been a hard one here, and I left Lala and the babies with her parents to make some money in the travelling show. The fortune-teller, she read the cards for me and told me my wife would be unfaithful to me whilst I was gone if I did not purchase her charm." He and Lala exchanged a look of mutual affection. "I told her to go to hell. Little did she know I had left Lala with another child starting, and she was sick as a calf!" He laughed up-roariously, slapping his knee and nudging Lala. She gave him an affectionate glance and he pulled her in for a re-sounding kiss.

When they pulled apart, Lala was pink with pleasure. "I have known women with the true gift of the sight," Ludo went on. "Your grandmother is the best I have ever known. This woman, she was a fraud. And the frauds have one trick only. They create fear and then ask you to pay them to get rid of it. It is a child's game, but a dangerous one."

"Did this medium ever get herself into trouble from it?" I put in quietly. Ludo canted his head and scratched himself lavishly.

"There was a bit of trouble with the local constabulary. She tried her little game with someone a bit too important and found herself in gaol for her trouble. The travelling show left without her. Pity, for the younger girl was a nice enough girl, but she stayed to help her sister. I think she would have preferred to go with us. But she was loyal and this is good. Family must be loyal," he added firmly.

"But you say her name was not Séraphine," Brisbane said, stirring his tea thoughtfully. He dropped his voice still lower, pitching it to a soothing register that was oddly calming. He stirred, his movements even and graceful, and I saw Ludo's eyes rest upon Brisbane's hand as it moved to trace the same circle with the spoon over and over again.

"I wonder if you would remember her name," Brisbane suggested softly. "You must think back to Bavaria, many years ago, when you were a young man. Lala is back in England with the babies, good strong babies that you miss. You miss Lala, too. You have only your bears to console you."

To my astonishment, tears began to well in Ludo's eyes, and one great, fat teardrop rolled down his cheek.

Brisbane never faltered. "It is cold in Bavaria, and the people are not always friendly. There is a girl, a French girl, and she is kind, but her sister is not. Her sister tells cruel fortunes for her own profit. She preys upon people, this sister, and you do not especially mind when she finds herself in trouble. Perhaps you say goodbye to the kindly French girl and tell her to be good. She wishes she could come away from this town with the cold people who have locked her sister away. But she must be loyal to her sister. She has a good heart, and she is loyal. She is loyal," Brisbane intoned again. "She is loyal to—"

"Agathe." The word dropped from Ludo's lips as easily as ripe apples will fall from the tree.

Brisbane stopped stirring his tea and smiled at Ludo. "I knew you would remember."

Ludo shook himself, as if shaking off a dream, and gave a broad smile. "I have a good memory, no?"

I nodded and smiled in return, feeling a shiver in spite of myself. It was not the first time I had witnessed Brisbane dabble in hypnosis, but it never failed to seem like some bit of sorcery to watch a subject slip unknowingly into a different place. We finished our tea and afterwards, Ludo introduced us to his bears, making them bow to me, which troubled me, for I did not like to see such beautiful wild creatures bent to the will of men. But I complimented him on the stoutness and handsomeness of his bears, and he seemed satisfied. Brisbane and I took our leave then, an undertaking of almost half an hour, for the children had returned and insisted upon being taken up in turn and kissed, and Lala pressed me to her immense bosom several times, calling me her sister.

I was exhausted and starving by the time we made our escape, but exhilarated.

"You realise what he said," I put to Brisbane as soon as we were out of earshot. "Agathe was the fortune-teller, not Madame Séraphine. Sometime after Bavaria, Madame must have adopted the role of medium and changed her name. What do you think it all means?"

Brisbane was walking quite quickly, his stride eating up the camp as I trotted beside him. "It means I have been a damnable fool," he said, his nostrils quite white at the tips. "I have never seriously considered Agathe as a possible culprit in her sister's death." He stopped and faced me, the wind on the heath tossing his hair and causing his shirt to billow like a sail. "Occam's razor—the simplest explanation is the likeliest. And yet I have ignored it from the beginning because I believed something far more dangerous was afoot. Can it really be so simple as sisterly jealousy?"

"You think Agathe might have arranged the root of the aconite to be served to her sister?"

"She might have put it in the kitchens herself," Brisbane said. "She was absent for some time during the séance, and God only knows what she did beforehand. She lodges in the Spirit Club. She would have the perfect opportunity to slip into the kitchens and introduce the root into the pile of horseradish." He swore and stalked off.

I trailed after him, thinking hard. It made sense, although I did not like the notion of a sister committing such an atrocity. My own sister Nerissa had often driven me to distraction, but I could no more imagine serving her poison than I could imagine walking on the moon. It was simply inconceivable, I told myself. Everything within me rebelled against it.

But as I walked, I considered it dispassionately. If Ludo's story was to be believed, Agathe had once been the shining star of their little duet. She had been the earner of their bread, although her talents sounded mediocre at best. Agathe had told me they were orphaned as youngsters. It had been her task to look after Séraphine. She had taken on the role of mother to her younger sister, protected her, provided for her.

And then something had happened to change that. Perhaps it was simply that Agathe was not suited to the work or perhaps it was the result of the arrest in Bavaria. Had it broken her spirit? Had Séraphine's star risen as Agathe's had set? Gaol was not a nice place. Ludo had not indicated how long Agathe had remained there, but even a few weeks might be enough to break a spirit that was not strong. It had happened to Brisbane's mother, I remembered. She had died imprisoned, regaining neither her spirit nor her freedom before her death. What if Agathe had been badly damaged by her experience? What was more natural than that the younger sister should move to the forefront, taking the lead in their affairs, reinventing herself as Madame? She had an affinity for the role, and Agathe did not. Did they settle easily into their new responsibilities? Or did Madame preen a little? Did she gloat over the sister she had supplanted? It would have been natural to do so. And it would have been natural that Agathe's resentment would grow, like a cancer, poisoning their relationship, until one day she could stand no more....

I shook off my reverie. A case could be made, but I still did not like it, and I hastened to tell Brisbane so.

"It is the likeliest explanation," he maintained, but he was clearly thinking the matter over. We said nothing further, for we had come to Granny Bones' caravan and she beckoned us with a smile. For the rest of the day, we stayed with her, chatting with the constant stream of family who came to pay their respects to Granny and her prodigal grandson. Once more I was put in mind of a royal court, for she gave the impression of granting audiences as the various relations came forward, sometimes singly, sometimes in groups, to murmur their greetings and stare openly at Brisbane and his *gorgio* wife. Some of them were thoroughly friendly, expressing themselves with wide smiles and words of welcome. Some were more restrained, offering the barest courtesies and taking their leave as soon as they could.

Even Rook paid his compliments, bringing me a gift which he dropped onto my lap with wide, unblinking eyes.

The little bundle of fur wriggled on my skirts and gave a tiny squeak.

"Rook, what the devil—" I broke off. "Good Lord, it's a dormouse!"

The tiny creature stared up at me with enormous black teardrop eyes, sooty against the pale gold of its fur. The whole of its little body trembled.

"Poor little thing, you're quite damp now," I observed with a repressive look at Rook. He had fairly drowned the poor fellow in his mouth, and I took out my handkerchief to dry it off.

Brisbane looked over my shoulder. "It seems sound enough. I don't think Rook did any real damage to him. Do you mean to make it a frock?" he asked, arching a brow as I wrapped the pitiful dormouse in my handkerchief.

"No, but it's had a terrible fright. Can you imagine how awful it must have been with those tremendous teeth coming down over him? It's a wonder he didn't die straight off from the horror of it."

"You do realise once you set him loose, one of the dogs will surely take him before he can make it home again?"

Brisbane nodded towards the pack of lurchers that skulked about the camp. The Roma used them for poaching, and indeed that would have been Rook's fate had he not been born pure white. No Rom would ever use a white lurcher for poaching, and so Brisbane had acquired the outcast dog; but from the little dormouse on my lap it was quite apparent that although his coat might be less than desirable, Rook lacked nothing in hunting skills.

"That's why I shall not set him loose," I said suddenly. "I shall keep him as a pet."

"Are you quite sure?" Brisbane asked. "Mice bite."

I put out a fingertip and the dormouse reached up and

touched it with a velvety paw, shaking hands as politely as a duchess.

"Quite."

Whilst Granny brewed tea, I asked Brisbane about the Roma who had been less than friendly as they paid their respects to the grandson of Granny Bones. By way of reply, he lit one of his favourite thin Spanish cigars and shrugged.

"I am not actually welcome here," he said simply.

"But we have spent the better part of the day being greeted by your family," I protested.

"Granny's family," he corrected. "They will do as Granny wishes and make the proper gestures. Some of them, like Ludo and Lala and Wee Geordie, will actually mean them. But the rest would just as soon see me hang."

"But why? You are one of them."

Brisbane's mouth turned upwards at the corners, but it was not a true smile. He took a deep draught of the pungent smoke. "I am half a Gypsy and half a Scot and neither side really wants to claim me. The Roma respect me a little because they think I spend my time solving the problems of silly *gorgios* and taking their money and because I am the son of Mariah Young. The rest of them—" He broke off and shrugged again.

"Was it really safe to come here then? If there are Roma who would betray you, perhaps we ought to go elsewhere."

"Betray me? Not in a thousand years," he swore. "I am still the grandson of Granny Bones and I am enough of a Rom that any man here would sooner die than give me up to an outsider. But within the camp—" he paused and his smile returned, a genuine one this time "—well, I always watch my back just to be sure."

"You do an injustice to your brothers," Granny scolded. She had returned with steaming mugs of wickedly strong tea and she folded herself into a sitting position on the steps of the *vardo,* as supple as a willow for all her years. She handed round the tea and took a deep draught of the stuff herself. As she did so, I realised my new charge had fallen asleep on my lap. I opened my bodice and tucked him inside, making a little nest of the handkerchief as Brisbane grinned at Granny Bones. "Surely you do not believe anyone here is going to slay the fatted calf for me."

"No one here would piss on you to put out the flames if you were on fire," Granny said flatly, "but there is not a body in this camp—man, woman or child—who would harm anything or anyone under my protection." She gave a decisive nod of the head to punctuate her declaration.

"True enough," Brisbane acknowledged.

"I am *shuvani,*" Granny told me. "You know this word?"

"I do. I had the pleasure of meeting Rosalie. She was very kind to me," I said, remembering the close relationship I had shared, albeit briefly, with Brisbane's youngest aunt.

Granny Bones gave a little snort. "Rosalie is a good girl, but she has no power. She brews her potions and crafts her love spells, but she does not work with the dark side."

"The dark side?" I was intrigued and a little frightened.

Granny tipped her head, giving me an appraising look with her bright black eyes. "If a *shuvani* is to be really powerful, she must learn to work with the dark as well as the light, little one. Granny Bones knows both sides of the coin."

"I can well imagine it," I told her.

She rose suddenly and put out her little monkey's paw of a hand. "Come, child. Granny will show you."

I flung Brisbane a questioning glance, but he merely sat, smoking his cigar as Granny drew me away.

"There is a child who is overlooked by the evil eye. I am

to cleanse him today. You would like to see this." It was not
a question, and Granny did not wait for a reply. She kept
hold of me and took me through the camp, calling orders
as she strode along. Women scurried in her wake, gathering
themselves and their children, and in a very few minutes
we were assembled at the edge of the pond. There were
no grown men, only women and children. A small boy of
perhaps two or three years was brought forward. He did
not stir from his mother's arms and his eyes were those of a
sleepwalker, vague and filmy. His mother looked to be no
more than seventeen, and she carried herself with painfully
erect posture and dry eyes, defiantly, but it was a brittle
sort of defiance, and I thought she might break from the
strain of it all. Another woman, the child's grandmother, I
expected, stood with the mother, her head bowed and her
eyes red from weeping.

Granny gave a series of orders which were instantly carried out. The child was divested of his clothing and made
to lie upon the ground. He made no sign of reluctance although the afternoon sun was weak and the breeze cool. It
ruffled the trees and raised gooseflesh on the boy, but he lay
still as a sacrifice.

Another woman came forward to bring Granny Bones
a vessel of water, and as I watched, a quantity of salt was
mixed in. Lala came to stand near me, murmuring expla-
nations.

"Salt is cleansing, as is moonlight. If the moon were full,
Granny would leave the water under the light of the moon
to purify it. White water is life-giving," she told me.

"Why?"

"Because it represents the fluid of the man when he
lies with his woman," she said with a thorough lack of
embarrassment.

I coughed so hard I began to choke and she struck me hard upon the back. I peeked in to look at my dormouse, but the blow had not disturbed him.

"Did you not know this?" Lala asked, her expression curious. "It is very good for the pores, as well, to make a woman's complexion beautiful."

"I beg your pardon?"

She began to mime the process then, and I touched her hands. "I think I understand now. Thank you."

She peered at my face. "Your complexion is very good, but you must make use of Nicky if it is ever a problem," she advised. "His would be good."

"Oh," was all the conversation I could manage for the moment.

"Because he is handsome," she said, speaking as if to a rather backwards child. "You would not want the stuff of an ugly man," she said, elbowing me with a meaningful nod.

"Of course not," I agreed.

Thankfully, at that moment, the preparations had concluded and Granny began the ritual. She walked clockwise around the boy, reciting an incantation, and each time she came to the head, she took a deep draught of the salted water and spewed it out in a fine spray over the child's naked body. Seven times she did this, each time louder and more vehement, until at last, on the seventh she lifted her arms and gave a great shout and the boy sat up with a gasp, his eyes wide. He was entirely himself then, for he looked at his mother and raised his arms and cried out.

Immediately, the women began to celebrate, falling upon the young mother, whose tears fell freely now. She scooped up her boy, wrapping him in a shawl and embracing him as the women praised Granny for removing the evil eye. There was much laughter and tears, and Granny instructed them to feed the child and watch him carefully.

The crowd dispersed then, and Granny Bones took my arm to return to her *vardo*. She was walking more slowly now, and I wondered what the ritual had taken from her that she seemed suddenly older.

"It requires great effort and energy to cast off the evil eye," she said before I could ask. "I am not so young anymore."

"It was remarkable," I told her truthfully.

"The old ways are the best. *Gorgios* forget that. They like their science and their fancy new machines and their engines and their houses. But we were not meant to live so far from the mother," she said, striking the earth with her heel. A little bit of the soil came up around her foot and she bent to take a small piece into her mouth. "Honest soil, the flesh of the mother. And we desecrate her when we forget."

We walked a moment in silence and to my astonishment, I felt a tremendous calm steal over me. I turned and saw Granny's lips moving soundlessly.

"Granny," I said sharply. "What are you doing?"

She made me wait until she came to the end of her recitation, then shrugged. "A little protection for you both. That is all."

"And you were not going to tell me?"

She paused and turned to me, putting both hands to my face. "You make him as happy as any woman could. I wanted a Roma wife for him, so his babies would be Roma and I could hold them upon my knee and sing them the old cradlesongs. But it was not to be, and I know better than to argue with the wind. It only makes you hoarse and the wind doesn't care," she said. "But he wants you and you must be kept safe if he is to be happy."

"Thank you," I told her, very moved by her words.

She dropped her hands and shrugged. "No matter. But if you ever make him unhappy, there is no corner of the earth far enough for you to hide from me."

Her eyes bored into me and it was quite like staring down a hawk. I had no doubt she would curse my very bones if I disappointed her, and in that moment, I was more than a little afraid of her.

"I shall remember it," I promised her.

"See that you do."

We walked on, saying nothing for a moment, and it was companionable, the silence that lay between us. But I felt compelled to confide in her, and we were still some distance from her *vardo* when I spoke.

"I worry for him," I said in such a low, small voice I was startled when she made me a reply.

"He was an old man even in his cradle," she said. "He knew what he wanted and he meant to have it. He has always been so."

I nodded. "I understand what you mean. It's that determination in him that frightens me sometimes. He will not accept himself for what he is, and the means he takes to forget..."

I broke off, remembering things I would happily have banished from my memory forever. Brisbane, crouching like a wounded animal, shielding his eyes from the light and the pain of the headaches that tormented him.

"I know he does not want the visions, but I wonder if the alternatives are worse," I burst out. "The things he doses himself with, the absinthe and the hashish and the opium."

She looked at me sharply. "He touches opium? Keep him away from it. He has had troubles with it in the past."

I hastened to reassure her. "He does not use it now, but

I know he has in the past, and I know it was not good for him." I did not mention the hypocrisy of my joining him in an occasional languid smoke from the hookah pipe.

Granny Bones was watching me out of the tail of her eye, her attention seemingly fixed upon a little bird pecking at thistle seeds upon the ground.

"Hey, nonny, little bird, peck, peck, peck," she said softly.

I pursed my lips in impatience. Granny had been sharp as a new pin for the whole of our visit until I had need of her advice.

"Be calm," she said soothingly, and I realised she was not talking to the bird.

"How am I supposed to be calm? I worry," I retorted.

She gave a snort. "Then you are more stupid than I supposed. Worry, what is that? A pointless thing is Master Worry—an intruder. He steals into your house and creeps into your bed and what do you do, child? Do you push him away and tell him to be gone and bolt the door fast against him? No, you move over and let him have the good pillow and the best quilt to warm himself." She flapped a hand in disgust. "Worry never did a man a bit of good. All he does is rob one's peace and make lines on the face." She peered at my skin then, scrutinising the corners of my eyes. "Myrrh. Throw a handful onto the fire and bathe your face in the vapours. It will soften those wrinkles."

"I do not have wrinkles."

She laughed—a rusty, wheezing sound—and slapped me soundly upon the back. "And now you worry again. Don't. It is bad for the digestion, too."

We walked on and I tried once more to make her understand my troubles. "Telling someone not to worry is a rather specious bit of advice, don't you think?"

She shrugged. "You are not Roma. I give good advice to Roma. You are a *gorgio*. I do not understand your ways."

"But I am asking about Brisbane, and he is a Rom," I pointed out triumphantly.

Granny paused again, crossing her arms over her low breasts and giving me a sigh. "You want an answer to a man who is not a problem to be solved. He is no equation of mathematics, child. He is a man and a complicated one. I will give you a willow-bark tonic that will help with the headaches, but besides this, there is nothing I can do. He chases shadows. He is haunted by what he cannot see, ghosts that are as fleeting as moonlight or smoke. There is nothing to be done for him unless he wishes it," she added, and as she finished, she set her jaw in a way that I had seen Brisbane do only too often. It meant finality, and I knew better than to press the issue further.

"Very well," I murmured.

Granny peered at me. "And don't sulk. It, too, is bad for the complexion. Remind me to give you a tonic."

The
SEVENTEENTH CHAPTER

I never heard so musical a discord, such sweet thunder.
—A Midsummer Night's Dream

There was a feast that night, a celebration of sorts for the child recalled to his senses, and much merriment ensued. Flasks of pear brandy were passed from hand to hand, and although I was offered mine in a cup—for my *gorgio* blood was unclean to them and would taint the shared bottle—it was kept full. There were stories told in a tongue I did not speak, but Brisbane murmured interpretations to me. There was dancing and music, violins scraping as skirts flew and feet stamped. Even the dancing bears came out, for Ludo brought them on gilded leather leashes, wearing their scarlet waistcoats and stepping as neatly as opera dancers at his commands. I longed to photograph them, and I was bitterly disappointed that I had come away without my camera. I wanted to capture them all, and I promised myself I would return as soon as possible to take photographs. In the meanwhile, I ate plateful after plateful of delicious things and drank a quantity of very good wine, which I suspected had been pilfered from a rather excellent cellar, and if anyone noticed that I occasionally passed little titbits inside my blouse they were polite enough not to remark upon it. The dormouse took each offering daintily as a princess, wiping each whisker carefully afterwards and blinking those wide black eyes as it stared up at me. Rook sulked a little until I found him another great bone to gnaw upon, and then he settled down happily. At one point, I noticed Brisbane was absent, but it was not out of the ordinary for the men to form groups of their own to gossip and tell stories, so I dismissed the thought and accepted another cup of pear brandy.

After I had eaten, Lala pressed her youngest child upon me, and the infant sat in my lap, clapping its sticky hands until I passed it along to someone else. But the precedent had been set, and from that moment on, I was seldom without a child in my lap or at my feet, particularly the girls, who seemed vastly interested in my pale skin and green eyes. The older girls scrutinised my clothes, which they considered hopelessly drab and dull, and pitied me my jewels. I had come away with few, only my wedding ring and the silver Medusa pendant that I accounted more precious than any of the emeralds and diamonds in my collection. But it was an unworthy thing to these girls, accustomed as they were to the warm seduction of gold. I was a curiosity to them, for although they often moved amongst the English for purposes of commerce, they had seldom if ever held a lengthy conversation with one. They had heard I was rich and that my father had a title, but they had expected better of me, I realised. They wanted pearls and satin and a great carriage with horses trimmed in plumes. Instead, I wore a tweed country suit and had arrived on foot with a carpetbag. I was a sore disappointment, I think, but they asked many questions and I was happy to answer them. They were particularly interested in the plumbing arrangements at our house, and turned shocked faces when I described the water closet.

"But it is unclean!" they cried, horrified at the notion of attending to nature in any proximity to where one slept, and if there was one thing I learned from my time amongst the Roma, it was how devotedly hygienic they were. There was a scrupulous system dictating where one washed, where one retrieved cooking water, where one's horses drank. They did not permit their horses to take water from the municipal troughs, for they found them dirty and stagnant, and their beasts were given only the same fresh running water that they themselves drank, although from farther downstream. For all their reputation for filth, they were cleaner and tidier than many aristocrats I have known, and I wondered briefly if that was where Brisbane had acquired his fastidious bent along with his musical talents.

"Penny for your thoughts," he murmured into my ear at one point in the evening.

"I was wishing you would play tonight," I told him. "It is seldom that you pick up your violin anymore."

Those witch-black eyes stared into mine, and he lifted my hand. Without taking his gaze from my face, he pressed a kiss to the palm, smiling a little at my sharp intake of breath.

"Brisbane," I murmured.

"I am yours to command," he said, dropping my hand and striding easily to where one of his cousins was tuning a violin. Brisbane said something to him, and his cousin surrendered the instrument with a smile and a slap to his back. Brisbane ran his hands over the silken curves of the wood, his brow furrowed as he applied his deft touch to every inch of the instrument. He plucked a string, sounding a note as plaintive as a sob, and then he picked up the bow. A hush fell over the crowd, and I saw the smiles of anticipation.

He waited a moment more, heightening the longing of every soul who waited, winding the tension higher and hotter until at last he touched the bow to the string. The first note was a cry of yearning. He conjured the voice of the violin, and it was as fluent as any human voice. It spoke, it sobbed, it wailed in anguish. And then, when it seemed as if no further agony could be wrung from it, the voice began to change subtly. At first it was the merest note slipping sinuously between the lamentations. But soon the notes came faster and closer together, strung together like pearls on a thread, each one round and ripe and luminous. He kept his eyes closed as he played, his fingers moving in a fashion I knew only too well. The melody was a seductive one, calling forth desires for dark pleasures and unshriven sins. The shadows hid my blushes, but I was deeply aware of the trembling that had taken hold of me.

Brisbane played on, tormenting me deliciously with the demands of that voice. It seemed to come from everywhere, surrounding me, whispering in my blood as the music flew on the night air. It was as if he meant to play for the moon itself and the stars bent near to listen. My lips parted and my thighs shook, and I was not surprised to see a few of the men take their womenfolk by the hand and disappear into the shadows. One or two of the girls rose and began to dance, stamping and clapping, and in the midst of it stood Brisbane, playing with such complete abandon he seemed not to see them at all.

Suddenly, the feverish melody seemed to scream its ecstasy, ending in a long, profound wail of satisfaction, the note spinning out until Brisbane could sustain it no further. He dropped the bow and the crowd erupted in cheers, passing him a bottle of pear brandy and calling for an encore. He played another piece then, this one a simple, beautiful bit of melody that conjured tranquillity with a touch of melancholy. It was a wistful lullaby from antiquity, haunting and unforgettable, but gently so. I was glad of the respite, and I fanned my heated cheeks as Lala leaned near.

"We have a saying, you know. When a musician plays like that, it's because the Devil is in him."

Her manner was arch and sly, and I suspected she knew precisely how affected I had been by Brisbane's music.

"Then I have nothing to fear," I said lightly. "Everyone knows the Devil takes care of his own."

It was some time before Brisbane was permitted to put the violin aside, and I had sufficiently recovered my composure when he rejoined me.

"So, wife," he said, "how like you the Gypsy life?"

"I find it astonishingly relaxing," I told him truthfully. "What simplicity! No house to worry over, no vast wardrobe to keep. No investments or property or staff to manage." I threw out my arms, growing expansive. "Only the sky and the stars and the earth itself."

Brisbane plucked the cup from my hand. "That is quite enough brandy for you."

"I mean it," I told him. "It is entirely unfettered."

"And wholly unstable," he added. "You have succumbed to the lure of Gypsy romance. Understandable," he hastened to add. "Most folk do if they spend a few days with them. But it is barely autumn now. Imagine this life when it grows cold, when the snow is so thick upon the ground you can find nothing to eat and the ice must be broken before the horses can drink. Or when it is high summer and the grass is burnt dry and there is no respite from the searing sun."

"Well, that does not sound very nice," I admitted.

"Or when there is only enough food for half the tribe and you have to fight with your own cousins to see who gets to eat that day," he went on, his eyes deeply shadowed. "When you have outgrown your only coat and you have to steal a newspaper to put inside your shirt to keep the cold out. When you pick a pocket and your mother whips you because your fingers were clumsy."

His voice had taken on a faraway quality, and I said nothing as he went on, half to himself. "Or the men come, *gorgio* men, with dogs and torches, turning out the *vardos* and throwing your only food upon the fire because the law will let them, and their children spit on you and call you names while their mothers smile. That is what it is to be a Gypsy," he finished.

"Sometimes I am very stupid," I said, my hand stealing into his. He lifted it, suddenly, pressing a hard kiss to the palm.

"Never stupid. You simply find the best in everything. I cannot comprehend how to do that," he added, shaking his head in wonder. "It is enough to be near it."

I turned my head, deeply moved by what he said, and gave a hard sniff. I turned back after a moment. "Yes, well, thinking the best of people is not going to solve Madame's murder or find our blackmailer," I reminded him.

He gave me a nudge. "Come, back to the tent. It is time to talk."

We slipped away to our tent and Brisbane dropped the flap, cocooning us into our own little world. It was cosy, and I rather liked it, but Brisbane had nothing but business upon his mind. He moved the bedding aside to reveal a patch of dirt and began to scratch it with his penknife.

"We have two points of enquiry in this investigation. First," he said, drawing a slash with the blade, "is the blackmailer's money. I brought five thousand pounds with me to Highgate, and yet there was no opportunity to leave it. The blackmailer was content to draw me out and equally content to leave without his purported goal—money. Why?"

"Because he had a greater purpose," I returned promptly.

"So it would seem. But why was the opportunity to attack you worth more than five thousand pounds?" He fell silent, musing a moment. "It tells us one thing," he said finally. "That he has no accomplice in whom he can place his trust. If he had, one of them could have collected the money whilst the other set the fire. He must be acting alone."

He made a second mark in the dirt. "The second point is Monk's enquiries into the finances of the guests of the Spirit Club. If they are in difficulty, it would prove a motive to blackmail."

"But not if the funds were never collected," I said, taking the blade to scratch a question mark next to his slash.

"And why attempt to break into the house when they believed you to be there? It would have made far more sense to do it when they knew both of us to be out."

He took the knife back and traced the outline of the ground floor of our house. Apart from the silver, all of our real valuables were kept upstairs, either in my dressing room or his. There was no profit to be had in setting fire to the house, only damage.

"I cannot see it," he muttered. "Why can I not see it?"

He closed his eyes. He remained quiet a long moment, then suddenly opened his eyes and hurled the knife towards the ground where the taut blade stuck fast, the handle quivering slightly.

"I cannot see it," he said again, his voice tight with frustration. "It must be revenge or manipulation. Either the blackmailer cares more about destroying Bellmont and you than money, or he wanted to ensure that I would stay to play his game by involving you. There is no other explanation."

"And no way to know which at present," I soothed. I took the knife again and made a fresh mark in the earth. "But there is another point I realised after our discussion with Ludo today. He said Agathe was a fraud as a medium, that she knew clever tricks, but nothing more. Yet when I left her, she mentioned my mother."

Brisbane's brows rose. "The Countess March?"

"She mentioned her by name, Charlotte. And she spoke of her perfume. Agathe knew who she was."

Brisbane gave a smothered roar of frustration. "Did you not think it might be significant to mention this to me at some point?"

"I just did," I pointed out.

He thrust his hands through his hair. "Julia, if she knew who your mother was, she knew who you were. That means she had to have made enquiries into your past *before you came.*"

I stared at him, suddenly quite cold. "That is not possible. She could not have guessed my identity. I was very careful."

"Did you sign the guestbook?" he demanded.

I pulled a face. "Of course not! At least not in my own name. I used an alias. Honestly, Brisbane, how stupid do you think me?"

He ignored the question. "Did you give her your hat?"

"Naturally. It is impolite for a gentleman to keep his hat once inside."

He said nothing, but merely waited for me to reach the proper conclusion myself. I gave a groan. "Oh, God, that is how she does it! Every gentleman must give up something—a hat, a coat, gloves, a walking stick. She takes them and examines them for clues, for information to pass to Madame to use in the séance. And the label in my hat says J. Brisbane," I related miserably.

"And she would have seen the label in your hat and noted it for the future."

"But why go to the trouble of investigating me?"

"The others she likely already knew. They were either clients Madame had seen before or they made appointments in advance to give Agathe time to learn as much as she could about them and relate those facts to Madame."

"But I was unknown," I mused. "An unknown who had given her a false name. That must have piqued her curiosity. From there, she would have noted the connection between my real surname and Bellmont. But wait—" I broke off, puzzling it over. "Would she have connected the Comte de Roselende with Lord Bellmont's *sister?*"

Brisbane mused a moment. "She would have at least noted the coincidence. And she would have been entirely prepared for your next visit in either guise. She would have spent hours researching your history, memorising just enough detail to be artfully dropped into conversation to persuade you of her talents. It is a classic medium's trick and vastly easier when one's clientele comes from a particular class whose movements are chronicled in the daily newspapers and society columns," he observed.

"Any lending library could provide her with the information, and no one would notice the nondescript Frenchwoman whiling away her time, nor would they connect her with Madame. A perfect system," I remarked.

"Perhaps too perfect," he said. He reached into his pocket and retrieved a newspaper clipping, which he passed to me. "I slipped away this evening to meet with Monk. He brought that."

I pursed my lips at the notion that he had gone to meet Monk without me, but even as my eyes dropped to the print, the words died stillborn on my tongue. The clipping was from the *Times* and reported the facts in stark detail. I thrust it back at him.

"Oh, God," I murmured. "I do not want to read it."

But I did. Brisbane passed it back wordlessly and I forced myself to read the facts dispassionately. And the facts were these—that a woman had been killed at Victoria Station by falling onto the tracks just as a train was pulling in. No one saw her fall. No one knew if she had simply lost her balance or thrown herself onto the tracks. She had been killed instantly, and papers on her person confirmed her identity as Agathe LeBrun, a practising medium currently holding sessions at the Spirit Club.

Agathe was dead. No matter how many times I repeated the words, I could not make sense of them. I had liked her far too well for the murderer of her own sister to have expected this.

"Why was she killed?"

"Because she knew something she oughtn't," Brisbane supplied.

Together, we talked the matter through, examining it closely from every angle. "She was privy to her sister's affairs," I recollected. "She knew her secrets."

"And they were partners in their profession," Brisbane put

in. "Madame could not have perpetrated her frauds without assistance."

"So that makes Agathe a valuable source of information, both about Madame and her clients," I continued. "She knew who came to see Madame and why. She discovered information that could be used against them." I hesitated, then lifted my eyes to Brisbane. "Do you think she knew about Bellmont?"

He paid me the compliment of honesty. "I think it possible."

"And do you think she was the blackmailer?"

"To what purpose? I could understand it if she took the money, but Bellmont's blackmailer did not. If the five thousand had been taken, I would have sworn to you that not only was Agathe culpable of blackmail, but that she was killed by one of her victims. But without the money, there is no motive."

I had felt the noose tightening about my brother's throat, and I gave a little lurch of relief. "So, all we can say with certainty is that Agathe knew too much. Knowledge is power. Agathe must have overplayed her hand and made the murderer nervous."

Brisbane stroked his jaw. It was heavily shadowed and I knew he missed his evening ablutions. It made him look even more the part of a Gypsy, and I found it rather dangerously attractive.

"It is no good," he told me. "We do not know if the murderer and blackmailer are one and the same. Until we determine that, we are wandering in the dark."

I turned that over in my mind. "Madame's murderer might have killed for one purpose—to remove Madame. That is all. Once his object was achieved, he might have disappeared.

The information left behind, the letters, Agathe's observations, those may be the root of the blackmailer's crime. But in that case, the blackmailer must be Agathe or a close associate. Or—" I sat forward, excitement rising. "Or, Agathe might have been blackmailing the murderer."

"Because she saw something she ought not and did not tell the police."

"Precisely! I was wrong. Agathe did not kill Madame, but she knew something about the person who did. She did not tell the police because she hoped to use the information to her advantage."

"Exposing one's knowledge to a murderer is a dangerous game," Brisbane reflected.

"But there was something rather clever about Agathe," I reminded him. "Doubtless she thought she could achieve her aim."

"Which was?"

"Money, of course. Isn't that always the aim of blackmail?" But of course, it was not. Hadn't Bellmont's blackmailer left the money untouched in his quest to course for bigger game? Too late, I saw the flaw in my hypothesis. "Oh. There would have to be two blackmailers! Agathe and Bellmont's, for—if as you say—money was her aim, she would not have left the five thousand uncollected."

"And we already decided that Bellmont's blackmailer had no accomplice, else he would have seen to it the money was retrieved whilst the fire was set," Brisbane put in.

"Damnation," I muttered. I had quite liked that theory. We fell silent again, and I nibbled at my lip as I thought. "Perhaps they were partners who did not trust one another," I said slowly.

Brisbane flicked me a glance and retrieved his cigar case.

He extracted another of his thin Spanish cigars and lit it, exhaling a narrow stream of fragrant, seductive smoke. "Go on."

"Imagine this. Agathe and Madame embark upon their professional partnership which requires Agathe to acquire knowledge, dangerous knowledge. Together they use this knowledge to pry money out of clients, either with promises of greater contact with the other side of the spirit world or with direct threats to expose their findings. One of the clients does not take kindly to this and manages to arrange for a delivery of aconite root to the kitchen of the Spirit Club." I paused and frowned. "You know, that in itself is quite telling, is it not? To poison all of the horseradish of the club was a reckless act. Either the murderer was quite certain only Madame would eat it, or he did not care how many died so long as Madame was dead."

"It would likely have suited his purposes if more than Madame died," Brisbane advised. "If half a dozen people were dead, it would make the intended victim almost impossible to identify with certainty."

"Oh, that is clever! And monstrous," I added. "Where was I?"

"Horseradish," he supplied, puffing out another stream of smoke.

"Yes, Madame eats it and dies. Agathe is left with a great deal of information that could be very valuable. But she is unaccustomed to working alone. She requires a partner. She confides then, in a friend, or perhaps even a lover. And she removes documents from Madame's possession that will aid her in her plans. She gives them to her new partner for safekeeping, but there is later a falling out. They quarrel, over how to proceed or money or any one of a hundred reasons, and they each choose a separate path. Agathe can unmask her sister's killer to the authorities or she can use the knowledge to fatten her purse. She goes to the murderer with a demand for money. He arranges to meet her at the train station. Maybe he says to her that he is leaving London altogether and it is her only chance to get the money. She is not a hardened criminal, but she is an opportunist," I went on, warming to my theme. "She agrees, and he pushes her onto the tracks, ending the threat to himself."

I sat back with an air of triumph. Brisbane gave me a slow-lidded stare.

"Then who blackmailed Bellmont?"

I thought for a moment. "Her partner. He had Bellmont's letters in his possession for safekeeping and realised he could make a fortune from them."

"Then why not actually take the money? And why set fire to our house?"

I nibbled at my lip again. "It was a warning. Agathe knows who we are. She would have told her partner. The relationship between you and Bellmont means that you would certainly work on his behalf to sleuth out the blackmailer. So you must be discouraged from participating in the case. You must believe I am in danger. And when you are busy attending to your wife, the blackmailer will strike Bellmont again."

The cigar fell from his mouth, scattering ash and sparks. Brisbane retrieved it with a smothered curse and fixed me with a smile that was very nearly accusing.

"That is a damned fine piece of logic," he said, almost grudgingly.

"Thank you." I smiled sweetly at him. "Your trousers are on fire."

He looked down and swatted idly at the lazy plume of smoke upon his thigh.

"Do not tell me you failed to think of it," I said once the fire was out.

He gave me a nasty look. "Of course I did. I sent word to Bellmont to reply to no further demands until he heard from me."

I felt a little deflated then. "Oh. Then why were you so astonished to hear my theory?"

"Because it was the same as mine," he explained. "All this time, you have stumbled into murderers and bumbled into solutions, and I thought it was an accident."

"I ought to be tremendously offended by that, but you are right. Most of my solutions were somewhat accidental."

"No, they were not," he maintained. "They were not the product of analytical reasoning, at least not that you realised. But you took in the information and created a working hypothesis and followed it through, the same as I do. Only the method is at a variance between us. I knew you were clever," he finished. "I just did not realise that you do have a methodology. It is entirely unique, but you have one."

I preened a little. "I will go even further and say that I think Madame's murderer will have wanted to be on hand when the murder was committed. I think it must have been one of the guests at the séance."

"I hardly think that General Fortescue or Sir Henry Eddington fit the bill."

I turned the notion over in my mind and was forced to agree. "No," I said slowly, "and I don't suppose Sir Morgan is a likely candidate, either. He has pots of money."

Brisbane went dangerously still. "Sir Morgan?"

"Hmm? Oh, yes. Sir Morgan Fielding. He was the last of my calls the day I visited the general and Sir Henry."

"Why?"

I wrinkled my nose, thinking. "I suppose I went there last because his address was the farthest from home."

Brisbane's voice was tight, as if he held a close rein upon his temper, but only just. "I mean, why did you call upon him at all?"

"Because he was there the night of the séance. But you knew that," I said rather unhelpfully.

"I did not. From my vantage point in the spirit cabinet, I could see only you and Madame and our American friend, Sullivan. I think you might have mentioned at least once that you had called upon Morgan Fielding in the course of your investigations." The last word was delivered with tight-lipped fury, and I adopted a soothing tone.

"Brisbane, really, you needn't fuss. I know he's a terrible flirt, but I was in no danger whatsoever. In fact, I discovered that we are cousins. As it happens, he is one of my Uncle Benvolio's by-blows. There is a family resemblance, I thought. He looks a bit like Plum."

Brisbane's jaw was clenched so tightly, I could hear the bones grinding. "I have no concerns about your fidelity, Julia. I have grave concerns about your intelligence."

"I do beg your pardon!" I sat upright and the dormouse, still nestled in my bosom, gave a little squeak of protest. "You just complimented me upon that very faculty."

"I withdraw it. You embarked upon a line of enquiry you insisted was essential without ever once giving me the name of the one person who is doubtless at the centre of the whole damn affair!"

I matched his heated tone with one of pure ice. "I believe I did attempt to relate to you the facts of my calls and you interrupted me with a rather magnificent display of temper, much as you are doing now. If you do not have all the facts of the case, perhaps you have no one but yourself to blame."

Brisbane opened his mouth and shut it with a snap. His mouth remained closed, but I could hear him muttering under his breath.

"What are you saying?"

"I am counting. To one hundred. In Cantonese."

That took the better part of five minutes, but once he was finished, he had a better grasp of his temper and we were able to discuss the matter more cordially.

"Perhaps, my dear," he began with exaggerated *politesse,* "you would be good enough to relate to me the details of your call upon Sir Morgan."

"I would be very happy to," I replied with equal civility. Hastily, I sketched the pleasant hour I had spent with Morgan, and Brisbane's expression grew blacker the longer I talked. But I omitted nothing, and when I was finished, Brisbane eyed me narrowly.

"Is that the whole of it?"

I sighed. "Really, you are the most exasperating man. Haven't I just told you everything? Now it is your turn. Tell me precisely why Morgan Fielding holds such interest for you."

Brisbane lit another cigar, taking several deep inhalations of the heady smoke before beginning his tale.

"To understand Morgan, you must know the history of the Spirit Club itself. At the height of the Regency, the Spirit Club was built as a brothel by one of the most notorious madams in London. It was unlike anything ever built before, and it was designed to cater to the most decadent fantasies of the most exclusive clientele. In particular, it was created as a haven for gentlemen whose tastes ran to watching rather than doing."

I blinked. "I beg your pardon?"

He slanted me a look full of meaning. "There is a certain species of gentleman who prefers to watch the goings-on rather than participate."

"Good heavens, why?"

Brisbane flicked me a smile and continued. "There were accommodations made for all sorts of tastes, but this particular one suited the madam, as well, for the various peeps and trapdoors installed in the house for her clients' pleasure also ensured she could keep a watchful eye upon her ladies. The house was extremely successful, and the proprietress took that success as a motivation to build another house. Only, this time she borrowed, heavily, and overextended her credit. She was forced to sell both houses, and after that, the original house passed through many hands and many incarnations before falling empty. It had been a brothel, a gaming hell and even a school at one point. But in the end, all of the ventures failed and it closed its doors until 1870."

"What happened in 1870?"

"Cast your mind back to Continental affairs at the time."

I furrowed my brow, and a sudden image of the Empress Eugénie sprang to mind. "The fall of Napoléon III?"

"Precisely. So long as Napoléon III was in power, there was an effective counter to Bismarck's rise in Prussia. But when the emperor was daft enough to start a war no one wanted and got himself thrown out of France, suddenly the entire Continent was no longer stable—an untenable state of affairs for any of us."

"What does Continental politics have to do with a club for Spiritualists?" The connection eluded me.

"Because the Spiritualist trappings of the club were only so much window dressing. It was formed as a sort of hive of espionage."

"Espionage!"

"The house was purchased by the British government in order to provide a place for coded messages to pass between English and French agents, a sort of cooperative effort against the Prussians."

I could scarcely take in what Brisbane was telling me, it all seemed so fantastical.

"Why a central point for their meetings? Would not a series of clandestine arrangements work better?"

"Yes, and that's why the club eventually fell into disuse. For a time, it was convenient. There were so many agents in England and France and no one knew what anyone else was doing. Spymasters have a passion for secrecy and obfuscation, even when it serves no purpose," he added with a wry twist of his lips. "The crux of effective espionage is that no one *can* know what anyone else is doing. This sort of front made things infinitely more complicated, which suited the spymasters whilst matters on the Continent were sorted. It was actually rather effective for a short while. The spymaster would give coded information to the medium who would pass it along to the operative at the next session. Because there were so many regulars, the mediums never knew to whom they were actually giving the message and neither did anyone else."

"If they did not know to whom to address the message, how did they pass it along?"

"Because the messages from the spymaster always began with a specific phrase. 'A message from a dark lady.'"

I sat bolt upright. "Brisbane! That is the message Madame delivered at our session!"

He swore softly. "If I had heard that at the time, it would have made this all a damned sight easier."

"Madame must have been involved in espionage," I said, catching my breath. It was almost painfully exciting.

"Except that the Spirit Club has not been used for that purpose in a dozen years," Brisbane told me gently. "It was a mad idea in the first place. Gathering all of those spies in one place seemed like a sound notion as it meant the English could keep an eye on their Continental opposites. In practise, it was utter chaos, and its best use was in keeping aristocratic dilettantes from doing any real mischief. Society gentlemen could play at being spies and feel they were doing their part without ever having access to the most important information. They were useful at best, but too often they bungled—and badly. They were always finding themselves embroiled in one fiasco or another. It took endless sorting out and finally, the whole thing got to be so much trouble, the government just packed it in and went back to the old ways."

"How do you know so much about the Spirit Club?"

Brisbane ground out the glowing tip of his cigar onto the sole of his boot. "Because just at the start of my career I had to sort out a very thorny problem that almost got me killed by an unhappy English spymaster. A terrified and very elderly widow hired me to protect her as she attended séances because she was quite certain she was being followed every time she left the club and she feared for her life."

"Was she being followed?"

"Yes," he answered in some disgust, "by a cotton-headed fool who thought she might be in Bismarck's pay. He did not take kindly to my interference, and I ended up the subject of a rather vigorous interrogation in the basement of the club."

"Oh, dear," I murmured.

"Not one of my happier memories," he reflected, rubbing at his chin.

I sat for a long moment, digesting all he had told me.

"What became of the club after the government disbanded it?"

He shrugged. "It became an actual haven for Spiritualists. There has been no reason to connect it with anything more—until now. There is one man in England who would know if the Spirit Club is once more being used as a rendezvous for spies," he said slowly.

"Sir Morgan Fielding?"

"Morgan was the spymaster who interrogated me in the basement of the Spirit Club."

I groaned and put my hands over my face. "And I interrogated him."

"I daresay Morgan found it all highly amusing," Brisbane told me. "And I will further wager that he deliberately charmed you and told you precisely as much as he wanted you to know and nothing more to set you haring off in the wrong direction."

I peeped through my hands. "You think that he made up the tale about us being related in order to get into my good graces? You think that Morgan may not be my uncle Benvolio's bastard?"

Brisbane's lips thinned into a bitter smile. "That Morgan Fielding is a bastard, I have absolutely no doubt."

"I still do not understand the need for all the theatrics. Surely Special Branch is up to the task of monitoring such activities."

Special Branch had been formed at Scotland Yard some six years previously to keep a watchful eye upon Irish agitators, but it soon became apparent that every corner of such a far-flung empire ought to be observed and their duties had been expanded.

Brisbane sighed. "Special Branch are overworked and undermanned. They are too new to be of any real use yet, although God hopes they will be someday. The truth is every bit of this ought to be taken out of amateur hands and left to the professionals. But there are those, the queen among them, who believe that the inherent superiority of the gentleman gives him a unique ability to serve his country in any capacity. Too often they are inbred idiots who merely muck up the field, and the professionals like Morgan have to clear up after them."

"I would have expected Sir Morgan to fall into the class of gentleman-dilettante," I argued.

Brisbane rolled back a sleeve, revealing a whip-thin scar that snaked from his wrist to his elbow, curving up the length of his arm like a serpent. I had often traced it with a delicate fingertip, but I had never asked him where he had acquired it.

"Morgan Fielding is no amateur," was all that he said. He rolled the sleeve back into place.

"I hope you returned the favour."

Brisbane gave me a slow, chilling smile. "I did."

I considered this and came to the conclusion that the less said upon the subject, the better. In fact, I had an entirely different matter of conversation already at hand.

"I am glad you played tonight. The music was most affecting."

He canted his head, his mouth curving into a slow smile. "Was it?"

"Yes, it was quite exhilarating. I cannot think when I have been so…stimulated by a piece."

"Show me," he commanded. And I did.

The EIGHTEENTH CHAPTER

Be it thy course to busy giddy minds with foreign quarrels.
—*Henry IV, Part Two*

The next morning we rose and washed and dressed ourselves, making as presentable a *toilette* as we could under the circumstances. We collected Rook and I tucked the dormouse into my décolletage once more. Granny gave us more of her rank tea and some cold meat for breakfast and walked us to the edge of the camp when the time came for farewells.

"You did not tell my fortune with the bones," I teased.

She shrugged. "Sometimes it is best not to look too closely at the future, child. Look to today." But she hugged me tightly, and when we broke apart, she put a finger to my brow, pressing firmly to the spot just between my eyes. She did the same to Brisbane and I realised it was a blessing of sorts.

"Thank you, Granny," he said softly, kissing her on both cheeks.

She wagged a finger at him. "Sometime Granny will ask you to pay a reckoning," she said. "You must not forget. *Ja develesa,* children. Go with God."

With that, we left, and I noticed Brisbane patting his pockets.

"What are you doing?"

"Making certain I still have my pocketwatch," he said drily.

I gave him a little push, but as I did, I felt something in my pocket bump against my leg. I put my hand into my pocket and drew out a small calico bag.

"What is this?"

Brisbane gave a look. "A charm bag. Do not open it or you will spill the magic."

I was not certain if he was serious, but I decided it was better to be safe. I tucked it carefully back into my pocket.

"What is in it?"

"Probably a feather, a stone, a bit of bone."

"Bone?"

He smiled. "Animal, not human. A few other things, as well. Granny will have said an incantation over it. Do not lose it. A charm bag is protection."

"From what?" I demanded.

But Brisbane said nothing more and I did not like to ask.

The morning sunshine was bright and the trees on the heath were ablaze with autumn colour. Juniper berries shone in the hedges, and here and there spotted scarlet caps of toadstools peeped through veils of green moss. A light breeze buffetted the trees, streaming the gold-and-red leaves like silken banners held aloft. It seemed impossible that we should have to investigate anything so awful as murder on such a day, but as soon as we reached the copse where Monk had hidden the carriage, Brisbane resumed his inscrutable mask and I knew he was pondering the case. We arrived in due course at Sir Morgan's house in St. John's Wood, and were shown in at once. I was surprised to find Morgan awake and ready to receive visitors. I would have thought him a late riser.

"Good morning, my dear Lady Julia. And I see you have brought your estimable husband this time. Good morning, Mr. Brisbane," Sir Morgan said, and there was a note of humour underscoring his polite greeting.

"I think we might dispense with the fiction that we are unacquainted, Morgan," Brisbane said coolly. "I have informed my wife of the origins of the Spirit Club and that I once had an investigation that took me under its roof."

Sir Morgan put up his hands. "My dear man, we cannot speak of such things before breakfast. Come and eat with me."

He ushered us out a pair of French doors and into his pretty little garden. It was cleverly designed with such careful plantings that the views of the surroundings were completely blocked by a tidy riot of flowers and greenery. I was surprised to find there were no exotics here, only a colourful mass of English cottage blooms. A neat path led from the house to the mews door at the back, and in the centre of the garden stood a comfortable arrangement of table and chairs. Dew still spangled the late roses, and it felt rather like an enchanted scene, so picturesque was the setting. We settled ourselves, and in a few minutes Sir Morgan's turbanned servant had presented us with a delectable breakfast of pastries, cups of chocolate and fruit besides the usual array of English dishes, and pots of tea. Sir Morgan busied himself with the chocolate service and the tea caddy, spooning up more of the delicious green tea and dishes of whipped cream to dollop onto the chocolate.

"So much more civilised than speaking on an empty stomach," Morgan said.

"I am sorry we troubled you so early," I said, reaching for a fragrant pastry. "I suppose we are lucky we did not find you still abed."

"Abed? Good lady, I have not yet been to sleep," he said, his green eyes twinkling. "I am sorry that Nin cannot come out to greet you, only I never permit her outside. Far too dangerous, you understand."

Brisbane's black brows winged upwards. "Nin?"

I darted him a quick glance. "Sir Morgan has the most extraordinary cat. A Siamese, he tells me. A souvenir of his travels abroad."

Morgan looked at me warmly. "Yes, and she is entirely smitten with Lady Julia. I have never seen her so devoted to anyone other than myself."

"I can just imagine," Brisbane said drily.

We fell to eating then, and Morgan and I chatted companionably over breakfast. Only Brisbane remained quiet, offering little to the conversation.

Morgan levelled a glance at him. "Tell me, my dear, do you not find his silences deafening?"

"I would rather have an eternity of his silence than five minutes' conversation with any other man," I said truthfully.

Morgan smiled, and when he did, it was touched with melancholy. "You are the most fortunate of men, Nicholas. I would give half the years of my life to hear a woman say the same of me." He looked to me. "She is an extraordinary individual. You must guard her with your life."

"I intend to," Brisbane said softly, and I would not have been at all surprised to see them draw swords and commence to brawling over the breakfast pastries.

"Yes, well," I said, dusting crumbs from my fingertips, "we have not come to discuss the past but the present, sir. Can you confirm for us that the Spirit Club is being used once more for the purposes of espionage?"

Morgan nearly choked upon his chocolate, and it took him some minutes to regain his composure. When he did, he looked to Brisbane who merely gave him a thin smile and folded his arms over the breadth of his chest.

"My dear lady, you are no wilting wallflower, are you? Straight to the heart of the matter. Very well, I will pay you the compliment of replying in kind. Yes."

I blinked rapidly. I had not expected this. "Really?"

"Really. The more arcane purposes of the club were revived earlier this year after the French government nearly fell to the Boulangistes. We felt the need to keep a closer eye upon the situation and also believed we had sorted some of the difficulties that once made the Spirit Club an impractical arrangement."

"And did you? Sort the difficulties?"

"Apparently not, since Madame is dead."

"Was she a spy?"

"No," he said slowly, "but she passed messages for us, relaying communications between our own agents and those of our allies. The communications were always coded and she never knew what they contained. She did not even know to whom she was relating the message, for she was only told what to say and to preface it with a key phrase."

"'A message from a dark lady,'" I murmured.

"Precisely. In that respect, it worked very well. Since her contacts only knew her and not the other way round, we thought the system quite safe."

"And it was not?" I guessed.

Morgan's handsome mouth turned down. "We recently

began to suspect that Madame was playing her own game. And unfortunately, that rather muddied the waters for us. We had hoped to use the sessions at the Spirit Club to draw out the agents from other countries, both friendly and otherwise. It is always best to know whom one is dealing with, and our German counterparts have been remarkably bashful about showing their faces. We sent out various 'messages from a dark lady' to prod them to action, but the gambit has proven less than successful, I'm afraid."

"What sort of game was Madame playing if she was not directly involved in espionage?" I ventured.

"We believe she was organising the fall of the Conservative government," Morgan said coolly.

I choked back a laugh, but I did not feel mirthful. To suspect it myself was one thing, but to hear the words fall from Sir Morgan's lips was chilling. I forced my voice to lightness. "Come now, sir. You expect us to believe that a medium who worked in travelling shows could topple an entire government?"

"Easier than you think," he said. "Our Prime Minister is a man of great probity and personal morality. It is that very morality that may prove his undoing. If any member of his inner circle were found to be consorting with the enemy, Lord Salisbury would be overthrown at once and the entire Conservative government would fall."

He had not spoken Bellmont's name, and I held my breath as he went on, his voice gentle. "And Madame had already accomplished the first part of her scheme. She had created an attachment between herself and one of Salisbury's most trusted advisers. I think you know whom." He paused and I said nothing. "Another cup of chocolate, my dear?" He rose and went inside the house a moment, returning with a bottle. "You need warming, I think." He added a tiny measure of something fervently alcoholic to the cup and stirred. "Drink that up. It will make this easier to bear."

I sipped and found the warmth of it shot clean to my belly. "You know?"

"I know, and I further know that you believed her goal was simply blackmail, to use her lover's letters against him as an insurance policy of sorts. The result might well have ruined him in society, but that was not her aim. She meant to bring down Salisbury, as well, and for that, she must demonstrate not that Lord Bellmont—" I winced at the name "—was an unfaithful husband, but that he was an unfaithful Englishman, a traitor."

"Impossible!" I cried. "No one loves England more than Bellmont. She could never have proved such a monstrous thing."

"She could have, if at the same time she gave her favours to Bellmont, she was intimately connected to a German," Morgan said simply.

I put my head in my hands and groaned aloud.

"Have you a specific German agent in mind?" Brisbane put in quietly. I dropped my hands and peered closely at Sir Morgan.

Sir Morgan shrugged. "Any one of a dozen. I'm afraid Herr Bismarck has been exceedingly busy. We have not as yet been able to identify the specific agent who might have shared Madame's confidence."

I cleared my throat. "We do know that Madame had formed an attachment that she expected to be quite lucrative. In fact, she seemed to think her connection with this person would secure her future—hers and that of her sister."

I said nothing of where I had heard that bit of information, nor anything about the button that indicated the

attachment was to a member of the kaiser's circle. If Morgan
had not discovered it for himself, I was in no mood to give
such information away freely, and a quick glance at Brisbane
confirmed it. He was regarding me with cool approbation,
and I knew he approved of my discretion. It had been a terrible shock to have my worst fears about the entire matter
confirmed by Sir Morgan. It was as if I had awakened from
a nightmare to find that the goblins I had fled had followed
me to wakefulness.

Morgan steepled his fingers together, fitting the point just
below his chin.

"That would make sense," he mused. "Madame would
need to get right out of England, preferably before the scandal broke. She would need a means of escape."

"Would she have been in danger of prosecution?" I
wondered.

Morgan's lips thinned to an unpleasant smile. "Madame
would have been in danger of quite a few things if she had
attempted her coup. But she was only an instrument. Her
German contact would have been directing matters and
would have arranged for passage to the Continent under
the protection of Bismarck."

I shuddered, thinking of that meddlesome, dangerous old
man in Berlin.

"I still cannot believe Bismarck would stoop to such
machinations to topple Lord Salisbury," I remarked.

"Lord Salisbury has been remarkably effective at putting the fear of God into the Germans," Sir Morgan replied. "The Naval Defence Act was the last straw. More
than twenty million pounds will be spent on building war-
ships. England's navy will be invincible again, and Bismarck
cannot risk that. As much as he despises Liberalism in his
own country, he must have a Liberal government in power

in England for Germany's protection. Otherwise he must spend millions to match our expenditures in armament."

"And if he does not?"

"Annihilation," Morgan said softly, and there was a hard note of satisfaction in his voice. I realised then that the effete and urbane character he put on in society was just that—a part he played to deflect suspicion. The real man beneath the façade was every bit as ruthless as Brisbane. Perhaps even more so.

I considered him carefully. "I wonder which of the faces you show to the world is the real one?"

His smile was genuine then, for the corners of his eyes crinkled in a peculiar way I had not seen before, and the years seemed to fall away, if only for a moment. "As little as I can possibly manage," he told me. "But I am your cousin. That much is true."

"I believe it. And I think your mother, for all her inconstant affections, must have loved Uncle Benvolio after her fashion."

He cocked his head, fixing me with his bright gaze. "How can you know that?"

"Because she gave you a Shakespearean name."

His roar of laughter was as charming as it was unexpected. "No one else has ever made the connection to *Cymbeline*. By God, I wish I had met you a dozen years ago," he said.

"Tread carefully, Morgan," Brisbane commented softly.

Their eyes locked, and something shifted then. The tentatively companionable mood of breakfast was broken, and in its place was something quite inexplicable. I only knew that these men were not enemies, but neither were they friends, and I realised then that they must have endured rather more during Brisbane's interrogation than either of them let on.

Sir Morgan spoke, his voice touched faintly with malice. "Tell me, Brisbane, have you ever told Lady Julia how you came to meet Sir Edward Grey?"

At the mention of my first husband, my ears pricked. I looked from one to the other. Morgan's manner was vaguely taunting, but if he meant to bait Brisbane, my husband did not rise to it. He merely spread his hands in a gesture of casual contempt.

Morgan turned to me. "You see, my dear, I knew Edward. Rather well. I made a point of befriending him because of some rather questionable dealings with a French wine merchant I suspected of misbehaving in service to his country."

I stared at Morgan in disbelief. "You thought Edward was a *spy?*" The notion was impossible, and Morgan merely smiled.

"Not at all. But the merchant was suspected of passing information along to English contacts, and it was my duty to investigate them. In a moment of weakness, Sir Edward poured out his troubles to me, stories of threatening notes that he had begun to receive. I put him onto Brisbane as just the fellow who could help him sort the business."

"You introduced them?"

"Poor Edward needed a champion, and by then I knew Brisbane was thoroughly reliable. I thought it might make for an interesting situation. So you see, my dear," he finished, looking from Brisbane to me with a fond glance, "I consider myself rather responsible for your current happiness."

I felt a sudden sharp prick of distaste for him. He reminded me of a marionette's master, twitching the strings to watch his creations dance, and it left me oddly unsettled to think that Morgan had known so much about my affairs whilst I had not even known he existed.

"Then I ought to make you a present of a nice bottle of port," I commented blandly. "I am only sorry we did not save you a piece of wedding cake."

He laughed again, and the image of a puppeteer working his magic disappeared. He was once more the charming and gracious fellow I had come to like, so much so that I could almost believe I had imagined the faint air of menace a moment before.

"My lady, you are a woman in a thousand. Has anyone ever told you that?"

"Frequently."

By the time Brisbane and I left Morgan's house, I was in a perfectly foul mood and I warned Brisbane so as we started for home.

"Yes, he occasionally has the same effect upon me," Brisbane observed.

"He is such a contradiction," I raged. "One minute he is a dilettante writer with a penchant for other men's wives. Then he is my illegitimate though charming cousin, then he is a spymaster who throws work your way!"

Brisbane said nothing, but I could tell from the curl of his lip that he did not think much of my last remark.

I went on. "I cannot credit that he knew Edward and that Edward confided in him. I thought I knew all of Edward's friends."

"There were many things you thought you knew about Edward," Brisbane reminded me.

"Yes, well, the least said about that the better. But I am deeply surprised to find that Morgan is the reason you and

I met in the first place. And I do not think I want to give him the credit for our marriage," I went on hotly. "I like to think we would have found our way to one another no matter what. Even if Edward had not hired you to investigate those notes, you would have had to have come into my life somehow. I cannot believe in a life without you," I said. A sudden chill crept over me.

Brisbane noticed and put an arm around me, holding me close to his chest. "It is nothing," I assured him. "A goose walked over my grave." I nestled close and deliberately changed the subject.

"Do you believe what he said about Madame? That she and a German agent were conspiring to overthrow Salisbury?"

Brisbane nodded. "It fits—exceedingly well. And Morgan is seldom wrong. I am surprised he has not been able to trace the German yet, but Bismarck has learned a few tricks in the past years, I imagine."

"And we beat Morgan to the mark," I reminded him. "We have the button."

"A button that indicates Madame was involved in some intimate capacity with someone very close to the kaiser," Brisbane acknowledged. "I suspect Morgan would rather like to get his hands on that bit of evidence."

"Do you mean to give it him?"

"I do not. Morgan is still hiding one or two things from us, I will wager, and if those are the rules, we shall play by them."

I glowed a little at his use of the word *us,* then sat up, my brow furrowed.

"What else do we know that Morgan does not?"

"Nothing yet, but I mean to find out," Brisbane told me, his expression grim. "He has not yet found the German operative, and that must be our first priority. Those letters of Bellmont's are still at large, and so long as they are out there, they remain a source of potential danger. To all of us."

I shook my head. "It seems so impossible, that Bellmont's stupid love letters could bring down an entire government."

"Governments have toppled over less," Brisbane reminded me. "Do not forget Sir Robert Peel."

The scandal had broke well before either of us had been born, but it was one of the most infamous moments of Queen Victoria's reign. Determined to retain her Liberal ladies-in-waiting, she had refused to appoint a single Peelite lady to her court. The resulting lack of confidence in Peel had undermined his ability to form a government and Lord Melbourne had been restored to power. It had been a shocking development at the time and the queen had been reviled for it, but it did serve as an excellent illustration of how a battle might be lost for the want of a horseshoe nail.

"Bellmont was astonishingly stupid to put anything in writing," I said. "One would have thought him too smart for that at least."

"One would have thought him smart enough to keep his vows to his wife," Brisbane returned, and the sentiment warmed me thoroughly. I was deeply gratified that Brisbane's own sense of morality dictated fidelity. I knew I maddened him, but I also knew that there could be no other possible woman for him, just as there could be no other man for me.

As if intuiting my thoughts, Brisbane spoke, his voice decidedly casual. "By the way, you might want to be on your guard with Morgan. He is rather too enchanted with you."

"Brisbane! What a curious notion."

"You do not deny it, and you are blushing," he observed.

"I am blushing because it is ridiculous and I most certainly *do* deny it," I returned.

"Then you are not half as observant as I credited you. I do not suggest his fondness is returned," he said evenly, "but Morgan is a slippery devil. His ulterior motives have ulterior motives. Be watchful."

"You are absurd. And you sound jealous, which does not become you at all."

He leaned closer to me, his words enunciated with great care. "Be. Watchful."

I said nothing more upon the subject, and mercifully, neither did he. We fell to discussing the case again.

"So, we have the button. We have the American reporter—Mr. Sullivan—to find, the German agent to run to ground, and it would not do us a bit of harm if we could find the veiled lady. Agathe mentioned she was a séance regular. I discounted her at first, but it occurs to me it is possible she might know something useful of the others," I said. "What news of the finances? Have you finished the enquiries?"

"Monk finished his enquiries. All as regular as we expected," Brisbane told me. "The general's purse is rather slender, but it has always been so and there are no pressing claims that would make his position untenable. Sir Henry is enormously rich, but expectedly so from his investments and less-than-scrupulous business practises. Morgan is possessed of an income from his family, as well as certain discreet payments made to a variety of accounts under assumed names, but all quite in keeping with his role as an agent of the Crown."

"You investigated the finances of England's spymaster." I stared at him in mingled horror and admiration.

Brisbane gave me a grin of grim satisfaction. "Even the best spies can turn their coats."

I pondered the statement for a moment, then sat bolt upright, my mind awhirl. "Oh, I think I have it! One of the séance guests was Madame's German connection, and it must have been the American."

Brisbane folded his arms over his chest and regarded me thoughtfully. "Why?"

"Madame conducts her séances with an eye to combining the business of espionage with actual sessions. We have an assortment of players at the table the night of her death, both those involved in the spy game and those there to hear messages from the other side. I am not under suspicion," I said, ticking off my fingers. "We know that the general, the veiled lady and Sir Henry were all there as legitimate guests seeking communication with the spirits. Sir Morgan was there to keep an eye upon his little web. That leaves Agathe and the American. Either might have killed Madame, and the American killed Agathe, perhaps because they quarrelled about the deed after it was done. Yes, the American fellow is actually a German masquerading as an American, I am certain of it."

I settled back onto the seat of the carriage with an air of triumph. As usual, Brisbane did not leave me long to enjoy it.

"It does not explain where the letters are or why the agent has not yet acted upon them," Brisbane countered. I flapped a hand.

"Perhaps he has," I said slowly. "Perhaps *that* was the cause of the fire."

Brisbane was swift to take my meaning. "If Bellmont's

blackmailer knew about the letters but did not have them in possession, he might have used the meeting at Highgate to lure me from the house in order to search the place, looking for some clue to their whereabouts."

My brow furrowed. "But we are back to the same question. Why search the house when I was sure to be home?"

"But you weren't," Brisbane said, passing a hand over his eyes. "We have talked over and around what the blackmailer might have thought and we surmised that he expected you to be at home. But what if his scheme went as planned? What if he anticipated that you would come with me to Highgate? The house would be left with only the staff in residence, meaning the family rooms would be vacant, an excellent prospect if he wanted to search the place."

I perked up considerably. "Oh, that does make me feel better! If he knew I was not at home, then the fire could not have been set with an eye to harming me."

But Brisbane's expression was grim. "It ought to chill your very marrow, my dear. If the blackmailer wrote that note intending that you should be out of the house, it means he knows us rather better than I would like."

I turned that over and felt slightly sick. "It means we have an adversary who knows us quite well indeed," I murmured, and for the rest of the ride home, I could not banish the picture of Morgan Fielding's laughing green eyes from my mind.

The
NINETEENTH CHAPTER

Come not between the dragon and his wrath.

—King Lear

We arrived at home to find yet another maid had given notice and the cook had quit after falling out with one of the footmen.

I clucked at Aquinas. "How tiresome. Which of the maids this time?"

"The second chambermaid."

I spread my hands. "I do not understand. We pay excellent wages. We are not particularly fussy people to work for. Why the devil do we have so much trouble keeping staff?"

Aquinas gave a discreet cough. "I believe the attempt to burn down the house might have had something to do with the girl's resignation, my lady."

I was indignant. "The house is almost never on fire. That was decidedly out of character for us. Besides, no one apart from us knows that the matter was deliberate. Everyone believes it to be an accident. The girl has no backbone," I told him stubbornly. "I want nice, sturdy girls with good character and no imagination or peculiarities of personal habit

or religion. Is that so very much to ask? And what happened
to Cook?"

"It appears that she has quarrelled with Swan, my lady."

"Whatever for?"

"I have discovered that Swan's avocation is cooking. He is
particularly interested in the new stove and spent too much
of his leisure time in the kitchens for Cook's liking. She has
resigned without notice in protest."

I huffed out a sigh. "I suppose you ought to use the
telephone to ring the agency and find us a new maid and
you can send out for meals until we find a replacement for
Cook."

Aquinas gave a discreet cough. "I can certainly do as you
have instructed, my lady, but as it happens, Swan is rather
accomplished in the kitchen. He feels terribly responsible for
Cook's departure. When she made her feelings known, he
did apologise—quite eloquently, in fact. He has put it to me
that he would be very happy to make amends by preparing
meals until a replacement may be engaged."

I waved a hand. "Do as you think best, Aquinas."

He bowed from the neck and withdrew, leaving me to
shake my head over the notion of letting our footman do
the cooking. I felt rather a failure just then, for it seemed
no matter what I tried, my household was destined to be in
uproar.

After attending to a few minor domestic details—including
giving Aquinas firm instructions on the care and handling of
my new dormouse—Brisbane and I bathed and dressed and
he ordered the carriage brought round.

"Where are we bound, dearest?" I enquired as I pulled
on my gloves.

He handed me into the carriage and took the seat opposite, his expression one of grim satisfaction.

"To the offices of the *Illustrated Daily News*."

I pulled a face. "I thought you had already spoken with the editor and found him less than helpful."

His black eyes were agleam. "Yes, but then he was speaking to Nicholas Brisbane, private enquiry agent. Now he will be speaking to Lady Julia Brisbane, daughter of the owner."

I gaped at him. "I do not believe it. After all this time, you have finally begun to see the advantages to having me along on an investigation."

He shrugged. "Your father at last did something useful."

He said nothing more upon the subject, and I fell to musing that it was difficult to know whether to be annoyed that Brisbane was clearly using my title and my position to retrieve information or to be delighted that I had, in some capacity, proved useful to him.

The newspaper offices, like those of its betters, were located in Fleet Street, and the din of the crowded street was very nearly deafening. Enormous wagons delivered great reams of blank paper ready for printing, whilst still more wagons carted off the finished product. There were newsboys shouting the latest headlines, and reporters dashing to and fro, coming and going as they broke the news from around the world. It was a maddening place, but the cacophony had a certain rhythm to it, and I could easily see why the men who worked there would find it exhilarating.

Brisbane showed none of my interest or enthusiasm for the place. He strode through the offices, scattering clerks and reporters in his wake, looking neither left nor right.

When he reached the office of the editor, he paused as an officious little fellow trotted up and flung himself in front of the door.

"You cannot go in there!" he said stoutly. "That is Mr. Froggitt's private office and you have no appointment."

Brisbane canted his head and offered the fellow a pleasant smile. "If you do not move out of my way instantly, I will open that window and hang you from it by your fingernails." He jerked his head in the direction of the closest window, and the fellow stood tall for a moment then fell back, clearing the way. A muted click sounded from behind the office door.

I poked Brisbane in the ribs. "That was not at all nice."

He cocked a brow at me. "I like to think I have many sterling qualities, my dear. 'Nice' does not number among them."

Without another word, he lifted one booted foot and drove it hard just below the doorknob, shattering the door.

"Brisbane, really! Was that necessary?" I demanded.

He pointed to the doorknob, still attached to the jamb. "He locked the door against me. Most inhospitable."

"And bloody useless," I muttered.

He raised a finger. "Julia, do not swear." He stepped over the splintered remains of the door and offered me a hand.

"Mr. Froggitt?" he called. "You might as well come out from under the desk. I can see your shoes."

I glanced down to find Brisbane was quite correct. From underneath the desk protruded the tips of two exceptionally scuffed shoes.

After a moment, there came a heavy sigh and a scraping noise as Mr. Froggitt emerged from under his desk, his clothing askew and his hair sadly disarranged. Or at least I hoped it was disarranged and not his habitual coiffure. He was balding, but three very long hairs had been draped over his greasy pate as if to simulate a full head of shining locks. The front of his waistcoat bore the traces of ink and the remnants of various meals, and I repressed a little shudder. The man did bear an unfortunate resemblance to a toad.

"How do you do, Mr. Froggitt?" I began. "I am happy to make your acquaintance. I am Lady Julia Brisbane. I believe you know my father, Lord March."

He swallowed hard, and when he spoke, his voice was hoarse. "I have met his lordship, yes."

"Lovely. That will make this easier. You have some information that my husband requires."

Mr. Froggitt set his jaw mulishly, the wattles at his neck shaking from side to side. "I have already told you I do not know anything more about Sullivan."

Brisbane smiled, the same bland smile that he had shown the official clerk in the outer office. I hurried to divert the coming storm.

"Mr. Froggitt, my husband is in no temper to be crossed. Now, if you would only be reasonable and give us the information we want, we could be on our way at once and this entire interlude will be over and I would have no reason to discuss it with my father."

Froggitt opened his mouth and closed it with a resounding snap. He threw himself into his desk chair and opened a desk drawer, rummaging through various bits of paper and ledgers. He opened one of the black-bound books and copied out a piece of information, fairly throwing the paper at us.

"There. That is all I know," he said flatly. "I have a paper to run. Leave me be."

I read the address he had copied out and handed it to Brisbane.

"Thank you, my dear." He handed me back over the wrecked door and turned back to Froggitt with a nod.

"Do send me the bill for damages."

Froggitt swore fluently as we left, and while Brisbane took exception to it, I could not. "Really, Brisbane, you frightened the man to death. Did you not see his hands trembling?"

Brisbane snorted. "Doubtless the effects of his morning dose of Mother's Ruin. Did you not see the signs of habitual drink upon his nose and smell the stink of it upon him? Your father has a drunkard in his employ."

"Will you tell him?"

"Absolutely not. His investments are his own business," Brisbane said coolly, and I knew better than to press the point. He was still mightily annoyed with Father's high-handedness.

He gave the address to the driver and we settled in for a lengthy drive. We discussed the various aspects of the case, and I thought of the wager we had placed. I could like Mr. Sullivan as the German agent if he had murdered Madame. It would mean one hundred pounds in my purse.

"Do you really think he is in the pay of Bismarck?" I asked.

Brisbane shrugged. "It is difficult to say. He is American, and one never really knows where they come from. Ah, here we are."

Mr. Sullivan's lodgings were in a disreputable street in an unsavoury part of town, and I was rather glad that Pigeon was perched on the back of the carriage should we have need of him. I was also quite happy to have finally perfected the self-igniting gunpowder I had laboured over for so long. I carried a small container of it in my reticule with an eye to surprising Brisbane should he have need of a rescue. In fact, I could not wait to use it.

We drove on, at length arriving at the lodging house where Mr. Sullivan lived. Next door stood a fish-and-chip shop, and the heavy, oily smell of it filled the air. My stomach gave a sharp growl as I followed Brisbane from the carriage and up the steps. He flicked me a glance and rapped smartly upon the door.

Whilst we waited, he gave me a look of admonition. "You did quite well with Froggitt, but this one is mine."

"Agreed." I was happy simply to be allowed to come along, and I smiled broadly at him as the door bounced back on its hinges.

The woman on the other side was a testament to artifice. Everything about her that could have been enhanced had been. Her hair had been hennaed a brilliant shade of orange and her brow was almost entirely covered by an elaborate frizette. Her slender bosom had been padded out to improbable dimensions, as had her backside. She was heavily rouged and her false teeth clacked as she talked.

"Well, hello to you both! I'm going to guess you aren't looking for a room, the pair of you, unless it's to get up to something you oughtn't." She leaned close and gave us a conspiratorial wink. "I don't let rooms for such goings-on, but my friend, Bet, up the street will. Just tell her Nell sent you."

She made to close the door, but Brisbane put out a hand.

"Miss Nell, if you don't mind, a moment of your time."

He coupled this with an expression of such forthright sweetness that she gave a little sigh and stepped back. "Of course, sir. Whatever I can do."

I smothered a roll of the eyes and followed him in as she showed him upstairs. He had merely murmured Sullivan's name and slipped a banknote into her greedy hand and she was halfway up the stairs before the money was even tucked into her bosom.

She paused at the first landing and nodded towards a closed door.

"This one."

Brisbane nodded and retrieved another note, a far larger one. "I am afraid there will be a little damage to the door."

She whistled soundlessly at the size of the note. "Not to worry. My boy, Bill, will have it fixed up in a trice for less than half of this."

"Then keep the rest with my compliments."

She giggled then, and gave him a little push. Suddenly, concern crossed her face. "You won't hurt him too badly, will you? He's quite good about paying his rent on time, and he's a nice enough lad."

"I promise to return him as good as new," Brisbane vowed. "Well, almost."

She giggled again and left us. I sighed, knowing what was coming, and stepped back as Brisbane kicked down his second door of the day.

"Honestly," I murmured under my breath. "You might have knocked."

"I do so enjoy the element of surprise," he called back to me as he vaulted over the broken door.

And surprised Mr. Sullivan certainly was. He was stretched out upon his bed in his underclothes, eating fish and chips from a twist of newspaper. He dropped them as soon as the door broke and scrambled upright, attempting to cover himself with the bedclothes.

"Oh, do not worry on my account," I assured him. "I have five brothers, Mr. Sullivan. I am not easily shocked."

He did not even pretend not to know me, and I certainly recognised him.

Brisbane took up the clothes that had been discarded upon the floor and flung them at Sullivan.

"Get dressed."

Sullivan slipped his hand beneath the pillow, but before he could finish what he had begun, Brisbane's hand darted out and clamped over the fellow's wrist. A quick twist, and Sullivan cried out, dropping the tiny revolver.

I went and retrieved it, shaking my head. "Really, Mr. Sullivan. You couldn't shoot a cat with that. You will want to invest in something more powerful."

He glanced in disbelief from me to Brisbane, who stood looming over him like a rather menacing god from antiquity.

"Let's try this again. Get dressed. We are going for a drive."

This time, Sullivan did as he was bade. I turned my back, but Brisbane did not, and in a very short time we had quit the house and were comfortably arranged in the carriage. At least, Brisbane and I were comfortable, but I suspected Mr. Sullivan was less so. His initial terror seemed to have abated, but his eyes still rolled and his knees were trembling.

I leaned forward. "Mr. Sullivan, you must calm yourself. We do not make a habit of abduction. You are quite safe with us."

I could feel Brisbane smothering a sigh, but I did not care. I firmly believed we would gather more flies with honey, and intended to make this experience as sweetly profitable as possible.

Brisbane instructed the driver to proceed, and he did so, leaving us to our interrogation. Mr. Sullivan's eyes flicked to the window to gauge our direction, but Brisbane instantly closed the shades. "For privacy," he told our captive, baring his teeth in a predatory smile.

Mr. Sullivan jumped a little, and I decided there was no

point in frightening the fellow to death if only because he would be vastly more difficult to question in that state.

I smiled kindly at him. "You have led us rather a merry chase, Mr. Sullivan."

He said nothing and I decided, as I had done with Sir Morgan, to grasp the nettle. "Mr. Sullivan, I deplore pretense, and I think we ought to dispense with yours. We know that your occupation as a writer of sensational newspaper stories is simply a ruse. You are engaged in espionage."

He gaped at me, his eyes starting in his white face.

I continued on, my tone deliberately pleasant. "We know that you had to adopt some more regular occupation to account for your presence in London, but we are curious as to why I should figure so prominently in your pieces for the newspaper. Would you care to enlighten us?"

He opened his mouth and closed it again, giving him a rather distressing resemblance to a freshly caught fish. At last, he found his voice.

"Sorry about that, ma'am," he said, and he did manage to look contrite. "And I am sorry for the things I wrote about you. I meant nothing personal, you understand. But I had to ensure that Mr. Brisbane stayed upon the case."

"Why? I should have thought Brisbane would have been a hindrance to you," I said bluntly.

"Thank you for that," Brisbane drawled.

"Not at all, ma'am," the American said. "In fact, I needed him."

"Needed him?"

Mr. Sullivan seemed to relax a little, so long as he was not looking directly at Brisbane. "Yes, ma'am. I knew Lord Bellmont had consulted with him, and I figured nothing would be more natural than a fellow in trouble appealing to his brother-in-law to get him out. I thought if I just kept

Mr. Brisbane in my sights, he would find the letters for me. He was my last hope."

I shot a questioning glance at Brisbane. "Then you do not have the letters? You are not the blackmailer?"

"I am the blackmailer," he said patiently, "at least, I sent Lord Bellmont the note demanding money. But that was because I needed help in finding the letters, and I knew if I approached any of you directly, I would never get them."

I shook my head. "I am entirely confused, Mr. Sullivan. Let us begin at the beginning. You knew there were letters in Madame Séraphine's possession that compromised my brother."

"Yes." He nodded emphatically to demonstrate his cooperation. He darted a glance at Brisbane, who sat glowering in the corner, saying nothing, but keeping a watchful eye upon the fellow.

"And you wanted the letters."

"I did," he said. He reached into his pocket, and in a flash, Brisbane was on him. The American gave a cry of pain as Brisbane bent his wrist back nearly upon itself. "Easy, fellow! I only want my handkerchief."

Brisbane dipped two fingers into the pocket and retrieved the somewhat grubby handkerchief. He inspected it, then dropped it on Mr. Sullivan's lap. The American took it up and mopped his brow with it. "Where was I?"

"The letters," I supplied.

"Yes. I had been attending the séances for some time. I was under strict orders to listen and report back to Washington what I heard, and that is all. But I started to get suspicious that something was up. So I started hanging around more, watching for regulars. I found two who interested me in particular, the first was General Fortescue."

I had blinked furiously at the mention of Washington. I

had truly believed Mr. Sullivan was an agent of the Germans, reporting to Bismarck, the old misery. It galled a little to learn that he was precisely what he appeared to be—a not terribly skillful American agent.

I left my musings about his allegiances as Brisbane seized upon his last remark. "General Fortescue? Why did he pique your interest?"

"He was a contact of ours from some years back, occasionally passing bits of information."

I bristled. "The general passed information to America? That treacherous devil! And to think I comforted him about his lost soldiers," I fumed, and Mr. Sullivan gave me a kindly smile.

"He never gave up anything significant," he assured me. "And I soon realised he wasn't giving up anything this time. He is exactly what he seems—a man who is haunted by the ghosts of his regrets."

"Who else captured your interest?" I asked, wondering if he would identify Morgan as his British opposite.

But he did not. "A certain woman who never spoke and who always wore a heavy veil she wouldn't take off."

"The veiled lady!" I cried. I was not entirely surprised that Morgan had been subtle enough to avoid detection by the Americans, but I was vastly annoyed that Brisbane and I had discounted the veiled lady so thoroughly. "I thought she was simply a client," I admitted.

"So did I," Mr. Sullivan assured me. "Until I realised she had managed to worm her way into five or six of the gentlemen's sessions and never said a single word. She came and Madame gave her messages about a dead son and an inheritance, but once Madame slipped up. She mentioned a dead daughter instead, and it was a tiny mistake, but it was all I needed to know. The veiled lady was a fraud, and

Madame was in on it. The likeliest explanation was that she was there to keep an eye on the rest of us, and at first I thought she must be my British opposite."

I choked slightly at the notion that the veiled lady might be mistaken for Morgan, but I swiftly recovered and he went on.

"I saw her nip up the stairs one evening after everyone else had gone. Madame opened the door to her room and I heard one of them say, *'Guten nacht,'* and that was all I needed to hear."

I dared not look at Brisbane. We had assumed Bismarck had dispatched a man for this job, but clearly he had a greater opinion of my sex than I had credited him.

Mr. Sullivan went on. "The veiled lady clearly had German connections. And Agathe confirmed it."

Brisbane stirred himself. "You befriended Agathe?"

Mr. Sullivan turned slightly pink and tugged at his collar. "I suppose you could say we were friends."

"Intimate friends," Brisbane pressed.

Mr. Sullivan shot a look towards me and flushed an even more startling shade of pink. "Damn me, must we talk about such things in front of a lady?"

"Think of her as a fellow investigator," Brisbane offered helpfully.

I gave Mr. Sullivan a cool smile to show I was not offended by the subject at hand, and he mopped his brow again.

"All right. Yes. We were intimate friends. I saw right off the bat I would never manage to worm my way into Madame's good graces. She wanted men who were either rich or powerful, and I didn't have anything in that way."

"Come now, Mr. Sullivan," I said. "America is a very wealthy young country. Surely your government could have

funded such a masquerade. You could have presented yourself as a railroad magnate or cattle baron." I looked to Brisbane. "Is that right? A cattle baron? It sounds strange."

"It is correct," he averred. "But I suspect Mr. Sullivan
was operating beyond the scope of his assignment. You set
yourself the task of unravelling Madame's plot, didn't you?
Without direction or support from Washington," Brisbane
guessed.

Mr. Sullivan wiped his brow again. "You don't know
what it's like there, all those stuffy old men pushing papers
around. It would have taken me a year to get the proper
permission, and that is only if I were the luckiest man on
God's green Earth. No, sir, if I had asked, my superiors
would have taken so long to argue about it that Lord Salisbury's government would have fallen twice over before I
could act."

"So you took the initiative to present them with a *fait accompli*," I finished.

He grinned, and it was a charming, boyish thing, his grin.
"I find it's better to ask for forgiveness than permission."

I led him back to the subject at hand. "So you set out to
seduce Agathe because you sensed she was an easier mark
than her sister."

"Yes, ma'am. And all she really wanted was someone to
listen to her. She used to be the headline act when they
first starting touring as mediums. But there was a dust-up
in Germany and Agathe lost her nerve. Madame Séraphine
stepped in and that was it. She just took over, and year by
year, Agathe dropped further back into the shadows. To tell
the truth," he said, dropping his gaze, "I felt sorry for her."

"Then you are a very poor spy," I commented, smelling
the deceit upon him. "They should have taught you never
to get personally attached to your subjects."

Again he offered up the grin, this time tinged with apology. "All right, I was not entirely sorry for her. Agathe was a bit of a shrew, if I may speak ill of the dead. She and Madame used to scrap like cats. And one of the things they quarrelled about was Madame's throwing in with the Germans."

That much made sense. After her experiences in Bavaria, Agathe would not look kindly upon Germans.

"So you learned from Agathe of Lord Bellmont's letters and concluded there was a conspiracy to use them to topple Lord Salisbury," I said.

He nodded. "And I knew I couldn't let that happen. The trouble again is Washington. If I had taken the time to let my superiors know, they might have told me just to let it play out. There are those who think America shouldn't involve itself at all in what you Europeans do, that it's going to lead us into a hell of a war someday, begging your pardon, ma'am," he added with a tip of his hat. "But I think England and America have always been real good friends and we ought to stay that way. A strong England is good for us, and frankly, I'm more than a little scared of Germany."

"As are we all," I murmured. "So you took it upon yourself to retrieve the letters."

"I told Agathe what I suspected was going on so she could search Madame's things for the letters. I figured if I enlisted her help, she could find them for me."

"And she failed, as well?"

"Madame found her looking and they had a big fight. Madame told her it was too late and that she had thrown in her lot with the Germans and that when the time came, England would be easy pickings for the Continentals. She said Bismarck was going to reward her with a title and a huge amount of money, her German friend had told her so."

"What else did you discover about this German friend of Madame's—the veiled lady?"

Sullivan looked disgusted. "Precious little. I only know that she pulled Madame into the plot on the orders of Bismarck and that she has some mighty powerful friends in Germany."

"Doubtless because she is a relative of the kaiser," Brisbane put in blandly. I bit back the oath that sprang to my lips. Leap of logic or brilliant stroke of intuition, I could not say, but in either event, it made perfect sense. Such perfect sense, in fact, that I could not believe I had failed to see it for myself.

Mr. Sullivan regarded Brisbane with awe. "How do you know that?"

"She wears buttons marked with the family name as a badge of honour. A rather indiscreet practise for a spy, but then I suspect she is an amateur, commissioned by Bismarck on the strength of her connections rather than her skills."

Sullivan looked dumbfounded. "The family?"

"Sigmaringen-Hohenzollern," I informed him. "A cadet branch of the kaiser's dynasty. One thing puzzles me. The scandal would indeed have been enough to sink Lord Salisbury if the letters had come to light. Why didn't they?"

He shrugged. "They disappeared the day Madame died. She and Agathe quarrelled about the letters, about the Germans, about me. Madame had found out Agathe and I had been seeing quite a lot of one another and she said some pretty cutting things about it. Agathe was as hurt and mad as I've ever seen a woman."

"Hurt and mad enough to kill her own sister?" Brisbane asked.

Mr. Sullivan's eyes widened, and his colour rose furiously. "Now, that's just a damned lie, that is. Agathe was all right. I mean, she was tight with a dollar and she could talk the ears off a rabbit, but she would never have hurt her own sister, and that's God's own truth."

I was touched in spite of myself. I had had the sense throughout the conversation that Mr. Sullivan was guarding himself carefully, telling only as much as he had to. But this spirited defence of Agathe rang true, and I liked him a little better for it.

"No, I do not think Agathe killed Madame," I said, sighing deeply. "Is it possible that she took advantage of her sister's death to find the letters and conceal them, even from you?"

"No, ma'am." The reply was adamant. "She was in a bit of a panic about it, actually, and we both figured the murderer must have taken them. I promised her we'd get them back. I knew that Lord Bellmont was connected to Mr. Brisbane and knew he would be after the letters, as well. I figured if I could get him to retrieve the letters, I would just steal them from him and be done with it."

Brisbane gave him a bland smile. "Nicely done, Mr. Sullivan, but I think we may excuse you of altruistic motives on that score. If I had found my brother-in-law's letters, I would have destroyed them in his presence. I hardly think you would have done the same."

Mr. Sullivan managed to look hurt. "No, but I assure you they would have never been used against him."

"You would have taken them to Washington, perhaps to keep as an insurance policy, perhaps as a tool to get what you wanted from Lord Salisbury," Brisbane pressed.

"I resent that, sir," Mr. Sullivan said, raising his chin. "My government would never resort to such methods."

Brisbane snorted, and I waved him off. "That is neither here nor there. The point is, you did not have the letters and

so you began to take steps to flush them out. Hence, following me about, writing articles for the newspaper. What
was the purpose in setting fire to our house? I presume that
was you?"

He had the grace to look deeply embarrassed. "I am sorry
about that. I wanted to search Mr. Brisbane's study for the
letters. I thought if I got you both out of the house, I would
have a chance. I managed to kick over a lamp on my way
in. I never got past the window," he said in some disgust.

"So you did not intend harm to me?" I asked pleasantly.

His expression was one of horror. "God, no! I figured
you would tag along with Mr. Brisbane to the cemetery.
That's why I chose Highgate. Agathe had made it her business to discover as much as she could about Lord Bellmont
and his family, and I knew if I put in that bit about your
husband's grave, you'd think there was a connection to you
and come along. I wanted you as far out of the house as
possible."

"And you arranged the little trap for us at Highgate?"

He ducked his head again. "I had to ensure you would
be out of the way for some time. I do apologise. If it's any
consolation, you made it out much faster than I expected."

"I am gratified," I said, smiling.

He returned the smile, and for a moment we felt like
comrades-in-arms.

"How touching," Brisbane said, chilling the warmth of
the moment, "but I wonder if you were quite so thoughtful
when you pushed Agathe under the wheels of an inbound
train in Victoria Station?"

Mr. Sullivan flushed again, then blanched as white as new
milk. "I had nothing to do with that. I swear upon my life,
my honour and my country. Madame's murderer must have

done it. I think Agathe may have pushed her luck a little," he said, hesitating.

I pounced upon his hesitation. "What did Agathe do? Did she perhaps overplay her hand?"

"That's exactly what she did," he said, his expression one of regret. "She told me she thought she might know who the murderer was—I mean, the veiled lady's real identity. She had done some research at the lending library and put a few clues together. She wouldn't tell me anything, so don't even ask," he told me, holding up a hand. "I couldn't imagine what it was at the time, but now I think she must have been using the insignia on the button to discover the lady's identity. I argued with Agathe for hours, but she was a stubborn woman when she made up her mind. She said she had sent a message to the lady, and if it turned out to be the murderer, she would be set for life. I think she planned to ask for money."

"Blackmailing murderers is a profoundly stupid enterprise," I remarked. But Agathe had not been entirely stupid. She had been cunning enough to get rid of the button itself, keeping the damning evidence of the veiled lady's identity away from the Spirit Club. Perhaps it had been an insurance policy of sorts, a guarantee that if something happened to her, at least someone would be able to deduce the villainess' name as she herself had done.

Mr. Sullivan nodded. "I'll say. I suspect Agathe found the veiled lady all right. She must have arranged to meet her at Victoria Station to get some money, and the lady decided to put an end to things before they even started. Pushing Agathe under the train was no more significant than snapping a loose thread from a hem, I have no doubt."

To his credit, I believed him, and I think Brisbane must

have been satisfied, as well, for he rapped sharply upon the roof of the conveyance and the driver pulled to a quick stop.

Brisbane leaned over and opened the door. "This is where you leave us, Mr. Sullivan."

The fellow peered outside and blinked. "Where are we?"

"That is a matter of absolutely no concern to me," Brisbane said pleasantly. He gestured towards the open door and Mr. Sullivan inclined his head to me.

"Ma'am, I do hope you will forgive me for inconveniencing you. As I said, it was not at all personal," he said.

He put out his hand and I smiled at his casual American manners. I shook his hand and he gave Brisbane a short nod as he left the carriage. Brisbane vaulted out after him and gave me a speaking look.

"I will be just a moment, my dear."

He closed the door firmly behind, and as the shades were still drawn, I could not see out. I toyed with the notion of lifting them, but from the sounds outside, I decided it was better to leave matters as they were. There were a few ominous thuds, a low groan, and at one point something hit the carriage so hard I was afraid we would be overturned. There was another groan and then Brisbane was back, wrapping a handkerchief about his knuckles.

"Drive on," he called, slamming the door decisively.

"Was that absolutely necessary?" I enquired politely.

"It was, and to his credit, he understood it. Said he would have done precisely the same if it had been his wife. And when it was done, I picked him up and shook his hand. We parted on excellent terms."

I crossed my arms and resisted the urge to throttle Brisbane. "Does it not seem entirely feudal to engage in such histrionics on my behalf?"

"Histrionics? You wound me," he said, but there was a gleam of satisfaction in his eyes that told me he was entirely pleased with himself.

"It looks as if Mr. Sullivan drew blood, as well." I nodded towards his bandaged hand.

He shrugged. "The fellow didn't know how to take a punch. He left his mouth open and his tooth cut my hand."

"I trust he knows better now?"

"Oh, he does." Brisbane smiled widely.

"Still, I think he gave us rather a lot of information. How much of it do you think was the truth? I shall be mightily put out with him if he lied about anything of significance."

Brisbane gave a short, humourless laugh. "Most days I am lied to half a dozen times before breakfast. You must learn to sift through the chaff to find the wheat."

"And the wheat of this particular conversation is that we know Mr. Sullivan is an American agent and that Madame conspired with the veiled lady, a German agent, to bring down my brother and Lord Salisbury with him. The question is why did she turn upon Madame and kill her before the deed was done?"

Brisbane shrugged. "We may never know, but such things are not uncommon amongst conspirators. Madame may have demanded too much money in return for her compliance. She may have delivered too little or threatened too much. It is enough to know that the situation was extremely dangerous and that Madame was not so clever as she ought to have been."

I nibbled at my lip. "I do think he was truthful about

Agathe not murdering her sister. He seemed quite impassioned upon the subject."

Brisbane smiled thinly. "He does not have the stomach to be a spy. He is far too sentimental and not half as good an actor as he ought to be. For example, did you detect that 'Sullivan' is a *nom de guerre?*"

I gaped at him. "I did not. How did you?"

"I have travelled some little bit in America. His name is Irish and he claims to be from New York, but his accent was entirely wrong."

"They have different accents in America?"

Brisbane smiled. "Just as we do here."

I waved a hand. "They all sound alike to me."

"They say the same of us," he told me. "Most of them would never notice the difference between your accent and mine."

"Impossible," I murmured. Mine was the expected accent of a well-born person whose childhood had been divided between Sussex and London. Brisbane's was threaded with the lilt of Gypsies and Highlanders, carefully schooled, but broader when he was angry. There was something both rough and elegant about his speech, and though I would never admit it, Brisbane spoke as I had always imagined Heathcliff would. I was deeply fond of Heathcliff.

"Nevertheless, they wouldn't. But I was intrigued by the accents of Americans, and I can assure you that Mr. Sullivan's accent is Southern, for all his attempts to mask it. His vowels are too liquid and he has a penchant for drawing out his words."

"Fascinating! And how did you deduce his name is not authentic? Wait—" I held up a hand. "Let me guess. You know that Irish immigrants are centralised around the northeastern metropolitan areas of the United States, and therefore it is less likely that Mr. Sullivan is of Irish descent." I was rather proud of that bit of deduction, but Brisbane shook his head.

"No." He flashed me a wicked smile and brandished a small leather folder. "I lifted his notecase. His papers identify him as Richard Beausavage of New Orleans."

"How precisely did you manage that?"

"When I helped him to his feet," he explained. "He was so busy staunching the flow of blood from his nose, I could have taken his shirt, as well, and he would never have noticed."

"And do you mean to keep it?" I demanded. "All of his identification papers are in there, as well as what looks to be a good deal of money."

Brisbane looked affronted. "Of course I shan't keep it. I merely wanted to ascertain the fellow's true identity. It was not my intention to steal it, merely to borrow it."

True to his word, Brisbane lifted the shade, lowered the window and flung the notecase out into the street.

"There. I have made an effort to return his property."

"The poor man. He will have quite a bit of trouble replacing his papers, to say nothing of the money."

"He ought to have thought of that before he brought you into this investigation," Brisbane said softly.

I opened my mouth to remonstrate with him, but Brisbane raised a finger and set it with gentle decisiveness upon my lips.

"He is lucky to have got off so lightly. His bruises will heal and his papers can be replaced, but every minute of trouble or inconvenience will remind him to have a care what he does in future. The next time, I will take his bones apart with my bare hands. Now, hush."

For once I did as I was told. I admit there was something

primitive and thrilling about having one's husband shed blood for one's honour, although it did me no credit whatsoever.

"It is thoroughly Darwinian," I muttered, and I realised with some disgust that my only real regret was that I had not seen Brisbane hit him. "You engage in rather more fisti-cuffs than I imagined when I first met you," I observed.

He quirked a brow at me. "Surely you have noticed I only resort to bare-handed violence when necessity demands."

That much was true. There was a Webley in his pocket and a knife in his boot, and poor Mr. Sullivan had seen the troublesome end of neither. But a point had had to be made, and I understood that Brisbane had actually used great re-straint in the making of it.

"Still, I cannot like it."

"You were not raised in a Gypsy camp," he reminded me. "Otherwise you would know better."

"Surely not. The girls cannot be expected to learn such things."

He snorted. "The girls were worse by far than any of the boys. A girl is taught as soon as she can toddle from her mother's side to take care of herself in any way she can."

"Dear me," I said. I fell silent for a moment, then bright-ened. "When do you think we will go back to the Gypsy camp to visit your family?"

"I have no plans to do so at present. Why?"

"It occurred to me that I might learn one or two useful things from the ladies," I said.

Brisbane smothered an oath. "Absolutely not. Anything you want to know, I will teach you."

"Really?"

"Really."

I felt buoyant with anticipation. "There is no time like the present. We will begin this afternoon."

By way of reply, Brisbane groaned.

"There, there," I said, patting his wounded hand. "It will not be so bad. I will be a very devoted student."

"That is what I am afraid of."

The
TWENTIETH CHAPTER

Now hear me speak with a prophetic spirit.
—*King John*

We returned to the consulting rooms where Mrs. Lawson brought the few things I ordered with very little grace and a good deal of grumbling.

"Are you quite sure you understand what must be done to clean the wound thoroughly?" she asked. "It has hitherto been my responsibility to attend to such things for Mr. Brisbane."

I summoned a smile. "I am quite confident, thank you, Mrs. Lawson."

She gave a sniff and retreated and I put out my tongue to her back. She was clearly envious of my role in Brisbane's life and felt her own usurped. She had spoilt him in his bachelor days, and I reflected, not for the first time, that Brisbane had a rather interesting effect upon women in his service. He invariably treated them with courtesy, far more than they were accustomed to receiving, and to a woman, they adored him. Maids, cooks, housekeepers. I had seen them all turn themselves inside out for a chance to polish his boots and cook his meals, and it was growing a little tiresome.

Besides, I reflected, Mrs. Lawson never attended Brisbane for the most critical of his injuries, for Monk was very accomplished with a needle and always set any stitches Brisbane required. But even I could manage a few gashes across the knuckles, I decided, and I carried in the tray to Brisbane with an air of brisk efficiency.

"Good God, what are you about?"

"I mean to clean that hand before it turns septic," I told him. I folded a fresh piece of white towelling and demanded the hand.

"Is this really necessary?" he asked. "I have work."

"Don't be stupid. You know that it is. Now, be quiet and let me get on with it." He gave an elaborate sigh, but I knew him well enough to know that he secretly enjoyed being fussed over, particularly by me. I put it down to having so little tender treatment as a child, and I made certain to move with gentleness as I bathed the injured hand in warm water. The gashes were not so deep as I feared, merely split knuckles, and I knew I could not bind them properly else he would not be able to write. Regretfully, I put aside the strips of linen I had torn for bandages and reached instead for the pot of salve. It was a preparation of yarrow and comfrey and smelled quite strong, but not unpleasantly so.

I daubed it gently, making certain to apply the salve just thoroughly enough to soothe the torn flesh. I was standing over him, my concentration fixed upon my task, when I realised he was watching me closely, his eyes never leaving my lips.

"Brisbane, I must finish," I said softly, but before I could quite manage the sentence, he had surged out of his chair and pinned me to the desk behind. I rather enjoyed the interlude that followed, brief as it was, for Brisbane had not quite achieved his aim when there came a noise from the doorway.

"Good God, man, she is my sister! I do not need to see that."

Brisbane looked past my shoulder. "Then get out," he growled at Plum.

Plum lounged into the room and dropped into a chair opposite the desk. "Would that I could. But I am at loose ends and you must give me work or I shall run mad. Julia, do something about your hair."

I put up my hand to find that my hair had almost entirely escaped its pins. "Oh, dear." I dropped to the floor to retrieve the pins where they had fallen.

Brisbane resumed his seat, and I saw from the evil glint in his eye that Plum was not to be forgiven for his intrusion. "Very well. I have just the job for you."

"I will not," Plum said flatly. "You cannot make me."

"You wanted a task, and Julia must be taught how to defend herself," Brisbane pointed out evenly.

"Yes, but like this?" We had pushed back the furniture in the main consulting room and Brisbane was instructing me in the finer arts of pugilism with Plum as my object.

"You haven't given her padded gloves," Plum put in. "And you told her to aim for my face."

Brisbane tossed him a velvet cushion. "Hold that up if she frightens you."

Plum swore fluently, and I positioned myself according to Brisbane's instructions. "Feet apart, knees loose, arms up," I recited.

"Very good. Now Plum will come at you with a right

cross," he instructed. He shot a piercing look to Plum who eventually complied, though with very little enthusiasm.

"Block it," Brisbane told me. "Now weight forward, lead with the flat between the knuckles of your right hand, stepping through the punch straight to the gut." We pantomimed the steps, and when my knuckles grazed Plum's waistcoat, he doubled over. "Turn your wrist to hit an uppercut straight to the jaw, then left cross. Then a right again."

I did as he told me, each time quickening the combination. He nodded. "Good. Of course, that will not help you if you have a left-handed fellow, and it will not aid you at all unless you have the element of surprise. No man will expect a lady to know how to do that, so it ought to stand you in good stead, but you must know a few other things, as well."

He then proceeded to teach me how to do several unspeakable things with my foot and my elbow and the heel of my hand, and with each new endeavour, Plum's face grew whiter.

"My God, Brisbane, you cannot teach her that! She is still a lady, for all her running about town like a savage."

Brisbane gave him a level gaze. "Anyone who would attack her will not care that she is a lady and this knowledge might well save her life. Again."

We walked through the steps again and again, until Plum finally cried off, pleading hunger. I was not quite ready to leave it, and at the last moment, I decided to apply what Brisbane had taught me to another part of Plum's anatomy.

Instantly, he collapsed onto the floor, deadly quiet and doubled over.

"Oh, that is *very* effective," I remarked. "Plum, dearest, are you quite all right?"

"He will be fine, but he may never father children," Brisbane put in drily.

Plum lifted a shaking finger towards Brisbane. "I blame you for this."

Brisbane had the grace to look slightly abashed. "I never told her to do that."

"You never told her not to," Plum put in before giving a deep groan.

"Julia, it is indeed effective, but not considered sporting for reasons that ought to be immediately apparent," Brisbane advised me.

I shrugged. "You were the one who taught me that in a street fight, one does not trouble with rules. Why bother with the rest of it when this does the trick so much more quickly?"

"Because you cannot always guarantee that you will be so fortunate as to land a blow in that particular area. Some men are a little quicker to protect themselves than Plum."

Plum muttered something unintelligible and no doubt profane, and I leaned nearer to Brisbane.

"Have I really hurt him? I mean, damaged him? He will be all right, won't he?"

"In time," Brisbane promised. He leaned over and clapped Plum on the shoulder. "Come back tomorrow. We start swords then."

Plum shuddered by way of reply.

We took Plum home shortly afterwards. He hobbled to his room and said he would have his dinner there on a tray, and Brisbane and I decided to do the same. A companionable meal taken in the privacy of our bedchamber always put me in mind of our honeymoon. True to his word, Swan proved an excellent cook and sent up an exquisite little meal with a bottle of superb wine as an accompaniment. We ate in our dressing gowns, chatting idly, and by tacit arrangement saying nothing of the investigation. We deserved at least a few minutes' peace, I thought, and Brisbane must have, as well, for it was not until the tray had been removed and we were settled before the fire and warming glasses of brandy that the subject came up.

"So, how does one go about finding an elusive German lady who has decided to make herself a proverbial needle in the haystack of London?" I enquired.

Brisbane rolled his glass thoughtfully between his palms.

"By tossing pebbles in a pond," he replied.

"I beg your pardon?"

"When you toss pebbles in a pond, you create ripples, some of which may be strong enough to come back to you. It is the same with detection. Put a few enquiries out, and something will shake loose. It has to," he finished firmly.

"I suppose we could retrieve the button from Stokes," I offered. "If he can tell us nothing further, we might show it to other haberdashers or even jewellers. It is a valuable little trinket."

"Possibly. We might also try an advertisement in the newspaper, mentioning Madame's death and alluding to the letters. The German still hasn't got her hands on those, and I suspect if she is still in London, it is solely to achieve her objective and retrieve the letters."

"You think there is a chance she has gone back to Germany already?"

"She may have, although I, for one, would not like to face Bismarck with work left undone. I suspect she is still here, biding her time until she can get her hands upon the letters. She must be frustrated by now," he mused. "Increasingly so.

Bismarck does not countenance failure. It would be dangerous for her to return to Germany without the letters."

I sipped, but the brandy tasted sour upon my tongue and
I put the glass aside and voiced a question that had been
nagging at me for the better part of the day. "Brisbane, if
you know Sir Morgan and he could vouch for you, are you
quite sure the police would be so quick to think the worst
of you if you interfered in an investigation? You said you
could be gaoled if they found you in the wrong place, but
surely Sir Morgan would speak on your behalf, use his influence to help."

Brisbane's gaze was inscrutable. "That shows precisely
how little you know Morgan Fielding. I assure you, if I am
apprehended by the Metropolitan Police, I am entirely on
my own."

"Too bad, really," I mused. "Seems a pity to know someone so well connected and be unable to make use of him."

Brisbane gave me a slow smile. "I find myself thoroughly
bored of the subject of Morgan Fielding. Come here."

He put his glass aside and I went to him. What followed
has no bearing upon the investigation, so I will pass on to
the next day.

At breakfast, Swan sent up an array of hot dishes—
coddled eggs and savoury kidneys and bacon coupled with
a warm fruit compote. Plum was up early and gone, set
off with Monk on an enquiry into the disappearance of a
sculpture from a private collection in Kensington, and Brisbane was very nearly finished when I descended, yawning
broadly.

"Good morning, my love. Tired?" he asked. He did
not raise his eyes from the newspaper, but a satisfied smile
played about his lips.

"Exhausted, as you can well imagine," I responded. "Really, Brisbane, you have the stamina of a domesticated farm animal. You cannot have had more than half an hour's sleep altogether."

He did not reply, but the smile deepened. He had availed himself of the generous breakfast, but I found I wanted only tea and a little toast.

I chewed slowly, dragging my feet as it were. For half a farthing, I would have retreated to my bed and slept the morning away. But for the first time in our relationship, Brisbane seemed not just reconciled to my involvement in our investigation but eager for it, and I was not about to be left behind.

I bolted the last of my toast and gulped at my tea, dashing out to find my hat and reticule. Pigeon and Swan were both in attendance as we left the house, and it occurred to me that the closer we drew to a conclusion in this case, the more dangerous it was. The veiled lady had already killed twice, if Mr. Sullivan was to be believed, and she would not scruple to kill again if it meant getting her hands on the letters.

We reached Mr. Stokes' shop in good time, and the tailor presented us with the button and an expression of despair.

"I have discovered nothing of significance," he said mournfully. "Except that it was most likely made for a woman's garment. There is a very slight difference in the execution of the design for the ladies of the kaiser's family in comparison with the gentlemen."

"Thank you, Stokes," Brisbane told him as he pocketed the button. "I am sure that information will be most useful."

Stokes preened then, and as we left the shop, I remonstrated gently with Brisbane. "We already had that information."

"It never hurts to be doubly certain," he assured me, "and next to one's wife, the most important person to keep happy is one's tailor."

I prodded him with my elbow, but he merely smiled and handed me back into the carriage. There had been a lightness to his tone, but as he settled himself, he reached into his pocket to retrieve his smoked spectacles.

"The headache?" I asked sharply.

He hesitated. "Only a certain sensitivity to light at present. It's just the beginning."

I felt a cold hand grip my heart. "You ought to have something now to head off the pain before it has a chance to establish itself." I was firm upon the point for two reasons. The first was that I dreaded to think of what might happen to the investigation if Brisbane were not in full possession of his faculties. I had seen him in the grip of a migraine and the various horrible cures he employed to deflect it. He might well be indisposed for some days as he wrestled with his demons. In that time, the veiled lady could easily find the letters and make her way to Berlin with them, imperiling my brother and indeed the entire government. The second reason was purely personal. I loved him, and it lashed me to see him in agony.

He gave me a thin smile. "I will be fine." But his face did not look fine, and as I watched, his eyes widened. He stared out the window of the carriage with unseeing eyes and did not blink. His breathing began to come fast and shallow, and there was a strange rattle in his throat.

"Brisbane? Brisbane, can you hear me?"

He made no response. He did not seem to be in pain, but

there was some distress, some detachment that frightened me deeply.

I would have pounded on the roof of the carriage had Monk been with us, and I cursed his absence just when I needed him most. He had more experience than anyone with Brisbane's odd fits and visions, and I craved his calm demeanour.

I put my hands to Brisbane's face, shouting at him. "Brisbane, can you hear me?"

He did not so much as blink. His concentration was complete. He saw something terrible in his mind, of that I had no doubt. His breathing was even faster now, and the gasping rattle of his inhalations frightened me.

I had to find a doctor, aid of some sort for him. I touched the handle of the carriage door, but before I could open it, his hand closed around mine, crushing it.

"Do. Not. Leave. Me." Each word was a struggle, ground out between jaws that did not move.

"I will not leave you," I promised him. "What do you see?"

His hands went to his throat, tearing at his neckcloth. He wrenched the fabric free, baring his throat, but still the awful gasping continued, as if each breath was a stolen thing and might be his last.

"Dying," he rasped.

And then he pitched forward into my lap, senseless.

I lifted his head. His eyes had rolled back into his head, and I rummaged in my reticule for a vinaigrette. I had seldom used one myself, but it seemed just the thing to restore Brisbane, and truth be told, I could not think of any other remedy for him. I opened the vial and held it beneath his nose, forcing him to breathe the foul vapours.

He jerked to his senses, coughing hard. "Are you actually trying to kill me?"

If I had been standing, my knees would have buckled at the swiftness of his recovery. A moment before, he had been reeling, gasping his last breaths it seemed, and now he pushed away the vinaigrette with great force and levered himself to a sitting position.

He took in his disarranged clothing and my face, which I have no doubt was white with shock.

"You had a vision," I said quietly. I took a discreet sniff of the vinaigrette myself before corking it and replacing it in my reticule.

"Christ. I am sorry." He restored his neckcloth and ran a hand through his tumbled hair. "How awful was it?"

"Not very."

"Then why are your hands shaking?"

I gave up my pretense then and threw myself into his arms. "It was horrible. You were making the most desperately awful noises, like a death rattle." I drew back and touched his face. "You seem well enough now."

"Yes, well, they go as quickly as they come sometimes. I am merely a little tired now."

"Do you remember anything of it?"

He said nothing for a long moment. "Only that I was suffocating. There was nothing but blackness all around me, pressing closer with each breath."

His voice was steady, but I noted the waxy pallor that had come over him. I still questioned his use of various substances to keep the visions at bay. Absinthe, poppy syrup, hashish. I had at times had my doubts about all of them. But when I saw him in the grip of his terrible visions, any remedy seemed better than the alternative.

I insisted upon dosing him with Granny Bones' willow-bark tonic.

"God, that's vile," Brisbane said, but I noted he seemed a trifle more energetic afterwards, and I corked the bottle and stowed it safely in my reticule. I had made a point of carrying it just on the chance it might be needed, and I felt rather smug at being properly prepared to take care of Brisbane in his time of need.

In light of his experience, we cut short our outing and returned to the consulting rooms in Chapel Street, where Brisbane read through the post while I fiddled with the tea things, pouring out too many cups and burning the toast.

After the fourth burnt piece, Brisbane sighed and took over the toasting fork. "What is it?"

I hesitated. "I just wonder if perhaps you ought to think about giving way to them more often," I began slowly.

"This again." His voice held no note of enquiry, only resignation.

"Yes, this again. Hear me out. You have these monstrous headaches that torment you beyond endurance. You dose yourself with all manner of nasty things to bear the pain. Now, I understand that the visions themselves are horrifying, but if the headaches are awful enough, as are the remedies, perhaps the answer is to simply endure the visions. At least then you might learn something useful."

He stared into the flames as they licked at the edges of the fork. The firelight played over the planes of his face like something out of Hell, and I remembered with a start the first time I read of the abduction of Persephone by the lustful Hades. He had come charging out of Hell itself to drag her down into the depths of the underworld—a fate worse than death, some would say. But my book had been illustrated with a painting of the event and I could see it still.

The pale, trembling figure of Persephone, clutched against the broadly muscled chest of her dark lover, one bared arm fast about her, protecting as much as imprisoning. And I had been struck with the notion that Persephone did not seem to mind all that much...

I wrenched my mind back to Brisbane and the matter at hand, trying very hard to ignore the writhing shadows over his face, casting him now in darkness, now illuminating him like a Renaissance saint.

"I cannot," he said, and in those two words was finality.

I put a hand to his arm. "I do not know if it is because you have pushed the visions aside for so long that now they can no longer be contained, or if it simply that they are growing stronger, but you cannot deny you have been more affected by them in recent weeks than ever before."

He said nothing and I pressed on, gently, ever so gently. I talked of my worries for him, my fears for his safety, for his sanity. As I talked, he became very still, his features schooled to immobility. Only his hand moved, twisting and turning the fork, thrusting the bread into the fire until it burnt to bits and the bits dropped into the flames and were consumed.

At length I paused, waiting for some reaction. And when it came, it rocked me backwards. He surged from the hearth rug where we had been huddled together like children. The first piece of furniture to hand was a chair and he took it up and broke it with a single blow of his hand, reducing it to kindling, which he threw upon the fire.

"Brisbane!" I said, shocked more than afraid.

He rounded on me then, clamping his hands at my shoulders and raising me roughly to my feet. "What? Are you afraid I have lost control? Let me discourse for you on the subject of control, wife. It is one I have had cause to think on most carefully these past months. And do you know what I have learned? That it is an illusion. All my life, I have prided myself on it. It has been the one constant in an otherwise precarious existence. No matter what else has befallen me, no matter who has left me, control over myself was my own choice. I staved off the visions because I could. It was all I had."

I opened my mouth, but his hands tightened farther still and he went on, his voice low and tight with emotion.

"Control was all I had and it is deserting me now, do you understand that? I vowed upon our wedding day to protect you and then I allowed myself, stupidly, to promise to involve you in my work. I thought I could do it. I thought I could control my fears for you, my terror that something unspeakable might happen to you, but I cannot, any more than I can control what happens to me when the visions come. I spend my whole life keeping these emotions at bay, forcing them back, and now I find that logic and control, my only real friends in this world, have deserted me. I built my life, my career, upon them, and they have fled when I needed them most."

He jerked his head towards the table where I conducted my experiments and gave a short, bitter laugh. "You play with science, and you think, as I once did, that you can reduce things to a formula. You think you can solve me as if I were an algebraic equation," he accused, and I blushed, thinking of Granny's admonition.

"I don't, not really," I began, but he raged me to silence.

"Oh, yes, you do. You think you have only to hit upon the right remedy and I will be fixed, cured of what ails me. But there is no power in Heaven or Hell can mend me. I have spent the whole of my life attempting to understand this affliction, and I will share with you the one thing I have learned—what I am, science has not a name for. I am an anomaly, a mistake, something undone."

The anger ebbed from him then, and in the space between us I heard nothing except a small crack that might have been what was left of my heart.

I slipped my arms out of his grasp and reached to put them about his neck. "Brisbane," I began.

He would not hear me. He pulled my arms down, gently this time, and walked to the door.

"Brisbane," I said again, this time through tears.

But he did not stop and he did not look back.

I waited for him to return, not entirely certain he would. I was heartsick and could not settle to much of anything. I scraped my latest efforts at the black powder into a pasteboard box and put it into my reticule, then tidied up after my experiments. I had no inclination to attempt more. I straightened stacks of magazines and plumped cushions, wondering how I could have failed to have guessed at Brisbane's true feelings. I had taxed him more than once with giving into his visions, but never before had he responded so savagely, and I could not blame him for it. He had carried the weight of self-loathing for a lifetime, and sometimes it was far harder to put a heavy burden down than it was to continue to plod on, mile after mile, one's back bowed against the weight of it.

I puttered in the attics, and as I did so, I reminded myself that Brisbane and I had shaken hands upon a wager. I was supposed to be unmasking Madame's killer myself, and a poor job I was making of it. But my sour mood at the raging scene with Brisbane had not yet abated, and I fretted as I picked up the various bottles and basins and set to work on my photography.

I tied on my darkroom apron and collected a series of negatives I had not yet developed. I slipped sheets of albumenised paper into wooden frames to put them in contact with the glass negatives. I then slid the whole contraption into the chemical bath, careful not to spill any of the vile liquids onto myself. As ever, the outside world began to slip away as I worked. There was something soothingly repetitive about labouring in my darkroom, and the dark, muffling draperies were curiously womblike. I worked for some time, feeling calmer than I had and even a little easier in my mind that Brisbane and I would find some way of resolving our differences.

Towards the end of the batch, I printed a particularly charming portrait of Jane the Younger. She was screaming, with her mouth open wide, but the expression of outrage upon her face was so entirely serious that I knew Portia would find it enchanting. I fixed it in a bath of hyposulfite of soda and water, then washed it and pinned it up to dry, well pleased with the work. I turned to the next portrait. This was of Auld Lachy. He had insisted on being photographed with his favourite seashell, the one he liked to carry about as if it were a child. It was ludicrous, of course, and the tea cosy on his head merely added to the absurdity, but something about the shadows upon his face gave him real dignity. There was humour in his gaze, and something otherwordly about his expression. It was a sorcerer's face, Merlin out of myth. He would be very pleased, and I pinned that one up, as well, promising myself that I would take it to him once I had got it nicely framed. I had no doubt he would hang it in pride of place in his hut.

I peered into the basin as the next image began to emerge, and I smiled. It was a photograph I had taken of our household staff. They were ranged upon the back steps, with

Aquinas standing in the centre, holding a bottle of wine
to denote his rank as butler. Next to him, Morag stood,
ramrod straight, eyes firmly closed. I had yet to manage
one of her where she kept her eyes open, I reminded myself
ruefully, although it did not matter in this particular photograph. Pigeon had been captured in the middle of a
sneeze, and the Swiss cook had turned her face at the last
minute, thoroughly blurring her image during the lengthy
exposure.

Something about that blur attached my interest. I leaned
closer, fishing the paper from the basin. I fixed the image,
then hung it to dry upon the clothesline that had been
pegged up for that purpose. I hurried to develop the next
plate. I had taken four in all, and in each of them, the cook
had moved, making it impossible to identify her. She was
insubstantial as a ghost, and I felt suddenly lightheaded. I
sat upon the floor, thinking hard. She had come to us suddenly, just after Madame's death. She claimed to be Swiss,
but German Swiss, and as Brisbane had observed, it was
difficult for anyone not a native speaker to detect a regional
accent. Was it possible that she was not Swiss, but was in
fact, German?

I cast my mind back feverishly to what I had observed
of the veiled lady at the séance. Medium height, medium
build, heavy veil obscuring her features and her hair. There
had been nothing to betray her, not age or colouring or
mannerisms. She was a cipher, as any good spy would be, I
reflected bitterly. She might be a marchioness or a milkmaid
or anything in between. She might even be a cook.

The more I thought of it, the more I liked the idea. Madame's German contact would certainly have investigated
Bellmont, would have knowledge of his family at her fingertips. She would have known that Brisbane would be

drawn into this web of intrigue, and by extention, me. What more natural than to take employment in our home?

She must have panicked, I reasoned, as soon as Madame had died and the letters had not been found. Her plot hung by a slender thread, and that slender thread was the hope that the letters might be recovered.

They must have quarrelled, I decided. I thought again of the séance and of the message from a dark lady that Madame had related. Something about patience. She had counselled encouragement and said that all things would come right in the end but that the recipient of the message must be generous. Had that been a thinly cloaked demand for more money? What if Madame had decided to hedge her bets, keeping the letters until all of her demands were met? She might have continually raised her demands, until finally her coconspirator could stand no more and killed her, realising too late that Madame had not left the letters accessible.

And how best to retrieve the letters? I mused. She would have turned to Brisbane. What better than taking employment in his house, in the servants' quarters where the gossip flowed like water? She would wait and watch, safe as a fox in her den. There was no need for her to find the letters if we did it first. She had only to be patient and Brisbane and I would do the work for her.

But then the fire broke out, I remembered. The fire would have been suspicious to her, a telltale sign that someone else was sniffing round for the letters. She had bolted then, giving notice and leaving the house whilst Brisbane and I were in the Gypsy camp, *just in time to throw Agathe LeBrun under the wheels of a train.* What had passed between them? Agathe and her sister were cut from the same cloth. Had she bluffed the veiled lady into believing that the letters were in her possession? Had she, too, overplayed her hand,

and—frustrated and frightened now—the veiled lady had killed her?

It all hung together beautifully as a spider's web, intricate and complex, but with a perfect order at the heart of it. I rose from the floor with trembling fingers and removed my apron and washed my hands. I had to tell Brisbane, and I had to do it instantly, and it was with a heavy heart that I suddenly remembered he was not there.

"Blast," I muttered. I hesitated. I ought to wait for him, but I had no notion of how long we had before the trail ran cold. I thought then of the hundred-pound wager and Brisbane's gnawing fears that I would not prove equal to detection and that decided me. I snatched up my hat and coat. Just as I put my hand to the doorknob, it turned and I shrieked.

The figure in the doorway shrieked back, clutching a basket to her bosom.

"Lady Julia! You frightened me half to death!" Felicity Mortlake's blue eyes were enormous in her fair face.

"I do apologise. You caught me unawares. I was just on my way out."

"Oh, I am sorry to have come at a bad time," she said. She lifted the basket in her arms. "I thought Mr. March might be about and perhaps a little hungry. A picnic in the park," she added with a becoming blush. "As he is not here, perhaps you and I might take luncheon together."

"Plum is off on a case, God only knows where," I informed her. "It was a sweet thought, and I would join you myself, only I am in a tearing hurry."

"Oh, I will not keep you," she said, her face a trifle downcast. I felt a thornprick of pity for the girl. She had become quite fond of Plum in the past days, and I wondered sometimes if he entirely returned her regard. He was a fool if he did not, I decided. She was quick and clever and it had taken great strength of character to leave her father's house.

I smiled at her to take the sting from my refusal. "We will do it tomorrow," I promised. "Only just now I am off to investigate a matter that cannot wait."

Her eyes widened farther still and she clutched the basket more tightly. "You will be careful, won't you? It's just that Plum has told me how dangerous the work can be." She blushed a little at the slip of using his familiar name, and I gave her a sisterly pat.

"Of course I will be careful."

She fell to nibbling her lip. "I wonder if you would take me with you."

I blinked at her. "Take you along? Are you quite serious?"

She put down the basket and squared her shoulders. "I am. Lady Julia, I must own what I feel and what I feel is that I am quite desperately in love with your brother. He means to be a detective and a good one, and if I have any hope of becoming his wife, I must learn to help him. I think he believes me too soft, too useless to do this sort of work, but I am not, really," she added, leaning towards me, earnestness writ on her face.

"Lady Felicity, this is not the sort of work one undertakes upon a whim," I began.

"I know that! And I have thought the matter over, quite thoroughly, I assure you," she said, her voice firm. "You have learned to become a proper partner to Mr. Brisbane, and I wish to do the same for Plum. Will you help me?"

I hesitated, taking in the shining eyes, the pleading expression. "Oh, very well. But bring the basket in the carriage. I am starving."

The
TWENTY-FIRST CHAPTER

One truth leads right to the world's end.
—*"Mr. Sludge, 'The Medium'"* Robert Browning

Lady Felicity proved an excellent helper in detection. She kept quiet on our drive to the domestic agency, asking no questions and handing over little sandwiches whenever I requested them. I had second and then third thoughts about involving her, and then reminded myself that Brisbane had drawn Plum into our investigations without so much as a by-your-leave to me. I did, however, take the precaution of telling her to wait in the carriage whilst I went to speak with Mrs. Potter, the owner of the domestic agency. The interview was brief and unsatisfactory. I demanded the name of the current employer of my previous cook and she refused it. No amount of cajolery or persuasion would change her mind, and I returned to the carriage to find Felicity munching contentedly on a plum tart, scattering crumbs over her skirts.

"I am sorry," she said through a full mouth. "It was the last of the plum tarts. Would you like apple?"

I waved her off. "No, I am at a loss and must think."

She brushed the crumbs from her gloves and fixed me with a reproving stare. "If there is one thing I understand, it is domestic troubles. My stepmother has been far too busy with her pregnancies to run the household. I have done it since Mama died. Tell me what you want to know from this woman, and I will discover it."

I gave her an abbreviated version of the truth, saying only that I needed to speak with the cook who had left my employ a few days previously and that I had no way of learning where she worked at present.

"The easiest thing in the world!" Felicity crowed. She handed over an apple tart and told me she had matters well in hand. She said nothing more, but waited a few minutes until we saw Mrs. Potter leave the agency, pinning her hat firmly in place as she walked. Mercifully, she did not look towards us, but I had taken the precaution of flinging myself to the floor of the carriage just in case. Felicity kept watch upon her and related her every movement.

"She finally has that wretched hat pinned down. She is walking towards Oxford Street, rummaging in her reticule. She has not looked back—oh! She has just hailed a hansom. No doubt she means to be gone for some little time if she has taken a horse cab. The time has come!"

With that pronouncement, Felicity alighted from the carriage and made her way up the steps of the agency. I struggled back to my seat just in time to see her enter. I waited, tapping my foot for the better part of a quarter of an hour until she emerged. She walked sedately back to the carriage, but just as she reached the door, she smiled broadly and brandished a slip of paper.

"Success!" She slammed the door behind her and shouted a direction to the driver. Her eyes were shining and her colour was high. Felicity Mortlake was having the time of her life, and I was glad of it.

"How?" I demanded.

Her expression was deservedly smug as she tucked the paper away in her reticule. "Well, I reasoned that Mrs. Potter would tell me nothing so soon after your enquiry, so I knew I would have to speak with an assistant. I hardly dared to hope that she would be so forthcoming! I had prepared an elaborate story about a Swiss aunt coming to visit and wanting to serve her some of her native delicacies and how I required a Swiss cook for a short engagement, but she was scarcely listening! I no sooner mentioned that I was there about a Swiss cook and she said, 'That will be Frau Glöcken. You'll be the second lady today asking after her. She is cooking at Lauderdale House.' Lauderdale House, can you believe it?"

Lauderdale House, once home to the earls of that title, had passed into other hands and not many years past been opened to the public for teas and other social events. It was perched on the edge of Waterlow Park, a very pretty green space dotted with ponds and little hills and extraordinary views of London. Rather a step up from our rented lodgings, even in Brook Street, and I said as much to Felicity.

She laughed aloud. "But surely not as prestigious as cooking for the daughter of the Earl March. Really, if she means to advance in private service, she would have been far better off with you."

It was on the tip of my tongue to explain to Felicity that I was not searching out the cook in order to settle any domestic troubles. But I could not imagine her shock if I were to explain that my cook was, in fact, an agent of the German government, so I said nothing.

A furrow knit her brow and she leaned forward. "I do

not mean to pry into your business, Lady Julia, but you have been rather adamant that you must find this person. Is she dangerous? Ought we to wait for Mr. Brisbane or Mr. March to accompany us?"

I was not surprised at her current attack of nerves. I had had my own doubts a time or two when I had faced down danger, but I thought again of the hundred-pound wager I had made with Brisbane and smiled.

"Do not fear, my dear. I am prepared," I said, patting my reticule gently.

Her eyes fairly popped from her head. "You have a weapon?"

"A small revolver, but deadly enough should we have need of it," I assured her.

She swallowed hard, but her next words were courageous ones. "I only wish I had known," she said stoutly. "I should have brought Father's duelling pistols."

We collapsed into laughter then, but as we drove on, we sobered. No more titbits from the picnic basket, no more girlish confidences. I knew I was taking a grave risk in confronting the cook by myself, but I also knew I dared not wait for Brisbane. She had spooked as easily as an unbroken pony at the fire in our lodgings. Who was to say she would not spook again? And if she fled, it would be impossible to trace her. I would not have found her even now if it were not for Lady Felicity's efforts, I reminded myself, and when the carriage drew up near to Lauderdale House, I realised it would be unfair to keep her sheltered from what would follow. She made no move to alight from the carriage, and I turned.

"I will leave it to your own judgement to accompany me or not, Lady Felicity. You have been a great help to me thus far, but I will not ask you to place yourself in harm's way."

She gulped once, then alighted to take her place next to me. She lifted her chin and gave a short, sharp nod. "Let us do this."

"Very good," I said. I led the way towards the front door, but as we drew near, Felicity plucked at my sleeve.

"Surely the back door," she suggested, nodding with her head to the side of the house. "If we mean to surprise her, we must approach without warning."

"An excellent notion," I conceded. We walked together around the side of the house, concealed by the shrubbery. Just as we reached the corner of the shrub walk, Lady Felicity grabbed my arm hard.

"What is it?" I demanded in a harsh whisper. "Do you see something?"

"Only a very stupid woman who has put herself entirely into my power," she said in a thoroughly unrecognisable voice. I jerked my head to find her pointing a rather lethal-looking pistol straight at my heart.

"Guten Tag, meine Liebe," she said sweetly. And the world began to spin.

"No, you don't," she said sharply. She reached out and gave me a sound slap on either cheek. "You will not swoon. You will walk quite naturally in that direction," she said, tipping her head away from Lauderdale House.

"There are people not fifty feet away inside the house," I reminded her. "I might scream."

"And I will shoot you before anyone can get to you."

It seemed a rather good plan, I was forced to admit, and I had no choice but to obey. I turned to walk, and she nudged my back with her pistol. "Not quite so quickly, my dear. I believe you mentioned a weapon in your reticule. I will have it, and mind you hand it over nicely."

I did as she bade and she tucked my little pistol into her pocket before we started off.

"Where are we bound?" I asked by way of making conversation.

"Towards the far end of Waterlow Park," she told me. We walked for some time across the pretty park, and if it was a fine autumn day, there were precious few others out to enjoy it. I saw in the distance a groundskeeper or two, but I dared not call out to them. I had no doubt Felicity would shoot me if I tried, and she would not hesitate to harm them, as well.

As we walked, I peppered her with questions.

"So you were Madame's German contact, the veiled lady," I began. "Why did you take up with the Germans?"

"Because of Mama," she returned impatiently. "Do you know nothing?"

I cast my mind back to the first Lady Mortlake. A pale and pretty blonde with an impenetrable accent. The gears shifted then, and a bit of the machinery of the plot slotted into place. "Your mother was a German."

"A Sigmaringen-Hohenzollern," she said proudly. "Distant cousin to the kaiser. She came with the Crown Prince of Germany's contingent when he married Princess Victoria. Mama stayed behind to marry my father, but she never forgot where she came from, and I bear her blood."

"So with the proud Teutonic blood of the Fatherland flowing in your veins, you thought you'd do a bit of spying for old Bismarck, is that the idea?"

The point of the barrel wedged painfully in my ribs. "Do not speak so disrespectfully of the Chancellor. He is a great man, and under him, Germany will rise."

I snorted aloud. "Oh, do leave off the flag-waving patriotism, Felicity. This has nothing to do with your mother's people. You are simply out to have your revenge upon your father."

Her pretty complexion flushed a dull red. "He made my mother's life a misery. He took up with that slut of a governess when Mama was alive, did you know that? And when she finally died of a broken heart, he married his whore within a year."

"It was badly done," I agreed, "but if everyone who had family troubles took up espionage as a hobby, where would that leave the world?"

The pistol pushed farther still, and I gave a sharp gasp. "Your flippancy does you no credit. Just because you cannot grasp true patriotism does not mean it fails to exist."

"I apologise," I said breathlessly. "But you have managed to kill quite a few birds with just the one stone, haven't you? I mean, you can have your revenge upon your father, further the interests of your mother's people, and—I imagine—line your pockets rather neatly at the same time. Not a bad day's work."

To my surprise, she laughed. "Day? I have been putting this scheme together for the better part of three years. It took quite some time to cultivate the proper contacts, then I had to gain Madame's confidence, persuade her that I could secure her future completely. She was not as easy to lure into conspiracy as I had imagined she would be."

Of course she wasn't, I thought to myself. Séraphine was far too accustomed to making her own way and fashioning her own schemes. She would have been wary, and it was a pity she had not clung to that wariness. It might have saved her life.

"Hmm, yes," I murmured. "Too bad about her. And about Agathe. I presume Agathe promised the letters and failed to deliver?"

"Time and again," Felicity said, her mouth twisting bitterly. "It reached the point where she became too much of a liability. I discovered she had told someone else about the letters, and I had to remove her."

My heart felt heavy then. I had not particularly liked Agathe. I had considered her a schemer and a charlatan, but no one deserved to die as she had, twisted beneath the wheels of a train, crushed by tonnes of steaming iron. Poor Mr. Sullivan had been lucky, I decided. If Felicity had known his identity, she might well have killed him, as well.

"And still you have no letters," I observed. "However will you proceed now?"

Again the shove between my ribs, and this time I felt a stay in my corset break, piercing the flesh. "I will proceed how I see fit. We have arrived, Lady Julia. Enter."

I looked up to see the looming gates of Highgate Cemetery. I had forgot the park bordered the cemetery. How fitting, I thought. And as I passed beneath them, I wondered if I would ever emerge.

We walked for some time through the cemetery, and I continued to annoy her with questions. "So my poor Swiss cook was entirely innocent of my suspicions?"

She gave a short, mirthless laugh. "Entirely."

"Little wonder you could not let me confront her," I mused. "You dared not let me accuse her for fear she would persuade me of her innocence."

"I could not let you accuse her because I do not know where she is," she corrected with exaggerated impatience. "I made up the story about Lauderdale House to get you to Highgate. It would have seemed terribly suspicious if I had just instructed the driver to take us to the cemetery, would it not?"

I marvelled in spite of myself. "You are quick on your feet, I will give you that much."

"I always have been. Why do you think the Mortlake emeralds ended up in Father's study? I had to have a place to hide them until I could find a jeweller to buy them. If I hid them amongst my things, it would have been damning should they be found. Amongst Father's things, they pointed only to him."

"You implicated your own father in a scheme to defraud his insurers! He might have gone to prison," I chided her.

"I believe I have made it quite clear that my father and I are not close," she returned blandly.

"Unnatural child," I muttered.

She guided me along the Egyptian Walk. The gates were still open, but there were no mourners, and I began to feel a little desperate. Had no one died recently? Was there no one to weep at the graves?

I half expected her to guide me to the Circle of Lebanon, to the same crypt where Mr. Sullivan had so thoughtfully laid his trap, but she did not. Instead she directed me to a small mausoleum that bore a familiar name. Mortlake.

She took a key from her reticule and brandished it with a thin smile. "One never knows when a quiet bolthole in the city will prove useful."

She handed me the key and gestured for the door. I unlocked it and entered. At her instruction, I struck a match and lit a candle that stood upon a little shelf. The light was dim in that cool expanse of dark marble, but it shone enough to permit a quick inspection of the place. I was not surprised to find myself surrounded by the dead, but it did strike me as odd that there should be clothing and a small supply of tinned food.

"Have you been living here?" I was curious in spite of myself.

"As I said, it is a useful place to collect my thoughts. I come here from time to time to rest or for a change of clothing."

She nodded towards the neat pile of garments lying in a basket and I recognised the garb of the veiled lady.

"My mother's things," she told me. I lifted one sleeve to find the buttons of the Sigmaringen-Hohenzollerns. The device matched that on the plaque of the nearest coffin. Beneath it were inscribed the words, "Kristina, Countess of Mortlake, Baroness von Hoefgen, beloved wife and mother."

"You must miss her very much," I observed quietly. "I lost my own mother. I understand."

Felicity rolled her eyes. "You understand nothing. And if you think to raise my sympathy by pointing out what we have in common, you have rather missed the point."

I shrugged. "It doesn't alter the truth. We have both of us lost our mothers."

"Stop talking," she ordered. "I have to think what to do next."

"This was rather impulsive," I agreed. "It is always best to have a plan if one can possibly arrange it."

She bared her teeth at me. "Do you have a plan?"

"I suppose it rather depends upon yours," I admitted.

"Good. Then be quiet. I am thinking."

Her voice had risen sharply, and I realised that if her cool composure deserted her, it would make her more volatile. She might make a mistake, but she might also become more erratic and therefore more dangerous.

I gave her a few minutes to think and then began again.

"It's curious that you and Mr. Sullivan both decided to make nefarious use of Highgate," I observed.

She made a moue of distaste. "Sullivan? You mean the ginger fellow. Is that his name? He followed me once from the Spirit Club when I came back here to change before I returned to the country. I lost him outside the gates of the cemetery, but he poked around here so long I very nearly missed my train."

"That would have been awkward to explain," I said, infusing my voice with sympathy. "In fact, you must have been very clever indeed to account for all your absences from Mortlake House."

"It did take some ingenuity," she admitted, preening a little. "I bribed my maid to make excuses for me sometimes and I made my way to the city alone. I had to be back in my own bed by morning, but I managed it. I think the stupid girl believed I had a lover," she said with a bitter smile.

"And that is how you managed to be at the séance the night the Mortlake emeralds were discovered. You pleaded a headache and retired to your room, only to slip out and take the train into London to attend the séance. You returned before morning, pretending as if you'd never been away. Neatly done, I must say. Tell me, did you care for Plum at all?"

"Of course," she said, and with such an air of matter-of-factness that I believed her. "Once or twice I even wondered what it would be like to give up my plans and become what I only pretended to be—a respectable and eligible member of society. But I could never see it. I could conjure a picture in my mind of Plum, of the house we should live in, of the parties we should give. But never once could I see myself in the picture."

Her expression was rueful, and against my will, I felt sorry for her. "You might have, if you had given it a chance."

She laughed at me then, and to my horror, I saw unshed tears shimmering in her eyes. "No, I think not. There is something broken within me. I know that now. I do not want the warmth of domesticity and love. I want the cold satisfaction of knowing I have fulfilled my plans. That is enough."

"It won't be if you fail to get the letters to Bismarck," I pointed out. "I suspect the Chancellor is a rather exacting master with very little patience for incompetence."

She gave me a nasty look. "Yes, I have considered that."

I sighed. "Well, what is the plan then?"

She spoke, the words slow and all the more horrifying for the calmness of her tone. "I must get away. To Germany. Bismarck will protect me, of that I have no doubt. I have failed him, but he will be merciful. He must," she said, perhaps a trifle too insistently. "And I cannot have you running loose to sound the alarm. So you will remain here. I will make one last attempt to secure the letters, and then I will leave."

"And me?" I asked politely.

"You will stay here."

She rose then and before I could open my mouth to speak, she was gone, slamming the door of the crypt behind her.

I vaulted to the door, trying the handle, but she had locked it soundly. And I was alone with the dead.

I do not know how many hours I remained there in the dark, locked behind the bronze door, but it was not long before I remembered Brisbane's remark about the sealed tomb when we had been lured to the subterranean vault by Sullivan. I realised that the air in the crypt could not sustain me. The stone walls and the heavy bronze door admitted not the slightest particle of air. I blew out the single candle, preferring the dark to the sight of those coffins arrayed against the walls. One effigy in particular seemed to be grinning, promising that I should be next. I slid to the floor and wrapped my arms around my knees, one word humming ceaselessly through my brain. *Brisbane.* I had no notion of when he planned to return to Chapel Street, and when he did, he should find me gone, disappeared with no trace left behind after that terrible scene between us. I could not imagine what his thoughts would be. Mrs. Lawson had not seen me leave with Felicity; the hansom could not be traced. Mrs. Potter could tell him that I had been on the trail of my Swiss cook, but that was a road to nowhere, even if Brisbane thought to enquire of her.

No, there was no hope that Brisbane would find me in time. *In time.* The words rang against the marble of the crypt, so I knew I had said them aloud. Was I mad then? I know I talked to myself, at first simply to break the awful silence of the place. I had tried screaming, but the shrieks only echoed back to me, and I knew no one would hear them. I searched every inch of the crypt for something, anything—a way out, a tool to pry at the door, a mechanism to open a hidden crypt. I ransacked my own reticule, and found only the tiny box of self-igniting black powder. I knew it would cause a cloud of smoke and spark, but it would take a far more powerful explosion to blow a bronze door from its hinges. I dared not detonate it and take the chance of failure, for if the door did not open I should suffocate myself almost instantly.

I continued to try, running my hands over every shelf, every coffin, every effigy that laughed at me in the darkness.

There was nothing. No crack of light shone through the inky blackness of the place, no bright sliver of hope to sustain me. Nothing but the enduring dark, and my own imagination.

The physical symptoms were to be expected. I felt hot and clammy and fatigued, and it was not long before a raging headache took hold of me. The mental aberrations were more unexpected and therefore more disturbing. I saw my mother during those long hours and others not so welcome. I saw my first husband, whose grave lay not far from this place, and I wondered if Brisbane would bury me there. I cried once, in my darkest hour of despair, and then I felt myself grow steadily calmer. Perhaps it was the lack of air that caused me to settle myself; perhaps it was simply that I was preparing myself for what must come. With the last of my ebbing strength, I pulled myself on top of the Kristina's coffin. The air was marginally fresher than that nearer to the floor, and I arranged myself as comfortably as I could atop the effigy of the late Countess of Mortlake. I lay there and breathed slowly, expecting each inhalation to be my last.

I drifted then, for how many hours I could not guess. I heard voices, but I made no attempt to answer them. I simply lay and let the sound lap over me, washing me out to the calm blue sea that beckoned.

Just as the sea broke over me, there was a shattering light, and I heard a voice louder then, shouting in my ear. Cool fresh air rushed in, and I struggled to sit up.

"For God's sake, just lie still," Brisbane ordered, and his voice broke as he said it.

I opened my eyes and Felicity was standing in the doorway, Plum and Morgan Fielding behind her.

"She is alive," Brisbane called over his shoulder. He slid

one arm under my legs and the other under my shoulders, hefting me as if I weighed no more than a child.

"What a lovely dream," I murmured.

"It isn't a dream, you daft woman," he growled in my ear. "I am rescuing you."

"How wonderful," I said, and he carried me swiftly out of the crypt.

To my astonishment, I saw that it was morning. The sun was slanted just over the gravestones and drops of dew hung heavy as jewels upon the grass. The air was crisp and intoxicating as wine, and I poked at Brisbane to set me upon my feet. My knees buckled instantly, but he did not move his arm, and I leaned heavily against him, breathing in the blessed sweet air.

"Lady Felicity Mortlake, I will see you charged with the attempted murder of Lady Julia Brisbane, as well as the murder of Agathe LeBrun," said Morgan Fielding. He looked every inch the government official now. The effete creature of society had been replaced by a stalwart man of action.

She appeared not to hear him. Her face was impassive as marble, and she did not look at Plum. He held his Webley in his hand, and I wondered if he would have the courage to use it against her if it became necessary.

Morgan took charge of the situation. "Mr. March and I will see to it that Lady Felicity is taken into custody, Brisbane. Take your wife home and we will speak later."

Brisbane agreed, and turned to help me. Just as Morgan reached to take Felicity's arm, she gave a little step and seemed to totter, crying out. I assumed she must have tripped over a broken bit of gravestone, for she doubled over to grab her ankle. Plum moved to help her, and as he moved, she rose and there came a sudden pop and a flash and Plum fell back with a scream of pain.

"Plum!" I rushed to him, but before I could touch him, Felicity stepped neatly in front of me and pivoted to put my body between hers and the rest of the group. I would have thrown her off, but she clamped her free hand to my shoulder.

"Stay where you are," she ordered, and I saw then that she held a revolver, a small but lethal thing, and she pointed it at each of the men in turn, holding them at bay.

I started to move, but Brisbane's voice rang out in command. "Do as she says," he ordered. "She is desperate."

"But Plum—" I could not finish the question. It was unthinkable.

"Mr. March is not fatally injured," Sir Morgan said coolly.

I felt my knees begin to buckle, but Felicity's fingers tightened on my shoulder, biting hard, and I did not fall.

"Are you certain?"

"Quite," Sir Morgan assured me. Just then, Plum struggled to his feet, holding his left arm. Blood flowed freely from his sleeve and his face so white I would have thought him dead if he had not risen.

"You bitch," he said succinctly.

Felicity pointed her revolver at him. "You were in the way. Do not make the same mistake again. Get over there, with Mr. Brisbane and your friend," she said, gesturing towards Morgan. She gave a nod of satisfaction.

"Now, I am leaving here with Lady Julia. She will be my safe conduct. When I have reached my destination, she will be released unharmed, you have my word." But I heard the desperation in her voice, and I knew her word was not worth my life. The others knew it, too, for Plum raised his good arm, levelling his revolver at her.

"For God's sake, hold your fire," Brisbane ordered hoarsely. "You might hit Julia."

That much was true. Plum had always been a fairly poor shot, and I did not like my chances with him for my liberator. And Brisbane dared not move, caught as he was with Felicity's weapon aimed directly at his heart. Morgan said nothing, he merely stood calmly, assessing the situation and waiting for her to reveal her gambit.

Felicity was not so cool as she pretended, for the hand upon my shoulder twitched a little.

"Perhaps I ought to just settle this now," she said, thinking aloud. "You have the advantage of me in numbers, and I do not much care for the odds." She cocked the weapon then, and I realised with a shattering roar of rage in my head that she meant to shoot Brisbane. She meant to shoot him, and there was no one to save him but me. I had no choice, and in that space of a heartbeat, my rage rolled away, smothered in the cool conviction that I must act.

I raised my reticule, and as I did, I heard Brisbane cry for me to stop. He had guessed my intention, but Felicity had not, and when I flung the reticule and its little pasteboard box of self-igniting gunpowder to the ground, the world erupted in a sheet of smoke and flame. Felicity was blown back against the crypt, her weapon wrenched from her hand, and I was flung backwards.

I could not see what happened to anyone else. I only knew that I was thrown up and then down again, into the wall of the crypt, hitting the stone with an audible crack before falling into the grass, the dew soaking my gown.

Brisbane was at my side in the space of a heartbeat. His clothes were streaked with soot and a long line of blood trickled from his brow. He gathered me onto his lap, touching the warm, sticky blood on my head and hands, demanding that I speak to him.

"I am alive," I said finally, wondering if it were actually true. "The powder was rather stronger than I anticipated."

He was holding me so tightly I could not breathe, or perhaps it was that I had cracked a rib or two, for breathing had never seemed such an ordeal before. I called his name and I felt his lips on my face.

"I am here, I am here," he repeated, chanting the words like a monk at prayer.

I felt broken, like a child's doll that is no longer wanted and has been flung to the ground. "It hurts," I murmured.

"I know. We must get you out of here," he said, and from the carefully schooled expression on his face, I knew all was not well.

"I will be fine," I promised him. "But I must look a fright."

"You are the most beautiful thing I have ever seen," he said harshly, and I knew he spoke roughly so I would not hear the break in his voice. "I am going to pick you up," he warned. "Lift your head a little."

He slid his arm under my neck and another under my legs and as he shifted me, I gave a cry. Something twisted in my abdomen then, a hot knife of pain lancing me inside.

"Julia! What is it?"

I put my hands to my womb just as I felt the first warm gush of blood between my legs. "The baby," I murmured. And then all went black.

The
TWENTY-SECOND CHAPTER

You are my true and honourable wife,
As dear to me as are the ruddy drops
That visit my sad heart.

—Julius Caesar

I do not like to think of the following days, for they were dark ones. I lost the child, and from what I was told, it was rather a near thing for me, as well. Brisbane's dear friend, Mordecai Bent, and my own brother Valerius worked like madmen to save me. At length, Mordecai was able to assure Brisbane that I would live but that I would never be able to conceive another child. Brisbane swore profanely, Mordecai told me, but not at the thought of my barrenness. He was outraged that Mordecai even thought he would care about such a thing when my life was at stake.

But I cared. As little as I had thought I wanted children, the knowledge that I had lost this one—unexpected as it had been—was bitter. I had only begun to suspect in the last few days before the accident, and I reminded myself over and over again that I could hardly mourn a child that had never been truly mine. It helped only a little. I dreamed incessantly of a black-eyed boy that had his father's tumbled dark locks and musicality and my sharp wit. Waking was little better. My injuries were extensive and painful. I had broken a pair of ribs and there were numerous lacerations and bruises to be nursed from a cracked cheekbone to a fractured bone in my foot. Brisbane came only occasionally to see me, for Mordecai kept me drugged with morphia until I finally threw the bottle away and said I would rather lie awake with the pain than endure any more of that strange twilight of the drug.

I demanded Brisbane and he came to me then, his face haggard, and fresh silver threading the hair at his temples. He said nothing for a long time, but climbed into bed with me and gathered me so very gently to him. It was only then that I was able to weep, soaking his shirt with my tears as he stroked my hair.

"I am sorry," I whispered.

"So am I," he said fiercely. "I failed you."

I struggled to sit up. He would not let me, but I managed to move my head to look him in the eye. "How can you say it? You saved me. If you had not got there when you did, I would have died. It was my own fault for using that gunpowder without testing it thoroughly," I said. "But I was so desperately afraid that she was going to shoot you. I had to save you."

His expression was one of wonderment. "You were trying to save me?"

"Of course. To lose you is impossible."

"It was not your fault," he said fiercely. "You acted for the best."

His eyes were haunted, and I put my hands to his face. "I absolve you. It was not your fault, and you are right. It was not mine. We did the best we could under difficult circumstances. And we are alive to tell the tale."

He held me close then, as close as he dared for all my bruises and bandages.

"I understand now," I said, my voice muffled against his shoulder. "I really do."

"Understand what?"

"What it feels like to see the one person you love most in the world in peril. I never knew it before, not really. And when I saw Felicity aim for your heart, I suddenly felt so very stupid not to have known."

"Known?"

"How savage it is. There is nothing reasonable or logical about it. You were so right when you said that control deserted you where I was concerned. I could no more have controlled what I did next than I could have flown to the moon. I set off that explosion because I had no thought in my head except to save you. I never counted the danger to myself or anyone else. Only you mattered in that moment. Only you. And I would have done anything to save you. I would have paid any price, committed any sin, sold my very soul to do it."

He stroked my hair and said nothing, but the hand upon my head stilled for an instant, and I felt it tremble.

I ventured a question then that I did not want to ask.

"Are you very upset about the child?"

He was silent a long moment, and I began to regret putting the question to him.

"It was an abstraction," he said finally. "It was not real to me, even when Mordecai explained that this one was gone and we could never have another."

"Did you never think of children then? Ours?"

His voice was thick with emotion. "I never expected in the whole of my life that God would be so generous as to give me you. I did not think to ask for more."

I had never heard Brisbane speak so poignantly of God, and something deep within me that had been tightly knotted uncoiled.

We talked a little of the details then, and we pieced together what we knew between us. It had transpired that the visit to Middlesex had been to call upon Lord Mortlake, who had finally seen fit to relate to someone his doubts about the loyalty and character of his eldest child. He had long suspected Felicity of German sympathies, but he had hesitated to call her out publicly until he discovered that she was living with Portia. Afraid of what havoc she might wreak amongst innocent folk, he had finally summoned Brisbane to confess his daughter's treachery.

"I could have throttled him with my bare hands for not telling us sooner," Brisbane told me.

"But at least he told you where to find me," I said, my eyes drooping heavily. The lingering effect of the drug was torpor.

"He told us no such thing," Brisbane corrected. "He only gave us the information that Felicity was not to be trusted. We had no idea where she had gone, or—more to the point—where she had taken you."

"How did you find me?" I asked sleepily.

"Never mind that now," he murmured, pressing his lips to my brow. "Sleep." And I did.

For the first time since the accident, I slipped into a deep and undrugged sleep. Oddly, I dreamed a more vivid dream than any I had had on morphia. I was wandering through a garden, a beautiful place, with the most exquisite blossoms. And as I put a hand to smell one, it closed, furling its petals tightly against me. I moved to the next flower, and it did the same, and it happened again and again until I reached the garden gate. I passed through and closed the gate, looking back only once to see the sea of blossoms, nodding sleepily on their stems. I locked the gate firmly behind me and walked on. I did not look back again.

Portia came to visit me soon after, and put the infant Jane the Younger into my arms.

"It is the best cure," she assured me, and to my astonishment, I found it oddly restful to hold the sleeping infant, and more restful still to give her back when she woke.

She passed the child off to Nanny Stone and arranged herself comfortably upon my bed. "I have brought you five new novels, an enormous box of chocolates, the latest edition of *Le Mode Illustrée,* and a cow."

"I thought you meant to keep the cow to have milk for Jane the Younger."

"Yes, well, this particular cow seems highly unsuited to city life. It moos constantly and keeps wandering into the dining room. Most unsettling. Besides, I found a very pretty little dairy quite close to the house that seems remarkably clean and the milk is sweet. It will do."

I sighed. "I suppose I could send her down to the Rookery. She will make a lovely addition to the menagerie I am starting. I hope she likes peacocks."

"And mice," she added with a nod towards my little dormouse. He was once more nestled into my bodice, peeping out with those black teardrop eyes. "Have you given him a name yet?"

I told her the name and she smiled. "I think it suits him."

I stroked the velvety head with a fingertip. This tiny creature had been a surprising consolation during my convalescence. He was quiet and thoughtful, at least as thoughtful as a dormouse can be. I continued to stroke his head as

Portia gave me a reproving glance. "You might have told me about the letters."

Bellmont, in true contrary fashion, had made a clean breast of the affair within the family. He was horrified to learn the lengths to which Brisbane and I had gone to retrieve them and the dangers we had faced. The knowledge that I had almost died and that Agathe had lost her life because of them was deeply sobering, and it was a humbled Bellmont who had sought forgiveness from us all. Adelaide had risen nobly to the occasion, and it was agreed that the news need go no farther, and even the children were kept in the dark. The fact that the letters had still not been recovered and might surface one day no doubt played into Bellmont's decision to reveal all to the family, but I think even if they had been published on the front page of the *Times,* he would have stood it like a gentleman.

Plum behaved with gentlemanly discretion, as well. He never spoke of Felicity again, not even to me, but he was most helpful in explaining how they came to find me on that terrible day.

"Mortlake was useless," he said with some disgust. "He had no notion of where she went on her own. He was just happy when she left the house. He always had some mad notion that she would harm her little brothers."

"Perhaps not quite so mad," I remarked.

Plum looked from his newly set arm to my swathes of bandages and shuddered. "Quite. In any event, it seemed possible that she had decided to bolt for Germany, and if so, she would be far likelier to get a good reception from Bismarck if she had the letters with her. Brisbane suggested she might try the Spirit Club one last time to search Agathe's possessions in case Agathe had hidden the letters. We simply went there and waited until she arrived. It was the most terrible wait, hours until she came, and the entire time Brisbane was very nearly incoherent."

"Incoherent? What happened?"

Plum looked distinctly uncomfortable. "His eyes would glaze over and he would start to speak, the same things over and over, about choking and suffocation, and not being able to breathe. We loosened his neckcloth and opened the carriage windows, but it didn't seem to help. I honestly thought the fellow was having an attack."

"He was, although not the sort you mean."

Plum gave me a narrow look but did not ask. "Then, when Felicity came, he recovered himself enough to come with us. I honestly thought that Morgan would be able to persuade her to tell us where you were, but nothing he promised, nothing he threatened did the trick. She said nothing at all, merely sat there with that same hateful smile, as if she knew it wouldn't matter because you couldn't be saved."

I thought of those last terrible hours in the crypt and despised her a little more. "How did you find me?"

Plum shook his head. "Even now I do not understand it. We had been questioning Felicity for hours it seemed. We had nothing from her, and Morgan actually suggested, well, what he suggested does not befit the treatment of a lady, but I considered it. Before Morgan could act, Brisbane seemed to collapse again. He folded in upon himself and crouched against the wall, he was breathing a horrible death-rattle sound, and his eyes were completely vacant, as if he could not see us at all and could only see something very far away. He could scarcely speak, he had not the breath for it. And then he said, 'Highgate. I see the word. We must save them.' And Morgan did not even hesitate. He pushed us into a carriage and told his driver to drive for hell. We fairly flew there, and when we alighted, Brisbane ran ahead, like a hound on the scent of a hare. He made straight for the Mortlake crypt, and when we found him, he was trying to take the stones apart with his bare hands. We had to pull him off to use Felicity's key."

It was not the first time Brisbane's second sight had alerted him to danger where I was concerned, and unnerving as it was, I blessed it.

"It was the most terrible thing I have ever seen, and so long as I live, I will never forget it."

I had no doubt of it. As I turned the words over in my mind, I wondered. Had Brisbane guessed about the child? Or had he known, in the same way that he had known where I would be? *We must save them.* There were things I would never know, and some threads of the case that would never be tied to my satisfaction.

The question of how much Mr. Sullivan knew was one such point. He was courteous enough to send a great basket of hothouse fruit to me during my convalescence, but as I considered the untidy scrawl of his signature, something unpleasant occurred to me. During our conversation with him, Mr. Sullivan had neglected to provide us with a significant clue—that he had once followed the veiled lady to Highgate Cemetery. It was possible that he harboured some hope of uncovering her identity himself and thereby securing the gratitude of his superiors. Or he may have, stupidly, written off the incident as nonsignificant. But I realised with a pang that if we had known of her connection to Highgate, Brisbane and I might have at least searched the place and perhaps turned up some clue to her identity. I did not like to mention the omission to Brisbane, but I suspect he realised it for himself. Quite abruptly, Mr. Sullivan stopped writing for the *Illustrated Daily News,* and when I remarked upon it

to Brisbane, he told me in a rather clipped tone that Mr.
Sullivan had been recalled to Washington by his superiors
and nothing more was said upon the matter. It would not
have surprised me at all to find Sir Morgan's fingers in that
particular pie. As I lay long hours convalescing, my mind
turned frequently to the events of the past weeks, and one
detail I had suddenly recalled was that on the evening of
the séance, it was Sir Morgan who prevented Sullivan from
following the others from the building. It was a perfectly
natural action—a gentleman checking the time and patting his pockets to find his cigarette case—but it effectively
blocked Sullivan long enough to ensure that none of the
three guests who had already departed could be trailed by
the American. Had it been intentional? Morgan had told us
that he had had difficulty in exposing the German agent,
but it was entirely possible that he knew Sullivan was working for the Americans and had taken steps to prevent him
from learning anything of importance. I smiled to myself.
In blocking the American operative—whether intentionally
or not—Morgan had unwittingly spent his own chance to
discover the identity of Madame's German contact for himself. The irony of it seemed entirely fitting.

To Brisbane's disgust, Felicity Mortlake escaped prosecution. She struck her head during the blast I had detonated,
and when she awoke, she remembered nothing, not even her
own name. Was it amnesia? Was it pretense? No one could
say. Sir Morgan and her father had her consigned to the care
of an asylum in Norfolk, deep in the fens, a secure place
where if she were not mad, she will surely be in time. Everything else was tidied up with the deft use of Sir Morgan's
influence. Not so much as a whisper of the affair found its
way into the newspapers, and if anyone wondered whatever

became of Lord Mortlake's eldest daughter, no one asked it aloud. Not a word of Bellmont's involvement in the Spirit Club was ever spoken. I appreciated Morgan's discretion in the matter. That and the enormous baskets of flowers he sent to my bedside. I always did love peonies to distraction.

Of course, Sir Morgan would never be an easy person to know, and this was borne home when, some weeks after the incident in the graveyard, Brisbane took me for a ride in the carriage. It had turned cold, and I was carefully bundled in furs, a heater at my feet. Brisbane would say nothing of where we were bound, but I was glad to be out and about. My excursions thus far had been to Portia's or to March House or to do a little shopping, and I was astonishingly bored of it all.

In a short time, we found ourselves in the mews behind Sir Morgan's house in St. John's Wood, and I watched in astonishment as Brisbane tried the garden door. It was a stout affair of good oak, but it yielded to his touch. He took a quick glance to make sure we were not observed and opened it.

"Brisbane, what are we doing here?" I whispered.

He put a finger over my lips and beckoned me to follow. We crept through the garden like thieves, and the metaphor was an apt one, for no sooner had we reached the house than Brisbane extracted a set of objects that made his intention instantly clear.

"No lockpicks?" I mouthed.

He shook his head and pointed to the complexity of the lock on the French doors. But while it was a good lock, it was poorly sited, and this made Brisbane's entry quite easy. I stood aside, plucking idly at a flower whilst he worked.

He took a piece of brown paper that had been liberally spread with glue and unfolded it carefully. He moistened it

with his own saliva and pressed it to the glass pane of the
door. Then he took the end of his walking stick and gave
a single sharp tap. The glass shattered, but silently, and the
glue ensured that the pieces came away in one tidy sheet. I
stared in admiration as he reached in and turned the lock
from the inside. We moved into the house, our feet soundless on the thick carpets. The crescent moon provided il-
lumination, and a moment after we entered we were at the
tea caddy.

Just as Brisbane reached for his lockpicks to work the
little lock, there was a hiss from the corner. I peered into
the gloom to see Nin advancing slowly, whipping her tail
back and forth like a cobra.

"This could be very bad," I muttered to Brisbane.
"Siamese can be very loud if the mood strikes them."

"Well, you are her favourite, according to Morgan.
Attend to her," he ordered, applying himself to the lock. I
suppressed a sigh and reached to my reticule to rip a peacock
feather free.

I dandled it in front of her, and just as the little lock
sprang open, I dropped the feather. Nin pounced upon it,
snatching it up in her jaws and trotting off as contentedly as
any retriever with her prize.

I turned my attention to Brisbane and the tea caddy that
he had opened. Inside was a packet of tea, and below that
a false bottom that he pried loose. Underneath lay another
packet, this one flat and bound with tape.

Brisbane replaced the caddy and gestured for us to leave.
We retraced our steps through the rooms, Brisbane shutting
the door carefully behind us. He did not bother to lock it,
for the missing pane would reveal soon enough that the residence had been breached. We moved through the garden
and back to the carriage, and once there, Brisbane rapped

sharply for the driver to move on. It was several minutes before he turned up the lamp and handed me the packet.

"Bellmont's letters," I breathed. "Sir Morgan had them the whole time."

"Very likely," Brisbane said. "I suspect he took them the very night Madame died. Everything else was so much smoke and mirrors."

"Then why not tell you?" I demanded. "Why let you continue to chase down that monstrous woman?"

"Because Morgan needed to flush her like a pheasant and he was using me as his beater," he said, his face expressionless.

"That is a vile thing to do! You might have been killed! How dare he show such a lack of respect for an innocent citizen," I raged. "What gives him the right to treat you so?"

"He is my employer," Brisbane said softly.

There was silence between us, and in that silence a world of things unsaid. I clutched the letters. "Sir Morgan is your employer? That would make you..."

"Upon occasion."

"How long?"

"Since I was eighteen. It was during my involvement with Fleur. She was suspected of being an agent of Napoléon III. They recruited me to discover what I could about her."

I shook my head. "No, it is too much. Not you. Not Fleur. Tell me she was not a spy."

"Only of the most innocuous variety and quite accidentally," he said by way of consolation.

"But you have not known Fleur intimately in over twenty years," I said, trying to make sense of it all. "Why are you still working for Sir Morgan?"

"Because I am rather good at it," he said simply. "My

detective business gives me ample opportunity to poke into the affairs of others, and anything I find out of note, I pass to Morgan. I am not so active as I once was," he promised. "More often now, I simply relay information he might require."

It was a clever version of the truth, I knew instantly, and had been heavily edited to allay my fears. But I was not to be put off. "It is not always so simple, is it?"

He opened his mouth to give me an easy answer, then snapped his teeth together. "No," he said finally. "Sometimes it is considerably more."

I said nothing for a long moment, realising that Brisbane had just done the unthinkable: he had trusted me enough to tell me that which he ought never to have revealed. He had, quite literally, trusted me with his life.

"You work for Sir Morgan," I began slowly. "For whom does he work?"

"The Prime Minister's office. He reports directly to the sitting Prime Minister, and he has a weekly, highly secret meeting with Her Majesty. I believe he is smuggled in and out of the palace in a laundry hamper."

The thought of the dapper and elegant Morgan Fielding stowed away in a basket of laundry boggled the mind, perhaps more than anything else about this entire matter.

"I cannot believe it," I murmured. "It never occurred to me that there might be clandestine agencies of which the average British citizen has no inkling."

"It is better that way," Brisbane said flatly. "And it will be better still when a proper bureau is established and Morgan can see to it that he has the manpower he needs."

"He doesn't now?"

"Do you really think he would have set up that elaborate farce at the Spirit Club if he had alternatives? He is given a handful of men and a budget that would scarcely keep you in slippers and fans. What he accomplishes is largely due to the force of his own personality and the loyalty of his friends."

"He will know the letters are gone," I pointed out.

"And he will know I took them. I rather think he intended I should," he said. "Otherwise he would not have left them in the tea caddy. He mentioned once that it was a useful piece, and he would know I remembered it."

"Intended? If he wanted you to have them, why not just give them to you?"

"Because Morgan would never take a straight path if the twisty one will do. He is as slippery a devil as I have ever met, but I would trust him with my life if the occasion demanded and, from time to time, it has. We understand each other."

"Do you think he would mind that you have told me?"

"I think Morgan would be distinctly surprised if I had not."

I nodded. "He knows you so well then."

"He does. And he knows you. And no man who has met you could fail to respect your single-minded determination to put your nose into anything that does not concern you."

I ought to have been insulted, I told myself, but instead I was conscious only of a deep satisfaction. Brisbane had confided to me the most dangerous secret, and he had done it of his own volition.

"And why tell me now? You had the chance, right at the beginning of the investigation when I noticed that you spoke with some familiarity of the Spirit Club. You said you could not explain then. What has changed?"

He turned away from me, and when he spoke, his voice was low. "Because I am selfish. I wanted just one person in this world to know me for everything I am. And because sometimes I find it difficult to believe that you could love me if you knew the whole of it. So I give you bits and pieces of myself, a mosaic of the man I am, and I lie awake at night and wonder which of them will cause you to leave me."

His voice was cold and bleak as a moorland wind, and I wiped the tears from my cheeks before I put my hand in his.

"Is there more? Things you have not told me?"

He said nothing, but he nodded. I took a deep breath of resignation.

"Well, you have told me this and I am still here. Leave the rest for another time."

I put my head upon his shoulder and rested it there. He crushed my hand in his, and I looked down to see the bruised petals of the flower peeping between our gloved hands.

"Brisbane, does it not strike you as odd that in the cemetery, Morgan said he would see Felicity charged with my attempted murder and the murder of Agathe LeBrun? He said nothing of Madame's murder." I dropped the broken bloom of monkshood into his hand.

"*Aconitum napellus,*" he murmured.

"Would Morgan have done such a thing?"

"Madame Séraphine had become a liability," he said simply. "Felicity knew she had been followed once to High-gate and that her identity had nearly been compromised. I suspect that Felicity was growing desperate and showed up at the séance in order to force Madame's hand and induce her to hand over the letters once and for all. Madame improvised with a message that Felicity would understand, a plea for time and money, and a message that was most definitely not of Morgan's construction. That proved she was playing at her own game and had established contacts of her own with the enemy. There is only one remedy for a spymaster when one of his operatives has decided to follow a different course."

"I do not think I care for the notion of you working for someone so reckless. He might have poisoned the entire club with that horseradish."

"Not likely. It would not be in keeping with Morgan's character to be quite so careless. I suspect the poison was never in the horseradish, but was in Madame's face crème instead. Remember, aconite is absorbed through the skin."

I plucked the poisonous flower from his hand and flung it from the window. "How could he have got the stuff into her room without detection?" I wondered aloud.

Brisbane pondered this a moment, then shook his head. "He must have been there before either of us arrived. I was on the area steps, and I watched everyone who came after me. Morgan did not."

"But he entered the public rooms of the club after I did," I recalled. "He must have been upstairs then. It would have been an easy thing to slip into Madame's rooms and poison the face crème." I shuddered at the idea. I had quite liked Morgan.

"I just thought of something. Sir Morgan knew Edward and the manner of his death. I wonder if it gave him the idea of how to dispose of Madame."

"We will likely never know," Brisbane said. "But Morgan forgets nothing. I would not be surprised if he filed away that particularly nasty bit of business with an eye to using it someday."

I gave Brisbane a severe look. "I do not care for the notion of your working quite so closely with a man capable of such things. And I ought to be entirely put out with you for not telling about your employment sooner. A lady should never marry a man without knowing he is a spy."

"Does it make a difference?" he asked, and I knew he held his breath as I pondered my reply.

I put my hand to his cheek. "Of course it does," I said softly. "Now I can really be involved in your work."

"Bloody hell," Brisbane said.

"And I just remembered the terms of our wager. Madame was murdered by someone at the séance," I said with satisfaction. "You owe me one hundred pounds."

Naturally, Brisbane saw no reason at all that I should aid in his efforts to protect the security of crown and country, and I knew the process of convincing him otherwise would take some time. No matter, I decided. I could wait. He also refused to settle the wager, arguing that as we had no actual proof of Sir Morgan's culpability, the case could not be considered closed. I accused him of pedantry and we agreed to double or nothing as terms for the next investigation that I took a hand in.

We worked at Brisbane's various cases and I continued to pursue my photography. Naturally, it was not until some weeks after the accident that I ventured back into my little studio at the top of the house on Chapel Street, but I was happy that I did. I had missed the cosy rooms devoted to my hobby, and I puttered away for some hours until Plum called to me that Mrs. Lawson had just brought up the tea and the post.

I made my way down to tea, relaxing as soon as I saw the cosy scene. Brisbane was at his desk, legs crossed at the ankles upon his blotter as he perused his post. He had a cup of tea at his elbow, and a plate of warm muffins with the butter melting in. Plum, freshly released from the splints of his broken arm, was toasting up a few for me, and I munched contentedly as Plum stroked Rook and sipped at his own tea. I applied myself to my letters, sorting the various notes and bills until I came to one in a familiar hand. I felt a rush of excitement.

"Bloody hell," I said. Plum blinked and Brisbane roused himself.

"What is it, my dear?"

I tore open the letter and skimmed it quickly. I brandished it at Brisbane. "We are going to Italy," I said. I gave him the letter to read, hopping from foot to foot as he came to the end.

"Bloody hell," he agreed.

"We must go," I insisted.

"We must not," was his equally firm reply.

I smiled, knowing that a battle would ensue, and equally confident I would win. I was already planning what to pack as we left for Rome and the new adventure that beckoned.

But that is a tale as yet untold.

★ ★ ★ ★ ★

ACKNOWLEDGMENTS

Tremendous thanks to my readers! You make me grateful every day, and I am so happy to share my stories with you. And heartfelt thanks to the booksellers and librarians who share my stories with others.

I am incredibly grateful to the MIRA Books team for their enthusiasm and the exquisite care they have lavished on my novels. Many, many thanks to the unseen hands whose work is often unremarked upon but so very essential—and much appreciated.

As ever, many thanks to my editor, the stylish and exacting Valerie Gray, whose commitment to my writing has been truly humbling in the best possible way. My life and my work are the better for knowing you.

And thanks most of all to my family—thanks to my mother for endless support and faultless proofreading, to my daughter and my father for their many kindnesses large and small, and to my husband, for everything and for always.

QUESTIONS FOR DISCUSSION

1. This novel sees the return of Nicholas and Julia to London, where they continue married life after an extended time away from the city. What are the most significant challenges facing Nicholas and Julia as they settle into domesticity? How does the setting influence the story?

2. This period in history saw tremendous change in technology, in social interests, in the world in general. Describe some of these changes and how they affected Victorian life.

3. With her lack of interest in domestic details, Julia is not a typical Victorian housewife. In some ways, she is not unlike a modern twenty-first-century woman. Do you agree and if so, what similarities do you find between Julia and the modern woman?

4. Several new characters are introduced in this book—most significantly, Sir Morgan Fielding. Describe his relationship to the established characters and what role he might play in the future.

5. What motivates Lady Felicity Mortlake?

6. Does Plum's presence in the enquiry agency change the dynamic of the working relationship between Nicholas and Julia? In what ways do you think Plum will be an effective enquiry agent?

7. Nicholas reveals more of his past to Julia in this novel. What does he reveal and how might it affect their

relationship? What do you think their marriage will be like in five years? In ten years?

8. How do the Roma characters fit your perception of Gypsies? How do they differ? How does Granny Bones fit into the development of Nicholas's character?

9. What are the difficult lessons learned by Lord Bellmont in this story? Then, as now, it is not uncommon for men in power to acquire female relationships outside marriage. Why do you think this happens? Why would someone gamble so heavily on their future in this way?

DEANNA RAYBOURN

"Let the wicked
be ashamed,
and let them be
silent in the grave."

These ominous words are the last threat that the darling of London society, Sir Edward Grey, receives from his killer. Before he can show them to Nicholas Brisbane, the private inquiry agent he has retained for his protection, Sir Edward is murdered in his home.

Determined to bring her husband's killer to justice, Julia Grey engages Brisbane to help her investigate Edward's demise. Together, they press forward, coming ever closer to a killer who waits expectantly for Julia's arrival.

Silent in the Grave

"[A] perfectly executed debut."
—*Publishers Weekly* (starred review)

Available wherever books are sold.

MIRA®

www.MIRABooks.com

MDR2817TR

The marvelous sequel to
the evocative *Silent in the Grave*

DEANNA RAYBOURN

Fresh from a six-month sojourn in Italy, Lady Julia
returns home to Sussex to find her father's estate
crowded with family and friends—but dark deeds
are afoot at the deconsecrated abbey, and a
murderer roams the ancient cloisters.

When one of the guests is found brutally murdered
in the chapel and a member of Lady Julia's own family
confesses to the crime, Lady Julia resumes her unlikely
and deliciously intriguing partnership with
Nicholas Brisbane, setting out to unravel a tangle
of deceit before the killer can strike again....

SILENT *in the*
SANCTUARY

"Fans of British historical thrillers will welcome
Raybourn's perfectly executed debut."
—*Publishers Weekly* on *Silent in the Grave*

Available wherever trade paperback books are sold!

MIRA®

www.MIRABooks.com

MDR2492TR

DEANNA RAYBOURN

In Grimsgrave Hall, enigmatic
Nicholas Brisbane has inherited a
ruined estate, replete with uncanny
tenants and one unwanted
houseguest: Lady Julia Grey.

Despite Brisbane's admonitions
to stay away, Lady Julia arrives in
Yorkshire to find him as remote
and maddeningly attractive as ever.
They share the house with the
proud but impoverished remnants
of an ancient family: the sort who
keep their bloodlines pure and
their secrets close.

A mystery unfolds from the
rotten heart of Grimsgrave—
one Lady Julia may have to
solve alone, as Brisbane appears
inextricably tangled in its
heinous twists and turns.

Silent on the Moor

"With a strong and unique voice,
Deanna Raybourn creates
unforgettable characters in a richly
detailed world. This is story-
telling at its most compelling."
—Nora Roberts, *New York Times*
bestselling author

Available wherever books are sold.

www.MIRABooks.com   MDR2614TR

DEANNA RAYBOURN

For Lady Julia Grey and Nicholas Brisbane, the honeymoon has ended…but the adventure is just beginning.

After eight idyllic months in the Mediterranean, Lady Julia Grey and her detective husband are ready to put their investigative talents to work once more. They travel to India to aid an old friend, the newly widowed Jane Cavendish, with discovering the truth about her husband's death.

Amid the lush foothills of the Himalayas, the Brisbanes uncover secrets and scandal, illicit affairs and twisted legacies. The danger is palpable and, if they are not careful, Julia and Nicholas will not live to celebrate their first anniversary.

Dark Road to Darjeeling

Available wherever books are sold.

A LADY JULIA GREY NOVEL

MIRA®

www.MIRABooks.com